GIDEON
The Cutpurse

BEING THE FIRST PART OF
THE GIDEON TRILOGY

LINDA BUCKLEY-ARCHER

SIMON & SCHUSTER BOOKS FOR YOUNG READERS

NEW YORK LONDON TORONTO SYDNEY

SIMON & SCHUSTER BOOKS FOR YOUNG READERS

An imprint of Simon & Schuster Children's Publishing Division

1230 Avenue of the Americas, New York, New York 10020

Simultaneously published in Great Britain in 2006 by Simon and Schuster UK Ltd.

First U.S. Edition, 2006

SIMON & SCHUSTER BOOKS FOR YOUNG READERS is a trademark of

Simon & Schuster, Inc.

Book design by Christopher Grassi

The text for this book is set in Adobe Garamond Pro.

Manufactured in the United States of America

2 4 6 8 10 9 7 5 3

Library of Congress Cataloging in Publication Data

Buckley-Archer, Linda.

Gideon the cutpurse : being the first part of the Gideon Trilogy / Linda Buckley-Archer.—

1st U.S. ed.

p. cm.

Summary: Ignored by his father and sent to Derbyshire for the weekend, twelve-year-old Peter and his new friend, Kate, are accidentally transported back in time to 1763 England where they are befriended by a reformed cutpurse.

ISBN-13: 978-1-4169-1525-6

ISBN-10: 1-4169-1525-7

[1. Time travel—Fiction. 2. Robbers and outlaws—Fiction. 3. Great Britain—History—George III, 1760–1820—Fiction. 4. Fathers and sons—Fiction.] I. Title.

PZ7.B882338Gid 2006

[Fic]—dc22

2006042204

For R., L., and I.

Contents

Contents

Contents

To the Reader

When I talked to Peter Schock about the part he played in all these events, he asked me to include some passages from the book that Peter himself found at Hawthorn Cottage in Derbyshire. Its title is *The Life and Times of Gideon Seymour*. It was written between 1790 and 1792, but it was never published, at least as far as I can tell.

Peter grew to love Gideon's stories. Lying on the grass under the shade of the oak tree at Hawthorn Cottage, Peter would let Gideon's soft voice take him to places and times he would never see for himself—and some of them he would not wish to. Peter told me that as there would not have been a story without Gideon, it was only fair that he be allowed to speak from time to time. I have therefore added some passages from Gideon's book to show his side of the story.

As for the writer of these volumes—the witness to whom the narration of these events, of such great consequence for so many, has been entrusted—until you have heard the entire story, it will be impossible for you to understand either my part in it or why this painstaking task fell to me. I have pieced together its many interweaving strands in the hope that its telling will serve not only as a grave warning but also as a celebration of mankind's infinite curiosity about his universe and the greatness of the human heart.

Peter asked if these books could be dedicated to Gideon's memory, and this I am very happy to do, for his part in all of this must not be underestimated.

IN MEMORY OF A GOOD AND BRAVE MAN
WHO SHALL BE REMEMBERED BEYOND HIS TIME:

GIDEON SEYMOUR, CUTPURSE AND GENTLEMAN

During those first days at Hawthorn Cottage, Peter felt abandoned by his father. It grieved me to see it, for I could understand the pain he felt. The rage he sometimes kept locked inside him was slow to lift, and he refused to give himself the comfort of speaking of it.

Once he said he wished that I had been his father. Then it was my turn to be angry. "What madness is this?" I cried. "What crime has your father committed that you would trade him for a cutpurse?"

"He has committed no crime," Peter replied, "unless a father can be punished for not loving his son."

—*The Life and Times of Gideon Seymour, Cutpurse and Gentleman,* 1792

ONE

The Birthday Treat

*In which Peter looks forward to his birthday
treat and subsequently argues with his father*

It was early morning on Saturday, the sixteenth of December,
the first day of the Christmas holidays. In a large house on the
edge of London it was beginning to get light. Peter jumped
out of bed and stuck his head underneath the curtains to look
outside. The sun glowed behind the houses on the other side of
Richmond Green, and the cloudless sky was palest blue—not
even a wisp of a cloud. "Yes!" exclaimed Peter, and flung himself
as hard as he could onto the mattress to get a good bounce.

Even torrential rain could not have spoiled this day, but crisp sunshine was better. When it was actually Peter's twelfth birthday, back in September, his father had been delayed in Venice on business and could not get back home in time. He postponed the birthday treat again at half term because of a business trip to New York, and had inked it in his diary for the first day of the Christmas holidays. Nowadays it was mostly like this with his father's promises. They hung, like mirages, shimmering in the future, and the closer you got to them the more you expected them to disappear. When his mother had gone over to work in the States for the first time and his father was supposed to have been making a special effort, Mr. Schock had still managed to turn up at Sports Day *after* Peter's big race. There was always another meeting, another client, another urgent matter demanding his attention.

But today was the day: sleighing on the dry ski slope, followed by lunch up in town, followed by a Premiership football match—a whole day with his dad, doing his favorite things! And nothing could stop it happening now. The smell of frying bacon and sausages that was drifting up the stairs confirmed it. You never got cooked breakfasts on ordinary days in the Schock household. Peter snuggled back under his stripy duvet, relishing the moment, and pretended to be asleep when the door opened.

"Wake up, Peter, time to wake up." Margrit was definitely the best in the long line of au pairs his father had employed since his mother had gone to work in Los Angeles. She was German and made brilliant meatballs. Her *W*s sounded like *V*s. "Peter,"

Margrit whispered into his ear. "I know that you are awake. We go on a journey this morning. You must get up now. Your father must speak to you."

She tickled Peter until he wriggled and his face cracked into a grin. But when his eyes met hers, she was not smiling. She looked uncomfortable.

"What journey?" he demanded. "What do you mean?"

When Margrit did not answer straightaway, he shot out of bed and flew down two flights of stairs to confront his father, who was cooking eggs in the kitchen. His father was already dressed in smart clothes chosen to impress. One look at his expression and Peter knew.

"It's not happening, is it?"

"I'm sorry, Peter, I really am. I'll make it up to you, I promise. I've just had a phone call. I have to meet the head of the studios, who is flying back to the States this afternoon."

Peter felt numb. This was not possible. Even his father could not do this to him a third time.

"But the good thing is that Margrit can take you up to spend the weekend on her friends' farm in Derbyshire. We'll do this when you get back. I know how disappointed you must be, but you've got to understand. . . . A lot of people's livelihoods depend on this meeting."

Father and son stood looking at each other over opposite sides of the kitchen table. All the morning's happiness started to seep out of Peter like a puddle onto the kitchen floor. But when his father walked around the table to put a hand on his shoulder, Peter quickly stepped backward out of reach. The adrenalin rush of sudden fury made Peter's fingers clench and his heart pound. He did not want to be understanding. He did not want to go and visit some strangers with Margrit. He wanted his father to cancel the meeting. He wanted to hammer his fists against his father's chest and tell him never, ever, ever again to break a promise he had made to him.

"I don't know why you bothered having a kid," he shouted. "You never want to do anything with me—I just get in the way!"

"If you're going to be like that, there's nothing I can say," snapped his father. "You know I'm here for you as much as I can be, but someone's got to earn the money to pay for all this." He gestured vaguely at the gleaming stainless steel kitchen and Margrit, who was polishing Peter's shoes. Margrit looked as if she wished she were somewhere else.

"Wait till you're a grown-up with responsibilities. You'd do exactly the same if you were in my place."

"No, I wouldn't! If Mum were here, she wouldn't let you do this to me."

This was a bad move and Peter knew it. But the words slipped out before he could stop them.

"Don't you *dare* take that tone with me." His father's voice had become steely with barely controlled rage. "How dare you say that, when it's your mother who's chosen to work on the other side of the planet." He picked up the frying pan and shoveled the now overcooked eggs angrily into the bin. "You'll go with Margrit. End of story. And I'll think about rescheduling your birthday treat *when* and *if* you stop acting like a spoiled brat."

The Birthday Treat

Peter hurtled upstairs, unable to cope with the feeling of help-lessness, the sense of injustice that surged up inside him. When he reached the first-floor landing, he turned round and leaned over the banister.

"I hate you!"

And those were the last words that passed between them.

Peter did not notice his father turning on his heel, wincing visibly. He fled into his bedroom, slamming the door so hard that frag-ments of gloss paint fell onto the carpet. Peter stood at the foot of his bed, kicking and kicking at the wooden leg until it hurt, holding back the tears, listening to the sound of crunching gravel as his father drove his car up the drive. He refused to give in to his impulse to rush to the window and cry, "Dad! Come back!"

TWO

Peter Misses an Important Telephone Call

In which Peter makes the acquaintance of the Dyer family and a hair-raising encounter with a Van de Graaff generator triggers an extraordinary chain of events

Margrit had witnessed many arguments between father and son but had never seen Peter this upset. She had grown very fond of him and did her best to cheer him up. Peter scarcely talked during the long journey up to Derbyshire. He stared out of the car window while Margrit sang German folk songs. He was too preoccupied to notice the hedgerows covered with hoarfrost or the cows huddling together for warmth, or the rooks cawing from the tops of giant trees, their nests clearly visible against the pale winter sky. Peter played all the games on Margrit's mobile, his thumbs striking the keys so fast and so hard that she had to ask him to stop before he broke it. London was left far behind, and by half past eleven a wilder, rugged landscape announced they were drawing near to the Dyer family's farm.

"I am sure you will like the Dyer children," Margrit told Peter. "There are six of them—four girls and two boys. You won't be bored this weekend, that's for sure."

"No," said Peter, unconvinced.

"And on the way back I'll take you to Lichfield, where I have some friends. Doctor Samuel Johnson was born there."

"Who?"

"You must know of Doctor Johnson! You are English! He lived in seventeen hundred and something, I think. He's the one who wrote the first—no, I will not tell you. If you find out by yourself, I will give you a present."

"What sort of present?" asked Peter, with a little more enthusiasm.

"Something that Doctor Johnson would approve of . . ."

"So not sweets, then."

"No!"

The Dyers' stone farmhouse, flanked by a barn on one side and an ancient beech tree on the other, stood huddled at the bottom of a long, deep valley crisscrossed with dry stone walls. A small, fast-flowing stream burbled alongside the road that led to the house.

"It's in the middle of nowhere," said Peter. "What a lonely

place! It's ages since we went past the last house—let alone shop. What do you do if you've run out of milk or something?"

"I don't think the Dyers ever have to worry about running out of milk!" said Margrit, pointing to some black-and-white cows in the distance. "Besides, you can get just as lonely in the city."

Margrit parked the car next to a mud-splattered Land Rover, and Peter got out and stretched his legs, stiff after the long journey. A biting wind whistled through the few dry leaves that remained clinging to the beech tree that towered above the house. Otherwise all was silent. Peter shivered, and not just because of the cold. This was his first visit to Derbyshire, yet the landscape seemed inexplicably familiar. The skin on the back of his neck began to tingle as if an invisible hand had stroked it.

"Are you okay, Peter?"

"Yeah . . . I'm fine."

Margrit reached over to smooth down his shiny brown hair, which wanted only to stand upright in the mornings.

"You need a haircut."

"No, I don't. I'm growing it," he replied, messing it up again.

Margrit smiled. "You're feeling better."

At the sound of Margrit's car the whole Dyer family trooped out into the farmyard to greet them. Margrit was delighted to see her friend, Mrs. Dyer, and they flung their arms around each other and talked breathlessly in a mixture of English and German, as though they were making up for lost time.

Mr. Dyer shook Peter's hand and made him feel welcome. He was a tall thin man with coarse red hair and so many freckles they almost joined up. With him were five children, who ranged in size from just above Peter's knees to somewhere below his shoulder. The biggest boy was Sam; next came twin girls, Issy and Alice; and then little Sean. The youngest, Milly, her cheeks glowing in the cold, stood unsteadily at Peter's feet, holding on to his corduroy trousers at the knees. Soon the sixth and eldest of the Dyer tribe arrived.

Kate was a little taller than Peter, and wisps of long red hair flew around her face as she bounded, breathless, into the muddy yard, closely followed by a golden Labrador.

"Katie!" Little Milly and Sean ran excitedly toward their big sister, and she lifted them both up high into the air before letting them clamber down her legs to the ground. She knocked Sam's woolly hat off before she noticed that the visitors had already arrived.

"Oh, *meine liebchen*, I can't believe how you've grown. You're nearly grown up!" exclaimed Margrit when she saw her. She kissed Kate and gave her a big hug.

Kate blushed, which caused Peter to smirk. He knew just what it felt like when grown-ups you could scarcely remember insisted on making personal remarks and kissing you. And you weren't supposed to wipe your cheek on your sleeve immediately afterward, either.

Why, thought Kate, *is that boy pulling such a stupid face at me?* Her expression changed into a lopsided frown. Margrit introduced them to each other.

"Hello, Kate," said Peter.

"Hello," she replied, warily, taking in his designer jeans and expensive sneakers, suddenly conscious of her own muddy ones. "How long are you here for?"

All the children were very proud and excited about a newborn calf and insisted that Peter should see her. The twins dragged him forcibly across the farmyard. The barn was dark and smelled of warm straw and milk and cow flesh. The black-and-white heifer was less than three hours old, and for a few moments everyone stood in solemn silence, suddenly conscious of the miracle of life. She lay close to her exhausted mother in a pool of weak light cast by a bare electric bulb. She peered at them through long black eyelashes.

"Isn't she the most beautiful calf you've ever seen?" asked Alice.

"It's the first calf I've ever seen," admitted Peter. "I mean, I've seen pictures . . . but it's not the same."

"Mummy's going to call her Einstein," said Issy.

"What's the mother cow called?" asked Peter.

"Erasmus Darwin," called out several voices.

"I see," said Peter, who did not.

"It's a family tradition," explained Kate. "Naming cows after scientists and astronomers, I mean." She pointed toward a young calf in the adjoining stall. "That's Galileo. She's three weeks old. . . . Erasmus Darwin was a famous scientist, in case you didn't know."

"Yeah, I know," said Peter, a little too quickly.

It was Kate's turn to smirk.

Little Sean reached out his hand for the calf to suck. Galileo swallowed his chubby arm practically up to the elbow, sucking noisily. Sean squealed with pleasure.

Peter watched from the edge of the human circle. He wanted to join in but was unsure whether he wanted such close contact with the animal. All of a sudden he felt his arm being pulled toward the calf. It was Kate.

"You're a real townie, aren't you? Don't be scared. It's not as if she's got sharp teeth or anything. Her tongue feels like sandpaper."

Peter pulled back his hand. "No, thanks."

Kate grabbed it again and held his clenched fingers near to the calf's wet nose. Peter looked round at Margrit for moral support. She was laughing! Peter flashed her a furious look. The calf licked his knuckles—her tongue really did feel like sandpaper.

"Kate likes to be in charge," said Margrit. "Isn't that right, Sam?"

Sam started to chant, "Bossy pants, bossy pants, Katie is a bossy pants!" and the little ones started to giggle.

Kate shoved him with her elbow. "Shut up, Sam."

"Nobody tells me what to do," retorted Peter, instantly wishing he had been cool enough just to shrug his shoulders.

"Well, we can all see that," said Kate, releasing his wrist.

When they stepped back out into the chilly farmyard, blinking in the wintry sunshine, Mr. Dyer was getting into the Land Rover.

"Where are you going, Dad? I thought you were going to take us to Dovedale this afternoon."

"I'll only be gone twenty minutes, nosy. I'll be back in time for lunch. Tim's gone away for the weekend. I promised to adjust the new generator on his blasted antigravity machine. I'll never hear the end of it if I forget to do it."

Kate suddenly turned to Peter, an excited gleam in her eye.

"Have you ever seen a Van de Graaff generator?"

"A what?"

"You'll see." Kate turned back to her father. "Can you take Peter and me with you? We could show Peter our party piece."

"I don't see why not . . . but we musn't be long."

"Can I bring Molly?" asked Kate.

"As long as you tie her up outside—we'll only be there a couple of minutes anyway. Run along and tell your mother we'll be back in time for lunch, will you?"

Peter got into the back of the old Land Rover and squeezed in between a child's car seat and Molly, who stretched herself out on a red tartan rug covered in golden hairs. There were empty drink cartons and comics and a bag of animal feed tucked underneath the front seat. Peter thought of his father's spotless car with its leather upholstery and how he wasn't even allowed to suck a sweet in it. Molly rested her head on her paws and looked up quizzically at Peter. He met the animal's kindly, thoughtful gaze and patted her head. Alone with his thoughts, Peter suddenly felt sad and lonely. Today could have turned out so differently.

If Mr. Dyer had checked his rearview mirror as the Land Rover juddered noisily down the uneven drive, he would have seen his wife running and calling after him, a mobile phone in her hand. However, he did not, and soon his wife had to give up the chase.

"I'm so sorry," she panted into the receiver. "You've just missed Peter, but I'm expecting them all back at about one o' clock. Can I take a message?"

"No, I need to speak to him," replied Peter's father. "I'm afraid we had a bit of a row this morning. I just wanted to talk to him, put matters right. I'll try again later."

The laboratory where Kate's father worked was only a short distance away by car, at the top of the valley, set in a small forest of pine trees. An inconspicuous sign at the beginning of the long drive announced: NCRDM—ALL VISITORS MUST REPORT TO SECURITY. Soon several high-tech buildings, apparently constructed entirely from glass, and invisible from the road, came into view. Two security guards waved them through with a smile and a friendly word. They addressed Kate's father as Dr. Dyer. *What is this place?* wondered Peter. *What does Kate's dad do?*

Dr. Dyer parked next to a long three-story building surrounded by fir trees. The frosty grass was littered with thousands of pine cones.

"Sit!" commanded Kate. "Stay! Good dog." Molly sat down obediently on the grass next to a door labeled: DR. A. DYER & DR. T. M. WILLIAMSON—DEPARTMENT OF COSMOLOGY. Kate's father keyed in a security code on a metal number pad, and the sleek electronic door swooshed open. "Welcome, Dr. Dyer," said a robotic voice.

"Poor Kate wishes she had one of these doors to keep the rabble out of her bedroom," remarked Dr. Dyer, amused at the expression of awe on Peter's face. "NASA—the American space agency—helps fund our research. We might not have discovered anything yet, but we have fabulous doors!"

They went into Dr. Dyer's laboratory, and Kate opened a window so she could keep an eye on Molly outside. There were papers everywhere—stacked on tables, in boxes on the floor, balanced on the windowsills—and there were *four* computers. But what immediately caught Peter's eye were the photographs. On every wall there were beautiful images of a blue Earth seen from space, of planets and their moons, and distant galaxies like jewels laid out on black velvet. Mathematical formulae were scrawled in green ink on two large whiteboards. Peter felt Kate nudging his elbow, and he turned to look at her. She had a grin on her face and was indicating her father with a nod of her head. Dr. Dyer stood lost in thought in front of one of the formulae. He had such a vacant look on his face that it made Peter want to laugh. Suddenly Dr. Dyer leaned forward, rubbed out something illegible with his forefinger, and scribbled something equally illegible in its place.

Kate cleared her throat.

"Right," said Dr. Dyer, oblivious that he was the focus of attention. "I had better see to Tim's generator before it goes out of my head. There's not a great deal to see, but you're welcome to come along."

Peter and Kate followed Dr. Dyer. They went down a long corridor and then descended a steep flight of stairs to the basement. Dr. Dyer opened a door, and they entered a large, cool room. Down here the windows were above eye level, and it felt gloomy compared to the ground floor. Kate and Peter watched as Dr. Dyer approached a machine in the center of the room. It was about the height and width of a man. The base of the machine consisted of a gray metal cube that displayed a series of digital readouts. Above it there was something that looked like an oversized streamlined lightbulb made of highly polished silvery metal. Metal brackets fixed it firmly to the base and to the walls of a Perspex box that encased it.

"Here it is," said Dr. Dyer. "Here's Tim's precious machine that's eating half our budget."

"What is it?" asked Peter.

"It's *supposed* to generate tiny amounts of antigravity—which it hasn't yet managed to do."

"I think it's lovely," said Kate. "It looks like a sculpture, like something you'd see in Tate Modern—a giant elongated tear."

"Mmm."

"It sounds like a fridge," said Peter.

"Well, it is in a way—though not so useful, if you ask me. It's the compressor that you can hear. There's liquid helium in there keeping it at absolute zero. Unless, of course, it's the nuclear generator that's humming, but I doubt that."

Peter took a step backward in alarm.

"Shouldn't we be wearing space suits or something this close to one of those things?"

Dr. Dyer laughed. "No, it's encased in a triple layer of lead and steel. In theory a generator like this could run safely for hundreds of years unless you did something stupid like dropping it—but even then it's got an inbuilt fail-safe. It'll only work if it's on the level."

Dr. Dyer then took out a piece of paper from his pocket, peered at it, and crouched down to look at one of the digital readouts.

"What does he want me to turn it up to?"

He looked at the paper again.

"Six point seven seven megawatts," he said to himself as he turned a knob and checked the digital display. "Temperature: minus two hundred and seventy-three centigrade—yes; speed: three thousand rpm—yes; vacuum: one hundred percent. Good, good. Mission accomplished. Let's go. I'm starving."

Back in Dr. Dyer's office Peter asked the researcher if he was interested in antigravity too.

"Only indirectly," replied Dr. Dyer. "Dark matter is more my line."

"Dark matter—"

"Dad," interrupted Kate, "please don't give him a lecture! You said we could do our party piece!"

Dr. Dyer gave Kate a severe look and continued. Kate sighed.

"People who spend a lot of time looking at space are no longer in any doubt that the stars and the galaxies just don't move in the way we'd expect. We suspect that something we can't see and don't understand is having an effect on the movement of the stars.

"Imagine, for instance, that it's the January sales in Oxford Street and you're walking through huge crowds of people. There's no way you could walk in a straight line, is there? You'd get pushed and shoved and you'd have to weave in and out to avoid bumping into everyone else. Now, just suppose that everyone else suddenly became *invisible*. The heaving masses would still be there, walking along and jostling you, but you couldn't *see* them. Now imagine that there were some people watching you from the top of a double-decker bus. What would they think?"

"That I was mad—or drunk, I guess," said Peter.

"I agree, but if the people on the bus observed you very closely, and they decided that you were neither mad nor drunk, how would they explain it? Can you see that they could conclude that you were moving in that peculiar way because of some invisible force? In other words they could guess at the existence of the crowd because of the way *you* were reacting to it. Does that make sense?"

"I think so."

"Well, we now believe that, just as the crowds in Oxford Street would alter how you moved, an invisible, mysterious force is having an effect on the movement of the stars. We think it makes up over ninety percent of our universe, and astronomers call it 'dark matter.'"

"Wow," said Peter. "What do you think it is? Is it here all around us?" he asked, grabbing fistfuls of air and staring at his empty hands.

"I wish I knew!" laughed Dr. Dyer. "But, believe me, this is the most exciting time to be alive in the history of science. By the time you and Kate are old and wrinkly, we will have discovered truly amazing things. Who knows, you might be part of it!"

A whirring, clicking sound made Peter turn to look at Kate.

She was cranking, for all she was worth, a handle attached to a shiny metal dome. She paused to catch her breath.

"Do you think that's enough, Dad?"

"Okay, okay, Kate, let's do the Van de Graaff thing. Peter, see what happens when you put your hands on the metal dome."

Peter walked over and did what he was told. Gingerly he put his hands on the shiny dome. A moment later he felt a bizarre prickling sensation in his scalp and he heard Kate screaming with laughter. He reached up to pat his normally floppy brown hair—it was standing on end! Kate was making so much noise that Molly got up on her hind legs and rested her jaw on the window to see what all the fuss was about.

"My turn!" cried Kate. Dr. Dyer took her place, and Kate put her palms on the dome. Kate's bright red hair, which reached almost down to her waist, started to float gently upward. Now Dr. Dyer increased his speed. He cranked the handle round so fast that his hands were one big blur. And as the static electricity flowed into her, Kate's hair rose half a yard above her head until it was perfectly vertical. It was as if she had been hung upside down—except that she was the right way up. Kate made her eyes roll upward to complete the effect, and Peter and her father doubled up with laughter. Molly, on the other hand, did not think this was remotely amusing. She was baring her teeth and growling menacingly. Suddenly she leaped through the open window. In one bound she was in front of the Van de Graaff generator, ready to attack. Kate immediately took one hand off the dome.

"It's all right, Molly, I'm okay." With one hand still on the generator, she reached toward the golden Labrador.

"Don't touch her!" cried Dr. Dyer, just too late. The static electricity flowing from the Van de Graaff generator through Kate's fingers set every hair on Molly's golden coat on end. The poor animal whimpered in fright and she shot like a bullet out of the laboratory door into the corridor before anyone could grab hold of her.

"Quick! Don't let her get away," shouted Dr. Dyer. "Heaven knows what mischief she could find to do in this place."

He raced toward the door and in his haste tripped over a box of printer paper. He fell badly and clutched at his knee, wincing in pain. Peter and Kate rushed to help him.

"Don't worry about me—get that dog!"

They tore after Molly, hearing the clatter of her claws as she skidded on the gray linoleum. As he ran, Peter watched Kate's red hair in front of him, swishing from side to side as if in slow motion, and every so often he caught a glimpse of Molly's solid form accelerating in front of them. He was dimly aware of hurtling along the long corridor and then down the basement stairs and through a half-open door, aware of just trying to keep up with Kate until, from one second to the next, the course of his life changed, and he charged slap bang into . . . nothing. The world dissolved for Peter. All sensation ceased. No pain. No noise. No heat. No great light. None of the things you might think would accompany such a momentous event—just an instantaneous, inexplicable, cavernous NOTHING.

A TERRIBLE DREAD CAME OVER ME AS I LAY CONCEALED WITHIN THE BUSH. ALTHOUGH I WAS WELL HIDDEN, TO BE SO CLOSE TO THIS FOUL CREATURE WHO HAD BEEN ON MY TRAIL FOR SO MANY DAYS WAS A TORMENT. I WATCHED THE TAR MAN EXAMINING HIS NEWFOUND TREASURE, HIS FAMILIAR GREASY HAT PERCHED ON HIS CROOKED HEAD. I DO NOT DENY THAT I WAS SORELY TEMPTED TO ESCAPE WHILE THE TAR MAN WAS THUS OCCUPIED WITH HIS UNEXPECTED BOOTY. YET I SAT BACK DOWN IN MY PRICKLY HAWTHORN BUSH, RESOLVED TO FOLLOW MY CONSCIENCE AND STAY WITH THE CHILDREN UNTIL THEY WERE OUT OF DANGER— FOR I KNEW WHAT IT WAS TO FEEL REMORSE. I HAD LEARNED THAT LESSON LONG AGO.

—*THE LIFE AND TIMES OF GIDEON SEYMOUR, CUTPURSE AND GENTLEMAN,* 1792

THREE

The Three-Cornered Hat

In which Peter finds himself in a
puzzling and precarious predicament

As he was either asleep or unconscious, Peter had no idea of the danger he was in. In his dream he was being sucked down a great, dark tunnel that had no end and no beginning. Spirals of light floated through him, and his whole body tingled as if he were being dissolved in sherbet. It was like a fairground ride, and he did not want it to stop.

He did not notice when the black-and-white cow with the long horns came over and licked the salt from his eyes with her meaty, pink tongue. Streaks of saliva dripped down his cheeks. Peter brushed the longhorn away in his sleep. The sudden movement startled her, and she moved away, giving him sidelong glances now and then.

Nor did Peter notice a menacing figure some five yards behind him, although there was someone else who did: a young, blond-haired man was crouching, fearful, in a thicket of hawthorn bushes some little way away. The frightening individual, whose every movement the young man closely observed, was a tall, powerfully built man who wore a vast, ragged coat and a black hat in the shape of a triangle. He carried his head at a curious angle, and his square shoulders were hunched over the end of a wooden cart to which was tethered a piebald horse. The man was cursing and blowing as he heaved a large, heavy object into position on the cart and attempted to secure it with some oddments of rope. The object appeared to be some kind of device or machine. All of a sudden the man leaped backward away from the cart as if he had received an electric shock. He then stood rooted to the spot for several minutes, clearly too terrified to move. At last he found the courage to approach the object once more.

It was easy to see why he had taken fright: All down the right-hand side, the ropes were sinking into the base of the machine as though into thick mud. And again, on this side but not on the other, the machine itself was becoming transparent, like dark glass. The man took out a fierce-looking knife and, with a trembling hand, struck the solid side of the object, which produced a sharp, ringing sound. Then he struck the transparent side. This time the blade sank instantly and silently into the object and then stuck there as if it were set in stone. The man pulled with all his might, then tried to jerk it out, but to no avail. Frustrated, he let go of the handle and stood scratching his head in bewilderment. As he watched, the knife blade started to slide smoothly out of its own accord as if repelled by the very substance from which the machine had been made.

Meanwhile Peter was beginning to emerge from his dream world and became aware of a terrible pain throbbing inside his head. It felt as though his brain had grown too large for his skull and was pressing up against the inside of his forehead. He lay quietly, unable to move, gradually becoming conscious of sunshine on his face and a cool breeze that ruffled his hair. He struggled to shift to one side of what felt like a large stone digging into his ribs. Things weren't making sense, but Peter was too dazed and confused to let that bother him. He listened to birds twittering and bees buzzing and crickets chirruping. When he heard a kind of snorting noise, he tried to take a look, but his eyelids refused to obey orders and remained firmly closed. Then he noticed that his legs felt really weird too—almost as if they weren't there. And he longed for something to drink. *Some Coca-Cola would be nice. Oh yes, some ice-cold Coca-Cola would be perfect.* He licked his parched lips and decided to go down to the kitchen to see what he could find.

As Peter concentrated all his efforts on opening his eyelids, a sharp, tweaking pain made him realize that he couldn't open them because his eyelashes were firmly stuck together, crusted over with some dried-up gooey stuff. He tried to work up some spittle in his poor dry mouth, and spat into the palms of his hands. Then he rubbed his eyes furiously. The world, in a blinding flash of sunlight, came into view. He opened and closed his eyes until they stopped watering and he could focus properly again. His eyes widened. This wasn't his home, this wasn't London, this wasn't what he'd been expecting. No, this was most definitely *not* what he'd been expecting.

The cow stood in front of him, tearing up great chunks of grass and snorting through her nose as she chewed. She flicked her tail and twitched her muscles in an effort to shoo away a cloud of flies that hovered around her. Beyond the animal a beautiful valley stretched as far as the eye could see. The grass was long and had turned to hay; dandelion seeds and thistledown floated through the air. Still too woozy to be seriously frightened, Peter reasoned that he was dreaming. The sun seemed terribly bright, and he rested his arm over his eyes to shade them.

And then, so abruptly that he did not have time to react, two gnarled, filthy hands landed on his chest and started to prod and press him through his padded anorak, as if he were a suspect being searched by the police. The hands worked their way from neck to toe, their cunning fingers sliding into every pocket, checking every crease. Peter felt his woollen scarf being pulled from his neck and heard the jingle of coins as his pocket money was removed from his trouser pocket. It was only his sense of self-preservation that kept Peter from screaming. He froze. He had the sense to close his eyes and go limp when he felt his arm being lifted away from his face. The owner of those black fingernails scrutinized him and pinched his cheek. Peter managed not to flinch, held his breath, played dead. A pungent smell of tobacco smoke and ale and stale sweat made him want to retch, but he fought the urge. He could feel those unseen eyes burning into him. By now his heart was thumping so hard he felt certain the man must be able to hear it, but a second later Peter's arm was allowed to flop back down over his eyes.

He let his breath out as slowly and silently as he could manage and cautiously opened his eyelids a crack. Now it was Peter's turn to scrutinize his attacker from under his arm. The man was crouching next to him alternately inspecting the pound coins he had stolen and biting them between his back teeth. Then he turned his attention to Peter's sneakers, stroking the material, examining the soles, pulling at the laces. Peter's heart started to beat even harder—what was so interesting about his sneakers? Was this man a thief, or was he just crazy? The man had a strong, angular nose and black hair that escaped in rats' tails from under a strange triangular hat. The thing that caught Peter's attention above all was a terrible scar, a startling white against his dark weather-beaten skin. The scar snaked down into the man's face in the shape of a crescent moon that started above his right eyebrow and reached down to below his jaw. There was something not quite right about his neck, too, for he held his head constantly tipped to one side.

Now the man stood up and stepped over Peter's legs, but not before giving him a sharp kick to his shins. To Peter's alarm, he could scarcely feel the impact of the kick. A terrible thought flashed into his mind. *Have I been in an accident? Can I walk?*

"Never try to hoodwink a hoodwinker," a slow, rasping voice

calmly announced. "I know that you are awake." The stranger leaned over and pulled Peter's arm from his face. The sun was low in the sky and when Peter opened his eyes, he was dazzled. He squinted at his assailant, who now knelt at Peter's feet, examining a handful of long bright-red hair. Peter heaved himself up on his elbows as well as he could to see where the hair had come from, and he saw that the body of a girl was draped over his ankles. He all but cried out in shock. Who was she? The man tugged on the hair, pulling up the girl's head from its grassy resting place. He examined her face dispassionately and then lowered the hair, letting the head drop back down into the mud. Peter watched in horror as the man drew out a long knife and pulled on the long red hair once more.

"No! No!" shouted Peter. "Please don't!"

The man turned to look at him, and as Peter stared into that terrible face, he knew, without a shadow of a doubt, that this was a man capable of anything.

"Life is not kind, young master. Nor fair neither. Haven't you learned that yet? Don't go expecting kindness from one who has been shown none."

Then the man laughed and pinched Peter's cheek again. This time Peter pushed his hand away. The man laughed again and picked up a few strands of the silky red hair and rubbed them between finger and thumb. He cut them and let them float to the ground.

"I could dine handsomely for a month on hair of this quality." He paused and then continued. "You have no cause to fear me— not so long as you're free with your information. If I'd wanted you dead, you'd already be at Saint Peter's gate. But tell me this, if you please: What manner of contraption is it that spews out children more dead than alive onto this desolate place?"

Behind them an unseen hand from within a large hawthorn bush aimed a stone at the flank of the piebald horse. The stone found its target, and the old mare whinnied in pain and shock. She strained to shift the heavy cart up the slope and was soon disappearing at a fast canter over the brow of the hill. The curious machine lurched precariously on the back of the cart.

The man looked from Peter to the escaping animal and back again, undecided what to do. Then he sprang up and set off in hot pursuit of his horse and cart. He was a powerful and surprisingly elegant runner. Peter had the feeling that, despite his wrecked face, this was still quite a young man. He turned at the top of the slope and shouted down to Peter so that his voice echoed all around the valley, "I have other, pressing matters to attend to. Find me at the Black Lion Tavern in Covent Garden if you want to see your infernal machine again—and if you have any sense, don't come empty-handed. Ask for Blueskin, though many do call me the Tar Man."

The Tar Man was now lost to view in the next valley, and Peter listened to the distant rumble of the cart growing fainter and fainter. He let his head sink back onto a clump of buttercups. He felt sick and faint, and the pain in his head throbbed unbearably. The Tar Man—what kind of a name was that? What infernal machine? He stared up at a hawk hovering above him in the pale blue sky and thought of nothing at all. The limp body of the girl was still bundled across his ankles, her bright hair trailing in the mud next to his feet. Soon Peter slipped out of the real world and lost consciousness once more. This time he dreamt that he was a spider caught at the bottom of a glass, and each time he started to climb out, he found himself sliding back to the bottom.

By the time Dr. Dyer had picked himself up off the floor and got down to the basement, there was no sign of the children. Molly soon reappeared, although she was trembling with fright. "Kate! Peter!" called Dr. Dyer at the top of his voice. There was an eerie silence. Dr. Dyer had the feeling in the pit of his stomach that something terrible had occurred. He looked round at Tim's laboratory, and his feeling of dread increased. The antigravity machine was gone! For a moment, where the machine should have been, Dr. Dyer had the strange sensation that he was seeing the blade of a knife, point down, floating in midair. He shook his head and looked again. It was gone. "Kate! Peter!" he shouted. "Molly's here. Where are you? Lunch will be getting cold!"

FOUR

The Howl of a Wolf

*In which the police and Kate come to some conclusions
about their predicament and the children spend the
night in a birch wood*

"Aaaaaaaaaaaaaaaaaaaaaaaaaaaaaaaaaaaaaaaaaaaaaaaaaaaaaaaaaargh!"

Peter was instantly awake again. He propped himself up on
his elbows and gawped at the strange girl who was silhouetted
against the crimson sky as the last rays of the sun lit up the
valley that stretched out before him. Her screams echoed all
around, bouncing off one slope after another until each one
repeated itself, deafeningly, three or four times. Peter watched
the girl staring in horror at a handful of hair that she held in

front of her. The sight of the red hair reminded him of something . . . a memory flickered tantalizingly on the surface of his mind, then vanished just as quickly. Peter's head throbbed even more sitting like this, and he slumped back down into the long grass.

As frightened as she had ever been in her life, Kate looked wildly around her, quite incapable of making any sense of what had happened to her. Where on earth was she? And what kind of creepy person would cut off a chunk of her hair? And where was that person now? She let go of the clump of hair, and the breeze carried it toward a giant thistle, where the long red strands got caught up in its spiky leaves, like horsehair on barbed wire. The sight of it was strangely upsetting. She screamed again.

"Aaaaaaaaaaaaaaaaaaaaagh!"

Peter put his hands over his ears. His head hurt far too much to cope with this.

Kate didn't particularly want to stop screaming, because when she did she was going to have to decide what else to do—and frankly that was going to be difficult. Where was her dad? Where was Molly? What—

"Shut up!" shouted Peter over the racket.

Kate's mouth remained open, but no more noise came out as she looked down at the skinny boy who sat gaping up at her. His dark hair was sticking up on end, and buttercup petals were sticking to his cheek. He looked as horrified as she felt.

"Oh no, it's you!" she exclaimed. Bits of straw and dry mud were now stuck to her matted hair.

"I don't know you!" cried Peter. "Who are you? What have you done to me?"

Kate walked unsteadily over to Peter. She sank down onto her knees next to him and tore the hair away from her face, showing a mass of golden freckles over pale cheeks, and frightened gray eyes. All the screaming had made her voice husky.

"What do you mean, you don't know me? I've only been forced to spend half the morning with you . . . except then it was winter and now it's summer, and then we were with my dad and now we're . . . in this place. I knew you were going to be trouble as soon as I saw you."

Peter looked at her in silent astonishment. He was so confused, he could not tell whether this was dream or reality. The girl looked familiar, but he really couldn't remember who she was.

"Are you all right?" Kate asked. "You're ever so pale. Did you know you've got a massive bruise on your forehead?" She touched him where a large purple bruise was blossoming on his temple, and Peter winced.

"And I've lost Molly! Oh, Molly, Molly, where are you?"

Kate was on the verge of crying again and quickly turned away from Peter and reached into her pocket for a handkerchief. She blew her nose noisily and sat quietly for a minute to compose herself. *There has to be a logical explanation for all this! I just can't see it right now. . . . And it must be because Peter's been hit on the head that he can't remember who I am.*

Peter turned to watch Kate get to her feet purposefully. She sprinted up the slope behind him, shading her eyes and scanning the horizon for signs of life. Then she whistled through her teeth like the farmers do at sheepdog trials. "Molly, come!" she shouted. "Molly, come!"

Peter lay watching this scene play out like a film at the cinema. It began to seem like this was happening to someone else, when, suddenly, an excruciating tingling pain started to run up and down Peter's legs like an electric current. He writhed in agony, rolling backward and forward in the long grass and clutching at the calves of his legs. It was Peter's turn to let out a piercing shriek that ricocheted across the peaceful landscape. He tried to stand up and immediately fell over. As his shoulder blades hit the ground, there was a suspicious squelching sound. Peter was in too much pain to take any notice for the moment.

"Help me! Somebody help me! Ow, ow, owwww . . ."

Kate was at his side in a moment. "Now what am I supposed to do?" she cried. She stood looking down at his squirming body, her jaw clenched and her lips pursed together. Despite Peter's continued moans she began to look more cheerful.

"I know what's wrong with you," she said. "I woke up lying over your ankles. You've just got pins and needles." And Kate began to rub his legs vigorously like she did when she helped her mother dry Milly and Sean after a paddle at the seaside. "Stamp your feet," she suggested. "By the way, do you know that you're lying in a cowpat?"

It was several minutes before Peter could bear to put any weight on his feet. Kate was now squatting in the long grass, staring into space. It was clear that she was thinking hard. Peter stood up and wiped his anorak on some long grass, taking a long sideways look at the unfamiliar girl as he did so. She noticed him

and her face went into a lopsided sort of frown with one eyebrow higher than the other. Peter instantly knew who she was. It
was as though someone had thrown a bucket of cold water over
his head—he recognized the girl and could remember her father
and all her brothers and sisters, and the Van de Graaff generator,
and Kate and himself chasing Molly down a long white corridor.
What he couldn't remember, or begin to understand, was *how*
he and the girl found themselves here in this beautiful, deserted
valley.

"You're Kate," he said.

"Yes, I know that," said Kate. "Why don't you tell me something I don't know, like how we got here?"

"But I don't know," replied Peter. "I can't remember."

"Well, try," said Kate. "Think back. Try and picture everything that happened between this morning and the last thing you
do remember, and look for clues. That's what I'm trying to do.
Something very weird has happened to us today. One of us has
got to work out what."

Molly could not be persuaded to leave Tim's laboratory. When
Dr. Dyer tried to pull her away, she bared her teeth and snarled
at him as if he were a stranger. Alarmed and fearful, he left her
there and ran out into the icy sunshine.

"Kate! Peter!" he cried over and over again until he grew
hoarse. But the only sound was the wind in the pine trees. He
rushed back to Tim's laboratory, where Molly was now howling
in a way that Dr. Dyer had never heard before—the animal's

unearthly cries chilled him more than the wind. What could possibly have happened to provoke Molly's heartrending howls of despair?

After half an hour Dr. Dyer decided that he had better call his wife. He did his best to disguise the growing panic that he felt, but Mrs. Dyer picked up on it immediately. When she arrived at the laboratory barely ten minutes later and saw the look on her husband's face, her blood turned to ice.

"Oh, no," she said in a small, thin voice. "Oh, no."

After another fruitless search the security guards contacted the police. Kate's parents sat side by side in the guards' room with more sickening fear in the pit of their stomachs than they would have believed possible to bear. And what could they say to Peter's father? The boy had been in their care. . . . They did not speak and they could not cry. Every time a pager bleeped or a telephone rang, they both leaped to their feet only to sink back down again when it was a false alarm.

It took the police two hours to track down Peter's father. It took another few minutes for what they were telling him to sink in, and then he got straight into his car and drove from central London to Derbyshire without stopping. He told himself that Peter would be there, safe and sound, when he reached the Dyers' farm. But what if he wasn't? How he wished he had taken Peter on his birthday treat instead of going to that useless meeting. How he wished Peter's last words to him that morning hadn't been "I hate you!"

•   •   •

The police arrived in force at the NCRDM laboratories at a quarter to three. Flashing orange lights illuminated fat flakes of snow before the flakes settled on the roofs of a line of police cars. Six uniformed police officers made a thorough search of the laboratories and grounds and questioned all the staff, but they found no trace of Peter or Kate and no clue as to where they might be.

When Mr. Schock arrived at half past five and was informed that Peter had not yet been found, he telephoned his wife in California, where she was still sleeping, and broke the awful news to her. She wanted to catch the first plane back, but her husband stopped her—after all, it was quite likely that as soon as he put the receiver down, Peter would turn up, right as rain. . . . She agreed to delay returning for three hours but no longer.

Meanwhile a policewoman had driven Mrs. Dyer back to the farm, and Dr. Dyer was taken to the police station at Bakewell, where he remained for the next three hours. The national and local media were alerted, and by six o'clock a senior police officer had been assigned to the case.

Detective Inspector Wheeler was a Scotsman by birth and was now close to retirement. He had been in charge of numerous high-profile investigations in his time, including several cases of missing persons, all of which he had seen through to their happy or tragic conclusions. He was well respected. He was also notorious for his bad temper, his dogged obstinacy, and his dedication to the job.

When Dr. Tim Williamson confirmed that the prototype for an antigravity machine that he was designing as part of a NASA-funded project had gone missing, it was suggested that the children might have been abducted when they came across thieves attempting to steal the equipment. Dr. Williamson argued that his machine was worthless—why would anyone want to steal a device that was barely at the testing stage? Detective Inspector Wheeler secretly formed the opinion that there was more to this machine than Dr. Williamson was prepared to admit. All his instincts told him that this was not going to be a straightforward case—but then, if there was one thing Inspector Wheeler relished, it was a challenge.

"Did you see what happened to my hair?" asked Kate.

"So I didn't dream it!" exclaimed Peter, whose muzzy head was finally beginning to clear. He told Kate as much as he could remember about the Tar Man and their conversation.

"He was going to *sell* my hair?" she repeated incredulously. "And what did this machine contraption thingy look like, then?"

"I didn't get a good look at it. I only saw it on the back of the cart when the horse was galloping away. Could have been anything. Sort of cube-shaped. Well, a cube that's taller than it is wide."

"A cuboid, you mean," said Kate.

Peter shrugged his shoulders. "If you say so."

"Could it have been Tim's antigravity machine?"

"Maybe . . ."

"What's the last thing you can remember before waking up here?" Kate asked.

"Chasing your dog down the corridor. You were in front of

me. I guess someone must have hit me on the head. What do you remember?"

"Chasing after Molly, like you. She was headed for Tim's lab. And I've got a picture of spirals, floating spirals of light. Perhaps I was hit on the head too." She felt her head, searching for lumps.

Peter and Kate fell silent and stood in the ever darkening valley, lost in their own thoughts, trying to understand their puzzling predicament. Both were tired and shaky and in need of food, especially Peter, whose face was gray with exhaustion. Yet they could not bring themselves to sit down, because both of them were waiting. Waiting to jump up and down and wave their arms about when the rescue helicopter or the police car arrived. After all, it was just a matter of time, wasn't it?

Kate stooped to pick a silky red poppy and a blue cornflower. Just how can it have been nearly Christmas at lunchtime and midsummer by late afternoon? And what godforsaken place was this? She was used to living in the countryside but had never been anywhere this isolated: no distant rumble of traffic, no electricity pylons, no roads, not even a hint of a vapor trail left in the sky by an airplane. And why, infuriatingly, could she not remember what had happened whilst chasing Molly down the corridor? Why, when she tried to recall what had happened next, did these shapes keep forming in her mind—long, loose, luminous spirals that seemed to pass right through her? And who precisely was this Tar Man person?

She looked over at Peter, who was kicking clods of earth high into the air. He had plunged his hands deep into his trouser pockets, and his head was drooping miserably. *I wonder how much help bean sprout over there is going to be,* Kate thought.

"You know what I think?" said Kate.

"What?"

"I think we must have both been hit over the head by thieves. The machine—I think they must have stolen it from the laboratory and had to take us with them because we were witnesses. I think we've been taken to Australia."

"Australia! You're not serious!"

"Or maybe New Zealand . . . Well, you explain why it's suddenly summer, then. Do you think it's more likely that we've been unconscious for six months?"

Peter scratched his head. "Mmm . . . but if they stole the machine, why did they dump it here for the Tar Man to find?"

"Well, I don't know," replied Kate. "Perhaps they couldn't carry everything. Or they were disturbed."

"And why bring us all the way here just to dump us? If they knocked us over the head, why didn't they just leave us at your dad's lab?" asked Peter.

"All right. I don't know. But I do think we're in Australia. And I definitely think we should stay here until they come to rescue us. They'll be searching everywhere for us."

Peter nodded. "They'd better be. . . . You don't have anything to drink, do you?"

"Don't you think I would have offered you some if I had? What sort of person do you think I am?"

Peter did not reply.

They both fell silent again.

"Maybe we should shout for help," suggested Kate after a while. "After all, the Tar Man must be long gone by now. There might be someone close by . . ."

Peter shrugged. "Okay. It's worth a try."

"Help!" shrieked Kate.

"You really do have a loud voice," said Peter, wincing.

"Good," Kate replied. "Aren't you going to join in?"

"Hee-eelp!" they both shouted. "Help!"

Whenever they stopped, the silence seemed even deeper. Discouraged, Peter started to yodel instead.

"Yo-del-ay-ee-o! Yo-del-ay-ee-o! Yo-del-ay-ee yo-del-ay-ee yo-del-ay-ee-o!" Kate grinned for the first time since waking up in this strange land. She added her voice to the din. They yodeled faster and faster until their throats hurt too much to continue. Then Peter just shouted out whatever came into his head: "Tottenham Hotspur! Lightning Conductor! Diplodocus!" Each phrase came diving back to him like a boomerang.

Kate answered, "Manchester United! Supercallifragilistic-expialidocious!"

Hidden in a tangle of hawthorn bushes and young birches, the young stranger woke up from a deep sleep at the sound of the children's yodeling. He peered through the foliage. A crescent moon had appeared in the evening sky. Two blue eyes focused on the children, and the stranger's face broke into a smile.

By now the children had moved on to doing animal impressions: Kate was imitating a cow in need of milking, and Peter was roaring like a lion. Then he howled like a wolf: "Aa-ooooh!"

The sound of another wolf rang out and echoed around the valley. "Aa-ooooh!" Its cry was strong and wild.

"Was that you?" asked Peter.

"No," said Kate. "Are you trying to scare me?"

"No, really, I'm not kidding. Stop playing about. It was you, wasn't it?"

"No, it wasn't!" insisted Kate.

"Aa-ooooh!" Another howl from the stranger's lips reverberated across the peaceful landscape.

A moment later Peter and Kate were charging blindly down the grassy slope, arms outstretched for balance. They bounded, panting and spluttering, down the steep incline, scattering groups of grazing rabbits, and eventually came to a shuddering halt at the edge of a small wood at the bottom of the valley. They flung themselves on the ground, incapable of doing anything save taking in huge gulps of air.

Inside the wood it was pitch black. The pale bark of the birch trees that grew at the wood's edge seemed to glow in the twilight. If there were wolves up above, thought Kate, what creatures would they find down here? There were sure to be deadly spiders and poisonous snakes. She would *not* go into the wood unless she absolutely had to. But then she looked back up at the dark slope behind her. The muscles across her chest tightened as she pictured having to leap onto a wolf's back to get away from its strong white teeth, imagined pulling at its shaggy, rank coat and kicking at it with all her might—anything to stop those fangs sinking into her, tearing at soft flesh . . . At the bottom of the valley, in the dark, everything pressed down on her. She covered her eyes with her hands in an attempt to shut it all out, and silent tears flowed through her fingers. *Where are you, Daddy, where are you?*

Meanwhile Peter, too, was straining to hear anything that could suggest a wolf was hunting them down. He listened so hard it almost hurt. At first Kate's panting was all he could hear. Gradually, though, he tuned into the sound of the leaves rustling in the gentle breeze and began to distinguish a different noise. . . . He was sure he could make out the trickling sound of a small stream.

"Water!" he shouted, and grabbing hold of Kate's sleeve, he pulled her into the darkness.

Water had never tasted so refreshing. They lay on their bellies and dipped their faces into the freezing water. Peter gulped down so much water he could hear it slooshing around inside his stomach.

"Come on," said Kate. "It doesn't look like we can count on anyone finding us tonight. We're going to have to find help fast if we don't want to spend the night out here."

They tried to press on through the black wood, stumbling over logs and walking into invisible branches that lashed at their faces. Whenever Kate felt the tickle of a leaf or a blade of grass against her skin, she became convinced it was a spider and came to a halt, rubbing herself down frantically and slapping the legs of her jeans just in case.

"Oh, this is hopeless!" exclaimed Peter after a while. "I can't see a thing—we could be walking around in circles for all we know!"

"Okay," sighed Kate. "Let's stay here until morning. But I'm not going to sleep, though."

"Well, I am."

Peter flopped down. His head was pounding and he felt weak with hunger. He looked up through the branches at the night sky. A carpet of milky stars hung over the valley. Could they really be in Australia? He began to convince himself that the night sky looked upside down.

Kate hesitated before speaking. "Earlier on, when I said that I knew you were trouble as soon as I looked at you . . ."

"Yes . . ."

"Well, that was a bit unfair—probably."

"Oh. Okay."

Kate lay on the bare ground next to him. "Roll over," she said. "I think we should lie back to back for safety and to keep warm."

"No way!" said Peter. "I'm not sleeping next to a girl."

Kate was too tired to argue and lay with her back against a young beech tree. She could just make out Peter in the dappled moonlight.

"My dad will find us, you know. He's really smart and he'd never let anything happen to me. He'll do whatever it takes to get us back, I know he will."

Kate, too, was in worse shape than she cared to admit to herself. She felt that she couldn't have got up again now even if she'd wanted to.

Peter wondered if anyone had yet dared disturb an important business meeting to tell his father that his son had got mislaid.

"Yeah," he said. "I'm sure you're right."

Kate did not reply. She was already asleep.

A Breakfast of Grilled Trout

*In which Peter goes fishing and
Kate gives her companion a fright*

As the sun rose, its rays started their slow descent down the valley's grassy slopes. Far below, a ghostly white mist hung above the stream, revealing the water's path as it passed through the middle of the wood where, under the green canopy, Peter and Kate slept on.

Kate was dead to the world, wrapped around the trunk of the beech tree, her white face streaked with mud and tears. Peter, though, was beginning to stir. He looked about him. Everything was covered in beads of dew that glistened in the half-light. How stiff and damp he felt after a night sleeping on bare ground. His T-shirt was sticking to his back, and a vague whiff of cowpat lingered around his anorak, reminding him of the events of the previous day. He looked over at Kate, whose back rose and fell in a slow, regular rhythm.

He decided not to wake her but to explore for a while on his own. It suddenly occurred to him that he had never woken up without a grown-up telling him what to do. What freedom! He followed the path of the little stream. Kicking his way through the bracken, Peter felt almost in a holiday mood. Somehow, this morning, he could not feel scared or miserable. He bet that the "wolf" they had heard the previous night was just a big dog locked out for the night. And even though it was still a puzzle how they'd got here, all they had to do was find a telephone, call home, and someone would pick them up straightaway.

He crouched down to scoop up some water with his hands— if there was nothing to eat, at least he could drink. *Plop!* Out of the corner of his eye Peter saw a fish break through the surface of the water to catch a fly. Slowly and quietly Peter stood up to see if he could catch sight of any more. His heart leaped as he counted five, six, seven beautiful brown trout swimming upstream among the bright green weed that splayed itself out like hair in the gentle current. The trouts' backs were an undistinguished greeny brown, but there was no mistaking their shimmering sides, speckled with dots of red, green, and gray. For a boy who had caught his first trout with his bare hands on the River Frome even before he had learned to read, breakfast suddenly seemed a distinct possibility.

A Breakfast of Grilled Trout

Trout-tickling as his grandfather had taught him was difficult and required endless patience, yet even as a small child he used to love to try—once set on something Peter was not one to give up easily. So now he lay on his stomach and slipped first his hand and then his whole arm into the freezing water. He made himself so still and quiet that he became one with the flow of the stream, the stony bed, and the rippling water. Eventually a plump, speckled trout drew near to his hand. Slowly and with the deftest of touches, Peter started to stroke its belly. After a few minutes he soothed the trout into a trancelike state. When Peter judged the moment was right, he flung the fish onto the grassy bank. He picked it up and killed it in one clean blow, as his grandfather had taught him, by knocking its head smartly on a rock. As he prepared to try his luck again, the crack of a twig breaking made him wheel around. All his senses went on full alert. Was there someone else with him in the sun-dappled wood? Eventually he decided that it must have been an animal, and his attention returned to the job at hand.

Half an hour later Peter set off to find Kate, very pleased with himself and with the three slippery brown trout that he had wrapped in dock leaves and stuffed into his anorak pockets. He was tempted to wake her by howling like a wolf, and grinned mischievously at the thought. Then he remembered how petrified she had seemed the previous night and thought the better of it.

When he reached Kate, she was still curled up in the same position, her hood pulled over her head and her knees tucked around the slim trunk of the young beech tree. Tendrils of red hair had escaped from her hood and were blowing gently in the breeze.

Peter crouched down, trying not to make a sound, and tipped his head to one side so that he could see her face. She looked pale through her freckles and was frowning. It made him sad to see her look so anxious even while she was still asleep. He was on the point of touching her shoulder to wake her when something happened that he could not begin to understand. She appeared to be fading or dissolving into thin air. Peter stared at her, unable to believe what he was witnessing. He blinked and rubbed his eyes. There was no doubt about it, Kate was distinctly hazy. He made himself look all around him, at the ground strewn with yellowing leaves, at the ant marching toward his shoe, at the huge cobweb with a great fat spider waiting at its center. Everything else was in sharp focus, yet Kate was like an image on a poorly tuned television, flickering and fuzzy. In fact, you could see the tree trunk she was huddled up against right through her body. Peter felt a dreadful sense of panic come over him. Was she going to disappear altogether? "Kate!" Peter shouted. "Wake up!"

At the sound of his voice she snapped instantly back into focus, and it was a solid Kate who was on her feet in a second. "What's wrong?" she gasped. "Have the wolves come?"

"No . . . no. It's just that you looked . . . funny."

"You shouted at me like that because I looked funny! You're worse than Sam! You really scared me. I thought we were about to be torn to pieces or something. . . ." Kate paused for breath; her fists were still clenched and her eyes burned into him. "What do you mean I looked *funny*?"

There was nothing remotely flickery or fuzzy about her now, and Peter began to doubt what he had seen. Could hunger make you imagine things? He decided to play the incident down.

"I thought you were looking a bit blurred around the edges, that's all," he said, failing to sound offhand. "It must have been a trick of the light."

Kate stared at him in disbelief. "A bit blurred round the edges!" she exclaimed. "Are you trying to wind me up? Because if you are, it's not working."

Peter was so preoccupied that he didn't notice how near to crying Kate was. *I must find out if she's still solid,* he told himself, and decided that the simplest course of action was to bump into her accidentally on purpose. Kate eyed him suspiciously as he circled around her before tripping himself up deliberately on a tree root and flooring Kate in the manner of a professional wrestler. Kate hit out at him and pushed him roughly off her. She shouted, "What do you think you're doing, you idiot?"

Large tears started to roll down Kate's cheeks and dropped onto the backs of her hands as she tugged at her cotton handkerchief. Her shoulders shook as she sobbed silently. Peter put his hand awkwardly on her arm.

"I shouldn't have pushed you over. I'm really sorry. I didn't think it would upset you that much."

Kate took in a deep breath to calm herself down.

"It's not just you," she said. "When you woke me up I thought I was standing in the kitchen at home. I saw Milly on the floor by the cooker, writing notes on pieces of newspaper and stuffing them into everyone's shoes. She does that a lot. Well, she can't write—she's only two—but she pretends. Then Molly trotted in. She stood there, sort of looking at me, but she didn't jump up or lick my face. She just whined. . . . It was as though she knew I was there but couldn't see me. And Milly didn't notice me at all. It was horrible. . . . It wasn't a dream. I swear it wasn't a dream. I was there."

Peter did not know what to say so he said nothing. Kate mopped her face with her handkerchief. Insects buzzed around them, and the birch trees rustled in the breeze. Then Peter remembered the trout.

"Look what I've got," he said, pulling out the fish from his pockets. "Brown trout. Delicious!"

"Wow! Did you catch those?"

Peter nodded.

"Do you know how to gut them?" asked Kate. "Have you got a knife?"

"Well, no," replied Peter.

"Have you got anything to light a fire with?" She was sounding a little less impressed.

"No, but I'm sure we'll think of something."

"I see—we can't cook them and we can't gut them. So how *are* we going to eat them? Suck them like lollipops?"

Peter managed to stop himself from snapping, "Find your own breakfast, then!" At least she had stopped crying.

If Peter had vague notions about making a stone knife out of flint, he soon dropped the idea when an extensive search yielded only a collection of smooth rounded pebbles. Meanwhile Kate gave herself friction burns rubbing two sticks together.

"Come on, I've had enough of this. Let's go and find a telephone," she said.

They left the trout for the crows and decided to retrace the course of the stream back up the hill. Once they were clear of the wood, the sun beat on their backs and they took off their anoraks and tied them around their waists. It was hard going, and when they were near the top, Kate flung herself down, panting. Peter followed suit and pushed his hair back from his damp forehead. His gaze settled absentmindedly on the wood where they had spent the night. It was his nose rather than his eyes that first alerted him to the plume of hazy gray smoke that rose up into the clear air.

"Look!" he cried. "Someone's lit a fire."

For the second time since their arrival, Peter and Kate hurtled down to the bottom of the valley. As they drew nearer to the source of the smoke they heard a man singing.

"My love she did a-wooing go. Fol-de-la-la-de-dah. My love she said she loved me so. Fol-de-la-la-de-dah."

They did not stop until they reached a small clearing where a mouthwatering smell of grilled trout greeted them. A man with a blond pigtail down his back was tending a wood fire. At the sound of their steps the man turned around to look at them. He had calm, deep blue eyes and a broad, handsome face, and he did not seem to be the least surprised to see them. For a second Peter thought he recognized him but then changed his mind.

The stranger advanced toward the children and gave a graceful bow.

"My name is Gideon Seymour. I hope I may be of some service to you in your trouble. I have, in any case, taken the liberty of cooking your trout."

SIX

Lost in Time

*In which Peter and Kate discover that
their troubles have only just begun*

Gideon handed each of the children a crispy-skinned trout that
he had skewered on a long stick. He motioned for them to sit.
"You need to eat," he said. "We can talk afterward." All three
sat in a circle around the crackling fire, glad to be putting food
in their bellies. Peter and Kate shot sidelong looks at Gideon
every now and then. There was a quiet dignity about him that
made them feel shy. Gideon ate his trout peaceably, and when

he intercepted one of Peter's curious glances, he smiled at him, an open, warmhearted smile.

Gideon stripped off the last morsels of pink flesh with his teeth, then flung the bones into the fire and wiped his mouth on the back of his hand. He wore a loose white shirt, soiled and torn after several days on the road, and well-worn boots, caked in mud almost to the knees, into which were tucked tight-fitting trousers. A small hawthorn twig had caught in his blond ponytail. On the ground next to him lay a three-cornered hat, less grimy, but of a similar shape to that worn by the Tar Man. Peter wondered why both people he had encountered since his arrival here looked and sounded like people in costume dramas on the television. An explanation for this popped into his mind, which he immediately dismissed as being too ridiculous to contemplate.

"Thank you for my breakfast, young master. I watched how you caught the fish. It is a rare skill that you have."

Peter looked at him in surprise. "You saw me?"

"When I saw the manner of your arrival I had to be sure I had nothing to fear from you. And I believe we share an enemy."

"Oh, please," burst in Kate suddenly. "I must phone home. My name is Kate Dyer and my parents will be going mad with worry. Do you have a mobile phone?"

Gideon looked at her, puzzled.

"Or do you know where there's a phone box?"

"I do not understand you, Mistress Kate."

Kate wrung her hands in exasperation.

"How *did* we arrive?" asked Peter. "What enemy?"

Gideon searched their eager, anxious faces. What should he do with these children? This was a strange predicament indeed. He looked at the sun climbing ever higher in the sky and stood up purposefully.

"Will you walk with me? I wish to reach my destination before nightfall." He swung a large bag over one shoulder and tapped his hat on his head. He looked over at Peter. "And may I ask *your* name, young sir?"

"My name is Peter, Peter Schock."

"Tell me," Gideon continued, "is it possible that our paths have crossed before this day? When I first saw your face I felt that someone had stepped over my grave. . . ." A look of concern swept across his face. "You are not, of course . . . *spirits*?" He made light of the question by laughing.

Kate and Peter remained silent, unsure whether this was a joke. Peter shook his head uncertainly. Gideon clearly felt awkward, for he set off up the slope at what seemed to the children a furious pace. At first they were forced to jog to keep up with him, but when Gideon noticed how little used they were to walking any distance, he slowed down. Eventually, as though he had been debating what to do, or what to say, or, indeed, what to believe, Gideon answered Peter's question.

"The enemy I spoke of is the Tar Man. He has stolen your property, has he not? And I—let us say, I have unfinished business with him. He has been pursuing me since I left Highgate, these six days past. Were it not for your timely arrival—which put all thought of my capture out of his head—he would have finally caught up with me, of that I am certain.

"I knew he was gaining on me and I had little strength left, so I concealed myself in a hawthorn bush, yonder." Here Gideon paused to point to the northern slopes of the valley where the children had first woken up. "Soon the Tar Man came into view on the brow of the hill, and as he looked out for me and I peeped out at him, we both witnessed you appear out of thin air like some devilish apparition. At first I feared you were both dead, for you were held as if by invisible ropes to that unworldly object, and your heads and limbs lolled down so that you looked like rag dolls. I could not move for I did not want the Tar Man to discover me. He sat on his cart and, by the look on his face, was as terrified as I. A moment later some monstrous force flung your bodies away from the contraption with such power that you landed a dozen paces away. You were lucky to have escaped more grievous injury. I heard the crack as Peter's head struck a rock."

Peter and Kate stopped walking and Peter reached up to touch his tender bruise, which was by now purple and yellow. To be abducted by thieves was one thing, but this seemed infinitely worse. Then, as Kate and Peter looked at each other in horror, their expressions changed subtly and both knew what the other was thinking—that Gideon was either mad or lying or mistaken and that it had all been a trick of the light and that there was a perfectly logical explanation for all this. They did not, of course, say as much to Gideon.

Kate lowered one eyebrow. "And so what happened to the, er, contraption that you were telling us about?" she asked.

"The Tar Man loaded it onto his cart. At one end it was a

plain thing, gray and unadorned. At the other there was a silver object that resembled for all the world a giant pear . . ."

Peter looked at Kate. "The antigravity machine," he mouthed. Kate nodded.

"Yet there was something magical about it," continued Gideon, "for when he tried to tie it down with rope, it began to dissolve into the air—I could make out the cart through it. It became glassy, like deep, still water. If the Tar Man had not leaped back in terror, I would have doubted the evidence of my own eyes."

"So the magic chest became sort of, blurred round the edges, did it?" asked Peter.

"Blurred, yes, and transparent, like thick glass. And when my gaze fell upon you, Master Peter, you, too, had started to dissolve into the air in the same ungodly fashion as your device."

"Me!" exclaimed Peter. "No! That's not possible!"

"I swear it is true," replied Gideon. "You all but disappeared in the bright sunshine—I do not know what called you back."

"This is unreal," said Peter under his breath. Kate gripped Peter's arm in distress.

"You weren't winding me up, were you? That happened to me, too, didn't it?" she asked in a whisper.

"Look, Gideon," said Peter, taking a step toward him and failing to hide how rattled he was, "we're really grateful to you for helping us out, but could you please take us to the nearest town, we have to get to a phone urgently."

"Phone? What or who is this phone? I do not understand you."

"Oh, come on, you must know," said Peter in frustration,

cupping one ear in his hand and pretending to chatter. "Tel-e-phone . . . Everyone knows what a phone is."

"I have told you that I do not," said Gideon, raising his voice in anger.

"We'll show you when we see one," said Kate hurriedly. "Please forgive us, we're a bit upset. Could you tell us where we are, please? Which part of Australia is this? Or is it New Zealand?"

Gideon seemed baffled for a moment, then spun round to look at her and, seeing that she was deadly serious, burst into laughter.

"Do you think you are in Austria? Ah no, Mistress Kate, this is not Austria."

Kate was about to protest that she meant Australia, when Gideon continued, "We are a stone's throw from Dovedale. As the crow flies, we are less than two hours' walk from Bakewell."

"Dovedale! Bakewell!" exclaimed Kate, her face radiant with relief. "But that's near to where I live. . . . Oh, Peter, we'll be home by lunchtime!"

"Could you excuse us a moment," said Peter, and he pulled Kate out of Gideon's earshot. He whispered urgently in her ear.

"I know you want to get home, but if this is Derbyshire, how come it's summer? Look, I do like Gideon, but how can we trust what he says when he doesn't even know what a phone is? And I'm not convinced he's heard of Australia, either."

Kate let out a deep sigh and opened her mouth to say something and then changed her mind and shook her head. "Oh, I don't know. I'm so totally confused. . . . I don't know what to think. Shall we just play along with him until we get to a town?"

Peter nodded. Gideon was pacing about impatiently, waiting for them to set off again. He seemed offended.

"I mean to reach Bakewell by nightfall. If you wish me to take you there, I would ask you to come now. I can escort you to the house of my future employer, where I can ask if you can rest before leaving for London."

"London?" repeated Peter. "Why London?"

"Do you not need the magic chest to return from whence you came? The Tar Man told you—he has taken it to Covent Garden. He lodges, I think, in Drury Lane. He drinks at the Black Lion Tavern, where I have seen him many a time with the Carrick gang. I urge you to find him before he decides to find you. The Tar Man will drive a hard bargain, of that you can be sure. But if he means to hand over the booty to his master . . . then your troubles have scarcely yet begun. His master is a man in need of constant diversion, and he has a taste for all things mysterious. So if he takes a fancy to it, you may never get it back. It will be lost in a wager or given as payment to his tailor or his wig-maker, or he will demand so high a price you will never be able to pay him. In any case he will deny all knowledge of it. Believe me—for I have cause to know—there is not a more skillful liar in the kingdom."

Gideon waited for a response but got none. Neither Peter nor Kate had any idea how to respond to this mass of baffling information. Gideon's patience was clearly at an end.

"I have delayed long enough. I'm off for Bakewell. Come or stay as you will."

He strode over the ridge of the hill and did not look back.

Peter and Kate hurried after their best hope of reaching civilization. Soon Gideon had disappeared into the neighboring valley.

"I don't care about the stupid chest," said Kate in annoyance. "I just want to go home."

Kate turned round to take a last look at the valley. She let out a gasp.

"What's wrong?" Peter asked.

"This *is* my valley," she said in a faltering voice. "I thought I was imagining it last night. This is the way the school bus comes—it's so obvious from this direction. My house should be beside the stream where we spent the night. This is my valley, but there's nothing here. There's nothing here!"

Peter saw Gideon glancing over his shoulder at them and realized that he was not going to wait for them. Kate stood with her hand over her mouth, her gray eyes filling with tears. Peter pulled her by the arm and attempted to reassure her while keeping her moving.

"How can that possibly be?" he said. "I guess one valley must look pretty much like another."

"What do you know?" cried Kate. "You're just a townie! Don't you think I'd recognize my own valley?"

"Okay, okay. Have it your way. There's no need to shout. Just hang on until we reach a phone—one call and all of this will be sorted out."

They walked without speaking, never letting Gideon out of their sight, putting one foot in front of the other through fertile summer meadows, treading over fresh green grass and clover and cow parsley and wishing that someone would pull them out of this bad dream.

Peter's mother flew back to England from California on Sunday. She arrived in the early hours of Monday morning, only just in time for the press conference that had been hastily organized in the assembly hall of Kate's school in Bakewell. It was a grim homecoming.

The television cameras focused in on Detective Inspector Wheeler, who announced to the press that the children had disappeared without a trace from the research center six miles away at midday forty-eight hours earlier. He said that there were now serious concerns about their safety. Dr. and Mrs. Dyer and Mr. and Mrs. Schock sat in a forlorn row behind a long table. It was more than Mrs. Dyer could bear to be sitting in these circumstances in the same place as she had seen Kate singing her heart out at the Christmas carol concert only one week earlier.

Police telephone numbers and images of the children flashed on the big screen and were beamed to televisions across the country: There was last term's school photograph of Peter with a silly grin on his face, and a video of Kate training Molly to shake hands.

At the end of the press conference Peter's and Kate's parents hurried away from the spotlights to cope with their anguish in private. While the cameramen packed up their equipment, Detective Inspector Wheeler stood staring out of a window, chewing the end of his pencil. He was perplexed. An experienced policeman, he could usually rely on his gut instincts, but with this case he felt he was receiving confused messages. When he had met Peter's parents for the first time, the unmistakable scent of money that wafted around them had made him suspect a kidnapping. Yet no ransom note had been delivered—at least not to his knowledge. Could Mr. and Mrs. Schock be hiding something? And then there was Dr. Williamson's machine, not to mention the representatives whom NASA was sending over from Houston. Why would they do that for some worthless bit of equipment? And, bizarrely, Detective Inspector Wheeler felt in his bones that both children were safe and sound and that, sooner or later, they *would* turn up. He would have liked to share his optimism with the distraught parents, but he could scarcely tell them to stop worrying because he had a funny sort of a hunch that Peter and Kate were all right. . . .

He chewed his pencil and stared absentmindedly at the playing field outside. The watery sunshine had melted most of last night's hard frost, but there were still lingering patches of ice under the branches of the ancient cedar tree that towered over the soccer pitches. Something caught the policeman's eye and he swung his gaze over to one of the far goalposts. The sun, already low in the sky, dazzled him, yet he was sure he could see a figure lying in the mouth of the goal. He squinted in the sunshine. It was a girl, wearing what seemed to be a long green evening dress. She was lying on her back with her knees up, the dress tucked around her legs. Her long red hair streamed out behind her on the muddy pitch.

"Good grief," he exclaimed in his soft Edinburgh accent. "She looks like the Dyer girl!"

He dropped his pencil and immediately ran out of the school and onto the soccer pitch, shouting at two constables to follow him at once. When they reached the goalposts, she had disappeared. Detective Inspector Wheeler turned around slowly, in a full circle, his breath turning to steam in the chill air as he carefully scanned the grounds, but there was no longer any sign of the girl who looked like Kate. He crouched down to search for fresh prints in the half-frozen mud between the goalposts, and he felt all the hackles rise on the back of his neck.

After two hours of hard walking under a hot sun, Gideon came to a halt and pointed. "The River Wye. We'll be in Bakewell within the hour." Gideon looked at Peter's and Kate's red, shiny faces and drooping shoulders. "We can rest here a moment and drink," he said.

He led them to a grassy riverbank where dragonflies of metallic blue swooped over the water. Kate kicked off her sneakers and unpeeled her socks from her aching feet. Peter followed suit, and they both dangled their toes in the icy water. Gideon filled a leather water bottle and offered it to the children before drinking himself. Then he stretched out luxuriously on the grass and put his three-cornered hat over his face.

"We will soon reach Sheepwash Bridge, if I am not mistaken," said Gideon from under his hat.

The effect his words had on Kate was electric. She leaped up and started to pull her socks onto her damp feet.

"I know Sheepwash Bridge. It's at Ashford-on-the-Water. My friend Megan lives there. We can telephone from her house!"

She set off at a run while Peter struggled to get his sneakers back on.

"Mistress Kate!" Gideon shouted after her. "Ashford is in that direction."

Kate turned round and started to run in the direction Gideon was indicating. She forgot her tiredness and sprang through the soft grass. Peter soon caught up with her, and after ten minutes they spotted a cluster of stone houses and a pretty bridge spanning a river.

"Look!" cried Kate. "That's Sheepwash Bridge."

They did not slow down until they were standing on the bridge, and then both of them came to an abrupt halt.

"Oh, no," said Kate in a crestfallen voice. "This can't be happening."

They were standing on cobblestones. A dirt road led from the bridge through the village of Ashford-on-the-Water that Kate thought she knew so well. Some of the mellow stone cottages seemed familiar but not much else. It was not just the absence of tarmacs, road markings, streetlamps, sidewalks, cars, and the hotel, where she had once had lunch, that was so upsetting. It was also the appearance of the villagers themselves. Kate and Peter saw an old man driving a cart and horse. White thistledown hair reached past his shoulders, and he wore a large soft-brimmed hat, filthy black coat, and knee breeches. Enormous buckles decorated his shabby shoes. Three barefooted boys in rags were teasing a cat that was backing, hissing, into a doorway. A woman in a straw bonnet and a long low-cut dress that displayed her ample bosom was carrying a basket of carrots. Soon each of the villagers had stopped what they were doing and were staring openmouthed at the strangers on the bridge. If Kate and Peter thought the villagers looked weird, the feeling was clearly mutual.

It's a film set. It has to be a film set, thought Peter, who had occasionally been allowed to see his mother at work. He looked around for the camera crew.

"We must find you some respectable clothes if you are not to make a spectacle of yourselves," said Gideon in a low voice from behind them. "Let me go ahead of you."

He pushed in front of them and bowed in turn to the woman with the carrots and the old man on the cart. "Good day to you," he said, pulling off his hat. "'Tis fine weather we are enjoying, is it not?" Peter looked down self-consciously at his T-shirt and jeans and adjusted the anorak that he had tied around his waist. The wretched cat had escaped its young tormentors while they recovered enough from their surprise to start pointing and jeering at Peter and Kate. Gideon marched through them, threatening to cuff one of them around the ear, and making as if to kick another's bottom.

"Mind your manners if you don't want to feel my boot on your behinds," he warned.

Peter waited until they'd reached the other side of the village before he asked the question that was on both children's tongues: "What is the date today, Gideon?"

"It must be the eighteenth—no, the nineteenth day of July."

"And the year?" Peter asked.

"The year?"

"Yes, the year."

"Why, the year of our Lord seventeen hundred and sixty-three."

"1763," mouthed Kate silently.

The shock of it was too much for Peter to take in, and for a moment he felt no emotion at all. Then he had a strong urge to giggle but found himself instead sinking to the ground. Kate kept repeating "1763" to herself as if to hammer the meaning home. She turned very pale and then said, "I feel a bit dizzy," and collapsed at Gideon's feet.

I WAS OVERCOME WITH WONDER AND AMAZEMENT WHEN PETER FIRST TOLD ME HE HAD COME HERE FROM THE FUTURE. THEN I SAW THE FEAR IN HIS FACE AND I REALIZED THAT HIS JOURNEY THROUGH THE CENTURIES HAD MADE HIM AN ORPHAN JUST AS SURELY AS I HAD BEEN ORPHANED BY THE FEVER.

—*THE LIFE AND TIMES OF GIDEON SEYMOUR, CUTPURSE AND GENTLEMAN, 1792*

SEVEN

The Hospitality of the Honorable Mrs. Byng

In which Peter and Kate make the acquaintance of the Byng family and Peter demonstrates his soccer skills

Kate was unconscious for barely thirty seconds. When she came round, her face was drawn and her skin was white as paper. She felt sick and weak and all she wanted to do was close her eyes and escape from a reality that she was not ready to face—at least not just yet. Gideon carried Kate to a shady spot well away from the road and laid her gently on the grass. He took a shirt from his bag and folded it into a pillow for Kate's head. Then he gave his water bottle to Peter, saying, "Stay with her. We are close to Baslow Hall,

Colonel Byng's house; I shall fetch a horse and will return as soon as I am able."

Peter took the bottle like a sleepwalker. His world had temporarily flicked out of focus, and he was quite happy for it to remain that way.

"Peter," said Gideon, putting a hand on his shoulder to get his attention. "Where have you come from?"

Peter looked up at him and realized he was going to have to decide whether to tell Gideon the truth. Could he trust him? He decided to follow his instincts.

"If this . . . is really . . . 1763," Peter said in a halting voice, "then everyone I know is living hundreds of years in the future. Kate and I come from the twenty-first century. I don't understand how we got here. And I don't see how we can get back. I . . ."

Peter couldn't find the words to say anything else. He suddenly felt desperate.

Gideon's face did not betray what he was thinking. He nodded slowly and paced up and down for a couple of minutes before answering him.

"I mean no disrespect when I say that I can scarce believe that what you have told me is true, and yet . . . my heart tells me that you are not lying. Fate put me in that hawthorn bush to witness your arrival, and I promise you that I will do what I can to help restore you and Mistress Kate to your families."

Peter felt a surge of relief and gratitude welling up inside him. Tears pricked at his eyelids. "Thank you," he replied finally. "I'm not lying to you, Gideon—I don't understand how any of this happened, but I swear to you I'm not lying."

• • •

Peter watched Gideon stride away to Baslow Hall. He set to wondering if his mother, so far away in California, had been told that her son was missing and what she would do. He had not seen her for nearly two months. Would she drop everything, tell the film studio that they would have to do without her, and get on a plane? Would she miss him if he got permanently stuck in 1763? Then it occurred to him that if he'd had a father who kept his promises, he wouldn't be in this situation now.

The shadows were lengthening by the time Kate heaved herself up on her elbows and helped herself to some water.

"Are you okay?" asked Peter. Kate nodded.

"Lost in time," she said after a while. "Why couldn't I see it before? Everyone in fancy dress and speaking funny."

"I thought that's how people spoke in Derbyshire," said Peter with a grin.

"Watch it," said Kate. "And before you ask, my dad and Dr. Williamson at the lab are *not* trying to invent time travel. That only happens in stories. They're studying how gravity actually works."

"Will," corrected Peter. "They *will* study how gravity works."

An air of unreality descended on them while they sat in the warm, still air, waiting for Gideon. Peter sat obsessively folding and unfolding a slip of paper that he had found in his anorak pocket.

"You're like Sam; you're a right fidget!" snapped Kate, irritated. "What is it anyway?"

Peter unrolled the grubby scrap of paper and read, "*Christmas homework. To be handed in to Mr. Carmichael on January eighth. Write five hundred words on: My Ideal Holiday.*"

They both burst out laughing but soon fell silent. Chance had thrown Peter and Kate together, and whether they liked it or not, each was now a key person in the other's life. But, of course, they had known each other for less than a day and a half, and neither had yet earned the other's trust.

After a while Peter said, "You know, it's got to be something to do with that machine thing that Gideon told us about. It might not be a time machine, but it's all we've got to go on. We're going to have to find the Tar Man, aren't we?"

"I don't know," Kate replied. "Maybe it would be better to wait here. . . . My dad will work out what happened. I know he will. He won't stop until he's found us."

Peter did not feel quite so optimistic about Dr. Dyer's ability to travel back through time. But he also felt a pang of jealousy—he wished the feelings he had about his own dad were less complicated.

"I didn't blur when I fainted, did I?" asked Kate.

"No, you didn't, why?"

"Just checking."

Gideon arrived not on horseback but sitting in an open carriage drawn by two glossy chestnut mares. Beside him sat a pretty, plump young woman in a severe black-and-white dress. She was perhaps twenty years old and she was balancing a basket covered with a muslin cloth on her knee. Golden curls escaped from beneath a cotton bonnet and tumbled over her rosy cheeks. The driver sat perched high up on a box seat. He held his back as straight as a soldier on parade and wielded a whip, which he cracked over the horses' heads as they strained up the steep track.

When they came to a halt, Gideon helped the young woman out of the carriage. They hurried toward the children. The woman dropped a neat curtsy in Peter and Kate's direction.

"This is Hannah," announced Gideon. "Mrs. Byng's personal maid. She has brought you refreshments and a cloak each to cover your barbaric garb." Then he raised his voice, and fixing them with his dark blue eyes, he spoke slowly and very pointedly to Peter and Kate.

"I have spoken to Mrs. Byng of your traveling to England from foreign parts and of your terrible encounter with an armed highwayman in Dovedale who made off with all your clothes and possessions. I have also enlightened Mrs. Byng as to your intention of traveling to London. I explained how you became separated from your uncle, who has doubtless made his way to Covent Garden, where he has urgent business."

"Yes, that's right," said Peter in such a stilted voice that Gideon had to turn away to hide his smile. "A terrible highwayman stole all our clothes in Dovedale."

"You poor, wretched children," said Hannah sympathetically. "Mr. Seymour told me that you were forced to wear whatever you could lay your hands on, yet I do declare I have never set eyes on a more outlandish getup. Why, a person would be ashamed to be seen in such clothes in respectable company. But, Mistress

Kate, you are not well. Let me help you to the carriage. Here, give me your arm and lean on me."

Kate did what she was told and looked over her shoulder quizzically at Gideon and Peter as she was maneuvered into the coach. Gideon leaned over and whispered in Peter's ear. "I do not think it wise to be open about your predicament. I fear that half the world will think you mad and the other half that you have been bewitched."

Tucked up in woollen cloaks, and swayed by the motion of the coach, Peter and Kate listened to the groaning of wooden axles and the rhythmic *clop, clop, clop* of the horses' hooves. The wild Derbyshire landscape, mellow in the setting sun, seemed to glide by. Hannah's basket, stuffed with hunks of bread, salty white cheese, and roast chicken, easily satisfied the children's ravenous appetites, although Hannah seemed to regard it as a small snack. She wanted to know if the highwayman could have been Ned Porter and if he was handsome. Thinking of the Tar Man, Peter told her that he was as ugly as a pig, with a big nose and greasy black hair, and that he stank. Hannah seemed very disappointed.

Peter heard Kate's sudden intake of breath and felt her hand on his arm as the broad stone facade of Baslow Hall came into view. Symmetrical and well proportioned in the same way that good doll's houses always are, the mansion was an impressive sight in the setting sun. The long curved drive cut through a great park, well stocked with stately elms and home to perhaps a thousand sheep.

"This is my school!" she exclaimed softly into Peter's ear. "This is where I go to school! I can't believe it!"

The coach crunched to a standstill in front of a flight of steps leading to a pair of imposing gilded doors. "Wow," said Kate to Peter under her breath. "It doesn't look this good now."

"It *won't* look this good," corrected Peter.

"You *will* get very annoying if you carry on like that," she whispered back.

As they all clambered down from the carriage, a small blond-haired boy in a velvet suit came careering around the corner of the house and skidded to a halt on the gravel of the drive. His mouth opened into a small O shape of surprise, and he let the misshapen leather ball he had been chasing roll toward Peter and Kate.

"We have visitors, Master Jack," Hannah called out. "Will you come and bid them welcome?"

The little fellow stood and stared at the strangers and began to walk backward, retracing his steps behind the corner.

"Hello," said Kate, kneeling down so that she was at the same height. "My name's Kate and this is Peter."

Peter walked toward the child's ball.

"Can I borrow your ball for a moment?"

He threw off his cloak, picked up the ball, and carefully placed it on the top of his right foot. Holding out his arms for balance, Peter kicked the ball to eye level then kept it in the air for a couple of minutes or more, first with his foot, then with his knee, and then he finally flicked the ball behind him, bent forward with his arms outstretched, and caught it deftly on the back of his neck. Master Jack was rooted to the spot, entranced; he had never seen such skill with a ball before. Kate was impressed too, although she couldn't quite bring herself to say so.

Jack ran forward and snatched the ball from Peter's neck.

"I like your game," he said. "I want to play it now." He smiled up at Peter, and dimples appeared in his chubby cheeks. Then his attention was drawn to Peter's anorak and he reached out to touch it.

"What is this?" he asked in wonderment, stroking the orange nylon and running his thumbnail up and down the fascinating metal zip.

"Where are your manners, Jack?" a refined woman's voice inquired. "Our guests have been attacked by a highwayman who has stolen all their good clothes."

"You poor souls," said Jack earnestly, and then added, breaking into a grin, "I should like to meet a highwayman."

"Hush, Jack," the woman's voice replied. "Do not wish for such a thing!"

Peter stood up to see who was speaking. He saw two women walking toward them: a handsome, dignified woman in a magnificent blue silk dress, and following her, a nurse carrying a baby swaddled in a lace shawl. The width of the lady's dress was nothing less than startling. *It must weigh a ton,* thought Peter. If she'd been standing on a sidewalk, there wouldn't have been room for anyone else. Peter started to get nervous. This must be Gideon's employer, the Honorable Mrs. Byng. What was he going to say to this grand lady? How was he supposed to behave? Thankfully,

Gideon and Kate joined him, and all three of them stood to attention in a little row.

"Bow!" hissed Gideon. Peter did a bow of sorts, though he did not know what to do with his arms and legs. If she noticed, Mrs. Byng had enough tact not to show that she had. Kate fared better with a curtsy, as her legs were hidden under her long cloak and she merely bent both knees before bobbing up again.

"Welcome to Baslow Hall," said the Honorable Mrs. Byng. "I am sorry that the master of the house, Colonel Byng, is unable to greet you. He is recently left for America, where he is to join his regiment. An uncivilized land, but he must needs do his duty for England and King George, and we must do without him as best we can. Come, Mr. Seymour, introduce me to our guests."

"May I present Mistress Kate and Master Peter Schock," said Gideon. "Alas the highwayman took everything and they now find themselves entirely without resources. He stole something of great worth that they must recover. They have been separated from their uncle, whom they believe has traveled on to London, where he has urgent business."

"A sorry tale indeed. My cousin, Parson Ledbury, dines with me this evening. You must give him a description of the foul fellow who committed this crime. Alas, Derbyshire is teeming nowadays with highwaymen and footpads and villains of all kinds. And yet, as Parson Ledbury says, we shall not be cowed into staying at home because the country is rife with wickedness. Are you brother and sister, may I ask?"

"No!" Kate and Peter almost shouted.

"Mistress Kate and Master Peter are cousins," said Gideon hurriedly.

"I see. And where do your families live?"

Gideon and the children looked at each other. Each was waiting for the other to make the first move.

"We, er, have estates in Germany, near Frankfurt, and also in the north of Scotland," blurted out Peter, reasoning that the richer they sounded the better they were likely to be treated.

"I have family in Scotland," said Mrs. Byng. "Perhaps I am familiar with your estate. What is the name of the nearest town?"

"Um," replied Peter, panicking quietly. "Glanadarry."

He hoped fervently there wasn't really such a place.

"No, I do not know it. Such a pity that Colonel Byng is not here—he would have enjoyed conversing with you in German. He has a good ear for languages."

"Yes, that is a pity," lied Peter, who did not.

They were saved from further inquiries by young Jack Byng, who, bored with all the talking, was trying to imitate Peter's skill with his ball. He kicked it high into the air, too high in fact, for it ricocheted off a windowpane. The glass did not shatter, and the ball was caught on the rebound by a tall black-haired boy who had just appeared from the side of the house.

"Jack Ketch, the hangman, will come and get you if you break a window," the tall boy drawled to young Jack. He then proceeded to mime putting a noose around his neck. Clutching at his throat with both hands, he made as if the breath was being squeezed out of him. He pretended to choke and let his tongue loll out and rolled back his eyes until only the whites showed. When Jack ran toward his mother and buried his head in her long swishing skirts, the black-haired boy laughed. Peter took an instant dislike to him but had to admit it was a pretty good mime.

"I wish you would not take such a delight in frightening your brothers and sisters, Sidney. Breaking a window is hardly a hanging offence, and I'll thank you not to teach young Jack that it is." She turned to Gideon. "Such a punishment would be excessively harsh, would you not agree, Mr. Seymour?"

"Yes, madam, although I have seen many a poor wretch strung up at Tyburn for scarcely more serious a crime."

"I see that you are plain-speaking, Mr. Seymour. It is a quality I shall value highly if you are to help me run the estate in the absence of the colonel. My brother Richard writes to me that you are reliable and resourceful and that you inspire men's trust. I am happy to take his advice and offer you a position here. You may settle the question of your salary with Parson Ledbury. I take it you are able to start your duties straightaway?"

"I am, madam. I am very grateful to you." A broad grin appeared on Gideon's face, and he gripped Peter's arm behind his back and squeezed it in happiness. *He must have really wanted this job,* Peter thought.

Mrs. Byng paused to reach into a drawstring purse made of the same blue silk as her dress. She took out a note sealed with wax and handed it to Gideon.

"Here is the letter that I mentioned earlier. It arrived but yesterday."

Gideon accepted it with a slight bow and tucked it into his pocket to read later.

"So you are often at Tyburn, Mr. Seymour?"

"Lord Luxon, my former employer, never misses a hanging day. He says that to see a man die makes him feel more keenly what it is to be alive. He hires seats in the covered stands—it was my task to see to the needs of his many distinguished guests. Lord Chesterfield's French chef would prepare sweetmeats, and the finest wines would be offered to the company."

"How fascinating! You will see little excitement of that type in Bakewell, I fear. Here we live very peacefully—too peacefully for some." Here she caught Sidney's eye.

"I should be content, madam, if I never saw Tyburn again in my entire life," Gideon replied.

"Then, I hope for your sake that you do not," said the Honorable Mrs. Byng.

Addressing herself once more to Peter and Kate, she said, "You are most welcome to stay at Baslow Hall and send word to your uncle in London that you are here. However, the day after tomorrow Parson Ledbury takes Sidney and young Jack to visit my brother Richard who lives in Lincoln's Inn Fields—a most convenient location. You might prefer to travel down to London with them. There is room enough in the carriage and four."

"Oh thanks!" Kate exclaimed. "That'd be so cool! Yes, please!"

"Yes, that'd be brilliant!" said Peter, and seeing the expression on Mrs. Byng's face, he added, "I mean, one would be most grateful to accept your gracious offer of a . . . er . . . lift."

Mrs. Byng looked as if she were wondering exactly which part of Scotland these children sprang from.

"Well, it is settled," she said. "I will tell Parson Ledbury to expect two extra passengers."

"Mama," interrupted Sidney. "If there is a hanging day while we are staying with Uncle Richard, perhaps I could ask Parson Ledbury to take me to Tyburn?"

"No, Sidney," replied his mother. "I forbid you to do any such thing."

Mrs. Byng ordered Hannah to arrange for rooms to be prepared for the guests and for Cook to prepare them a light supper. A footman wearing a tightly curled white wig guided Peter and Kate through the airy entrance hall to a dining room lined with oak paneling. The footman stood to attention at one side of the room. Neither Peter nor Kate could guess whether they were supposed to make conversation with him. Kate tried to catch his eye and smile, but he stared right ahead so they sat in silence. Soon a kitchen maid appeared wearing a starched white apron over a worn gray dress. She carried a silver tray crammed with dishes. While the silver was gleaming, Kate could not help noticing that the servant girl could definitely have done with a wash. As the girl bent to arrange their supper in front of them, Kate saw a black rim of dirt above her collar. The kitchen maid curtsied and left the room, closing the door behind her. Peter and Kate sat in silence, feeling awkward, unsure whether they should help themselves to supper or wait to be asked. There was a bowl of steaming cabbage, a golden-crusted pie, and a pretty china dish containing a kind of stew or casserole: Some pale gray lumps were swimming around in some grayish broth. When Peter noticed the islands of congealed fat floating on the top of it, he thought he would plump for a slice of the pie. The footman came forward and picked up a heavy serving spoon. He turned to Kate.

"The stewed carp or the pie, ma'am?" he inquired with a bow of his head.

Kate looked doubtful.

"Hmmm . . . What are you having, Peter?" she asked.

"I know what carp is, because I've caught plenty, but I've never eaten one. They're supposed to taste a bit muddy," he whispered.

"The pie looks nice," said Kate brightly to the footman. "What sort of pie is it?"

"Calf's head pie, ma'am. It is a favorite of the Byng family."

Kate gulped and exchanged a desperate look with Peter. "May I have some cabbage and fish, please?"

"And the same for me, please," said Peter.

They ate without speaking, partly because the presence of the footman unnerved them, but mainly because the excitement of the day had utterly exhausted them. The carp was edible but was not nice—Kate managed to swallow it, but Peter pushed it around his plate with his fork until finally he gave up any pretence that he was going to eat it, and pushed it away. The pudding was better. The kitchen maid arrived with a dome-shaped mound of yellow custard stuck with so many almonds it looked like a hedgehog. As she carried it in, the pudding quivered so much it made Kate laugh.

"It's alive!" she said, and then added suspiciously, "What is it made of?"

•   •   •

The Hospitality of the Honorable Mrs. Byng

When supper was over, it was with relief that they followed Hannah to their bedrooms. Members of the Byng family gazed down at them from gilded frames as the children climbed up the sweeping staircase that overlooked the hall with its black-and-white marble floor. *What a shame,* thought Kate, *that in two hundred and fifty years all this will be replaced by a gray linoleum floor, row after row of lockers, and a pile of unclaimed sneakers.*

Alone in his attic room, and with a full stomach for the first time in a week, Gideon pulled off his boots and flung himself on the bed. He stretched out luxuriously and then remembered the letter that Mrs. Byng had given him. He sat on the edge of the bed and read it by candlelight. As his eyes moved down the page, the look of tired contentment drained from face and was replaced by distress, which soon turned into anger. He crumpled up the letter and flung it against the wall.

EIGHT

The Tar Man's Tale

*In which Peter and Kate plant a cedar of Lebanon
and Gideon tells the story of the Tar Man*

At breakfast, melted butter dropped off Peter's hot muffin onto
the old red hunting jacket that had been found for him to wear.
He tried to wipe it off surreptitiously with his napkin but only
succeeded in smearing the greasy stain over the ruffled cuff of his
shirt, too. He tugged repeatedly at the collar that Hannah had
fastened with an ornate bow. Through the tall windows he could
see the sun beating down onto broad lawns, already scorched by
the summer's heat. Surely they didn't really expect him to wear

this getup on such a day? He was already boiling hot, and his breeches were cutting into the backs of his knees. What was so *barbaric* about a T-shirt anyway? Neither Sidney nor Jack looked uncomfortable, but he supposed they must be used to it.

No grown-ups were in evidence around the breakfast table, but Peter counted eight Byng children, not including the infant Byng, whom he had seen the previous evening. He was introduced to all of them but quickly forgot who was who. All these talkative Emmas, Sophies, Elizabeths, and Rachels were a little overwhelming. A small army of maids must have been responsible for all the ringlets and ribbons and cascades of lace. Despite the lavish use of lavender water, an underlying odor of unwashed bodies pervaded the crowded dining room. Peter was beginning to realize that in an age before deodorants and power showers, it was only natural that everyone was going to have their own, individual smell.

The six Byng sisters greeted Peter kindly enough, asking how he had slept and inquiring whether he had grown up abroad, on account of his strange way of speaking, but they ignored him after a while, preferring to talk about the handsome Mr. Seymour who was to help Mama run the estate while Papa was in America.

The eldest of the Byng children, Sidney, sat at the head of the table gazing out of the window through half-closed eyes, with an expression on his face that said all the tittle-tattle was of absolutely no interest to him. Young Jack Byng sat opposite Peter but was absorbed in watching motes of dust dance above him in a narrow sunbeam that passed over his head. Every so often he would poke a plump finger into the ray of sunshine and watch how it affected the movement of the dust particles. It put Peter in mind of Dr. Dyer talking to him about dark matter.

When Hannah and a kitchen maid, no older than twelve or thirteen, came in bearing fresh muffins, the girls demanded to know where Gideon was going to stay. Hannah told them that he would probably stay here at Baslow Hall until Hawthorn Cottage was ready.

Sidney roused himself to speak for the first time: "I don't know why you girls"—which he pronounced "gels"—"are making such a to-do about Mr. Seymour," he said. "He's not a *gentleman*. Indeed, he's scarcely more than a servant. Papa says that people in our position should take care to avoid an excess of contact with our . . . social inferiors."

If one of the elder girls had not blushed with embarrassment and exclaimed "Sidney!" Peter would not have realized that Sidney was staring directly at him. Was Sidney saying that neither he nor Gideon were worthy to mix with the Honorable Byng family?

Before Peter could work out how to react, Sidney had thrown down his napkin and excused himself from the table.

"I'll leave you to the ladies, sir," he said with a curt nod to Peter.

Who does he think he is? thought Peter. *And why does he speak as if he's got a Ping-Pong ball in his mouth? I'm not sitting next to him on the way down to London.*

"Please don't pay too much attention to our brother," said one of the *gels* to Peter. "When Papa is away, Sidney feels the responsibility of being the man of the house very keenly."

"Sidney is always a terrible prig," said another. "Whether Papa is here or not." She was shushed by her sisters.

"I'm sure Sidney did not mean to be unkind," Peter lied.

He was beginning to feel unpleasantly outnumbered by this eighteenth-century crowd and wondered where Kate had got to. The door opened and Hannah bustled in, saying that the girls' governess was ready to begin lessons, and herded them out of the room.

"You can finish your breakfast in peace, Master Schock," she said. "Young Jack can keep you company until Mistress Kate arrives. We've been searching the whole house for stays that will fit her."

"What are stays?" Peter asked Jack when Hannah had gone.

Jack sniggered and hid his face in his napkin.

When Kate arrived, Peter and Jack were sitting at opposite ends of the long table throwing pellets of bread into an empty milk jug. When the twenty-first century children each saw how the other was dressed, they fell about laughing.

"Look," said Peter, "they couldn't find any shoes big enough to fit me, so I'm having to wear sneakers with white stockings and breeches. Have you ever seen anything so stupid?"

Kate lifted up her long skirts to reveal that she, too, was wearing sneakers. Peter snorted with laughter.

"Don't make me laugh. I can't breathe as it is!" Kate gasped. "They've put this leather thing round me and laced me up at the back. I think my ribs are going to break."

"Ah, those will be the stays."

"How did you know what they're called?" asked Kate.

"Oh, everyone knows that," Peter replied.

"Is there a mirror in here?" asked Kate. "I want to see what I look like."

She looked about the morning room and saw a large gilded mirror above the fireplace. As she drew out a chair to stand on, Jack's piping voice declared, "You look ravishing, my dear."

"Is that what your father says to your mama?" asked Kate, trying to keep a straight face.

"Yes." And then, to Kate's great dismay, Jack's small face crumpled and he started to cry.

"I want Papa to come home," he sobbed.

Kate put her arms around his shoulders.

"I understand," she said.

"How old are you, Jack?" asked Peter.

"I am five. I am very ill."

"Are you?" said Peter. "You don't *seem* too ill."

Jack grabbed Peter's hand and placed it on one side of his throat. It was true that there was a slight swelling.

"I have the King's evil," he said proudly.

Peter quickly removed his hand and looked at Kate to see if she knew what Jack was talking about. She shook her head.

"Does it hurt?"

"No."

"Well, that's something," replied Peter.

Kate picked up her skirts and balanced precariously on a chair to study her reflection. She wore a dress of soft green silk; pink roses were embroidered on the bodice and it was edged in ivory lace. Her hair had been piled up on top of her head and strands of hair had been curled and artfully arranged around her face. She looked beautiful.

"I wish I had a camera—I'd love to show Mum; she's always trying to get me to wear dresses." Kate's voice cracked. "Do you think we'll ever . . ."

"You *will* see her again," said Peter quickly. "We'll find a way."

Peter did not want Kate to start crying—she was actually all right when she wasn't crying or being bossy.

Kate nodded and tried to smile. "You must miss your family too."

"I do . . . but my mum and dad are always away on business anyway."

"Don't you get lonely?" Kate asked.

"I can look after myself."

"I've been talking to your au pair, Miss Stein," said Detective Inspector Wheeler. "She told me that Peter was extremely upset the morning he disappeared."

He was meeting Mr. and Mrs. Schock for lunch at the Peacock Hotel, where they were staying. This was a mistake, he soon realized, because although he was ravenous, he could hardly wolf down his steak and chips when Mr. and Mrs. Schock had pushed away their plates without even touching their food.

"It would have been helpful if you could have mentioned the argument you had with your son. In the light of what Miss Stein said, I think we need to consider the possibility that Peter has run away."

Mrs. Schock looked at her husband in alarm. "What argument?" she asked. "What is all this about?"

Peter's father clenched his jaw in a vain effort to keep calm.

"There was a meeting I couldn't get out of. I had to cancel Peter's birthday treat . . . again. There was nothing else I could do. Peter didn't take it too well. He said he hated me. . . . Don't look at me like that! If you hadn't swanned off to work in LA, this wouldn't have happened!"

Mrs. Schock dropped her hands onto her lap and let her chin sink to her chest. She closed her eyes. Then her husband put his hands over hers.

"I didn't mean that. I'm sorry. All of this is my fault. I know it is."

Mrs. Schock shook her head and looked up at Detective Inspector Wheeler.

"I know my son," she said. "I don't believe that Peter would have run away. He gets angry, just like his father, and then he gets upset. But he doesn't run away. It's not his style. I don't believe it."

Mrs. Byng had invited Peter and Kate to join them in the gardens after lunch. It was a family custom, she explained, to plant a tree in honor of the birth of each of her children.

Three-month-old Alexander Byng was held by his nurse to watch the ceremony. Two gardeners held a small evergreen tree level while all the children took it in turns to throw a spade of earth into the hole that had been dug to accommodate the tree's roots.

"The colonel got Mr. Powell of Holborn to send up the tree. I have never seen a full-grown cedar of Lebanon, but Mr. Powell assured the colonel that they are long-lived and grow into majestic specimens. He guarantees that this cedar tree will outlive us all."

"Yes," said Kate wistfully, "hundreds of years from now children will still be playing in the shade of its beautiful broad branches. They'll eat their lunch, leaning their backs on its massive trunk. And if they can manage it without getting caught, they might even carve their initials into its thick bark. I can picture the scene quite clearly."

"A pretty speech, Mistress Kate, thank you," said Mrs. Byng. "And now I must finish the preparations for your journey tomorrow. Hannah will find a change of costume for you to take with you to London. In the meantime I suggest that you take your ease in the gardens—your journey tomorrow will be long and uncomfortable."

As Mrs. Byng returned to the house, the children saw Gideon approach her. He took off his three-cornered hat and bowed low. He seemed preoccupied and concerned. They saw Mrs. Byng listening carefully to what he had to say. They could not hear Gideon's low voice as he had his back to them, but Mrs. Byng's clear, resonant voice carried toward them on the breeze.

"Ah, but that is unfortunate, Mr. Seymour. The harvest will soon be upon us and I was counting on your help. Can your business not be delayed?"

Gideon shook his head and spoke again.

"Then of course you must go. I would be the last person to counsel otherwise. Hurry back as soon as you are able."

Gideon kissed her hand.

"At least," Mrs. Byng continued, "I shall rest easier now there is to be another man to accompany the party. My nerves have been quite rattled with all this talk of highwaymen. Parson Ledbury is as brave as a lion, but his bluster is no match, I fear, for a gentleman of the road's pistol. While Sidney, for all his airs, is still a child."

Mrs. Byng disappeared into the house, and Gideon turned and strode over to where Peter and Kate were sitting. There always seemed to be a calmness about Gideon; even when he was rushing, he never seemed in a hurry.

"I couldn't help overhearing," Peter blurted out. "Are you coming to London with us?"

"Yes, it seems we are to follow the same road once more. Mrs. Byng is happy for me to accompany the party."

"Yes!" said Peter, punching the air.

"Hurrah!" said Kate.

Gideon seemed pleased. "I am happy to be traveling with you. But are you recovered, Mistress Kate?"

"Yes, I feel much better, thank you."

"I am glad. Mrs. Byng's dress suits you well. And you, Peter, I scarcely recognized you. You look quite the gentleman, although a pair of decent boots might improve the picture!"

"I'm glad you think so, because at breakfast Sidney as good as said I wasn't worthy to sit at the same table."

Gideon laughed. "The Byng family is old and respectable, yet they would not appear on the guest lists of half the noble families I had dealings with in London. It is understandable that the eldest son takes pleasure in claiming his superiority when he believes he can."

"Don't you think I'm a gentleman either, then?" asked Peter. He was beginning to feel a bit put out.

Gideon's eyes twinkled, but he would only reply, "A gentleman is as a gentleman does. We shall soon find out. . . ."

"Gideon," asked Kate, "who is this Tar Man who we must track down in London?"

Gideon's smile faded and he sighed as if just the thought of the man cast a shadow over his mood.

"He is a bad man. But that much you will have worked out for yourselves. Everyone who knows him fears him, and for good reason. He is the henchman of . . . a powerful man. If someone needs to be found, he will find them. And when he does, just as a cat with a mouse, it is his habit to play with them a little. . . . And he is persistent. By heaven, he is persistent. Once set on something, he never gives up. You two should have little to fear from him as long as you give him what he demands, but at all costs do not try to double-cross him."

"He sounds terrifying!" cried Kate. "And he's the man we've got to find? What if we haven't got what he wants? What do we do then? Oh, this is not good."

"It gives me the creeps just to think about him," said Peter. "I don't want to see him again if I can help it."

"I know his history," said Gideon. "It is no surprise that he is angry with the world."

"Why? What happened to him?"

"I do not care to dwell on such a cruel story on this fine, sunny day."

"Oh, you've got to tell us now!" exclaimed Peter.

Gideon was reluctant, but Kate, who was pretty persistent herself, eventually convinced him that he might just as well tell them the truth because they'd only have nightmares imagining worse things if he didn't.

The three of them sat on the grass at the foot of a yew hedge, and Gideon told them the Tar Man's story.

He had lived in a small village, the eldest of a large family, and life had not been easy. In those days he had a name: Nathaniel. His father died when he was still young, and thereafter the only money the family had came from his mother's skill as a needle-woman. Nathaniel was mostly left to shift for himself, and he was almost always hungry. He soon took to stealing food, and by the time he had reached his teens, he had become a petty thief. He was not greedy and was far too cunning and secretive to ever get caught—a few pennies, an old jacket to keep out the cold, a chicken for dinner—but people were suspicious of Nathaniel, and his dark, sullen looks were against him.

One January night a stranger was attacked and robbed outside the village and left for dead. When he recovered, he accused Nathaniel of the crime. Nathaniel swore that he had never seen the man before in his entire life. However, despite the lack of evidence, Nathaniel was tried and found guilty and sentenced to be hanged. Anxious to protect his siblings from the shame and horror of such a thing, his mother stayed away from the execution. And so, at the tender age of fourteen, he was to face those last terrible moments of his life alone.

It was a bitterly cold day in January when Nathaniel was hanged, and the hangman, who had a streaming cold, did not wait the usual thirty minutes before cutting him down. Nathaniel's body was bound and covered in tar-soaked calico, as was the custom, and taken in a wagon to the village green, where in the early evening he was suspended from a post to serve as a warning to other wrongdoers.

On the other side of the green, villagers were dancing and making merry in a hall lit by candles. Outside, a fierce cold wind blew and unforgiving rain spattered against the windowpanes. A tired farmer, returning from market on horseback, heard groans as he rode past Nathaniel. The farmer peered into the darkness, and when he caught sight of this ghoulish, slimy creature swaying in a strong gust of wind, he let out a yelp of fright. The farmer was sorely tempted to ride on but decided that the least he could do was to cut the poor wretch down. So, with a heaving stomach, the farmer positioned his horse under Nathaniel and cut the cords that bound him. Nathaniel slithered to the ground, where the farmer loosened the ropes that cut into his hands and feet. Then the farmer lost his nerve and rode home at a gallop.

Barely conscious and half-blinded by the tar, Nathaniel managed to get to his feet. Drawn by the candlelight and the sound of feet drumming in time to a fiddler's tune, Nathaniel made his way across the green and staggered into the hall. The music stopped abruptly as did the cheerful babble of the crowd. It was replaced by gasps and screams and finally by silence. Through streaming eyes Nathaniel saw a circle of horrified villagers, most of whom he had known all his life, each one backing away from him, expressions of horror and revulsion on their faces. Nathaniel's neck, whilst miraculously unbroken, was severely injured, and his head drooped grotesquely to one side. To speak was agony, but still he tried. He opened his mouth to beg for help and reached out to his neighbors with tar-covered arms. Not a single soul was willing to come to his aid, and soon the whole gathering had retreated as fast as their legs could carry them into the wintry night, away from this monster in their midst. Nathaniel was left alone, howling in anguish at a world without pity.

When Gideon finished his tale, the children sat for some time lost in thought, and shivered in the warm sunshine.

"And that," concluded Gideon, "is why he is called the Tar Man. I suppose he is fearless because he has faced the worst a man can face and still survived. I have never seen him truly fear another mortal soul, nor have I seen him show pity or compassion. I do not like to recall the things I have seen him do. Most rogues' hearts are not completely black, but his heart is buried so deep I doubt it will ever see the light of day. Beware of him, children; he is always two steps ahead of you while appearing to be two steps behind, and he has powerful connections."

"You seem to know a lot about him," said Kate. "How do you know him?"

"I believe we've had enough stories for one day," Gideon answered.

"Some people like to be mysterious," said Kate.

"And others like to be impertinent," Gideon replied.

Kate pulled out the pins that were sticking into her scalp, and shook out her long hair with relief. "That's better," she said, and stretched out on her back, tucking the full skirts of her dress around her knees. She wished she could have unlaced the stays, too. *I probably shouldn't be lying on the grass in this dress,* she thought, *but I don't think I can get up now.* She yawned and her eyelids closed.

"Do you think the Tar Man did rob that man?" asked Peter.

"No," said Gideon. "I do not. He insists that he was innocent of the crime, and I believe him. The injustice of it still gnaws away at him. It robbed him of his family and his future. But he has more than made up for it since."

"What do you—" Peter stopped abruptly. "Oh, no," he cried, "look at Kate!"

Gideon swung round, and both of them watched as Kate's form dissolved in front of their eyes.

"Quickly," said Gideon. "Let us sit in front of her so she cannot be seen from the house."

Peter and Gideon sat cross-legged next to what was left of Kate, shielding her from sight.

"Kate!" said Peter as loudly as he dared. "Come back!"

For several minutes they watched the transparent flickering form, a fluid amber spectre in the strong sunlight. Peter could see the daisies through her. Suddenly her shape shifted, and though Kate was still transparent, they realized she was pushing herself up on her elbows. Her eyes were open and she was shouting something in the direction of the house. She looked straight through them. Peter felt terrified and desperate.

"Kate," he cried out, "don't leave me here on my own!"

And in an instant she was back, solid as before. She sat bolt upright and said, "I blurred, didn't I?"

Peter nodded.

All the blood had gone from Gideon's face, but he asked, "How are you, Mistress Kate?"

"I was back at school," she sobbed. "I was lying in between the goalposts on the soccer pitch. The cedar of Lebanon was there, much taller than the house. And there were three men running toward me as fast as they could. Two of them were in policemen's uniforms. They could see me, I know they could. I must have looked like a ghost to them. A future ghost. I cried out to them for help. Oh, why did you call me back? I was home! I don't want to be here! I want to go home! I just want to go home!"

N I N E

The Journey Begins

In which the redoubtable Parson Ledbury insults
Gideon and the company sets off for London

Kate's spirits were very low after the blurring episode. She and
Peter ate with the Byng children that evening. Sidney was not
present, however, having been asked to dine later with his mother,
Parson Ledbury, and some friends invited for a farewell dinner.

Cook had prepared a special dinner for the children, too, and
the table groaned with roast meats, poached fish, baked custards,
junkets, flummeries, and pies. Flies crawled over everything, and
the dark specks in the pastry turned out to be roast flour weevils,

but no one seemed to mind. Kate hardly spoke. If her body was present, she was elsewhere in spirit. Peter felt he had to talk twice as much to make up for her.

They went to bed early, in preparation for their long journey. They said their good-byes to Mrs. Byng before going upstairs, and Peter gave a small speech of thanks. Kate tried to join in too, but it was so obvious how sad and distracted and homesick she felt, that Mrs. Byng stopped her. "My dear," she said, "we need to get you to your uncle so he can dispatch you home with all haste. I believe your encounter with the highwayman has unsettled you, as well it might any young girl."

Mrs. Byng's tender concern almost provoked the tears that Peter hoped would not come, and he stood, balancing first on one foot and then on the other, while Kate was held in the lady's maternal embrace.

"Thank you," said Kate to Mrs. Byng, but the expression of gratitude in her eyes was thanks enough.

Why, thought Peter, *must she* always *cry?*

Kate slept a long and dreamless sleep that night, but Peter slept fitfully. Images of a monstrous bellowing figure dripping with tar kept intruding into his dreams. The sound of voices outside woke him after an hour, and he got up to look out of the window.

It was a hot night, with scarcely a breath of wind, and the clear sky was grainy with stars. When Peter hoisted himself up onto the high window ledge of his attic room, an amazing sight met his eyes. Twenty or thirty flaming torches illuminated the garden, causing the many trees to cast giant inky shadows behind them. A long table, placed on the lawn two floors below him, glowed with so many candles it seemed a raft of light against the dark grass. Peter could easily make out the diners' wigs, their powdered faces, and their sumptuous costumes in shades of turquoise, peach, and yellow. Sidney, looking half-asleep and wearing a ridiculous long wig, sat next to his mother, who gave him a sharp tap on his back with her fan every time he slouched. White-gloved footmen patrolled the table, replenishing glasses and serving the guests from silver platters piled high with roast meats of every sort.

Peter listened to the buzz of conversation punctuated by occasional gales of laughter. One voice in particular swept up from the table and echoed off the walls of the house and into the night.

"Damn your eyes, sir!" exclaimed a stout, hearty gentleman whilst removing his wig and wiping his bald head with a lace handkerchief. "I'll wager you ten—no, twenty!—bottles of my best port that the bay mare is in foal before her sister."

"I accept your wager, Parson Ledbury, as the whole table can bear witness," declared the man sitting opposite him. "And as you boast you keep the best cellar in these parts, I shall look forward all the more to consuming my winnings."

"Gentlemen," said Mrs. Byng reproachfully, "I hope your passion for gambling does not lead you down the same path as my husband's friend Lord Arlington. He lost a king's ransom last month betting that one raindrop would reach the bottom of the windowpane before another."

Parson Ledbury roared appreciatively.

"What is a life without risk? A sorry one, I should say, madam. How much did the young feller lose?"

"Three thousand guineas."

Wow! Peter said to himself. *They sure are fond of betting.*

The parson slapped his thigh. "Sidney," he exclaimed, gripping the boy's arm in his meaty fist, "by the look of disapproval on your dear mother's face, I believe she is beginning to doubt the wisdom of entrusting her jewelry to me. My dear Charlotte, do you think me capable of betting your diamond necklace on a raindrop?"

Mrs. Byng laughed. "All I ask is that you have the clasp properly repaired and the necklace returned safe to me in time for the Harvest Ball. In any case, if I could not trust you with my precious necklace, I should scarcely be entrusting you with my two precious sons."

The parson's fleshy face folded into a roguish smile. "I see your reasoning, cousin, although it occurs to me that Sidney here is a strapping young fellow. Now that it is the custom in London to wager one's relatives when one's purse is empty, what is to stop me losing your son and heir in a bet?"

Sidney shot to his feet, affronted, and the whole table burst into laughter.

"The parson is teasing you, Sidney," said his mother gently. "You know he cannot stand to be serious for more than five minutes at a stretch."

Peter chuckled into his sleeve. This was a different Sidney from the one he had seen lord over his sisters at breakfast. Parson Ledbury gave Sidney a friendly punch to the shoulder, causing him to spill his glass of wine, which Peter suspected was the parson's intention. A footman appeared out of the shadows to mop up the mess, although Peter noticed that nobody bothered to say thank you.

Peter watched the parson turn serious all of a sudden as he leaned toward Mrs. Byng. He lowered his booming voice, although it was still perfectly audible to everyone.

"You will not, I hope, mention the necklace to Mr. Seymour, given his history."

Peter's ears pricked up. *What's the parson got against Gideon?* he wondered.

"My brother says we are lucky indeed to have him," said Mrs. Byng. "He ran a great house in London as well as an estate in Surrey with a thousand acres. Richard insists that he is a good man who has been ill used by Lord Luxon."

"A leopard does not change his spots, madam. I don't trust him and I don't like him. I shall be on my guard, of that you can be certain."

"You are too harsh," replied Mrs. Byng. "I believe Mr. Seymour to be sound."

"What has Mr. Seymour done, Mother?" asked Sidney.

"Nothing, my dear, nothing at all. It is of no consequence."

The parson grunted. Peter was so keen to hear what they were saying about Gideon that he lost his footing momentarily and his chin came crashing down onto the windowsill, causing him to bite his tongue. He gasped in pain and inhaled all the dust that had collected in the corner of the window. The dust irritated Peter's nose and he let out not one but four explosive sneezes one after the other, which rang out across the garden. When Peter opened his eyes, every face at the table was turned up toward him. He thought he had better wave and say something.

"Good night!" Peter shouted down. "Looks like you're having a smashing dinner."

And with that he slammed down the window, leaped into bed, and covered his face with a sheet, the sound of Parson Ledbury's laughter ringing in his ears.

The farewell dinner had ended some time before, and now Baslow Hall was silent except for the occasional hooting of an owl. Gideon Seymour alone was not asleep in his bed. On his bed lay the crumpled letter. He stood motionless at an open window high above the gardens fragrant with lavender and roses. Above his head, silhouetted against a hunter's moon, bats flitted in and out from under the eaves.

"To think I escaped his clutches only to learn of this!" Gideon's eyes burned with such intensity and hatred that an observer would have thought he was talking to a living being. Yet it was into the empty night air that Gideon directed his words, and whatever he saw in his mind's eye was clearly causing him great distress.

"He lies, Joshua! He lies! He does not hold you in high regard. He does this to lure *me* back; he has no other aim!" Gideon cried. "Will Luxon not rest until he has taken everything from me? Why can he not let me go in peace?"

Peter was dreaming about his mother and father. He was trying to tell them something, but they could not hear him, no matter how loudly he spoke.

"Peter! Peter! Wake up!"

Someone was shaking his shoulder. He blinked his eyes open, and the bare whitewashed room came into focus.

"Oh. It's you," he said, and slumped back on the pillow.

"Peter, I can make myself blur!" said Kate. Her hair was loose and she was still dressed in a long white nightgown. Her face was lit up with excitement. "Just watch."

She closed her eyes and shook out her body until her limbs were floppy. Peter lay on the bed watching Kate. She looked so comical standing there that when nothing happened after a couple of minutes, he started to chuckle.

"Oh, you've put me off now," said Kate crossly. "It's a knack. I know I can get better at it. I've been practicing since daybreak. It's like those 3-D pictures—at first everything's flat, but if you relax and just keep on looking, after a while the picture pops out at you and you can't imagine how you couldn't have seen it before."

Kate walked toward the window and stood in the sunshine, her red hair gleaming.

"Don't put me off this time," she ordered, and relaxed her body again. She closed her eyes and let her head fall forward a little. She put Peter in mind of a meditating angel.

A moment later Kate seemed to melt into the morning air. The sun shone directly onto Peter's face. He lifted up his hand to shade his eyes. The next moment Kate had vanished altogether. A buzzing bluebottle zigzagged in the bright space where she had stood.

"Oh, no! Kate!" Peter called out. "No!"

Peter's heart started to beat frantically, and that sixth sense that tells you if you're in someone's presence told Peter, even before he looked around him to check, that the room was empty. Kate had gone. The thought of being stranded in 1763 all alone was terrifying. She might have her faults, but he and Kate were in this together and she couldn't just abandon him like this, could she? Peter flung himself onto his stomach, feeling wretched beyond words, and punched his pillow, again and again, shouting "No!" with each thump.

"Temper, temper," said Kate from his bedroom door.

Peter froze in midpunch and looked over at her, open-mouthed.

"How did you do that?"

"I walked," she replied and burst into a fit of giggles.

"Stop laughing and tell me what happened," said Peter in exasperation.

But Kate could not stop laughing and collapsed on the bed, holding her stomach, tears running down her cheeks.

"Your face," she gasped. "Those girls' faces!" She buried her head in the sheets, but her body still vibrated with laughter.

"What girls? Oh, Kate, do get a grip!"

Kate slowly sat up and tried very hard not to laugh. "I walked the length of the room . . . ," she started, but it was no good, she was having an attack of the giggles and the crosser Peter looked, the more she laughed.

Why does she have to be so annoying? Peter thought, already forgetting how pleased to see her he had felt. Finally she stopped.

"Do you know you're sleeping in a Year Eleven common room? It was full of bossy prefects in overalls holding scrubbing brushes. Someone had scrawled really rude comments about the teachers all over the walls, and they were having to clean it off. Miss Gunn, the deputy headmistress, was there—she's really strict—sitting reading a newspaper. Every so often she'd look over her glasses and say, "Come on, girls, a bit more elbow grease. This is my holiday too, you know." The sports captain was there, right next to me. She winded me with a net ball the other week just because I was daydreaming. When she looked round, I stuck my tongue out at her. It was so cool. She screamed and screamed. She looked like she'd seen a ghost; they all did."

"Well they had, sort of," said Peter.

"But I'm not dead," Kate replied cheerfully.

"How are they supposed to know? We must be presumed dead by now. And look at what you're wearing—a perfect ghost costume."

Kate's face dropped. "They'll tell Mum and Dad and they'll think that I'm dead. Oh, no, what have I done?"

"We'll just have to get back and show them we're alive, won't we?" said Peter, getting in quickly in case Kate got emotional. "You know," he continued, "it was difficult to see properly because of the light, but I think you just about disappeared this time. Did you look solid in the classroom?"

"I'm not sure—I couldn't see myself. But I could see stuff through my arm. I guess I must have looked kind of filmy, not fully formed somehow. But they all looked so terrified, I must have looked like a ghost. The funny thing was, all the time I was there, I was still aware of you in this room. It was like having one foot in the past and one foot in the future."

"Why did you come back?" asked Peter. "Could you have stayed there if you had wanted to?"

"It felt like it was taking all my strength to stay there as long as I did. I don't know how to describe it. . . . It's as if I have a giant elastic band tied round my waist, which is attached to a hook here. I can go quite a way straining against the band—and I suspect that I could go farther and stay longer—but sooner or later I am going to ping right back."

Peter kicked the bottom of the bed absentmindedly.

"Don't do that. You'll scratch it," said Kate.

Peter gave her a look and kept on kicking. "I wonder if you've always been able to blur, I mean even though you didn't know you could. Or perhaps whatever happened to us has changed you in some way."

Kate shrugged her shoulders. "Oh!" she exclaimed suddenly. "I'll write 'I'm not dead' on a piece of paper and take it with me when I blur. Then they'll know I'm all right."

Peter thought for a moment and screwed up his face. "A ghost saying 'I'm not dead'? I don't think so somehow."

Kate sighed. "Yeah, well . . . I'm going to keep practicing blurring, anyway. If I do it enough times, maybe I can figure out how to unhook the elastic band, and then bye-bye 1763."

"Do you think I could blur?"

"Gideon said you did."

"Well, I can't remember."

"Try! Lie on the bed and relax and think of home. Imagine your mum's face and try to let go."

"All right," said Peter, unconvinced, "I'll give it a try."

He stretched out and made an effort to let his muscles go slack. He tried to picture his mother bringing him up a glass of milk at bedtime, sitting on the edge of his bed, and talking to him while he drank it. He clenched his fists as he forced himself to conjure up her image, but no picture would come into his head. His throat constricted and he grew tense and anxious. Why couldn't he see her?

"I can't even remember what she looks like now!" Peter burst out.

Kate looked at him, concerned; he seemed upset. "Okay, okay . . . think about your bedroom, then," she suggested. "I think it's really important not to feel stressed."

Peter took in a deep breath and released it slowly. He thought of lying on a beach as Margrit had once taught him. He imagined the roar of the surf as his shoulders and neck, then his arms and legs, started to feel heavy and sink into the firm sand. Now he was calm. It was the memory of his stripy duvet that popped into his head first. He held the picture as steady as he could, and before long his mind was full of stripes, dark blue on white. They were curiously soothing, and soon, ever so gently, the stripes started to ripple and vibrate, as though some great engine were being started up a long way away. After a while the stripes turned into spirals, and gradually they became more luminous. Peter had the sensation that they were passing right through his body and that he was leaving this world behind. Then, unbidden, his mother's pretty face appeared in front of him, smiling and sweet; she was brushing the hair out of his eyes. He felt a surge of happiness when he saw her face. How much he had missed her and how long it had been since he had allowed himself to give in to that feeling. All the sadness of wanting his mother to come home burst out of him in one big sob of pain. He sat up with a start.

"You started to fade for a moment there," said Kate. "I think you can do it, Peter. You can blur too."

The morning of departure had arrived, and the whole Byng family and most of their servants had been milling about on the gravel forecourt since breakfast. The July sun was already beating down mercilessly. Kate and Peter longed to set off, and all this waiting seemed interminable. Sweat trickled down Peter's back, but he did not dare remove his jacket. Kate, too, was suffering under the weight of her complicated attire, and was fanning herself madly with the painted fan Mrs. Byng had given to her. Mrs. Byng had explained about the language of fans—if you held it in this way, it meant "I like you," and in another it meant "go away." Whatever else Kate's frantic fanning signified, it principally said, "I am suffocating. *Please* let me undo these awful stays."

Four sturdy chestnut horses were harnessed to a gleaming black carriage. The horses stood patiently, chewing on the iron bits in their mouths while footmen clambered onto the roof of the carriage, fastening down trunks. One of them lost his grip on a heavy crate and nearly sent it crashing to the ground. There was the sound of clinking glass as he dived down and grabbed it just in time.

"Well caught, Andrew," called out Mrs. Byng. "That would have been unfortunate, indeed," she observed to the older children. "That chest contains Parson Ledbury's supply of port. He is convinced that every tavern keeper between here and London will water down his wine."

Peter watched a stable boy arrive with two horses. Gideon, who had been helping organize the trunks, now came forward. He walked slowly around the stable horses, stroking their heads and talking quietly to them. He examined their eyes and their hooves and pulled up their gums so he could see their teeth. Then he got the stable lad to run around the forecourt with them on a long lead so he could watch them canter.

"I will take the black stallion," Gideon said to the stable boy. "What is his name?"

"Midnight, sir. He's fast and strong, sure enough," replied the boy, "but there's not one of us stable lads he hasn't kicked."

"Good!" said Gideon. "I like an animal with some fight in him."

Poor Jack Byng was clearly not keen on the idea of traveling to London. Despite all his sisters' efforts to cheer him up, he was clinging to his mother's skirts like a sailor to a mast in rough seas.

"Uncle Richard writes he will take you in a rowboat to Eel Pie Island and that you will ride on a donkey at Vauxhall Gardens, where you will see all the fine ladies and gentlemen," said one sister. "We girls are all jealous because we simply long to go."

"And King George will touch you and cure you of the scrofula," said another.

"I am better already," protested little Jack through several layers of fabric.

He steadfastly refused to leave his mother, and Mrs. Byng was forced to drag him around like a third leg. Only when Peter offered to have a game of footie with him did he peep out from the folds of her dress. Mesmerized by his fancy footwork, Jack followed Peter as he dribbled the ball onto the lawn. Mrs. Byng mouthed her thank you to Peter and suggested to Sidney that he join in. Sidney merely looked on in a very condescending fashion, striking a pose with one foot forward, a hand on one hip, and his chin thrust into the air. *What a plonker,* thought Peter, booting the ball right at him so that he had to catch it.

"Gadzooks, sir!" Sidney exclaimed. "You might have dirtied my waistcoat!"

Jack immediately struck the same imperious pose as his elder brother and repeated in his own high voice, "'Gadzooks, sir. You might have dirtied my waistcoat!'"

All his sisters laughed so hard and for so long that the servants had to bite their lips in order not to join in, and Sidney, furious, stomped off into the house.

Peter suddenly felt Kate's hand on his arm.

"I'll be back in a minute," she whispered into his ear.

"Why? What are you going to do?"

"I'm going to leave a clue for my friend Megan," Kate replied.

"What do you mean?" asked Peter.

"Never mind. It probably won't work anyway."

Kate made her way to the back of the house and found the stairs that led to the coal cellar. She crept slowly down them, touching the rough brick walls and marveling at how new and clean they looked. She was used to seeing them black with centuries of coal dust and glistening with damp. Kate remembered when she had first come here. It was after a gang of Year 8 girls were mean to her during her first ever week at the school. They said they could smell that she lived on a farm and that her lace-up shoes were so uncool even grannies wouldn't wear them. . . . Megan had eventually found her here. They both ended up skipping science and got detentions. This became their special place. Kate crouched down in the exact spot where she and Megan always sat on their backpacks when they wanted to be alone.

A long strand of red hair tumbled down as Kate removed an iron hairpin. She started to scratch at the soft brick with it, biting her lip in concentration. Every so often she would blow the dust away to inspect her handiwork. *Oh, Megan,* she thought, *what would you say if you saw me in this stupid dress? I wish you were here too—No, I don't. Then you'd be stuck in 1763 as well.* Kate finished her message and wiped the red dust off her hands.

"I'm counting on you, Megan!" she said out loud. "Tell my dad!"

All the preparations were complete by the time Kate returned. It was only then that the cheerful red face of Parson Ledbury appeared at the front door. He stood in the sunshine and wiped away the remains of breakfast with his handkerchief. He bid the assembled company a good morning, and Mrs. Byng's comment that she was grateful to him for rising *so early* went straight over his head.

"Splendid!" he commented, surveying the carriage laden with luggage and provisions, and the well-groomed horses. "Is there anything more pleasing in the world than the prospect of a fine day's traveling in good company?" he asked. "Watch out for the off-leader, there," he advised the coach driver. "She shied at a hen in the road last month and nearly had us all floundering in the ditch."

When Mrs. Byng introduced him to Peter and Kate, he bowed low to Kate and squeezed Peter's hand a little too firmly. "I hope your cold in the nose has improved, Master Schock, although the loudness of your sneezes are such we could use you in fog to warn other travelers of our presence."

Peter reddened a little, and the parson gave him a friendly thump on the back that almost sent him sprawling.

"Damn shame about your encounter with that scoundrel in Dovedale. Still, lightning doesn't strike twice in the same place."

Parson Ledbury leaned down and picked up little Jack, who gladly sat on the big man's shoulders and pretended to ride a horse.

"Well," the parson continued, "it seems that we are to be a proper party on our way to London, and I cannot say that I am sorry, for the road is hard and dangerous. We shall make a brave show to any footpad, highwayman, or cutpurse that crosses our path, shall we not?" Here he paused to glare at Gideon. "We've got enough bottom for an army, eh, Master Jack?" he roared, causing the little lad to put his hands over his ears. Kate and Peter looked at each other and smirked. "Bottom?" Peter mouthed.

"Don't you know what bottom is?" exclaimed the parson.

"You must come from the most out-of-the-way place. A man without bottom, sir, will soon go to the wall. Bottom is *courage*. And I shall expect every member of the party to show their bottom on this journey!"

The parson deposited Jack on the ground and walked over to Gideon, leaving Kate and Peter chuckling silently about the quality they were required to exhibit for the trip.

They saw Gideon look up expectantly at the parson, who neither bowed nor extended his hand to him. Instead he said in a quiet and deadly serious voice that everyone could hear, "I have my eye on you, Mr. Seymour, and do not forget it. You have Mrs. Byng's trust, you do not have mine. One step out of line and you'll rue the day you ever set foot in Derbyshire."

The children saw the color drain from Gideon's face and heard Mrs. Byng's sharp intake of breath. For a moment everyone thought Gideon would strike the parson, and a terrible hush fell upon the gathering. Gideon mastered himself, never taking his eyes off the parson.

"As God is my witness," Gideon declared, "the Byng family, who has shown me such generosity, can expect nothing less than my devotion and loyalty. And for the sake of Mrs. Byng and her good brother, Sir Richard, I will not, on this occasion, hold this ill-judged threat against you. But know this, Parson Ledbury, I answer only to God and my own conscience. If you insult me in this way again, be prepared to accept the consequences."

Gideon turned his back on the parson and continued making adjustments to Midnight's saddle. The parson walked back to the carriage, and everyone started talking hurriedly as if nothing had occurred. Mrs. Byng, however, throwing a thunderous glance in her cousin's direction, went over to have a quiet word with Gideon. A moment later Gideon had mounted the black stallion and was galloping up the drive.

"You will be pleased to know, cousin," announced Mrs. Byng with some irritation, "that Mr. Seymour prefers *not* to ride to London with the party in the circumstances and intends to travel alone."

"I feel sure that Mr. Seymour will now think twice before trying to pull the wool over our eyes," said the parson.

"Where is your Christian charity, cousin?" asked Mrs. Byng. "Must he forever be judged on what he did when little more than a child? Besides, you are basing your concerns on mere rumor and speculation. You are wrong to tar him with the same brush as Lord Luxon . . ."

"Then tell me why the fellow must be so mysterious about his reasons for returning so suddenly to London, when he has scarcely just arrived?"

"He was not mysterious with *me*," Mrs. Byng replied, "but I saw no cause to share his reasons with all the world when he asked me to be discreet."

The parson appeared a little awkward for the first time. "I am sorry, madam, if, in my enthusiasm for your welfare, I have acted in such a way as to displease you."

Mrs. Byng hesitated, then smiled and held out her hand. "Come, cousin, I know you intended well. You have a long journey ahead of you; let *us*, at least, be friends."

Peter and Kate exchanged crestfallen looks. How were they

going to find the Tar Man without Gideon? What would they do when they got to London?

The Byng sisters said their good-byes to Sidney and managed to peel Jack from his mother's embrace and deposit him in Hannah's lap. Mrs. Byng bid Peter and Kate write to her when they were safely reunited with their uncle, and wished the whole party Godspeed.

The parson and Sidney squeezed onto the narrow bench on top of the carriage with the coach driver. Parson Ledbury insisted on taking the reins while the driver cracked his whip over the horses' heads and clicked his tongue to get them moving. The rest of the party sat on slippery leather seats inside the stuffy carriage, now full of the sounds of creaking wood, groaning axles, and the clinking of Parson Ledbury's bottles of port. They all leaned out of the windows to wave their good-byes. Baslow Hall, the elegant figure of Mrs. Byng, and the row of sisters fluttering their handkerchiefs aloft slowly receded into the distance, and Peter realized how lucky they had been to have encountered these kind folk. The horses picked up their pace, and the broad carriage wheels seemed to thunder over the stony track past mighty elms, rolling green fields, and vast flocks of bleating sheep. Soon they were headed for London and the open road.

The warm July wind blew through the open window and fanned Peter's face. He stared at the breathtaking scenery without seeing it. *Gideon couldn't even be bothered to say good-bye,* he thought. *He said he was going to help—yet another grown-up who says one thing and does another.*

TEN

Attack!

In which Dr. Dyer meets the NASA scientists
and the travelers make an unwelcome acquaintance

A thick bank of cloud hung over the valley in the gathering gloom. Inside the farmhouse the relentless *tick-tock* of a grand-father clock measured out the seconds that had passed since Mr. and Mrs. Dyer had last seen their eldest child. Although it was only a quarter to four, it was already nearly dark. Outside in the farmyard Margrit, who had stayed on to help, could be heard counting to a hundred while the four youngest children scurried about finding places to hide out of the cold wind. A sickly yellow light seeped into the dusk from an upstairs window. Sam, who was nearly ten, had refused to come out of his room since lunch-time, and his parents had thought it best not to force him.

Dr. Dyer broke the silence. "It's almost the longest night of the year."

Mrs. Dyer sat looking out of the front window and was staring at the gray landscape through red-rimmed eyes. "And it will be Christmas day this time next week. . . ." She lifted a cup of tea halfway to her lips, then lowered it down again, as if just sitting propped up in the high-backed chair was taking up all her energy. She let the cup drop heavily onto the saucer with a clink, and the tea slopped over the sides. She pushed it away. Kate's disappearance had hit her so hard, the pain of it was almost physical. Every motherly instinct was screaming at her to go after Kate, to defend her from attack, to protect her from harm, to tear the countryside apart until she could stroke her daughter's lovely red hair again. But there was nothing for her to do but endure the anguish of waiting. All she could do was wait and hope. Above all she must not give up hope, for everybody's sake she must not give up hope.

"*Do* you think that Peter could have been unhappy enough to run away?" Mrs. Dyer asked her husband.

"He didn't seem particularly upset to me . . . but then, I don't know him. Margrit says he was about as worked up that morning as she'd ever seen him. I'm sure Detective Inspector Wheeler is right to take that into account. But there's no way that Kate would have run away with him. She wouldn't have even gone after Peter to stop him before coming back and telling me first."

"No, of course she wouldn't," said Mrs. Dyer. "She's far too sensible."

"And they both seemed so happy a moment before, laughing at Molly and the Van de Graaff generator. Why would Peter choose that moment to do a runner, in a building surrounded by security guards and fences? No. I don't buy it."

They sat in silence again and listened to the wind wuthering down the chimney. When the telephone rang in the hall, they both jumped.

"It'll be another reporter," said Mrs. Dyer, desperately trying not to get her hopes up, for with each phone call she imagined the inspector's gruff voice announcing that they'd found Kate at last. Dr. Dyer walked over to answer it. Mrs. Dyer heard him say, "Of course I will, I'll come over straightaway."

"What is it?" asked his wife, all alight with hope.

He shook his head quickly. "No, no, still no news. It was Tim. The NASA scientists are over at the lab; they wondered if they could have a word. They offered to come over here, but I didn't think you'd feel like being sociable."

The NASA scientists—Dr. Jacob, a youngish man with thinning blond hair, and Dr. Pirretti, a neat dark-haired woman in her late thirties—were dressed formally as a mark of respect, but they looked uncomfortable in their dark suits. Their golden tans and rich West Coast accents seemed exotic in this chilly Derbyshire laboratory. They were embarrassed about bothering Kate's father at a time like this and spent a long time saying how sorry they were about the children's disappearance, asking about Mr. and

Mrs. Schock, and offering to help in any way they could. In the end Dr. Dyer stopped them.

"You must have had a compelling reason to fly over here to see me," he said. "Please tell me what it is, because I don't want to leave my wife alone for too long at the moment."

"I'm so sorry," said Dr. Pirretti. "I'll get to the point directly. You see, Tim Williamson has been working on an antigravity project very similar to one in the States—which is why we were particularly happy to fund his research here. We hoped that one project would complement the other. Anyway, Russ Merrick, at MIT, built a device that was different in design from Tim's but that had pretty similar aims. They were both working on the premise that the *casimir effect* isn't just theoretical—although Russ was using static metal plates inside the vacuum chamber rather than a mirrored belt moving at high speed. Russ, like Tim, felt that he was getting nowhere fast with his experiments. He hadn't managed to generate any measurable amount of antigravity. But—and this is why we're here today—a couple of months ago he contacted us to say that his machine had vanished. Russ assumed that someone had broken in and stolen it, although he couldn't work out why someone would want to risk breaking into a high-security lab for such a low-profile experiment. However, on precisely the same night as the theft, one of the cleaners who was scheduled to clean Russ's lab disappeared without a trace. Up until now we had not connected the two events—and, sure, the chances are there isn't any connection. But, hey, if there is, we really want to know about it."

Dr. Dyer's eyes widened. "Does Detective Inspector Wheeler know about this?" he asked.

"No. And if it's not asking too much, I'd prefer he didn't. Unless some concrete evidence turns up. I'm sure you understand. . . ."

"I'm not sure that I do understand," replied Kate's father. "What do you think could have happened? Why don't you want the police to know?"

"Obviously we don't *know* what happened, but until we've investigated the incident ourselves, we'd prefer not to have the interference of the police, who, with no disrespect, could only be a hindrance. We'd just be glad if we could count on your cooperation just in case . . . something turns up."

"Yes, of course I'll cooperate," replied Dr. Dyer. "Why on earth shouldn't I? But tell me, for pity's sake, what do you think *could* have happened?"

Dr. Jacob cleared his throat and looked at Dr. Pirretti. "Shall I tell him?"

Dr. Pirretti nodded.

"It's a shot in the dark, you understand, but we have got to at least question whether these disappearances are linked."

"How could they be linked?"

"What if the theory that minivirtual wormholes are spontaneously created and destroyed in a quantum vacuum turns out to be true?"

"You're talking about space-time foam?"

"Yes. Well, just supposing you wanted to turn a virtual wormhole into a real wormhole. In theory, although it's never been proven, you would need *anti-energy*. We're considering the possibility that both Russ's and Tim's machines have provided the anti-energy needed to do just that."

Dr. Dyer frowned and shook his head. "I don't get it. How is a machine that—on a subatomic scale—*may* have an effect on virtual wormholes going to make people disappear?"

"Let's just say that we're thinking along the lines of the relationship between *gravity* and *time*."

Dr. Dyer sat down in a chair with a thump. "But that's ridiculous! Surely you'd need massive amounts of anti-energy to create a wormhole big enough to warp time. You're not serious?"

Dr. Pirretti slowly nodded her head. "Well, it's not exactly a case of *warping* time, but, yes, we are serious."

"Good Lord," Dr. Dyer exclaimed. "I can see that you are."

"Russ is rebuilding his equipment in Houston as we speak," said Dr. Jacob. "And we'd like Tim to return to the U.S. with us to recreate his experiment. We need to throw every test we can think of at these machines. It is almost certainly a red herring, but we cannot discount it—yet."

Dr. Pirretti put her hand on Dr. Dyer's arm. "Can we count on your discretion? We felt that we owed it to you to share our thoughts, but we must ask you to talk about this to no one—not even your wife. Even though it is highly unlikely that this gravity-time hypothesis will come to anything, we all know that if the newspapers got hold of something like this, all hell would break loose."

"You can imagine the headlines," said Dr. Jacob. "'NASA scientists inundated with requests to become time traveler test pilots,' 'Paleontologists beg for the chance to prove their theories,' 'More dangerous than the atom bomb—Protect our history!' 'Worldwide demonstrations against new invention.'"

Dr. Dyer nodded. "I see what you mean. No, you needn't worry. I won't say anything. I wouldn't want to say anything to my wife that would upset her any more than she is already. Besides, what you say is so far-fetched, I find it difficult to take your fears seriously."

When Mrs. Dyer heard the key in the lock, she ran to meet her husband. He could tell that she had been crying and that she was now having to try very hard not to.

"What is it?" he cried, fearing the worst.

"Kate's friend Megan just telephoned. She said that half of the Year Eleven prefects were in hysterics at school this morning because they saw a ghost walking through the common room. . . ."

Mrs. Dyer covered her face with her hands.

"A ghost! But you don't believe in ghosts!" Dr. Dyer exclaimed. "What's that got to do with us?"

"They all swore the ghost was Kate—they said she was wearing a long white gown!"

Kate gave a huge yawn and stretched her arms high above her head. The sound of sixteen hooves striking the cracked earth for mile after mile was hypnotic. It was all she could do to keep awake in the stifling heat with Peter falling asleep in the opposite seat and Hannah snoring quietly next to her. She and Jack had both given up leaning out of the window, because the dust thrown up by the wheels made their eyes water. Kate invited Jack to sit on her knee. It was the heavy, warm weight of a young child on her lap that provoked a sudden pang of longing to see her family again. She could rarely watch television or sleep late on Sunday mornings without Milly or Sean or the twins snuggling up to her. And poor Sam—he was such a worrier. If she was ten minutes late from school, he would start asking Mum to phone the school secretary. He was going to be beside himself by now. Jack sensed her distress and turned round to look at her. He stared at a small tear running down her cheek.

"Why are you crying, Mistress Kate?"

"I've got some dust in my eye. . . . Why don't you tell me what nursery rhymes you know, Jack?"

Kate had never heard of some of the songs he wanted her to sing. They both knew "Three Blind Mice," although they could not agree on the words. With the unmoving stubbornness of a five-year-old, Jack insisted that Kate's version was not just different, it was wrong. In the end Kate learned his version to keep him from complaining. At least the tune was the same.

> *Three blind mice, three blind mice,*
> *Dame julienne, dame julienne,*
> *The miller and his merry old wife,*
> *She scraped the tripe, lick thou the knife,*
> *Three blind mice, three blind mice.*

Kate was a good singer and her high, melodious voice rose through the roof of the carriage to where Parson Ledbury took up the rhyme and sang it as a round, starting one line as Kate and Jack had finished it. Then the carriage driver joined in, and together they made a fine noise as they progressed through the Derbyshire countryside.

Kate and Jack had just taken in a deep breath to start the round again when Jack let out a shrill cry. Looking up, Kate saw why. Directly opposite them the dozing form of Peter was beginning to blur. Terrified yet fascinated, Jack hid his head on Kate's shoulder but could not resist peeping out with one eye open a tiny crack. "Why is he doing that?" he whimpered, pointing a small accusing finger at Peter's flickering, liquefying form. "I don't like it."

Aware that Hannah was beginning to stir, Kate kicked out in panic at Peter, who was now smiling in a most disconcerting fashion and looking around from side to side as if he were sightseeing. When her foot entered the space apparently occupied by Peter's left leg, Kate felt the sensation of intense cold, as if all the living heat was being sucked out of her. Her knee was pushed up and backward as she felt her foot being expelled with some force from Peter's blurring body. At the same time, luminous spirals started to form in front of her eyes. She felt a strong urge to join him, to detach herself from this reality and . . .

"Make him stop it!" cried Jack.

The parson was still singing "Three Blind Mice."

"Peter!" Kate cried out as loudly as she dared. "Peter, come back!"

Hannah opened her eyes at the same moment that Peter, whose face had turned a livid greenish white, said, "I think I'm going to be sick." Peter promptly hung himself over the window, and the rest of the carriage watched as his back heaved.

"Oh, the poor soul!" Hannah exclaimed, and rapped sharply

on the roof of the carriage. "By your leave, Parson Ledbury, Master Schock is ill; will you kindly stop the carriage as soon as you are able?"

Jack tugged at Hannah's skirts. "Hannah," he said, "Peter turned very strange while he slept."

"Well, Master Jack," she replied, "it is what happens to some people on long journeys. You are fortunate it did not happen to you."

Jack's eyes grew very large.

The whole party got down to stretch their legs. Peter stood trembling and pale in the shade of some bushes.

"You look terrible," Kate remarked.

"Thanks a lot," said Peter.

Hannah came over and poured some clear amber liquid from a rather dirty glass bottle into a tumbler and told Peter to swallow it in one gulp.

"It will make you feel better," she urged.

Peter looked at it suspiciously but did what he was told. The medicine certainly brought the color to his cheeks, but he did not feel exactly better. He clutched his stomach.

"Not found your sea legs, yet, eh, Master Schock?" said Parson Ledbury without a great deal of sympathy. "Perhaps you had better sit up on top as long as you can keep the contents of your stomach to yourself!"

Peter dived into some bushes.

"Upon my word the journey to London is going to seem an eternity for that poor child," said Hannah.

"How long will the journey take?" asked Kate.

"It will take no time at all with horseflesh of this quality," declared the parson, patting the flank of one of his chestnut mares. "Why, you shall be supping in Lincoln's Inn Fields this Wednesday evening."

"Two and a half days!" exclaimed Kate.

"Indeed," agreed the parson, "an amazing short time, is it not?"

Kate nodded her head. "Amazing."

Kate was tactful enough to wait for a moment before going after Peter to see how he was doing.

"Please don't ever, ever do that again," he said. "I thought I was going to die. When your foot went into me, it felt like I was being turned inside out. Stop laughing! I'm serious—it felt really dangerous. I wondered for a moment there if I was going to disintegrate. Like every molecule of me was unsure which way to go."

"I'm sorry," said Kate. "I didn't mean to do it. Did you blur deliberately or did it just happen?"

"I'm not stupid enough to try and blur in a carriage full of people!" snapped Peter, who still looked distinctly green.

"Okay, there's no need to get so cross!" retorted Kate. "Where did you go, anyway? For a moment back there you looked like you were having a nice time."

"Yeah, I was. Actually it was great. I was floating over a country road at the same speed as the carriage, only minus the carriage. It felt like flying. It was only spoiled when a farmer spotted me and insisted on driving right up next to me in his tractor with his jaw open like this." Peter put on a half-baked expression and let his mouth sag open. Kate giggled.

"And when you decided to invade my body space," he said, knitting his eyebrows together, "it hurt so much I couldn't see. The farmer probably drove into a ditch, for all I know."

"Look, I said I was sorry. I won't do it ever again, I promise. Come on," she said, "we'd better be getting back."

"Kate . . ."

"Yes?"

"I'm not going to dare go to sleep now."

"It doesn't happen every time, but I know what you mean. If I'm going to blur, I want to know it's happening," Kate replied.

"What are we going to do?"

"I don't know. Get very tired I suppose. The sooner we get that machine back the better."

"Only if we can get it to work," said Peter.

"Yeah, well, I don't think we've got much choice—though maybe one of these times we'll blur back to the future and stay there. Then it doesn't matter if anyone sees us."

"It's as if there's a homing device in us, isn't it?" said Peter. "Like dogs that get lost on holiday and then walk hundreds of miles back home."

"Or maybe that machine damaged us in some way," said Kate. "I don't know. But I bet my dad has got it sussed. He'll come back and get us, you wait and see. Anyway, we'd better be getting back."

Peter did not understand why he felt quite so irritated when

Kate went on about her dad like this, but he did. *If he was so totally wonderful, how come he let this happen in the first place?* he thought.

Once they were back on the road, Parson Ledbury announced, "I know a tolerable inn some three or four miles hence. The inn-keeper's wife is as ugly as sin, but she cooks like an angel. I dined handsomely off a plate of tripe the last time I was there."

"What's tripe?" whispered Peter to Kate.

"Believe me, if you're still feeling sick, you don't want to know," she replied.

Half an hour later they found themselves seated around a long wooden table in the dining room of the New Inn. In comparison to the sweltering heat outside, the inn felt blissfully cool and comfort-able. It was a large low-ceilinged room with oak beams, and sawdust scattered on the scrubbed wooden floor. There were half a dozen large tables crammed into the room, although Peter and Kate's group were currently the only guests. A serving wench brought out jugs of foaming ale and water, and the parson whispered something into her ear that made her smile and blush and scamper back into the kitchen. The innkeeper was busy stacking bottles in the cellar, and through the open trapdoor came the sound of his cheerful song echoing in the cavernous space—although he could not keep in tune from one note to the next. So it was the innkeeper's wife who pre-sented them with a whole loin of pork roasted with potatoes. She had pretty blond hair and fine blue eyes, but every inch of her skin, even that on her eyelids and the palms of her hands, was horribly pockmarked, covered in deep pits and craters like a lunar landscape. It was impossible for Jack to stop staring. Hannah did her best to distract him, but to no avail—his wide blue eyes swiveled constantly back to the woman's disfigured complexion.

"Don't you fret at him, mistress. If I was apt to take offence, I'd never come out of the kitchen. There's not many that's had the smallpox as bad and lived to tell the tale. My mother lost two of my brothers and my only sister at the same time. When I took to feeling sorry for myself, she always said to me, 'Better to have skin like a honeycomb than be six feet under.' And of course she was right. Count your blessings, for you never know when they might be taken away."

"Well said, madam!" said Parson Ledbury, his chin glistening with pork grease. "You set an example to us all. Life is what you make of it. But tell me, why is your establishment so unseasonably quiet? I have never seen it so empty. I trust your husband has not taken to singing to his guests."

The woman laughed. "No, sir. Much as I love him I've too sharp an eye for business to let him do that. No, it's on account of a highwayman. He's struck five times between Derby and Lichfield this past fortnight. Folk reckon it's Ned Porter that's responsible, though they do say that there's a vicious gang of footpads abroad too. I advise you to take extra care and arm yourself in case of need."

The parson drew out a wooden cudgel from his belt and brandished it in the air.

"Do you have a pistol, sir?" asked the innkeeper's wife. "He is armed to the teeth, so they say."

Everybody stopped eating. Peter and Kate looked at each other in alarm, and Hannah clasped Jack to her. Sidney stood up suddenly and cried out, "Fear not! The parson and I will show no mercy to any gentleman of the road foolish enough to waylay us!"

"Bravo, my lad!" shouted the parson.

"Well, I admire your bottom, young sir," said the innkeeper's wife, ignoring Kate's snigger. "But if you change your mind, there's a gunsmith's shop in the village."

"You don't think we're in real danger, do you?" whispered Kate to Peter.

Peter shrugged his shoulders. "How should I know? But I shouldn't worry. Sidney here will protect us!"

By late afternoon they had left the hills and valleys of Derbyshire and passed into Needwood Forest in Staffordshire. For two hours they rode through humid, dappled shade, where the air was thick with clouds of midges. Banks of tall bracken lined the dirt track and large blue butterflies of a kind that were unknown to Peter and Kate flapped their iridescent wings and sunned themselves in the rare pools of sunshine. In the silence of the forest the wheels of the carriage seemed to thunder over the rough ground, announcing their presence for miles around.

More troubled than he cared to admit at the news of highwaymen and footpads in the district, Parson Ledbury was quieter than he had been in the morning. When the carriage arrived at a crossroads, he asked the driver to stop. A peddler was selling spoons and tin pans and the parson shouted down to ask him if he knew where the narrower road led. The peddler said that the main road led straight to Lichfield through Kings Bromley, if that was where they were headed—though he had heard tell that a gentleman had had his throat slit from ear to ear on that very road not two days past—whereas the lesser road led to Lichfield but meandered through several villages on the way. He then tried to interest the parson in a set of tin pans, but the parson brushed the man to one side like a buzzing fly and paid no more heed to him. The peddler gave the parson a sly, disgruntled look, wished the company good day, and disappeared into the forest.

"He's not going to sell much there," commented Kate. "Why doesn't he set up his stall in a village instead of in the middle of nowhere?"

Parson Ledbury plucked off his wig and wiped his perspiring head with a handkerchief. He reached into his inside pocket and fingered Mrs. Byng's precious necklace. Then he stroked little Jack's golden curls, warmed by the sun, and sighed deeply. He sat, frowning, on top of the carriage for some time. Jack took hold of the parson's hot fleshy hand in his.

"I promised your mother," the parson said to Jack, "that I should get her family to London without anyone harming a single hair on their heads, and I am a man of my word. I have therefore decided to be prudent. We shall avoid the main road to Lichfield and by way of precaution we shall take the lesser road. It will make our journey longer, but a highwayman is certain to lurk by the main road in his search for easy victims. So we shall outwit him by taking the less direct route. We should, in any case, still reach the George Inn by nightfall."

Hannah was concerned that Jack had sat in the sunshine for

too long, and so the parson lifted him from the top of the carriage and posted him, upside down, through the window. Jack giggled. The driver was not so happy. He gave one look at the state of the small track through the woods, and his heart sank. However, he knew better than to express an opinion to his superiors, so he cracked his whip and directed the horses into the overgrown road leading into the woods. The road must have been scarcely passable in winter. As it was, the carriage bumped up and down over the uneven surface, and the passengers bounced up into the air and slapped back down again onto the black leather seats as the wheels sank into deep ruts and potholes. It was exhausting for everyone, especially the horses, but they could not stop if they were to reach the George Inn before dark. A couple of times fallen branches blocked their path and the driver had to climb down to heave them off the road. After an hour the parson left Sidney and the driver to it and joined Hannah and the children in the carriage. The sky grew pink, and the balmy air grew gradually cooler and damper. The party inside the carriage had grown tired of singing songs and talking and had slumped, finally, into silence. Even Jack had given up asking how long it would be before they could stop, and was now leaning against Hannah, half-asleep. Peter and Kate were both desperate to keep awake in the crowded, stuffy carriage, and both kept looking up to check that the other had not succumbed to blurring.

Then, without warning, the carriage juddered to a halt, throwing all the passengers forward. For a moment the labored breathing of the horses and the jingling of brass on the leather tackle were the only sounds to break an uneasy silence.

"What is it now?" bawled the parson. "I shall not be sorry to leave this confounded road. I think I should rather face a highwayman than have my bones rattled by one more pothole!"

The driver's head suddenly appeared at the window. It took everyone a fraction of a second to notice the blood pouring from a wound of the top of his head and to realize that he had been propped up against the side of the carriage like a sack of potatoes.

"Oh, Parson Ledbury," exclaimed Hannah in a terrified whisper, "I think you should be careful what you wish for!"

Someone pulled the door open abruptly, and the unconscious driver collapsed at their feet. All eyes looked down at the injured man and then back up again to the door. No one, not even Hannah, who had a strong urge to scream, made a sound. A pair of impertinent green eyes stared back at them from the doorway. He was a rosy-cheeked man, dressed like a gentleman who had been unable to change his clothes in a fortnight, and he was wearing the sort of smile the Big, Bad Wolf might have given Red Riding Hood from her grandmother's bed. He removed his three-cornered hat and stood before them, head slightly bowed, in a pose that would have been respectful were it not for the gleaming pistol that was aimed directly at the parson's heart.

"I am sorry to impose myself on your charity, ladies and gentlemen," he said, chucking Jack under his chin.

Hannah jerked the child away and sat him on her knee. The highwayman looked at her, taking in her every detail, and Hannah returned his gaze defiantly until he blew her a kiss, at which point she looked down at the floor.

"Be calm, mistress. I take no pleasure in unnecessary violence, I assure you. I merely find myself out of pocket this evening. I do hope that it is not too great an imposition to ask if any of you gentlefolk could grant me the honor of a small loan?"

"Loan, my eye!" shouted Parson Ledbury, although there was a noticeable tremor in his voice. "Go to damnation, sir! I take it you are the infamous Ned Porter—your reputation precedes you, yet you don't fool me! You're naught but a common thief!" And he plucked the wooden cudgel from his belt and took a powerful swipe at the highwayman. The highwayman reacted like lightning, cracking the parson over the knuckles with the butt of his pistol and easily relieving him of his weapon. The parson howled with the excruciating pain of it and bit his lip to stop himself crying out any more. He cradled his bloodied knuckles in the palm of his good hand. Shock and the desire to help the parson caused Peter to leap to his feet. He had not thought what to do but tried to look as defiant as he could. Ned Porter pretended to be scared, and then laughed heartily, pointing the gun in Peter's direction all the while. He kept the cudgel hovering close to the parson's skull.

"Don't be foolish, lad," the highwayman said to Peter in a quiet, silky voice. "'Twould be a shame to leave the world without tasting manhood first. You've a handsome face—think of all the pretty maids you might have stepped out with."

Peter glared back at the highwayman, his cheeks burning. He felt small and helpless and stupid but was unwilling to back down. The parson motioned to Peter to sit, which he reluctantly did after as long a pause as he dared.

"John!" called out the highwayman. "Would you come and help these good folk remember where they've put their valuables?"

"I can't, Ned, not unless you do something with this 'un," replied a gravelly voice. As Ned stepped backward, they saw Sidney being manhandled by a scrawny man whom Kate instantly recognized. "Look," she whispered, "it's the peddler we saw at the crossroads!" John, Ned's accomplice, had his black-nailed fingers clasped over Sidney's mouth and was jerking Sidney's head backward to try to control him. At the same time he held him in a tight armlock, and, if the smothered yelps were anything to go by, Sidney was in considerable pain.

"Let the boy go, you filthy scoundrel!" thundered Parson Ledbury. "You'll hang for this!"

John must have loosened his grip involuntarily for a second, because Sidney managed to bite his hand, drawing blood as he did so. The next moment, uttering a stream of oaths, John released Sidney, who struggled to regain his balance and then staggered toward the carriage. Ned Porter waited for him to come within spitting distance and calmly delivered a brutal blow to the side of his head with his pistol. Hannah and Kate screamed whilst the parson, gray with horror, stood up and made as if to get out of the carriage. Sidney crumpled, unconscious, onto the stony ground, face first.

"Stay where you are!" shouted Ned Porter. "The next person to try my patience gets a bullet through their heart. Empty your pockets!"

Peter and Kate looked to the parson for guidance.

"Oh cousin, oh cousin, what have I done?" muttered the distraught parson. Then he called out, "For pity's sake let me see to the boy!"

Ned pointed the gun at the parson's head and squeezed the trigger. The parson reached into his jacket and pulled out a purse bulging with gold coin. The highwayman snatched it from him and weighed it appreciatively in one hand before passing it over to John, who was sucking at the row of scarlet tooth marks inflicted on him by Sidney. Ned now turned his attention to Hannah. The poor driver was still slumped at her feet, groaning gently. There was now a small pool of blood on the floor of the carriage that was soaking into the hems of Kate's and Hannah's skirts.

"And you, madam, what little treasures do you have to tempt me with?"

Hannah hurriedly dug into her drawstring purse, holding Jack protectively against her. Peter looked up at the parson, whose uncharacteristically pale face was shiny with sweat. His attention was suddenly taken by something that sparkled on the parson's forehead. It was slithering very slowly down from beneath his wig like some glittering snake. *Oh, no!* thought Peter as he realized what it was. *It's Mrs. Byng's diamond necklace. He's been hiding it under his wig!*

Hannah held out a plain cotton handkerchief, a comb, and a few pennies for the highwayman's inspection. Peter tried to gain the parson's attention by nudging his foot beneath the dead weight of the driver.

"Keep your pennies, my dear," Ned said to Hannah, "and

your handkerchief. I'd rather have a kiss. And one from your flame-haired young charge too."

Ned looked over at Kate, who tried to disappear into the corner of the carriage. At last Peter managed to catch the parson's eye and frantically tried to alert him to the danger by staring fixedly at the escaping strand of diamonds on his forehead. The way the panic-stricken Parson clapped his hand to his forehead was too sudden for the highwayman's suspicions not to be aroused. Ned Porter tore back the parson's hand, and the whole carriage saw Mrs. Byng's diamonds glittering like a small constellation of stars over the parson's wrinkled brow.

With a sharp tug the magnificent necklace dropped heavily into the highwayman's palm.

"John!" he shouted out in delight, dangling the necklace from the barrel of his pistol. "Lady Fortune smiles on us this day!"

Abruptly the highwayman's features were contorted in pain. Confused and bewildered, the five terrified passengers saw a white-shirted arm slide around the highwayman's neck and squeeze.

"Don't be so sure about that," said a familiar voice. "I fancy Lady Fortune has changed her mind."

They watched as a man with blond hair grabbed hold of Ned's pistol and forced him, out of sight, to the ground. Peter leaned out of the window to see none other than Gideon Seymour struggling to pin the highwayman to the ground.

"Gideon!" Peter shouted, overjoyed.

"Help me!" Gideon cried. "Sit on him!"

Peter leaped out of the carriage and did as he was told. Gideon aimed his pistol at John and fired. It missed its target, and a second shot rang out in reply. With a whiff of gunpowder a lead shot lodged itself in the carriage door a couple of inches from Kate's head. A moment later the sound of a horse at a gallop indicated that John, together with the parson's gold, was escaping as fast as he could. Kate, Hannah, Jack, and the parson all tumbled out of the carriage and threw themselves, very willingly, over the struggling highwayman.

"You are a very bad man," scolded Jack as he sat roughly on Ned's head.

"Gideon!" exclaimed Peter, his face wreathed in smiles. "You came back!"

"Oh, Mr. Seymour," breathed Hannah, "you have saved us!"

"Scarcely that," replied Gideon, "or I should have got here *before* you were attacked."

Gideon ran over to Sidney and carefully turned him over. His mouth was bloodied, but he was beginning to stir. Picking something up from the ground between finger and thumb, Gideon said, "He'll live, but I fear he has lost a couple of teeth."

"I'll live too," said the coach driver barely holding on to the carriage door. "And I've a mind to relieve this rogue of some of *his* teeth." He lurched over to where Ned Porter lay pressed into the earth under the combined weight of the party. Ned watched the driver's vacillating foot with terror in his eyes as he took his uncertain aim.

"Come, friend," said Gideon, taking hold of the coach driver's arm. "He'll be hanging by the neck before the month's end. Leave him his teeth so he might make a pretty speech to the ones he leaves behind."

Ned Porter closed his eyes with relief but grimaced as Jack bounced on his head as hard as he could.

Gideon settled Sidney and the driver inside the carriage and asked Hannah to tend to them. Then he untangled the diamond necklace from the long grass where it had fallen and handed it to the parson without a word. Parson Ledbury took it from him and placed it in his pocket.

"Thank you, Mr. Seymour. I am in your debt," said Parson Ledbury.

ELEVEN

Lord Luxon's Tragedy

*In which Detective Inspector Wheeler's suspicions
are aroused and Gideon recounts how he met Lord Luxon*

"It's nice to see a spot of sunshine at last," commented Detective Inspector Wheeler.

"Yes," replied Kate's father distractedly.

Detective Inspector Wheeler and Dr. Dyer were walking alongside the narrow stream that rippled and burbled into the heart of the valley.

"You live in a nice part of the world, Dr. Dyer."

"Yes."

"Look," said the inspector awkwardly. "I don't quite know how to say this and I apologize if it causes you distress, but there's a girl from Kate's school who insists that she saw a ghost yesterday, the figure of a girl in a long white dress of some kind. She also said that the—apparition—was a dead ringer for—sorry. Slip of the tongue. I meant that she looked very much like . . . Kate."

"I know," said Dr. Dyer. "I've already heard about it through the grapevine. I don't believe in ghosts, Inspector. I can't explain it, but I'm not going to give up on finding my daughter alive on the evidence of one hysterical girl."

"No. Quite. It is strange, though, because a total of five girls reckon they saw Kate. The teacher who was present saw nothing, however. Perhaps, as you say, it's simply a case of mass hysteria. The headmistress says that the whole school has been traumatized by Kate's disappearance. One of the girls said that Kate—I should say the ghost—stuck out her tongue at her."

Dr. Dyer raised an eyebrow.

"What would you say," continued the inspector, "if I told you that after the press conference on Monday, I, along with two constables, saw a girl answering Kate's description lying between the goalposts on the school's soccer pitch? Whoever it was gave us quite a scare—there and somehow not there, if you know what I mean. I don't wish to use the word ghost, but the term could fit. I'm afraid she disappeared before we could get to her."

Now the inspector had Dr. Dyer's undivided attention. "What happened? Where did she go?" asked Kate's father without pausing for breath. "Did she say anything? Was she in white?"

The inspector looked quizzically at Dr. Dyer.

"We saw her from a distance. She had red hair and looked like she was wearing a long, green dress. An unusual garment— not that I know much about fashion, but it looked more like something out of a costume drama than an evening dress. It was certainly not the sort of dress I'd expect to see a twelve-year-old wearing. Anyway, if the constables hadn't seen her, I might have thought I'd imagined her. We searched the grounds but there was no trace of her. Dr. Dyer, is there anything you would like to tell me about this case that you hadn't thought to tell me already?"

"No. Why?"

"I thought you said you didn't believe in ghosts."

"No, I don't—which doesn't stop me looking at the same evidence through a different filter and coming to my own con- clusions."

"Well," said the inspector, "if you do come to any conclu- sions, I hope you'll feel able to share them with me. Obviously you and Mr. and Mrs. Schock will be the first to know of any new developments in our investigation."

"Thank you, Inspector."

An hour later the inspector received a phone call from one of his team assigned to surveying the NCRDM laboratory. He told him that Dr. Dyer had indeed turned up and had been seen entering Dr. Williamson's office where the NASA scientists were currently based.

Detective Inspector Wheeler chewed his pencil thoughtfully. *Brilliant scientists they might be,* he said to himself, *but they're sadly mistaken if they think they can keep a secret from Dan Wheeler.*

Then the policeman got into his car to drive to the nearest supermarket to stock up on ready-made meals-for-one for his freezer.

With infinite patience Gideon coaxed the horses down the tortuous dark path back to the main road. If Mrs. Byng could have seen the sorry state of her loved ones after only one day's traveling, she would have insisted they all return to Baslow Hall at once. As it was, Hannah did what she could for Sidney, Parson Ledbury, and the driver and wrapped Jack up in her cape and sat him on her lap. After all the excitement the little boy's teeth were chattering with cold and tiredness. He was such an uncomplaining child that it was easy to forget that Jack was not in good health. Sidney and the driver fell asleep almost as soon as the carriage started moving, but Parson Ledbury sat in silence in the darkness, crestfallen at what he had allowed to happen to his charges. After half an hour he reached up for one of his bottles of port and soon began to feel more cheerful. He resisted the temptation to offer some to Gideon. He may have arrived in the nick of time, said the parson to himself, but Mr. Seymour was only Mrs. Byng's servant and not to be trusted. No, by heaven, a leopard doesn't change its spots that easily.

As Peter and Kate had come through the ordeal relatively unscathed, they sat up on top with Gideon. It was their job to peer into the darkness and look out for branches that could slash at their faces or topple them off their high seats. Each time the carriage dipped into one of the deep ruts in the road, Ned Porter, who had been bound tight down like another piece of luggage, let out an involuntary groan. The motion of the coach had nearly lulled Kate to sleep, and she was now leaning heavily on Peter. He didn't mind; she was keeping him warm. He breathed in the night air, cool and sweet after the heat of the day, and looked up at the sky. Through fluttering layers of birch leaves he glimpsed the canopy of stars twinkling down at him from the other side of the universe and remembered what Dr. Dyer had told him about dark matter. Then Peter glanced up at Gideon's face, calm and intent as he balanced the reins between thumb and forefinger and talked to the horses. *This is not my time,* Peter thought. *I shouldn't be here. But I don't want to go back—not just yet.*

"I'm glad you're traveling with us again, Gideon," he said.

Gideon's arm suddenly shot out and broke off a branch that would have smashed into Peter's face.

"I promised I would help you," he said.

Once they were back on the main Lichfield road, traveling became much easier. Peter started to feel drowsy. He decided that this beat driving in a boring car down a boring motorway glowing with orange streetlights any day.

Peter must have fallen asleep because the next thing he knew a terrible metallic crashing sound made him jump. Next to him, Kate, too, woke up with a start. When he opened his eyes it seemed that he was looking at the world through smoked glass.

"Peter!" cried Kate. "We're blurring at the same time. Oh, this could be it! We're back!"

At first all Peter saw was a grid of yellow lines painted on tarmac. Then, as he looked up, it became clear where he was. He met the horrified gaze of a mother who had just allowed her overflowing supermarket trolley to crash into the side of a shiny red sports car. Her two toddlers were pointing at Peter and Kate and were trilling with delight. Delight, however, was not the first emotion the grown-ups were feeling. The irate driver leaped out of the sports car and started shouting at the mother.

"They should bring in driving licenses for those things! Why can't you look where you're . . ." When a boy and a girl in eighteenth-century costume floating a yard above Sainsbury's car park caught his attention, his voice trailed off in midsentence and his jaw dropped open in a peculiarly unattractive way. Kate could not resist giving him a little wave.

Peter cast his eyes around him, taking in the dull, overcast sky heavy with snow, the row of artificial Christmas trees on the roof of the supermarket, the growing group of shoppers who stood, rooted to the spot, staring at this bizarre apparition. Someone started to scream. One man took a camera out of his pocket and aimed it at Peter and Kate. Kate jerked her head around as the camera flashed. And then, as though someone had used a remote control to change channels, Peter now focused on that other scene, which had always been skirting around the edges of his awareness. This was the scene that consisted of a starry sky and swaying trees and horses snorting and stamping their feet. For a moment he could flick between the summer's night and the wintry car park at will. Then an anxious voice rose to the surface of his consciousness.

"Master Peter! Mistress Kate! You are fading. If it is your

intention to leave this world, fare thee well. . . . I wish you Godspeed."

But at the sound of Gideon's voice, Kate and Peter were sucked back to 1763 with a sickening, lurching thump. Gideon had stopped the carriage and was staring at them, waiting for their forms to settle.

"No!" cried Kate accusingly. "Why did you call us back?"

"I am truly sorry, Mistress Kate, I meant only to wish you farewell," Gideon replied.

"What did you have to say that for?" hissed Peter. "It wasn't his fault."

Kate did not seem convinced, and said nothing. Gideon clicked his tongue and pulled on the reins, and the four horses strained against the weight of the carriage once more. They sat without speaking for a long time and then all three turned round abruptly when they heard Ned Porter speak. They had all but forgotten he was there. His voice was muffled for he could only manage to lift his head an inch or so.

"I had a feeling in my bones that it was those two. I've been told to keep a weather eye open for them. You've got a mighty valuable cargo there . . . Mr. Seymour."

"Who told—" Gideon stopped himself.

Ned laughed. "So it *is* you. You're in great demand it seems, Mr. Seymour—at least in some circles. Though I should not care to be in your shoes, not for a casket of diamond necklaces."

"Open your mouth one more time and you'll find a gag in it," warned Gideon.

Ned, however, would not be put off.

"I hope you had good reason to cross the Thief-taker and his henchman, for I do not rate your chances of getting away. The Tar Man has promised to wring the necks of every rogue between Lichfield and Covent Garden if they do not peach on you. Although a certain diamond necklace might be enough to persuade me to keep my mouth shut."

"Enough!" cried Gideon.

Ned did not utter another word, but Peter did not care for the amused expression that by the light of the moon he could make out flickering across the highwayman's face.

Kate leaned over and spoke softly into Peter's ear: "What did he mean? Who *is* Gideon? Parson Ledbury is very suspicious of him. Do you think *we* can trust him?"

Peter turned round to look at her, an expression of fury on his face.

"How can you say that after everything he's done for us?" he practically spat at her in a violent whisper.

"Okay, okay," mouthed Kate, holding up her hands in appeasement. "Sorry I spoke. And what's a thief-taker mean, anyway?"

"I don't know! And I'm not going to ask Gideon now."

When they reached Lichfield, Gideon asked the nightwatch—a bent and decrepit old man who would have been lucky to hold his own against a child, let alone a hardened criminal—for directions to the magistrate's house.

It was past midnight when they arrived at a substantial four-story house built of thin red bricks. Parson Ledbury rapped firmly on the door with his good fist. When there was no response, the parson's thunderous bellowing echoed around the small front yard, and this did not fail to arouse the irritable magistrate from his slumbers. A pair of wooden shutters on the second floor opened.

"Who the devil makes such a noise at this hour?" shouted a voice from inside the dark house. Then the shutters creaked closed again and they could hear movement in the house and see candle-light through the wooden slats. The company waited in subdued, exhausted silence. Above them a million stars shone down from a sky swept clean by a warm southwesterly wind. The three spires of Lichfield Cathedral, inky black against the night sky, were sharply silhouetted against the twinkling universe beyond. Presently the magistrate appeared at the door. He peered out into the darkness, bleary-eyed and dressed in a long nightgown and turban. His tiny wife and a burly-looking servant carrying a lantern appeared at his side, and all three cowered in the hall.

The magistrate protected his guttering candle from the wind and looked out suspiciously.

"A good evening to you, sir," said the parson, stepping toward him. "Our party has been attacked by a highwayman whom we have captured and whom we now deliver into your custody."

"A highwayman, indeed? Let me see the scoundrel! Give me the lantern."

His servant took his master's candle and gave him the brass lantern, whereupon the magistrate began to inspect each member of the company one by one as if on a military parade. He held the light up to their faces, and when he got to Kate, the sight of the magistrate's mistrustful, hawklike features made her want to laugh. She kept as still as a statue until he moved on to scrutinize Sidney's bloodied face, and then she allowed herself to giggle silently—and a little hysterically on account of her tiredness—under cover of the night. The magistrate stopped when he got to a young man trussed up like a chicken with some old rope.

"Is this he? Is this the highwayman?" he asked.

When he was informed that this was indeed the infamous Ned Porter, the magistrate could scarcely contain his excitement.

"Upon my word!" he exclaimed. "Ned Porter is wanted in five counties. What a fine catch you bring me, ladies and gentlemen."

Ned remained smiling and pleasant even when he was bundled roughly into the magistrate's cellar without a candle, and even when the coach driver spat at him. Then he wished everyone a good night as the trapdoor was bolted down on top of him.

"Is there anything more profoundly distasteful," exploded Parson Ledbury, "than a base criminal who apes the good manners of his betters. The sooner the world is cleansed of Ned Porter, the happier will I be. When is the next hanging day, may I ask, sir?"

"There is the small matter of his trial first, Parson," commented Gideon.

Parson Ledbury shot a withering look at Gideon and then turned to the magistrate.

"I will return in the morning to give you my full account of this rogue's offences against our property and persons. And now, if you will permit us, we will seek out our lodgings for the night. Perhaps your servant can accompany us to the George Inn."

The magistrate bid them good night, looking very pleased with his unexpected booty, and ordered his servant, still in his nightclothes, to take the party to the George Inn on Bird Street.

The next morning the party woke late to find that the torrential rain that had disturbed them during the night had not abated. The George Inn did not offer luxurious or even comfortable accommodation. Nor was it particularly clean. They had shared rooms—and beds. Parson Ledbury, Sidney, and Peter were crammed into one, whilst Hannah, Jack, and Kate took the other. After half an hour of the parson's stomach rumbling from lack of supper, not to mention his snoring and Sidney's whistling through his missing teeth, Peter had crept down to join Gideon and the driver, who were sleeping in the barn with the horses. It might have stunk enough to make your eyes water, but at least Peter had escaped the worst of the fleas and the constant dripping of rain through the leaky roof.

"This bread is more chalk and ashes than flour," growled Parson Ledbury. Gideon and the driver, despite his injuries, were seeing to the horses. The rest of the party drooped over a bare wooden table eating a meagre breakfast. The mood was subdued. The parson's face was puffy and pale and his hand badly swollen. Everybody was scratching madly. Jack had pulled up his shirt and was peering at the pattern the itchy red bites made across his chest.

"You're worse than a band of monkeys," said the parson. He

tried to laugh but his heart wasn't in it. He was watching Sidney, who stood at a casement window in the low, dark dining room that smelled of damp. He was examining his injured jaw and his teeth—or lack of them—in a small looking glass. There was no denying the fact that his face was a mess. Sidney looked mortified. Even Peter felt sorry for him. The parson heaved himself up and strode over to the window. He patted Sidney roughly on the back.

"Never fear, my lad, I know of a shop in St. James that can fit you with wooden teeth prettier than those you have lost. Your dear mama will never know the difference."

Sidney nodded his head, yet it was difficult to tell who was more upset—Sidney, or the parson, racked with guilt at his failure to keep his cousin's family safe.

The appearance of Gideon and the coach driver shook the parson out of his despondency, for he was not a man to remain downhearted for long. He turned and greeted them.

"How do find your head this morning, Martin?" he asked the driver.

"No worse than if I'd supped half a gallon of cider, sir," the driver replied. "And it'll be an adventure to tell the little ones."

"Well said, Martin. You shall receive an extra shilling at the end of the month."

"Thank you, Parson," said Martin, tipping his hat in acknowledgment. "We got him good and proper, did we not, sir?"

"Aye, that we did, Martin."

Thanks to Gideon! thought Peter indignantly.

"'Tis a pity his sidekick got away with your gold, sir," added the driver.

The parson slapped his thigh. "Ha!" he roared. "Well, you need not worry on that account, for see what I have here!"

The parson pulled out a purse bulging with coins from his waistcoat pocket and jingled it so that everyone could hear the clink of metal.

"*This*," he said, "is my gold. Ned's accomplice ran off with the counterfeit coins that I had procured expressly for this eventuality. Those coins are worthless. I told you we were more than a match for any gentlemen of the road!"

Everyone laughed and cheered and thumped the table. Only Gideon did not seem to want to join in.

"Why the sour face, Mr. Seymour? Do not tell me that you of all people disapprove."

Gideon swallowed his irritation. "With respect, sir, aside from it being punishable by death, is there any better way than carrying counterfeit coins of announcing to the world that you do indeed have something worth stealing?"

"Pish pash, sir. You worry like an old woman. With Ned Porter behind bars, his accomplice would not dare come within a mile of us."

"Then let us hope he does not have any friends. . . ."

"So, Mr. Seymour, you would have me hand over my hard-earned gold to that ruffian?"

"In which case, sir, you would perhaps concede that there are occasions when even good men are sometimes pushed into breaking the law of the land?"

The parson did not reply.

"If you will permit me, sir," continued Gideon, "I should like to ride ahead to scout the county. I am persuaded that Ned Porter is not the only villain hereabouts."

"Can I go with you?" Peter burst out.

"A capital idea. Take the boy for some exercise," said the parson. "The remainder of the party can rest while I complete my business with the magistrate. Meet us back here before noon."

"But . . . ," said Kate, looking pleadingly at Peter.

"Gideon can't carry two on his horse," said Peter reasonably.

Kate scowled at him. "But you're a townie. You don't know how to ride a horse."

Everyone looked incredulous, as if she had said Peter couldn't use a knife and fork.

"I'm sorry," Kate said quickly. "I was joking. I just wanted to go too."

"It will be my pleasure to keep you company, Mistress Kate," said Sidney, smiling his ragged smile at her.

Kate raised her eyebrows at Peter, which he correctly interpreted as meaning: I'm going to get you for this.

Peter was not sure whether it was tact or merriment that prompted Gideon to look away while Peter tried to mount Midnight. It took him a good five minutes, and then Midnight promptly threw him off again. Why, oh why, thought Peter, had his parents always said no to riding lessons? Gideon finally took pity on him, climbed up himself, and reached down to pull Peter up. When Gideon said that Peter could hold on to him if he felt unsteady, Peter refused, saying that he had a good sense of balance. However, when Midnight headed off at a gallop, Peter couldn't help grabbing hold of Gideon's shirt. Five miles later

Peter's legs, stretched out over Midnight's muscular back, were sore and stiff, and he felt a little seasick, but he was beginning to get the hang of this riding business. He started to enjoy himself.

"Imagine a carriage moving on its own without horses, only much, much faster," Peter said to Gideon. "And then imagine roads that are smooth and hard and never get muddy. When we drove up from London to Derbyshire it took less than three hours—and that was in the middle of winter."

Gideon looked suitably impressed.

"And so," Peter continued, "if we were attacked by a highwayman in our time, all we'd do is call 999, and then within minutes a car with flashing lights and sirens full of armed policemen would arrive to rescue us."

"And how would they deal with the highwayman?" asked Gideon. "Would they carry him to a magistrate or would they hang him?"

"Hang him? Oh, no! No one gets hanged nowadays. Not even murderers. Not even mass murderers. The police would cart him off to prison. He'd probably have to stay there for the rest of his life, though."

"I once had the misfortune to visit someone in Newgate Gaol. If your prisons are as foul as Newgate, it would be more merciful to hang him."

"Why? What was it like?"

"It is hell on earth. There is the foulest stench that makes those with the strongest stomach retch. And the air is thick with cries and moans that make your heart stop with the horror of the place. But worst of all is the look in the eyes of those who have languished there any time. Please, God, I never have the occasion to see Newgate Gaol again. But tell me, can it be true that in your time the authorities hang *no one*? No matter what crime they have committed?"

"Yes," Peter replied.

"But if bad men need not fear Jack Ketch and his noose, are not the streets thronged with assassins?"

"I don't think so—well, I've never seen one."

Gideon grew thoughtful and then rode Midnight to a vantage point on high ground where they could see for miles around. Midnight was breathing hard and his flanks were steaming in the cool, misty air. They dismounted to give him a rest. Rain dripped onto their backs from a great oak tree under which they were taking shelter. Suddenly Gideon let out a great cry that rang out over the surrounding fields strewn with poppies. "Nine! Nine! Nine!"

Peter started to chuckle quietly, but when Gideon turned to him to comment that calling "999" did not work in these days, Peter positively exploded. Tears ran down his cheeks and he could scarcely breathe. Gideon, momentarily affronted, pushed Peter over into the wet grass.

"All this is fancy!" Gideon shouted, laughing himself. "'Tis naught but the imaginings of a mischievous"—here Gideon rolled Peter over with the toe of his boot—"young"—another roll—"rogue!"

"But it's true! I swear it's true! I meant that you call 999 on the telephone."

"This tel-ee-phone again," said Gideon in mock exasperation. "Confound your tel-ee-phones."

"It's not difficult to understand," said Peter, miming the actions. "You just key in a number—999 if you want the emergency services, but everyone has their own special number—and then you put the telephone to your ear and you speak to someone who is . . . somewhere else."

Gideon laughed out loud. "Enough! The future is a foreign country to me. Unless I see it with my own eyes I shall not believe it."

"But I've hardly started yet," protested Peter. "I haven't told you about television and computer games and DNA and the Hubble telescope and nanotechnology . . ."

Abruptly Gideon's expression changed and he held up his hand indicating to Peter that he should be quiet.

"Wood smoke," he said. Peter followed him as Gideon set off purposefully down the slope, leaving Midnight to graze on the long grass. There, in a deep hollow that would have provided shelter from the worst of the wind and rain, they came across the smouldering remains of a large bonfire. All around it the grass and bracken had been flattened in a wide circle. The stripped carcasses of roast rabbits and some kind of bird, probably pigeon, lay scattered about. Two small wooden chests, empty apart from a soiled, torn nightgown, had seemingly been abandoned.

Gideon's eyes darted everywhere, taking in every detail. He picked up a discarded flagon and sniffed at it. "Brandy," he said. "And no sign of horses . . . these were a gang of footpads. Six of them at least, I'll warrant."

"What are footpads?" asked Peter.

"Footpads roam the country in search of innocent travelers. They are oft-times more to be feared than highwaymen, for they attack in groups and are likely as not more vicious—for without horses they cannot make a swift escape and so must overwhelm their victims."

"But how can you be sure these are footpads?" asked Peter. "Perhaps these were just tourists having a picnic."

Gideon looked puzzled. "Tourists? Picnic?"

"Never mind," said Peter. "Maybe they were just travelers stopping for breakfast."

"What traveler would leave good chests like these behind? No, Master Peter, these men were interested only in what these chests contained. We have discovered a gang of footpads."

Gideon bent down to pick up a small rag, which he shook out and held by one corner. Traces of blood streaked out from a central crease in the material.

"Never let another man's blood blunt your blade," commented Gideon in a curious, deep voice as if he were thinking of someone. It put Peter in mind of the Tar Man. Gideon flung the rag onto the glowing embers of the fire. Peter shuddered.

"Let us hope that Ned Porter and his accomplice were not in league with them," said Gideon. "Come, we must return to inform the parson. This is ill news indeed."

Midnight carried them back to Lichfield through the drizzle. The horse had picked up his master's mood. His velvet nostrils flared and his very coat seemed to bristle with nervous anticipation. Gideon constantly scanned the horizon for signs of the gang of footpads, every sense on full alert. But if the footpads were there, invisible and watchful, they chose to remain out of sight, screened by trees or hedges or stretched out at their ease at the bottom of ditches. Peter held on tight as they galloped back, and he felt the tension build up in Gideon's back each time they rode through woods and copses, and afterward his relief when they emerged unscathed.

"They are out there. I can feel it in my water," said Gideon.

"But aren't we safe from them on horseback?" asked Peter.

"It's easier than you might imagine for a group of men to pull over horse and rider. And the bones in a horse's leg are not difficult to break." And then he quickly added, "Do not fear, Master Peter. Sadly, I have needed to learn how to hold my own against bad folk."

Peter, however, was not as scared as Gideon supposed. Why should he be, sitting on the back of this magnificent animal in the company of a man who had defeated a notorious highwayman single-handedly?

By the time they were within a mile of Lichfield the roads became much busier, and Gideon felt that there was now little likelihood of attack. Midnight's pace slowed down and they fell to talking again.

"Mistress Kate suffers grievously, I think, from being wrenched from her family. Do you not feel sick for your home and your time too?"

"I do . . . but I don't see so much of my family in any case. Mum and Dad work abroad a lot. Margrit, the au pair, looks after me while they are away."

"Your mother works?"

"Yes. Lots of mothers work in my time."

"And yet you have a servant?"

"Yes," answered Peter, puzzled. "Well, sort of. Why shouldn't we?"

"If you have the money to pay a servant, why would your mother need to work?"

"She doesn't just work for the money—she likes it."

"Perhaps work is different in your time. And your servant is an Irishwoman? I like the Irish. They are always ready with a song or a jest."

"I don't understand."

"Mistress O' Pear. Is she Irish?"

"Er . . . our au pair is German, if that's what you mean. Anyway, things are different for Kate—it's hard to explain. She comes from this big family. They're quite close, I think. My parents have really important, stressful jobs. I guess they're just too busy to notice me most of the time."

"I have few memories of my mother in moments of idleness," said Gideon kindly. "I think it is in the nature of things that parents are forever occupied." He pointed to the swallows skimming low over the fields through clouds of midges. "Look at the birds in search of food to feed their chicks from dawn to dusk. Parents mostly do not have the leisure to be with their children. It is why you have brothers and sisters to play with."

"I'm an only child."

"Ah . . . ," said Gideon. "Lord Luxon," he continued, "in whose employ I remained for almost seven years, was an only child. He had a father so wealthy he never knew anything but leisure. And yet his son was none the better for it."

"Was he the one you told Mrs. Byng about? The man who always went to Tyburn for the hangings?"

"The same. When Lord Luxon was on the verge of manhood, just a little older than you are now, his father cut open a ripe red apple at dinner and found that a worm had eaten deep into its flesh. His father was always hard on him. Without warning, his father turned on him in a great rage and said, 'You are like this apple, rotten at the core. I can never be proud of you. I doubt that I ever shall.'"

"What had he done that got his father so angry?"

"I do not know. I heard the story from his servant. But what boy has done nothing of which he is ashamed? Nor is it uncommon that a parent asks more of his child than the child has it in his power to achieve. And it seems to me that it is often the eldest child who suffers most in this way. . . . Alas, Lord Luxon's father died soon afterward. It is a hard thing to have lost the respect of one's father. It ate into Lord Luxon. I believe it is his tragedy."

"Why did you work for Lord Luxon if he's such a bad man?" asked Peter.

"I had no choice in the matter."

"Will you tell me about it?"

Gideon nodded. "If you like. It is not an extraordinary tale. Many children have had far worse fates."

Gideon took a few moments to gather his thoughts. Peter hoped they would not reach Lichfield before he arrived at the end of his story.

"My mother and father and eight out of my nine brothers and sisters are all dead," he began.

Peter gasped. "That's awful!"

"It happened many years ago."

"Then who brought you up?"

"My mother until I was ten and then . . . someone whom I have no reason to remember with affection."

Gideon told Peter how his father, a skilled cabinetmaker, died when he was two, leaving his mother to bring up her large family alone. Shortly afterward one of his elder brothers died suddenly, and the whole family left Somerset to settle in Surrey, in a small village called Abinger, where his mother's only surviving sister lived. His mother remarried an Abinger man, Joshua Seymour, and they had two children—a boy, Joshua, and a girl. One March, when Gideon was ten, the village was blighted with a virulent outbreak of scarlet fever. After a bad winter when food had been scarce and bronchitis had already weakened several members of the family, the scarlet fever could not have arrived at a worse time. Only ten-year-old Gideon and his young half brother, Joshua, then six and a half, survived. The two boys watched ten members of their family buried in the same week. On her deathbed Mrs. Seymour wrote to the rector begging him to find a home for her two youngest boys. They were both, she wrote, honest, God-fearing boys who knew their letters and were not afraid of hard work.

And so it was that the local squire acquired two slaves in all but name. Unpaid, mostly hungry and cold, and regularly beaten, the Seymour boys had a wretched childhood, but at least they had each other. Only when the squire was away on business, or on Sundays, when they were dressed in good clothes and displayed in church as an example of their master's generosity, did they know any respite.

On his fifteenth birthday the cook gave Gideon a tankard of cider to celebrate the day. Unused to strong drink, Gideon sent a Japanese bowl crashing to the floor in the stone-flagged entrance hall at the same moment that the squire returned empty-handed from a frustrating morning's pike fishing. The squire dragged Gideon outside, tore the shirt from his back, and beat him until he bled and then, when Gideon fainted, revived him with a bucket of icy water. Poor Joshua watched, helpless, from the scullery window, tears streaming down his face.

That night Gideon vowed to run away and start a new life, swearing to young Joshua that he would come back for him at the first opportunity.

"But why didn't you tell somebody?" Peter wanted to know. "Surely the local police or magistrate or whatever you call them could have made the squire stop beating you. It's against the law to beat children like that in my time. They'd put you in prison if you were found out."

"Against the law! If that were the law of this land, there would be more people in prison than without! But that is wondrous to hear—no hangings! No beatings! Why, the future must herald paradise on earth!"

"Well, not exactly. . . . So did you escape in the end?" asked Peter.

"I was foolish. I ran away that very night. I should have waited for the spring. I headed for London but did not get even as far as Esher."

Gideon described how he soon finished the provisions of bread and cheese he had brought with him. He avoided the roads in case the squire's men came after him. He became hopelessly lost crossing the interminable farmland under sunless skies and almost died of cold, sleeping rough under frozen hedgerows. Twice he begged poor farmers for something to eat but both times he was chased off their land. Finally, after ten days, weak from a feverish chill and lack of food, he came to a decision. He must either steal something to eat or die. He sank to his knees onto grass stiff with frost and prayed for forgiveness. He reasoned that he had promised to rescue Joshua, and that if he died, his young half brother would be forever at the squire's mercy.

Arriving at a small farm close to Oxshott, Gideon observed the house from a distance until he saw the farmer walk off into the fields with his dog. He crept into the farmyard and, drawn onward by the tantalizing smell of baking, found himself at the kitchen door. His heart pounding, Gideon peeped in through the grimy window. On the scrubbed wooden table he saw three pies. There was no sign of anyone. Gideon slowly pushed open the door, which creaked alarmingly, and stole into the kitchen. He almost changed his mind and got ready to run out again, but then he remembered Joshua. He grabbed hold of one of the pies. Fresh out of the oven, it was red hot and he was forced to drop it back onto the table with a loud clatter. Convinced he had alerted the house to his presence, Gideon froze, straining to hear footsteps, but all was silent once more. Then he snatched a spoon off a dresser and broke through the thick suet crust. A cloud of steam rose out of the pie, along with an irresistibly savory aroma. He lifted a spoonful of meat and rich gravy to his lips and blew on it to cool it down. What bliss it was to feel hot food in his belly. He swallowed another spoonful and then another and another, knowing that he ought to make his escape while he had the chance.

It was the deep growling of the dog that he heard first. The farmer's wife, who had been tending a sick calf in the barn, had seen Gideon enter the kitchen and had run off after her husband to fetch him back to deal with the intruder. Now the farmer stood at the kitchen door, wielding a scythe in one hand and restraining his dog with the other. The dog, a large mongrel with a rank, shaggy coat, was baring its teeth and straining to leap at Gideon's throat.

"No food has passed my lips these five days past! Have mercy!" cried Gideon.

It took the farmer half a second to make up his mind, and then he released his hold on the dog. Gideon hurled a wooden stool at the animal and dashed into the inner hall and out through the front door. He headed into the barn and jumped onto a pile of firewood stacked at one end. The dog was at his heels and, with the adrenalin rush of fear spurring him on, Gideon hurled himself upward and managed to catch hold of one of the supporting beams. His legs hung precariously above the dog's snapping jaws. After several attempts he succeeded in swinging both legs over the wooden beam. He locked his ankles together and inch by inch started to heave and slide himself over to the nearest corner of the barn, where he could see chinks of light breaking through gaps in the rough slate roof.

The farmer, whose shriveled face told of a life full of hardship, started to shout at Gideon to come down, telling him that there was no escape and that he'd teach him to steal his supper.

"What is he doing to our roof?" shrieked his wife as Gideon thumped desperately at the slate tiles with his bare fist. They heard the crash as first one and then three or four slates smashed onto the cobbles in the farmyard below. Gideon hauled himself through the hole he had made and clambered up the steeply pitched roof. He straddled the ridge, one leg over each side, and looked down at the irate farmer far below, as he tried to get his breath back. The foul dog barked incessantly. Then Gideon noticed two things in quick succession. He watched the farmer stoop down and pick up a stone and take aim. At the same time, in the narrow lane in front of the farmhouse, Gideon could see an elegant figure on horseback wearing a splendid sky blue jacket. The gentleman's attention had clearly been drawn by all the commotion. The stone whizzed through the air and found its target. Half an inch nearer and Gideon would have lost an eye; as it was, the stone stung his cheekbone and it was his grip that he lost. Gideon slithered down the roof, grasping hold of the edge of the hole he had made. The sharp slate cut into his fingers, and his legs jerked this way and that trying to find a foothold.

Suddenly two tiles gave way under his weight. Gideon slid down the roof, his nails screeching down the slate, as his fingers scrabbled after anything to hang on to. *This is the end,* he thought. *My neck will be broken. This is punishment for my wickedness.*

Time itself seemed to slow down and in that instant Gideon saw everything with a terrifying clarity: There was the dog, foaming at the mouth in a frenzy of excitement; next to it the farmer who was craning his neck upward, an expression of triumphant expectation on his face. And then there was the *clip-clop* of hooves as the fine young gentleman rode his black mare into the cobbled yard. . . . It was at that moment that Gideon glimpsed a rusting pulley attached to an iron bar that jutted out of the barn wall. Instinctively Gideon shot out his arm and seized hold of the bar. He swung like a pendulum perhaps six feet above the yard. This was the dog's chance. It leaped up and sank its teeth into Gideon's left calf, opening up a gaping, bloody wound as the animal fell back to the ground. Screaming with the pain of it, Gideon struggled to lift up his knees out of reach of the dog.

"Call that dog off, sir!" shouted the young gentleman. "The lad cannot defend himself!"

Startled at the gentleman's sudden appearance, the farmer turned around to look at him. "What is it to you, my lord? This thief stole my supper!"

"And he must pay for his supper with his legs? Here, take that. It will buy you a dozen suppers."

The gentleman threw down onto the muddy yard a handful of coins, which the farmer's wife quickly retrieved.

"Call off your dog at once if you don't want to feel my whip on your back."

The farmer scowled at the gentleman but made no move. Gideon, who was fast losing his grip, was by now no longer able to raise his knees. The dog attacked again. This time the other leg. Gideon let out an agonized scream as its teeth tore into his flesh. A shot rang out as the gentleman fired his pistol into the air and the petrified dog sped out of sight. The gentleman positioned his horse under Gideon and commanded him to drop.

"You'd better come with me. Can you ride?"

"Was that Lord Luxon?" asked Peter.

"It was he. He saved me."

"He can't have been that bad if he'd do a thing like that."

"On that day and on many others I saw him display great character. When I asked him afterward why he had shown me such kindness, he told me, 'Any fool could see you were starving. I do not condemn you for trying to keep alive even though there are those who would.' I have never forgotten it. It is one of the sorrows of my life to have witnessed how Lord Luxon squandered the fine qualities he was born with."

"Were you badly injured by the dog?" asked Peter.

Gideon pulled down a stocking for Peter to see the scars running like white rope up his calf.

Peter gulped. "That's bad. That's really bad. You're braver than me. I couldn't have stood that."

"No. Physical pain is over as soon as it stops. Other things take longer to heal."

The three spires of Lichfield Cathedral rose up majestically above green meadows. They rode past the cathedral pond and onward toward the George Inn. As they rode into the yard, Kate ran out to greet them. "The parson's just returned with the news. Ned Porter escaped from the magistrate's cellar during the night!"

I WAS STARVING. I HAD NEVER KNOWN HUNGER LIKE IT BEFORE OR SINCE. ANYONE WHO HAS NOT FELT HUNGER CLAWING AWAY AT HIS ENTRAILS UNTIL HE FEARS HE WILL GO MAD WILL NOT COMPREHEND WHAT I FELT. I BELIEVE I WOULD HAVE DONE ANYTHING FOR A MOUTHFUL OF THAT BEEF PIE. I KNEW IT WAS NOURISHMENT PREPARED BY A STRANGER'S HAND AND NEVER INTENDED TO SUSTAIN ME, BUT THE TEMPTATION WAS TOO GREAT.

I HAD NOT THOUGHT OF MY MOTHER IN ALL THE DAYS SINCE I HAD RUN AWAY, AND YET IT WAS THEN THAT HER FACE APPEARED TO ME. *IN ANOTHER MOMENT,* I SAID TO MYSELF, *I SHALL BE A THIEF, LET THE LORD FORGIVE ME.* AND THEN I REMEMBERED JOSHUA AND I ATE.

I HAVE OFTEN WONDERED SINCE, WHAT MY FATE WOULD HAVE BEEN HAD I RESISTED, FOR THAT FIRST CRIME LED TO OTHERS. WOULD I HAVE DIED THAT BITTER WINTER OR WOULD I HAVE LED A BETTER LIFE?

—*THE LIFE AND TIMES OF GIDEON SEYMOUR, CUTPURSE AND GENTLEMAN,* 1792

TWELVE

A Parliament of Rooks

*In which Detective Inspector Wheeler is perturbed
by a photograph, Kate talks to a famous scientist,
and Peter sees something very shocking*

Peter's mother was talking to the head of the Hollywood film studios that were financing the film she was working on. Mrs. Schock told him that she would not be returning to California until Peter was found. She listened to what he had to say and then put the phone down slowly with a quiet click.

Peter's father was waiting for her in their car outside the hotel, the engine running. They were due to see Detective

Inspector Wheeler at the Dyers' farm at half past two.

"How did he take it?" Peter's father asked as he drove off.

"Well, he made the right kind of sympathetic noises but the delay in shooting has already cost them a quarter of a million dollars. It sounds like there's already a long queue of people willing to step into the breach."

"I bet," said Mr. Schock. "I thought it wouldn't be long before the vultures started to circle overhead."

The narrow road clung to the shoulder of a high peak, and suddenly a magnificent vista swept into view. The previous night's snow still clung to the high ground despite the sunshine, and a bitter cold wind buffeted the car. Mr. Schock tried not to think about Peter and Kate being caught out in these conditions—or worse.

"He said that as I'd lived and breathed this film for five years, no one could really replace me. Which hasn't stopped him terminating my contract. He's appointing another producer this afternoon."

"I'm so sorry," said Mr. Schock, resting his hand on hers.

"Are you? I didn't think you would be. I'm not. You can replace a producer, but you can't replace a mother. The film as good as robbed Peter of his mother from the age of seven." She tried hard not to cry but the tears came anyway. "I wish I'd stayed at home with him; I wish I'd walked him to school; I wish I'd invited his friends over for tea and made them chocolate brownies, and now . . . and now I might never see him again to say that I am sorry for being a bad mother."

The tires squealed as Mr. Schock pulled over to the side of the deserted road and switched the engine off.

"Don't say that!" he shouted at his wife. "We are *not* going to give up hope. Peter's out there. I don't know where, but he is. And you are *not* a bad mother. Sure, your career hasn't made things easy for any of us, but you've only got one life and if you'd have stayed at home with Peter, I believe you would have gone mad. Don't torture yourself like this—neither of us is a perfect parent, but we love him and we've done the best we can in the circumstances. I know he misses you but he's *proud* of you too. You *will* see Peter again, and when he grows up he *will* understand."

Beneath an overcast sky Parson Ledbury and Gideon talked earnestly in the cobbled courtyard behind the George Inn. Peter and Kate were each perched on a dolphin—a low post to which horses could be tethered at the entrance to the narrow alley that led from the courtyard into Bird Street. The three spires of Lichfield Cathedral could be seen towering above the rooftops. Peter had been telling Kate about the footpads' abandoned camp, and then Kate had told Peter how the magistrate had arrived with the shocking news of the highwayman's escape minutes after Gideon and Peter's departure.

"So how did Ned manage to get out of the cellar, then? There weren't any windows, were there?"

"No, and the trapdoor was padlocked from the outside. The magistrate took the only key to bed with him. It's a total mystery," said Kate.

"Didn't they hear anything?"

"No."

"If we were locked up, I bet we could blur our way out," remarked Peter.

"You're right! That'd be so cool! I'm going to try it out when I get the chance. . . . By the way, you haven't blurred since the supermarket car park, have you?"

"No," replied Peter.

"No, neither have I," said Kate. "It's weird because I was beginning to think it only happens when you are either about to fall asleep or about to wake up. But it didn't happen to me last night or this morning."

"Have you tried to blur again on purpose?" asked Peter.

"No, there's always been someone around. I just hope we can manage to blur our way out of this without the machine, because I'm telling you, I don't want to meet the Tar Man again if I can help it."

"When we get back to our time, do you think we'll start blurring back to the eighteenth century?" said Peter.

"Ooh," said Kate. "I hadn't thought of that."

"It'd be great in history lessons," said Peter. "'Who can tell me the date of the French Revolution, boys?' 'If you'd just give me a moment, miss, I'll go back and check. Anything else you'd like to know while I'm there?'"

Kate suddenly looked serious. "What do you think would happen if we let slip what we knew was going to happen in the future? I mean, do you remember the way Mrs. Byng talked about America, like it was this unimportant, wild country. She said the best thing about America was that it saved money on prisons—you could just transport criminals there to work on the plantations."

"I thought they sent prisoners to Australia," said Peter.

"They did but I don't think Captain Cook has discovered Australia yet. Can you imagine what the Byngs would say if we told them America was going to become a superpower and send men to the moon and be the richest country on earth? They'd faint."

"Parson Ledbury wouldn't believe us," said Peter. "I heard what he thinks about America." Peter imitated the parson's deep, booming voice: "'That bothersome little colony is more trouble than it's worth. King George may be monstrous attached to it, but I say the day America amounts to anything I'll eat my hat!'"

Kate laughed. "Is that what he said?" she asked, a grin spreading over her face.

"Yes."

"Oh, I wish we could tell him! It'd be so cool to see the expression on his face."

"Maybe we shouldn't talk about the future at all," said Peter. "If we did say something, they'd only think we were mad—but who knows what effect it could have."

"Yeah," agreed Kate. "We'd better keep our mouths shut. It's tempting, though."

Oh, no, thought Peter guiltily, *maybe I shouldn't have told Gideon about telephones and police cars and stuff. Oh well, it's too late now.*

Hannah appeared presently, coming out of the stable door at the rear of the inn, Jack trailing behind her. She was carrying a basin.

"Ah, you're back, Master Schock," she said with a friendly smile, "just in time to eat some pork pie with us." Hannah looked at the contents of the bowl and then looked back at Kate and Peter.

"I do hope you two children do not have delicate stomachs. Perhaps it's best you look away, for the good doctor has seen fit to bleed Sidney and the driver."

Hannah walked over to the gutter at the bottom of the yard. After what she'd said, Peter, Kate, and Jack trooped after her, of course, as she tipped the basin and poured quantities of dark red blood into the stagnant rainwater in the blocked gutter. Dozens of wasps and flies seemed to appear out of nowhere and buzzed around it.

"He bled them?" Kate exclaimed in disgust.

"He did it as a precaution on account of both them having had hard blows to the head. Better to be safe than sorry. Jack held the bowl for the doctor, didn't you, my little master?" asked Hannah.

"He pricked their vines until their blood fell *plop, plop, plop* into the basin," commented Jack, his face very proud and serious. "I held Sidney's hand."

"They are called veins, not vines, Master Jack, veins like weather vanes," explained Hannah.

"Oh, that is so gross," exclaimed Kate, her voice echoing around the courtyard as she watched the blood flowing down the slimy gutter. "What an awful thing to do to someone who's already feeling ill. Is he a proper doctor?"

Peter tugged on Kate's sleeve. She turned to look at him and he gave a slight backward nod with his head.

Parson Ledbury and Gideon were standing with a plump, youngish gentleman in a heavily powdered wig and snowy white shirt. He was wiping his hands with a cloth, and he gave off an air of quiet calm and competence.

"I hope you will excuse my young charge's impertinence," said Parson Ledbury. "She does not understand how honored we are by your attendance on us."

"I assure you I take no offence, Parson Ledbury," replied the gentleman. "The sight of blood is always alarming to those unused to it."

"Master Peter Schock, Mistress Kate," announced Parson Ledbury grandly, "this gentleman is none other than Dr. Erasmus Darwin, whose medical prowess is such that even the King of England would have him as his physician."

Gideon, who stood behind the doctor and the parson, gestured to Peter to bow, which he did. Kate, though, stood there openmouthed and neither curtsied nor said a word.

"I am happy to make your acquaintance, children, and can assure you that young Sidney and your driver are perfectly comfortable and, after another hour or two's rest, will be ready to resume their journey."

"You are Dr. Erasmus Darwin?" asked Kate incredulously.

Bemused, the doctor nodded his head and smiled. "I am none other."

"Oh, how my parents would love to meet you! We have named a cow after you on our farm, sir," she said, which made both the parson and the doctor laugh out loud.

"Now that is indeed an honor, is it not, Parson?" said Dr. Darwin. "I trust she is a good milker!"

"And," continued Kate, "you will become a great scientist and

[173]

inventor and your grandson, who will be called Charles, will discover something that will change the world forever."

"Uh-oh," said Peter under his breath. "Now she's done it."

Dr. Darwin stopped laughing and, rather taken aback, looked
searchingly into Kate's face. The parson, unusually, was at a loss
to know what to say, but Gideon stepped forward.

"Some of the members of Kate's family have the gift of second
sight. They can predict the future. Although I am sure Mistress
Kate would be the first to admit their predictions do not always
come to fruition."

Kate looked at Gideon and shook her head as if she had just
woken up, and suddenly looked confused and embarrassed.

"Oh, I'm sorry," she said to Dr. Darwin. "Please take no notice
of me. I didn't realize what I was saying. It's all nonsense."

Dr. Darwin smiled at her and to save her embarrassment knelt
down next to Jack and started up a conversation with him.

"So, Master Jack, you hope to see the King and have him lay
his hands on you to cure you of the scrofula?"

"Yes, sir, I have the King's evil."

Dr. Darwin gently felt Jack's neck while he spoke to him.

"You do, Jack, but I am happy to say it is not a serious case.
I fancy you are resisting the infection. I attended the mother of
Dr. Samuel Johnson, who lived in Lichfield until her death," said
Dr. Darwin, "and she told me that her famous son also suffered
from the King's evil as a child. But unlike you, Dr. Johnson suffered grievously from the infection. You cannot help but notice
the scars he has carried from it for the rest of his life. When
he was even younger than you, two years old or thereabout, his

mother took him to London in order that Queen Anne could lay her hands on him. Her Majesty gave him a gold touchpiece, which he hangs around his neck to this very day. And look at Dr. Johnson now: a respected man of letters, the author of the first dictionary of the English language, and, according to some, although *I* remain to be convinced, London's greatest wit."

"So that's who Dr. Johnson was, is, I mean," whispered Peter to Kate. "He wrote the first dictionary. Margrit said if I found out what Dr. Johnson was famous for, she'd buy me a present."

"*Everyone* knows that," whispered Kate back.

"Oh yeah? Well, I might not know who Dr. Johnson is but at least I know when to keep my mouth shut," Peter replied.

Kate looked shamefaced. "I'm sorry; it just came out. It won't happen again. Anyway, I bet I know what present Margrit would give you."

"What?"

"A dictionary!"

Peter pulled a face.

Dr. Darwin was still talking with Jack, crouching down on the cobbles next to him. "Sidney says that the sweat of a hanged man would cure me too. He wants to go to Tyburn to get some," said Jack.

"It is not something I would recommend, Master Jack, neither for you nor for him. But by all means go to the Court of St. James. You will like King George, and I am quite certain that he will like you. You must tell him that Mistress Kate has named a cow after Dr. Darwin in Lichfield—it will amuse him. He is so fond of farming that some of his courtiers call him Farmer George."

"There, Master Jack," said Hannah, "you might tell King George about your cabbage patch and how you and your mama frightened away the rabbits." Then in a lower voice so Jack might not hear, she asked, "How ill is he, Dr. Darwin?"

"The swellings in his neck are small and there is no sign of ulceration. He has good color, nor is he too thin. Let him eat well, retire early, take moderate exercise and, if he can be persuaded, cold baths. If he suffers too much from night sweats, you should have him bled. Nothing is certain in this life, but the King's evil does not seem to have the better of young Jack."

"Did Queen Anne's touch cure good Dr. Johnson like it did Mrs. Byng's own father?" Hannah asked.

"I cannot say for certain, my dear," replied the doctor. "Although I do know it gave Mrs. Johnson great comfort. In any case, as the whole world knows, even with a scarred face and blind in one eye and deaf in one ear, Samuel Johnson has achieved more in one lifetime than most men would in six—with or without the scrofula!"

Dr. Darwin took leave of the party and wished them Godspeed. The parson shook his hand warmly. He clearly had enormous respect for Lichfield's celebrated doctor. As Dr. Darwin passed Peter and Kate to walk through the narrow alleyway into Bird Street, he stopped for a moment to speak to Kate.

"And what, pray, do you foretell my distinguished grandson will discover?"

"Do you really want to know?"

"I do."

Kate hesitated for a moment and gave a sidelong look at Peter. "Then you must swear not to tell anyone," she said.

"Very well. I swear."

"Charles Darwin discovered something called *evolution*. He discovered that human beings weren't created, they *evolved* from apes. Once they found that out, it changed everything."

Dr. Darwin looked as if he had been given a strong electric shock. He gulped and said, "Why did you say it *changed* everything? Why not it *will change* everything?"

Peter clapped his hand to his forehead in exasperation.

"Slip of the tongue," said Kate hurriedly. "I told you I was tired."

Over a light luncheon the parson announced that in view of Gideon's discovery of the footpads and Ned Porter's escape, there was to be a change of plan. He had intended to drive Mrs. Byng's carriage all the way to her brother's house in Chiswick, but in the circumstances, he felt it would be safer to drive to Birmingham and catch one of the nonstop stagecoaches to London. It would be faster, for they changed the horses regularly at staging posts, and safer, as the stagecoach men were armed with blunderbusses. As he spoke, Gideon nodded strongly in agreement. The journey from Lichfield to Birmingham should not, he told them, take much above two hours. They were to set off at six, by which time Sidney and the driver should be fit for travel.

The sun came out after lunch and, with the exception of Gideon and the two invalids, the party decided to take a stroll around Lichfield. A warm, blustery wind had blown up and as they strolled through the pleasant streets thronged with the good folk of Lichfield, it gave the children much amusement to see what a strong gust of wind could do to a three-cornered hat, a wig, or a skirt the width of a small car. They half-expected to see some of the more fashionable ladies being carried up toward the clouds like brightly colored balloons.

Parson Ledbury gave them a tour of Lichfield Cathedral, scarcely lowering his booming voice, which seemed almost indecent in this hushed, vaulted, glorious space. Kate stood in the Lady Chapel, bathed in the tinted sunlight that streamed through the richly colored stained-glass windows, and offered up a silent prayer for their safe return to their own time.

Afterward they walked through the Cathedral Close, past Dr. Darwin's house, and on to the Minster Pond. It was the most normal thing the children had done since arriving in the eighteenth century, for both Kate and Peter were used to being dragged around historic towns on holiday. It was hard, though, not being able to go off and buy an ice cream or a can of fizzy drink.

Peter was lagging behind, convinced that he had seen a green woodpecker in a great elm tree overhanging the pond. He was standing, staring up into the lofty branches, shading his eyes, when he heard peals of laughter. Looking over at his companions, he saw that the wind had blown Parson Ledbury's hat onto the pond, where it was floating farther from the edge every second. After the longest stick the parson could find proved too short, he waded without hesitation into the murky water in his white stockings and buckled shoes and retrieved his hat. Water trickled down his face, and his stockings were streaked with green weed, but he seemed very pleased with himself.

"Upon my word that cools the blood!" he laughed, and taking off his hat once more, scooped up some more pond water and doused himself with it. Hannah shrieked and cried with laughter, turning quite pink, and Jack begged the parson to do the same to him—which he would have done had Hannah not cried, "No, no, sir, think of his condition. He could catch a chill in this wind!"

Peter joined in the laughter from some fifty yards behind, until he caught sight of something that made him stop at once. He stepped behind the trunk of the great elm tree and took another look to confirm his first impression. Farther around the edge of the pond, positioned between two bushes in such a way as to be invisible to his companions but clearly visible to Peter, stood the Tar Man. Peter shrank back behind the tree trunk, his heart thudding in his chest. He turned his head until he could spot him again, and he peered shakily across the water at the man he had hoped never to set eyes on again. He took in the crescent moon scar, visible even from here, the dirty black coat, and, above all, that air of detached cruelty and total focus on his prey. Peter was put in mind of a wary old lion stalking unsuspecting game at a waterhole on the savannah.

Before he knew what he was doing, Peter was running toward his friends waving his arms and whooping madly. "Come and see this woodpecker!" he shouted at the top of his voice. When he looked over at the space where the Tar Man had been, it was empty.

•   •   •

Detective Inspector Wheeler gave Dr. and Mrs. Dyer and Mr. and Mrs. Schock each an enlarged color photograph to look at and sat back in a scuffed kitchen chair waiting for a reaction. The photograph depicted a boy and a girl in eighteenth-century dress, floating at shoulder height in a supermarket car park.

"Oh my Lord!" gasped Mrs. Dyer. "It's Kate!"

"What's going on?" demanded Dr. Dyer. "Where and when was this taken?"

"Are you implying that this could be Peter?" exclaimed Mrs. Schock.

Everyone was speaking at once.

"I think perhaps you'd better tell us what this is all about, Detective Inspector," said Mr. Schock.

"I only wish I *could* tell you what this is all about," said the inspector. "But you've answered one of my questions already, Mrs. Dyer. The girl in the picture appears to be your daughter. Now, this is clearly a somewhat unusual image and we would have dismissed it as a hoax except that there are apparently several witnesses to the incident."

The policeman observed the four heads as they bowed over the kitchen table. This was a strange case and no mistake. He had now ruled out kidnapping. The Schocks were well off but not seriously wealthy, and there would have been a ransom note by now if the children had been kidnapped. As for the other possibility, that Peter had run away, he could not rule it out entirely, as the boy was obviously angry at some level with both parents. But he had never run away before and why should he take Kate with him—a girl he had only just met? No. It did not add up. As for a madman of some description suddenly taking it into his head to harm these children, conceal them, and then escape from the lab without any witnesses at all within a time gap of what—three or four minutes at most? That idea beggared belief. He kept coming back to the same conclusion: These children had simply disappeared into thin air.

The photograph was the first lead in the case—and what a lead! What possible conclusions could he draw from this bizarre picture? And yet he still had this hunch—which he could neither explain nor share—that the children were safe. He was also increasingly convinced that the girl's father was holding back some information, and it was Dr. Dyer's reaction above all that he observed.

"But where was the photograph taken? How did you get hold of it? Where is she now?" Mrs. Dyer was becoming extremely agitated. Dr. Dyer put an arm round her shoulder. The inspector looked at him. *He seems shocked,* thought the inspector, *but excited too. Really excited. Just what exactly are you hiding, Dr. Dyer?*

"The subeditor of a local newspaper in rural Staffordshire faxed it to me this morning. They were planning to publish a piece on a supposed sighting of ghosts—"

At this, Mrs. Schock burst into tears.

"I'm sorry if this is upsetting, Mrs. Schock," said the inspector. "May I continue?"

"Of course. I'm sorry, please do," she replied.

"There is actually not much more to say at this stage. The man who took this photograph swears that he saw two ghosts in

Sainsbury's car park. The subeditor at the newspaper thought she recognized Kate and checked with me before publishing it. I've confiscated the photograph and the negative and have implied that there is a logical explanation for this. I'm sure my sergeant will think of one to satisfy them presently. . . . Three officers are on their way to Staffordshire as we speak. Rest assured that you will be informed of any developments."

"But could the boy be Peter?" asked his father. "And how are they floating? And what on earth are they doing in eighteenth-century costume?"

"I couldn't have put it better myself," said Inspector Wheeler. "If any of you know how to explain this, I will be delighted to hear it, because for the present, unless I accept that these fig-ures are ghosts—which I certainly don't—I have no idea what to make of this picture."

"Can I keep hold of this photograph?" asked Dr. Dyer.

"Be my guest," replied the inspector. "Here, have an envelope to put it in. Please keep it confidential, though. I don't want the press to get hold of it before we've had a chance to investigate."

Driving away from the Dyers' farm, the inspector made a call to the officer in charge of surveillance at the NCRDM laboratory. "Let me know if Dr. Dyer turns up this afternoon—I'd be inter-ested to know if he's got a large brown envelope with him."

The driver declined the parson's offer of a seat inside the car-riage, saying that he would feel more at ease riding on top. Squeezed between the driver and Gideon, Peter watched the driver's head droop as he grew drowsy, and soon the motion of horses had lulled him to sleep. Only when he started up a slow, rhythmic snoring did Peter dare tell Gideon what was on his mind.

"When we were out walking this afternoon I saw the Tar Man. He was spying on us. And then, on our way out of Lichfield, we passed a tavern and I'm pretty sure I saw him again. He sat at a table surrounded by a big crowd of men. But I might have imagined it was him."

Gideon's tranquil expression vanished. After a moment he replied, "I asked myself why you were forever looking over your shoulder. Did you see anything?"

"No, nothing. And I've told Kate to keep a lookout from the carriage too."

"I had thought he was already in London and we were out of harm's way," said Gideon. "But then, his employer has a hundred paid informants who could track you down from land's end to John O' Groats if he so wished."

"Gideon . . ." Peter hesitated before asking his questions, for fear of offending him. "Gideon, if you don't mind me asking, why is the Tar Man following you? Who *does* he work for? . . . And what did Ned Porter mean when he said that he wouldn't be in your shoes for a casketful of diamonds?"

"Ha! Ned Porter," growled Gideon. "I have a theory about that slippery villain now that I know the Tar Man has been in Lichfield. I'll wager that Ned Porter's miraculous escape has something to do with the Tar Man's miraculous skill in picking locks. The Tar Man will certainly have put the word about that he would make it worth any rogue's while to give him news of a certain Mr. Seymour and two children with magical powers. And Ned saw you and Mistress Kate blur—"

"But we don't have magical powers! It's not like that! We're not witches or anything," cried Peter.

"I know that, Master Peter, but if the Tar Man is to get a good price for his booty, it will be to his profit to excite interest in his magic box."

"But he said he'd sell it back to us!"

"Ha! Do you think he would sell it to you if he could get a more handsome price elsewhere?"

"Then what's the point of us going down to London? We haven't got any money—he'll never give it to us. How are Kate and I ever going to get home?"

For the first time Peter felt a terrible panic rise up from deep within him. He had not seriously considered before the possibility that he could not get back. Now the thought of being cut off from his home, friends, school, everything he knew or cared about, made his heart skip a beat. Never to taste ice cream or peanut butter sandwiches again, never to watch television nor ride on a double-decker bus, never to finish the last fifty pages of *The Lord of the Rings*, never to see a jumbo jet thundering overhead above Richmond Green . . . never to have his mother take his face in her hands to kiss him good night. And then he remembered that the last thing he'd said to his father was "I hate you." His throat tightened. He looked straight ahead without speaking. The summer landscape, instead of seeming wild and free and inviting as it had only a few moments before, now appeared unbearably empty and unfamiliar.

Gideon urged the horses to go faster and cracked the whip, which made the driver stir in his sleep and lean on Peter. The driver's unshaved cheek grated on Peter's neck, and his breath smelled very bad. Gideon reached over and pushed the driver away from his young friend.

"We will find a way to get you home, Master Peter. No matter how long it takes, we will find a way."

Peter bit his lip and nodded his head vigorously in thanks, not capable of speaking just yet.

"You asked me who the Tar Man works for. And as it seems that our fates have been woven together, it is right that you know. The Tar Man and I had the same employer: Lord Luxon. He is Lord Luxon's henchman."

Peter sat up, appalled at the thought that Gideon might have had to work alongside such a monster. "But why would Lord Luxon send someone like that after you?"

"Lord Luxon believes that I know too much to be allowed to walk away from his service. He is very angry with me for having left his employ."

"But why? He can't expect you to work for him if you don't want to."

"He saved my life."

"Yes, but that doesn't mean that he owns you!"

"Soon after Lord Luxon took me in," said Gideon, "his father, the old Lord Luxon, died. We lived in Tempest House, in Surrey, a mansion with thirty rooms, set in a thousand acres. Within a year Lord Luxon had taken against nearly all the servants and those employed to run the estate. I think he still felt his father's disapproval of him through their eyes and it was true that many of them were too used to thinking of Lord Luxon as a wayward boy to treat him in the manner that their new master demanded. Lord Luxon got rid of them all one by one and hired new ones. He trusted me, above all, for I owed him my life and I had a talent for bookkeeping and handling the staff. By the age of nineteen I was all but running Tempest House. In return he paid me well and arranged for my half brother, Joshua, to be apprenticed to a well-known artist and engraver, Mr. Hogarth, at his studio in Covent Garden Piazza."

"What's Joshua like? How old is he?"

"He is nineteen. You remind me a little of him. You have the same coloring and both of you are slow to smile, but when you do . . ."

"Thanks, Gideon! My mum always says I take life too seriously."

Gideon laughed and then looked sad. "Joshua can catch a likeness better than anyone I know. . . . Mr. Hogarth is in ill health and Joshua is anxious about his position. Joshua does not understand . . . why I left Lord Luxon's service. . . . In the letter that was waiting for me at Baslow Hall, Joshua wrote to warn me that my employer was angry that I had left. He also told me that Lord Luxon had arranged with Mr. Hogarth that he should leave his employ and move to Tempest House. Lord Luxon promises to entrust Joshua with the task of making a set of drawings of his various properties and those of his friends. My brother, of course, is flattered and delighted to be accorded such an honor. But he must not go! He must not go! Lord Luxon does this to draw me back into his web, and I do not like to think of the role that Lord Luxon intends for poor Joshua. . . . Nowadays Lord Luxon's mind forever teems with plans and stratagems. He is not the man he was."

Gideon fell silent and would not speak for some time. Peter wished the driver would stop snoring.

"And what about the Tar Man?" asked Peter when he dared. "Why on earth did Lord Luxon employ a thug like him?"

"Lord Luxon took to gambling. He spent his time in the company of wastrels and scoundrels who cared nothing for him but who lived off his generosity. He became a member of White's Club in St. James's. Within a year he had built up a mountain of gambling debts. As I kept the accounts, I soon realized that he was losing a king's ransom every night. Finally I had to tell him that he was only weeks away from ruin, but he did not seem to care. 'Don't lecture me like an old woman, Seymour,' he told me, 'but fetch me a short sharp blade. I fancy I have a plan.'"

Gideon stopped and sighed heavily.

"What was the plan?"

"To my eternal shame, Master Peter, I became a cutpurse for him. I did not know how to refuse him—then. He would invite his fair-weather friends down to Tempest House for days at a time. They would drink too much and gamble all night, waging bets of hundreds, even thousands, of guineas on the most foolish things—racing snails and dropping feathers from ladders and suchlike. It turned my stomach to see how Lord Luxon, whom I had admired so much, was living up to his father's prediction. I believed he had it in him to be a fine and honorable gentleman. At the end of each night I would be sent for, and if any of his guests had won too much, I would be sent after them to bring back their winnings to Lord Luxon."

"You stole the money back!" exclaimed Peter.

"I did, Master Peter. I was Lord Luxon's cutpurse. For nearly a year I did as he bid. I never came even close to being caught. My victims would scarcely feel the breath of air as I brushed past them; only later would they reach down and find their purses cut. I have stolen diamonds from a countess's neck and pulled gold watches from the pockets of sleeping gentlemen too drunk to stir—and no doubt I shall burn in hell for it."

Peter did not know what to say. No wonder Parson Ledbury did not trust him if he had known Gideon to be a thief. Conflicting emotions coursed through Peter and he struggled against a feeling of disappointment and disbelief. Gideon the Cutpurse—this did not tally with how Peter had come to think of him. Gideon the Brave, Gideon the Strong, Gideon the Dependable, yes—Gideon the Cutpurse, never.

"But Lord Luxon made you do it, didn't he?" exclaimed Peter. "It wasn't your fault!"

"He commanded me to do it, and yet it was in my power to refuse him. I was weak and did what I was bid."

"But he might have done something bad to you if you'd refused," Peter rejoined.

"Yes, but who is to know if I might have saved my master had I stood firm. He told me that I was a thief when he saved my life, and now, by becoming a thief once more, I could save his."

"How could you say no to that?" said Peter.

"Indeed, that is what I told myself. But there is not a day

that goes by when I do not regret what I did. On the eve of my twenty-first birthday I told Lord Luxon that my conscience would not allow me to steal for him any longer. I thought he would turn me out of Tempest House but for the second time he surprised me with his compassion, for he agreed to my resuming my former duties. The space that I left was filled shortly afterward by the Tar Man, who inspired fear in everyone he encountered. The Tar Man brought with him two qualities which hastened, I believe, my master's fall. The first was his desire to take vengeance on his fellow man for the misfortunes life had heaped upon him—and you know his sorry history, for I have told you. The second was the Tar Man's knowledge of London's vast army of villains, whose influence stretches over the city and beyond: pickpockets and footpads, highwaymen and plumpers, cutpurses and assassins."

"You don't mean you actually worked with the Tar Man?"

"Our paths rarely crossed but, yes, we had the same employer for over two years—until Mrs. Byng's brother, Sir Richard Picard, wrote to his sister on my behalf asking if she could offer me employment at Baslow Hall. Sir Richard bought several horses from Lord Luxon and, as I made all the arrangements, he got to know me well. Lord Luxon would not accept my resignation, but I left, to his great anger, some three weeks since."

"Well, I can see why you don't want Joshua to work for him. But . . . but . . . you're not still a cutpurse, are you?" asked Peter, feeling the need to be clear on the point.

Gideon looked so saddened by his question that Peter wished

he could have crawled into a hole for asking it. Nevertheless Gideon replied.

"No! . . . No. I am not," he said, and cracked his whip over the horses' heads and looked straight ahead without speaking again.

The carriage rumbled on through mile after mile of farming country. Rain had not fallen in this part of Staffordshire, and the roads and fields were dusty and parched. Sometimes they passed laborers in cotton smocks, toiling in the heat, their faces blackened by the sun. In one field Peter saw a great flock of rooks, easily a hundred or more, all gathered together. The large black birds were grazing on what was left after a pea crop had been harvested. An empty wagon had been left abandoned in the middle of the field and a lone rook perched on its end. The rook opened its white beak and made a raucous *Caw! Caw!* sound and bobbed its head to one side toward the carriage, occasionally flapping its wings. The sun sparkled in its black eyes and Peter fancied it was talking about them. The other rooks were silent and paused from rooting about in the earth to stare up at the lone bird. They appeared for all the world as if they were listening to a speech.

"Look," said Gideon to Peter, "a parliament of rooks."

The driver, who had been slowly coming round for the last half mile, was suddenly wide awake. "Mr. Seymour, sir!" he cried. "Listen! It is the front axle if I'm not mistaken."

Above the *Caw! Caw!* of the rook an ominous creaking and splintering of wood was audible. Gideon and the driver looked at each other in alarm.

"It's going to go, sir! You mark my words."

A moment later, as one of the wheels juddered over a rock in the road, the axle broke in two with a terrible *CRACK!* The carriage lurched heavily and Gideon reined in the horses, who shied and kicked and whinnied in fright. Someone flung open the carriage doors, and screams and shouts came from within. Startled by the noise, the rooks flew into the air in a dense black mass, circled the carriage three times, and alighted noisily in a giant oak tree to one side of the road. A dreadful *Caw! Caw! Caw! Caw!* from a hundred beaks resounded over the fields and seemed to make the very air vibrate. Inside the carriage little Jack covered his ears with his hands and buried his face in Hannah's skirt.

An hour later the party listened disconsolately to the driver's judgement that after two failed attempts to brace the axle, there was no way on earth the carriage would be in a fit state to get them to Birmingham.

"I am hungry, Hannah," said Jack.

"And so are we all," lisped Sidney. "And thirsty."

"I have some good red apples, Master Sidney, crisp and juicy. Here, there are enough for everyone."

Hannah handed them out and Peter and Kate tried very hard not to exchange glances as Sidney tried to bite into his without the benefit of front teeth. Hannah tactfully offered to cut it into segments for him.

"By heaven, Lady Luck is against us!" exclaimed the parson. "Still, we passed a village not more than two miles back, where we can hire a wagon from one of the farmers. What say you, Mr. Seymour?"

"The village was Shenstone, Parson Ledbury. A very small

hamlet indeed. If we push on a little farther, I believe we will reach Aldridge, where we are more likely to be able to procure a carriage of the size we need. I fear that we must all walk there for we dare not risk dividing the party."

"Mr. Seymour," said Hannah, "I do not like the look of Master Jack—see how his eyes are turned glassy. I fancy he has one of his fevers coming on. And, pardon me for saying so, but surely Master Sidney and Martin would be ill-advised to go for long walks over rough country—"

"Come, Mr. Seymour," interrupted the parson, "take that anxious look off your face. It is broad daylight and we are in open country. Surely you cannot doubt that Martin, Sidney, and I are capable of defending the women and children for half an hour! Go! And take Master Schock with you!"

Gideon did not look convinced. "I do not like this place," he replied. "It is true that we are in open country and that makes it difficult to surprise us, and yet this works against us too. We stand out against this landscape. We could not have chosen a more exposed spot if we had planned it."

"Pish pash, Mr. Seymour," exclaimed the parson. "We have learned our lesson. And besides, if we all go to Aldridge with you, who is going to guard our valuables?"

Gideon sighed and walked toward Midnight. "Come, Peter," he said. "The sooner we start, the sooner we will return."

Kate shot Peter a withering look and whispered sarcastically, "Well, don't mind me, will you? I can always have a nice chat with Sidney."

Peter shrugged apologetically. "What can I do? It's not my fault you're a girl and have to wear long skirts."

"Don't say another word!" said Kate under her breath.

Then she sighed and gave a weak smile in the direction of Sidney, who was giving her coy, furtive glances and seemed very pleased at the prospect of having Kate all to himself again.

Midnight galloped toward Aldridge. Holding on to Gideon's shirt to keep himself steady, Peter turned around to look back at the companions they were leaving behind. Hannah, Jack, Sidney, and Kate had set off for a stroll over the fields. The driver was seeing to the horses and the parson was sitting against the oak tree, his hands clasped over his belly and his hat over his face. Above him the branches were laden with rooks. Every so often one of them would fly up and settle down again on a different branch. Because the farmland that stretched for miles around was flat, the tall oak tree was a prominent landmark. The broken carriage, piled up with luggage at the foot of the trees, was clearly visible from a great distance. The party seemed horribly exposed. *If the footpads are nearby,* thought Peter, *they will be a sitting target.* And he could tell by the speed at which they were galloping that the same thought had occurred to Gideon.

"We shall not ride to Aldridge," said Gideon. "We shall stop at the first farm and pay them to fetch a carriage for us. We need to get back as quickly as ever we can. It is likely that someone cut through the axle before we set off. The parson has a pistol, but I fear he is not a fighting man, and the driver has not recovered his strength. We need to act quickly and keep a steady nerve."

THIRTEEN

Pandora's Box

*In which Dr. Pirretti shows her true colors
and Gideon tells the story of his namesake*

Sergeant Chadwick watched the four figures striding across the playing fields. He nibbled on a bar of chocolate and took a pair of binoculars from his coat pocket. He hesitated before telephoning Detective Inspector Wheeler at this time in the morning but decided that his boss would be angrier still if he did not phone.

There was a spring in Dr. Dyer's step as he guided the two NASA scientists and Tim Williamson over the sodden grass toward

Kate's school. "I hope this is early enough not to draw attention to ourselves," said Dr. Dyer as he looked around at the deserted hockey pitches.

When they reached the towering rear wall of the school, he pointed to some worn stone steps leading to a coal cellar. Someone had stretched some wire across the steps in a halfhearted attempt to keep the girls out. Dr. Dyer stepped over it and motioned for the others to follow him into a dank little alcove.

"Megan—who has been Kate's best friend since nursery school—tells me that this is their special place. They creep down here at break time to be by themselves and to get out of the wind. Yesterday Megan was missing Kate so much she came here for a while to think about her friend—which is lucky for us because that is when she noticed *this*. Look. Come closer."

They all crouched down around Dr. Dyer, who took out a torch from his coat pocket and directed the beam close to an emerald green fern that had taken root in the wall. The mellow red bricks were covered in a tracery of carved names and initials. At the center of the beam of light was an ancient-looking piece of graffiti—still perfectly legible because it had been so deeply etched into the soft brick:

Kate Dyer wants to come home!
July 21st 1763

Underneath was a circle with four smaller circles grouped above it. "It's Kate's trademark signature—Molly's paw print," explained Dr. Dyer. "My clever Kate has left us a message. I don't think I need any more proof that your hunch, Dr. Pirretti, about the link between time and gravity, was justified."

There was a very long pause while the scientists took in the earth-shattering significance of Kate's simple message.

"Whoa!" breathed Dr. Jacob. "This is kind of . . . momentous. I never thought to witness this in my lifetime."

Tim Williamson stared, unblinking, at Kate's message. "She's gone back in time!" he exclaimed. "Somehow I've managed to make the first time machine! This dawn meeting at Bakewell will go down in history. People will write about this moment."

"Only if anyone gets to hear about it," said Dr. Pirretti under her breath.

Suddenly, as Tim realized that he had played a part in without a doubt the most important scientific discovery of this century—no, of this new *millennium*—he started dancing and punching his fists in the air. Dr. Pirretti, on the other hand, looked grim. She opened her mouth to say something but then pursed her lips together.

"Believe me, Andrew," Tim Williamson said to Dr. Dyer, "I'll work night and day to rebuild the antigravity machine to the nth specification. We'll reproduce the precise conditions. If we can do it once, we can do it twice—we'll get the children back."

Dr. Dyer had tears in his eyes. "We're going to bring them home!"

Dr. Pirretti clearly could contain herself no longer. "Get real, Tim! You didn't 'do it once.' It was a freak accident. We have no way of knowing for sure how to reproduce the same conditions. Meanwhile we have two defenseless children stranded in the eighteenth century."

"Don't underestimate Kate," replied her father. "She's intelligent and resourceful—"

"You know," interrupted Dr. Jacob, who had been so deep in thought he had not been following his colleagues' conversation, "after concentrating so much of our efforts on the relationship between gravity and dark matter, it really does bring up the question: Is there a link between dark energy and time? It's going to be so fascinating working on this—"

"Listen to yourselves!" Dr. Pirretti cried. "You're already seeing your names in the history books, congratulating yourselves on being part of this astounding new scientific development! Can't you see what this really means? This is a disaster! This is a tragedy for mankind! This is a million times worse even than the invention of the atom bomb! Don't you understand that we are playing the part of Pandora opening her box and releasing undreamed-of horrors into our universe. Look what terrible things we do to each other every second of every day all over the world. Before today the one thing that was totally safe was the past. Do you *want* to live in a world where the past will always be open to infinite future interference? If we don't do the right thing *now*, most of humanity, quite rightly, will curse us forever!"

"What are you saying?" asked Dr. Dyer, his fists clenched. "Do you mean that we should not try to go back and get them?"

Dr. Pirretti's eyes met those of Kate's father and softened. "No, Andrew. I don't—necessarily—mean that. We have a duty to Kate and Peter. I'm sorry to be brutal—I have a daughter too—but ask yourself this question: Would you put the safety of your children above the right of each and every individual on this planet to a secure history? What I mean is, somehow we have got to find a way to *undo* what has happened and leave history none the wiser."

Dr. Dyer covered his face with his hands. "Oh God! Why did this have to happen to Kate?" The other two men looked stunned at the ferocity of Dr. Pirretti's outburst. Dr. Williamson shuffled from one foot to the other uncomfortably. Dr. Jacob cleared his throat and said, "I had not realized how strongly you felt about this, Anita."

"Well, you do now. Until we've all thought this through and the consequences of going public, no one must find out about what we have seen today. No one. Not the police, not NASA, not even Peter Schock's parents. Is that agreed, gentlemen?"

They all nodded, although there was some hesitation on Dr. Jacob's part. Then Dr. Dyer said, "But, of course, Megan knows. And my wife—I couldn't not tell her mother."

"No." Dr. Pirretti sighed deeply and took out a penknife from her handbag and began scraping away at Kate's message until it was a pile of reddish dust at the foot of the sooty wall.

They rode bareback. Peter instinctively adjusted his position with every change in Midnight's speed or direction. At first he had found himself clinging rigidly to Gideon's back; now, after only a little tuition, he sat upright and easy, only grabbing hold of Gideon in case of real need. He watched the parched sandy fields fleeing before them and felt the impact of Midnight's hooves as they pounded the earth. Peter had never before experienced such freedom. He'd seen a picture of his father on horseback in his grandparents' photo album. If it had been okay for his dad to do it, why did his father always say that Peter might end up breaking his neck if he tried to ride? He wished his mum and dad could see him now.

"You've lost your fear, Master Peter," commented Gideon. "I fancy you might make a horseman yet. Hold on to me. Let us see if Midnight is as strong as I think he is!"

Gideon dug his heels into Midnight's sides, and the stallion erupted into a high-speed gallop despite his double load. The sudden acceleration took Peter's breath away. He held on tight to Gideon but then whooped with the thrill of it.

"So there is something that pleases you about my time," shouted Gideon over his shoulder. And it was true, thought Peter. A few hours earlier he would have given anything to be back in suburban London. Now, suddenly, he was not so sure.

After a couple of miles they spotted a boy balanced precariously on the back of a black-and-white carthorse. He was reaching up into the branches of a spreading cherry tree, picking off the last of the overripe black fruit that had been spared by the birds. The horse flicked its mud-spattered tail at some wasps that hovered drunkenly over rotting cherries at the foot of the tree.

"I don't think we need announce ourselves," said Gideon with a mischievous look in his blue eyes. He slipped off Midnight and glided noiselessly toward the boy almost as if in slow motion. The horse noticed him but, unconcerned, continued to tear up the sweet, yellowing grass. Peter watched in awe and could not help thinking about Gideon's previous profession. *I can see why he made such a good cutpurse,* he said to himself. *No wonder he never got caught—he moves like a cat.*

The boy was straining to get to a couple of luscious black cherries that were just out of arm's reach.

"Good evening, young master," said Gideon very loudly. "'Tis true that forbidden fruit always tastes the sweetest."

The boy nearly shot out of his skin, and lost his footing. Gideon caught him in midair and, laughing, set him down gently on the grass.

The boy was perhaps seven or eight, and his grubby face was stained with cherry juice. He attempted to run away, but Gideon reached out and caught hold of his shirt. The boy was none too pleased with Gideon and he kicked him angrily about the shins.

"Are all the lads hereabouts made of such stout stuff?" asked Gideon half-amused, half-wincing as he held the boy at arm's length. The boy kicked him again.

"That's enough, lad! I am flesh and blood! How would you like to earn yourself a shilling?"

The boy stopped kicking him and eyed Gideon suspiciously. "What must I do for it, sir?"

"We are in urgent need of a likely lad such as yourself to fetch help. Our carriage is broken, the axle snapped clean through."

Gideon described the giant oak and asked if the boy knew it, which he did, saying that it was a landmark thereabouts. Gideon reached deep into his jacket pocket and gave him a sixpence. The boy set off at once on his lumbering carthorse in the direction of Aldridge, fingering his treasure as he went.

"Don't dally, lad," Gideon called after him. "There's another sixpence waiting for you."

They watched the boy disappear out of sight. The sky was already growing pink and the sun sinking low on the horizon. Swallows called to each other, so high in the sky that they were barely visible as they swooped and soared through the clear, dry air in search of midges. Gideon squinted up at them, his arm shading his eyes.

"We need not fear rain tonight at least," commented Gideon.

"How many sixpences are there in a pound?" asked Peter, who was wondering how much the boy could buy with his earnings.

"Forty. Twelve pennies in a shilling, twenty shillings to the pound."

"Money's a lot easier to work out in my time. What can you buy for a sixpence, then?"

Gideon thought about it for a moment. "Well, you can dine handsomely for sixpence. Or have the barber cut your hair. And sixpence will buy a quantity of wine sufficient to put even Parson Ledbury under the table."

They remounted Midnight and began the journey back. Before long the great oak tree came into view in the distance. Above it hovered a curious black cloud, which was moving swiftly in their direction. It was the rooks. Soon all they could hear was their raucous cries. *Caw! Caw! Caw!* The great black birds passed right over their heads in a dense flock, and a feeling close to dismay came over Peter. What were they flying away from? Gideon pulled sharply on the reins and dismounted. Peter followed suit. The giant oak tree and the broken carriage beneath, silhouetted against the empty fields, were scarcely visible. Gideon reached into the inside pocket of his jacket and pulled out a small brass spyglass, which he put to his eye. He screwed up his face in an attempt to focus on the broken carriage.

"I cannot tell for certain what I see," exclaimed Gideon, heaving an exasperated sigh.

"Can I have a look?" asked Peter. Gideon handed over the spyglass to Peter, who strained to keep his hand steady, supporting it with his other arm.

"My hand keeps wobbling. I keep missing the cart."

Peter trained his gaze toward the oak tree until something caught his eye. Then he let out a gasp.

"What is it that you see?" Gideon shouted, seizing hold of the spyglass again and directing it toward their companions.

"How many of them are there?" asked Peter after a moment.

Gideon's lips moved as he counted silently. "Five. And a boy," said Gideon. "I believe they are tying the parson to the tree, but I cannot be certain from this distance. I can't see the others."

"You don't think they'll hurt them? I mean, they wouldn't touch Kate and Hannah and Jack, would they? They'll just take the diamond necklace and the parson's gold and go, right? It's only money that they're after?"

Gideon would not answer but stood staring at the distant oak tree. A wisp of wood smoke curled up from behind the carriage.

Then he took hold of Midnight's reins and, patting him on the neck, led him quietly to a thicket of young birches. Between the thicket and the broken carriage was open land without a scrap of shelter. Peter's mouth became dry with fear.

Gideon reappeared next to Peter. "They are armed and we are not," he said. "Save for my knife. But there are too many of them to risk an attack. I do not doubt that the Tar Man or Ned Porter—or both—pushed these footpads to strike here and now, a good league from the nearest aid. When they find that we are missing, they will surely question my whereabouts and yours. I pray with all my heart that our companions have had the good sense to tell them we have ridden on ahead, for at least then we might have the advantage of surprise."

Gideon suddenly picked up a large rock and flung it with all his force into the bushes behind him. "Have I learned nothing these past five years! I knew he would send them! I knew it! He is like a cat before the kill: He cannot deny himself the pleasure of toying with his victims. He is not content to hunt me down. He must attack and rob those who help me! Did I ever have a more foolish and reckless notion? To leave the party thus exposed, for all the world to see . . . like lambs to the slaughter! The Tar Man will allow the footpads to keep their loot for *I* am the prize his master bids him seek. I promised to help you and Mistress Kate, but I have done naught but drag you further into danger!"

Gideon picked up another stone and smashed it so hard into the trunk of a tree that it cut deep into its bark. "Damn his eyes!" he shouted, and strode away, unable to contain his rage and frustration.

Peter sank to the ground and put his forehead on his knees. He was rattled by Gideon's outburst; his face was pale and his hands clammy. If Gideon did not know what to do, then he certainly did not. He closed his eyes. After a quarter of an hour he heard Gideon's footsteps and felt a hand on his shoulder.

"Do not be afraid—it is what they count on. All is far from lost. The footpads have made a fire. I'll warrant they are making camp for the night. We shall wait for cover of darkness and then we shall see what we can do."

Peter took the spyglass and peered at the distant oak tree. The carriage hid the footpads from view, and apart from the occasional flicker of movement there was no indication of what was happening to their friends—so close and yet so out of reach—on the other side of this vast, empty field. Gideon tethered Midnight to the trunk of a tree, and then tried to persuade Peter to sit and rest while he had the chance, for they would soon need to have all their wits about them. So, for a while, they sat side by side under the shelter of the whispering birches, Gideon chewing on a piece of long grass and Peter obsessively looking through the spyglass at the plume of white smoke that rose up into the sky from behind the carriage. They did not speak as they watched the darkness slowly dissolve the ribbons of scarlet and gold that stretched across the horizon.

"Come," said Gideon, breaking the silence at last. "We passed some reeds a way back. There must be a spring nearby. Let us find Midnight some water."

Gideon untied the horse and they walked, retracing their steps to the reed bed. It was becoming cooler now. Peter rested his hand on Midnight's neck; occasionally he stooped down to pick him handfuls of dandelions and choice green grass, and as the horse chewed his offerings, Peter could feel his hot breath on his outstretched palm. There was something about the presence of the animal—his warmth, perhaps, and the familiar smell of horseflesh—that made Peter feel a little less afraid.

The ground grew marshy as they approached the reeds and they soon found a small bubbling spring that fed into a pond. They watched Midnight drink eagerly, standing knee high in the muddy water. The light was fading fast but Gideon took care to scan the landscape through his spyglass in case they had been spotted by unseen eyes. "It belonged to my father," said Gideon, indicating the spyglass. "He gave it to my eldest brother, and when he died it came to me."

"Was that when most of your family caught the scarlet fever?"

"No, not then. I have no recollection of my eldest brother. He died some years before we moved to Abinger. My mother never liked to talk of it. I believe it was some kind of accident. I do know that my mother never recovered from the shock of it. He was her firstborn—it must have been a grievous loss to bear."

Gideon pulled out an object a little larger than the size of his hand from his jacket. Its polished surface gleamed.

"What is it?" Peter asked.

"Can you not guess? It was carved by my father's own hands from the horn of a ram when I was but an infant. It was on account of my namesake. Listen."

Gideon put the object to his lips and blew very gently—a series of clear, soft notes came from the horn.

"Who is your namesake?" asked Peter.

"Do you not know your Bible? Have you not heard of Gideon and the Midianites?"

Peter admitted that he had not.

"It was Gideon who led the Israelites against the Midianites—"

Gideon came to a halt abruptly in midsentence. "I believe my father's horn has provided us with a solution to our dilemma! Yes, by heaven! Now I see what we must do!"

He smiled triumphantly at Peter, who was puzzled but glad that Gideon seemed to have a plan of some kind.

"If I tell you the story of Gideon, you will understand," Gideon said. "The Israelites were far outnumbered by the Midianites, who were defending their camp with a large army. Yet God spoke to Gideon and told him to pick only a small number of his best fighters for the attack. Do you know how God told him to make his choice?"

Peter shook his head.

"Drink some water, Master Peter."

"What, now?"

"Yes."

"All right . . ." Peter lay on his stomach at the side of the pond and hoped the murky water was safe to drink. He plunged his head into the water.

"No!" exclaimed Gideon. "My namesake would not have chosen you. This is how a soldier drinks."

He bent his knees and, keeping his back straight, lowered himself to the ground while he cupped his right hand, which he carefully dipped into the water. Then he stood up and lapped up the water from his hand, looking around him all the time for any signs of danger.

"That is how Gideon chose his men: He bade them drink. Those who drank without regard to possible danger were left behind. The few who remained alert and watchful while drinking from their hands, he chose for the attack.

"God told Gideon to wait until the middle of the night before bidding his men encircle the camp. This Gideon did, and then, on his order, the Israelites, each of whom carried a trumpet and a flaming torch inside a jar, made a terrible noise, blowing their trumpets and smashing their jars and shouting. The Midianites were so maddened and confused, they began to kill one another.

"Now do you understand what I mean us to do?"

Peter nodded and smiled.

FOURTEEN

Gideon's Strategem

*In which the parson preaches a curious sermon
and the party shows their bottom*

It should have been a peaceful scene. The swallows swooped over
a landscape turned pink and gold by the setting sun, crickets
chirped in the long dry grass, and a warm breeze agitated the
leaves of the great oak. . . . But peaceful it was not. The wrecked
carriage sat like a giant carcass in the road, surrounded by scattered trunks, their contents strewn all about. Parson Ledbury was
bound to the tree, a double length of rope wrapped around his
broad girth. The driver and Sidney were tied to two wheels of

the carriage. Kate, Hannah, and Jack sat huddled together on one side of the tree whilst opposite them Ned Porter and the foul thugs who held them at their mercy sat around a wood fire. Whenever the breeze changed direction, they were choked by smoke. Jack started to cough.

"Hush, Master Jack. If we keep quiet and brave all will be well," whispered Hannah. "Put your face in my lap so you cannot see the ugly, wicked brutes, and I will sing you a song."

Hannah tried to sing but her voice trembled so much she soon gave up and hummed quietly instead. She slowly stroked Jack's back, and gradually, soothed by Hannah's touch and with his head hidden in the folds of her skirt, Jack fell fast asleep. Hannah leaned over toward Kate and spoke into her ear.

"I think he is not quite well. He has a slight fever. I do not like him being in this chill evening air—"

"Who said you could speak!" barked the leader of the foot-pads, who was striding toward them. "One more word and you'll feel the back of my hand."

"I was only saying that the child—oww!"

Hannah cried out in pain as a handful of acorns smacked into her face from the other side of the fire.

"Leave her alone, you great bully!" shrieked Kate.

The other two footpads looked on and laughed. Now the leader began advancing angrily toward Kate. She clenched her fists and for a split second a surge of adrenalin made her believe that if he so much as touched her it would be the footpad who would come off worse. But the footpad grabbed hold of both Kate's arms as if they were two twigs and bent them behind her back until she cried out in pain. She struggled and screamed, but he may as well have been holding a kitten for all the effect her kicks and wriggling had.

"And the same goes for you, you meddlesome baggage," he growled. "If you can't behave, you'll get tied up like the rest!"

He held her against him and forced her to walk toward the others. She was dimly conscious of the parson shouting something to her and Sidney straining against the ropes that tied him to one wheel of the carriage, but it was none other than Ned Porter who came to her aid.

"Let her go," he said sweetly, his green eyes glinting in the light of the fire. "A gentleman of the road would not behave in such a low fashion, and while you're with me I'd prefer it if you didn't mistreat the ladies."

Ned gave a wry smile in response to the footpad's defiant stare and waited patiently, arms folded and buckled foot slowly tapping. Unable to move, Kate became suddenly aware of the rank heat of the footpad's broad chest. Through the fine cotton of her dress she could feel the thumping of his heart. Nausea and fear all but overwhelmed her. The footpad was like a pit bull terrier straining on its leash, and she could sense his intense dislike of Ned Porter. His grip tightened for a moment and then he shoved her roughly back toward Hannah and Jack. Ned acknowledged Kate with a slight nod of the head. Hannah grasped hold of her hand and squeezed it. Kate felt a trickle of cold sweat drip down her back, and closed her eyes.

• • •

The light was now beginning to fade and the fire glowed more brightly under the tree's canopy. Bound tightly to a carriage wheel, the driver looked blankly in front of him—either resigned to his fate or feeling too ill to care—but Sidney's face alternated between terror and fury. John, Ned's accomplice, took delight in putting his face right up against Sidney's and clicking his front teeth. He rubbed his hand, which still bore the traces of Sidney's lately lamented incisors.

"I hope I was tasty, for I was the last dish those teeth will ever bite into!" he said to Sidney, laughing heartily at his own wit.

Sidney's eyes narrowed and he struggled against his bonds.

"Sticks and stones, dear boy!" called out the parson.

It seemed to Kate that every second was a minute and that every minute was an hour. Kate wondered how long your heart could thump this frantically in your chest without it bursting. *Where have Peter and Gideon got to?* she asked herself constantly. *Why haven't they come?*

Deep breaths, Kate, deep breaths. It was her father's voice that suddenly came into her head. She made herself breathe slowly, in and out, in and out, and felt a tiny fraction calmer. It was what her father had said to her when she had telephoned home in the middle of the night and begged him to come and get her. She'd been in the last year of junior school, and her class was spending a week in an activity center in the High Peak. He refused, saying that he would be doing her no favors if he did. Some kids from a rival school had made life so miserable for Kate in particular (her hair had always drawn attention) that on the second night she escaped and walked through isolated roads in the pitch dark to find a phone. Don't act like a victim, he had advised. If you feel like crying, wait until they can't see you. There's a solution to every problem, he told her. Keep a clear head and work it out. You're a smart girl, Kate. Trust yourself, because you know that you can. . . . And so, with moths fluttering around the yellow light of the telephone box, father and daughter had talked through her dilemma. Half an hour later Kate broke back into the center with no one any the wiser.

The solution to that particular problem could hardly be replicated here, she thought, but the memory of it brought the shadow of a smile to Kate's face. Her father had made the two-hour round trip before breakfast in order to smuggle a special package past reception. Later that morning, miles from the nearest corner shop, big kids were queuing up to thump anyone who gave Kate Dyer trouble, in return for a share of the biggest stash of sweets any of them had ever seen.

Deep breaths, Kate told herself, *you're going to be okay.* There had to be some way out of this situation, and she was going to find it. She sat quietly and took everything in.

At first Kate had thought that the footpad who had grabbed hold of her was the Tar Man. He was a thickset bristly man with a dirty, gray ponytail. As time went on and she listened to their ill-humored banter, Kate gradually began to work out who was who. In fact, this was Joe Carrick. The Carrick gang was composed of the three Carrick brothers: Joseph, Stammering John, and Will. Joe Carrick seemed to be the leader. He was the youngest, but it was he, above all, whom Kate feared. When Joe looked in her direction, the hairs stood up on the back of her neck. He was aggressive, foulmouthed, and unpredictable: calm and reasonable one moment and ranting and raving over nothing the next. He was the one to keep an eye on. There was also a silent, skulking boy whose name she had not yet managed to catch.

From what she could gather it was the Tar Man who had sent Ned Porter and the footpads to find Gideon Seymour and bring him back to London. *But why,* she asked herself, *hadn't the Tar Man come in person to get Gideon? What hold did he have over these vicious villains who willingly carried out his orders?*

Ned Porter appeared none the worse for wear after his short spell in the magistrate's cellar and strutted about in a sky blue jacket with matching silk waistcoat, doubtless acquired from one of the good residents of Lichfield. Ned made it plain that he considered himself a cut above these loutish unshaved footpads. As for the footpads, they, in turn, let him know that they were only here under sufferance because you could not say no to the Tar Man. They made it equally clear that if they did not get their fair share of the pickings, it would be Ned Porter who would suffer the consequences.

"If it is Mr. Seymour that you seek," Parson Ledbury announced, "there is no point dallying here. I do not trust him and have told him so to his face. We have had a falling-out, and he and Master Schock have ridden on to London alone."

The parson is lying to protect Gideon! thought Kate. *Does that mean he's changed his mind about him?* And then it occurred to her that it could be just to give Gideon and Peter the advantage of surprise when they came back.

When they heard that Gideon had left for London, the foot-pads were keen to take the loot and the prancers (as they called the horses) and head off back to London themselves. After all, Will commented, it had been over a month since they had seen the inside of the Rose Tavern in Drury Lane. Ned Porter, however, remained unconvinced by the parson's explanation for Gideon's absence.

"Even a man of the cloth is capable of a little deception when it suits him. So you will forgive me, Parson, if we tarry a while in case Mr. Seymour and young Master Schock have a change of heart. For I can scarce believe that they would leave their lovely companion behind—even in such distinguished company."

Here he made a show of bowing to Kate, sliding one leg forward and dropping his gaze to the ground while he fluttered a handkerchief in his right hand. Joe Carrick raised his eyes to heaven in disgust at such affectation.

So the disgruntled footpads threw themselves back on the ground and were obliged to wait while Ned engaged the parson in conversation prior to relieving him of his valuables. Kate wondered how long it would be before the Carrick gang's patience broke. Soon everyone's stomach started to rumble, and since the footpads had not eaten since the previous evening, Stammering John, who was their best shot, was sent off with his catapult to find something tasty for their supper. The boy, who looked older than Peter and Kate but was a good three inches shorter and was all skin and bone, went with him. He had large dark eyes in a mobile face whose expression was one of constant anxiety. His shoulders were hunched up toward his ears as though anticipating the next blow.

It was Stammering John's catapult that put the rooks to flight. Believing them to be birds of ill omen, he had taken a potshot at them as they roosted in the great oak tree. When he and the boy returned with four plump young rabbits, they found that Ned Porter was still lecturing Parson Ledbury. Kate remembered the parson's remark about Ned aping his betters at the magistrate's house in Lichfield, and it suddenly became clear to her how much the parson's insult had got under his skin. The parson refused to respond in any way, a tactic which was, to his great satisfaction, driving Ned wild.

"You are wrong, indeed, to dismiss me as if I were some common thief. If misfortune had not overtaken my family, I should have gone into the professions. I could have been a doctor, or a lawyer, or indeed a parson. . . ."

Joe Carrick gave a loud burp. His two brothers roared with laughter.

"Pardon me, your lordship," he said. "I did not mean to offend your fine sensibilities."

"Give us a s-s-sermon, then, Ned," called out Stammering John.

Ned flew around with such ferocity that even Joe Carrick was taken aback. He grabbed hold of John by the neck and cocked his pistol. The other brothers immediately stood up, but Ned was in no mood to back down. Beefy Will Carrick, who was lame in one leg, stopped skinning the rabbits next to the fire and limped over, holding his bloodstained knife at the ready.

"Those that pitch themselves against Ned Porter only discover their mistake when it's too late." Ned's blazing eyes bore into

Stammering John until John dropped his stare. Only then did Ned let go of his collar. Joe motioned the others to sit down.

"Where's this diamond necklace, then, Ned?" asked Will, breaking a long silence and trying to change the subject. "Let's fork him. Look in his jacket."

"Look under his wig, more like," said John, Ned's sidekick, known to the rest as Stinking John to avoid confusion. "That's where he hid it the last time."

With that, Stinking John whisked off the parson's wig, revealing his bristly white scalp. There was no necklace.

"You are an educated man," said Ned to the parson, "and will have as little taste as I for the company I am currently obliged to keep. However, let me offer you some advice in your dealings with these fellows. It will avoid much unpleasantness if you tell us without more ado where you are concealing the necklace and your money. The Carrick gang are not known for their mild manners."

Kate looked at Joe Carrick, who was tapping his foot impatiently. *Oh, tell him! For goodness' sake tell him! They'll find it soon enough anyway!*

The parson did not speak and for a moment the only sound was Will Carrick's knife as he skinned and jointed the rabbits. There *is a man*, thought Kate, *who knows how to use a knife*. The parson's internal struggle was evident. It went against everything he held dear to give in to these villains, but it was plainly useless to resist. He glanced over toward Sidney as if by way of apology and then gave a heavy sigh.

"My gold is in a wooden casket with the brandy. Mrs. Byng's necklace you will find in my jacket."

Joe and Will untied the parson so they could get at his jacket. Joe pulled off the parson's jacket and Will pulled down his trousers for good measure. Hannah looked away out of respect, although not before noting with satisfaction that the washerwoman at Baslow Hall had done a fine job with the parson's undergarments. The footpads soon found the necklace, and their mood improved instantly. Joe and Stammering John searched through the chests and cases that were littered around the broken carriage and split open the crate of brandy. Joe took out the bag of gold coins and weighed it in his hand.

"A tidy sum," he said. "I reckon near on fifty guineas, give or take."

"Fifty-seven guineas," admitted the parson through gritted teeth.

"Look how she sparkles," said Will appreciatively, as he examined Mrs. Byng's diamond necklace. "Even after the fence has taken his share, we'll get a king's ransom for this one."

"It's not going to the fence," said Ned. "We've had our orders. The rhino we can share out between us. The necklace is going to the Thief-taker."

Will opened his mouth and shut it again as though he realized that there was no point arguing with Ned.

"The Thief-taker will make it worth our while," said the highwayman, reaching out his hand for the necklace.

Will reluctantly dropped it into Ned's hand, then limped over to Joe and said in a whisper everyone could hear, "We don't have to hand it over. You can tell him we never found it."

"Ay, that was n-n-never part of the b-bargain," said Stammering John.

"Use your head, lads," said Joe, staring at Ned. "Remember Four String. The Thief-taker gets to know everything in the end. One way or another."

Will grunted.

"And remember when Laurence Rose was tried at the Old Bailey," continued Joe, "it was the Thief-taker what paid the straw men to swear he was somewhere else at the time. And they don't come cheap. We might need him one day. That's what he would have us believe, eh, Ned?"

Ned did not reply. Kate looked over at him. He stood on the opposite side of the fire from the footpads, whistling softly as he nudged a large log farther into the flames with the toe of his boot. He seemed as relaxed as if he were on a picnic, but Kate noticed how his hand hovered over his pistol.

"Oi, lads, who wants some of the parson's bingo!" called out Stinking John as he walked over toward the fire carrying three bottles of brandy in each hand, dangling the stems between his fingers. He gave Ned a meaningful wink.

"Bring your cups, boys, this'll keep out the cold. Tom, you keep a lookout. Up the tree with you."

So he's called Tom, thought Kate. The boy scrabbled up the tree, getting his footing by using the rope that once more bound the parson. Tom wedged himself between the trunk and a low branch and stared out over the fields. Below him Ned, Stinking John, and the footpads sat around the fire and drank, mostly in silence, wiping their mouths with the backs of their hands and spitting into the fire. It was nearly nightfall, and the flames cast a yellowish glow on the villains' faces. Behind them their long shadows stretched into empty darkness.

"Did you ever see an uglier bunch of men in your whole life," whispered Hannah to Kate. "They're enough to turn milk sour. Though I don't include Ned in that."

"What's a thief-taker?" asked Kate.

"Don't you know that, Mistress Kate? Why, it is someone who recovers property that has been stolen, though mostly for the reward, and sometimes, if it is worth his while, he will hand over the villain too. Though 'tis said that more often than not the thief-takers are worse than the rogues they live off. The magistrates need them and the villains fear them, and the thief-taker plays one off against the other. The one they speak of must be mighty powerful to hold footpads like these in his thrall."

Will had constructed a make-do spit out of branches, and the smell of roasting rabbit was making the footpads dribble. Now that their attention had shifted for a while from their captives, Kate felt a little easier. The boy, Tom, however, seemed to have his eye on her. Every time she looked up, his gaze met hers before he looked away. Suddenly Kate had an idea. She edged backward deeper into the shadows and half-closed her eyes. She was going to try to blur. What else could she do? Whether she could relax enough in this predicament was a different matter. . . .

• • •

After a while Stinking John nudged Ned and pointed to Will.

"What ails thee?" Ned asked Will.

Will Carrick was weeping into his brandy. "It's on account of Four String George."

"What kind of name is that?" asked Ned. "Who is he?"

"Was," replied Will tearfully. "He was scragged at Tyburn, this April last. We called 'im Four String on account of the colored ribbons he wore at the bottom of his breeches. He was a bingo-boy all right. When he was lappy after a few glasses, he was the merriest man in England. Lord, I do miss him."

The footpad sniffed noisily, and streaks of clean skin appeared where he wiped away the tears. "Give us a wipe, Joe."

His brother threw him a handkerchief that might have been white once.

"The dead are dead, Will," said Joe. "It's the living you've got to worry about."

"He m-m-made a g-g-good show at Tyburn, though, did F-F-Four String," said Stammering John. "He n-n-never showed no fear. The crowd loved 'im. Once J-J-J-Jack Ketch had the noose round his n-n-neck, they pulled on him to g-g-give him an easy end. They honor their own, the Tyburn crowd."

Will cried all the more at the memory of it and soon he and Stammering John were sobbing on each other's shoulders.

"And now he'll be burning in hell and the rest of us will soon be joining him!" said Will between sobs.

"And we'll n-never see our m-m-mother again, who is in heaven, and she'll be waiting all eternity for her d-dear boys to join her," howled Stammering John.

Despite her fear Kate laughed silently in the dark and then forced herself once more to picture the kitchen at her farm in Derbyshire.

"I d-d-dreamed last night that we was d-done for and that all the folk we had ever hurt were c-c-crowding round and a-pushing against us, crushing the v-very breath out of us. P-P-Parson Ledbury, sir, would the Lord forgive men as w-w-wicked as us? Is there any hope for us?"

The parson looked down at them and paused a while before replying. He took a deep breath and, tied up though he was, endeavoured to stand taller.

"It is time," he boomed, resplendent in his underwear and bald head, "that you wretches make your peace with God before it is too late. Our Lord is all-forgiving but for him to forgive, you must repent! Come to me and repent your sins as little children!"

Joe Carrick stood up unsteadily.

"Hold your tongue, Parson. This is no time for Sunday sermons."

The parson's brandy, however, seemed to have released Joe's brothers' appetite for spiritual matters, and they insisted on untying Parson Ledbury so that he might speak to them at his ease.

"Have it your own way," snapped Joe, and he collapsed heavily back down to the ground.

The footpads did indeed sit at the parson's feet like attentive children (except for taking the occasional slug of brandy), and even Tom crept down from the tree to listen. It seemed that the more the parson called them the wickedest wretches in the whole of Christendom, the more they cried but the more they liked it—and no one noticed Kate's form blending into the shadows and finally disappearing into the night altogether.

As they edged closer to the giant oak tree, keeping the carriage between them and the footpads as much as possible, Peter had the sudden impression that they had come across some sort of traveling circus. He caught glimpses of a circle of upturned faces, illuminated by the fire and transfixed by the comic figure of the parson, wigless and half-dressed, who was making sweeping gestures toward heaven with his powerful arms. And then, on the other side of this little scene, he saw a whole troop of horses, tethered peaceably together for all the world as if awaiting their turn to trot around the ring. All the same, Peter was sure that if any member of this particular audience spotted them, they would be done for.

It was Gideon who first noticed Kate, and he slapped his hand over his mouth to stop himself crying out in fright. He watched as her form slowly settled, and he finally regained enough composure to clap his hand on top of Peter's head and twist it around until the boy's eyes fell on his friend.

"Kate!" shrieked Peter, nearly jumping out of his skin.

"Sshh!" hissed Gideon. "Be quiet, I pray you, we are within earshot."

Kate shook her head violently as though coming out of a dream.

"How did you get here?" said Peter in a loud whisper.

"I blurred, of course," Kate replied.

"That was well done indeed, Mistress Kate," Gideon said

softly. "You could not have bettered your timing—although I cannot deny that the sight of you in that terrible state turns my insides to water."

All of a sudden Kate started to thump Peter, banging her fists on his chest. Peter pushed back, bewildered, until Kate's arms dropped to her sides. Tears ran silently down her face.

"What have *I* done to you?" whispered Peter angrily. "Whatever's up, why are you taking it out on me?"

"She cannot help herself, Master Peter. Can you not see how she trembles?"

"Where were you?" Kate asked Peter. "I thought we were all going to die! I thought you'd gone. I thought you'd blurred back to the twenty-first century. Why did you have to go off with Gideon again? You didn't give me a second thought."

"How can you say that? That is so unfair," said Peter.

"Is it? Don't you know what it feels like to be left behind? Isn't that what you say your dad does to you? That's the trouble with being an only child, you don't think about anyone else's feelings."

"It's impossible to ignore your feelings, the amount you cry!"

"In my family letting your feelings out doesn't mean that you can't be brave or strong. I suppose you think that keeping them all bottled up and getting screwed up on the inside is better?"

Outraged, Peter opened his mouth to reply, but Gideon put his hand on Peter's shoulder and said sharply, "This is not the time for arguments. Our companions have need of us."

Some people might actually be pleased that someone is trying to rescue them, Peter thought furiously. *But not Kate!*

"Mistress Kate," Gideon continued. "Is anyone hurt? Do they have the necklace? Tell me everything that has happened."

When Kate had finished speaking, Gideon declared that they would have to make their move quickly before Kate's absence was noticed. They were all crouching, huddled together about twenty feet behind the carriage. The bonfire crackled and spit, and its orange glow spread out toward them over the rough grass.

"Wait here," Gideon said softly. "I intend to recover Mrs. Byng's necklace."

Peter and Kate both looked alarmed.

"But it's you that they want, Gideon!" whispered Kate.

"Then they shall have to catch me first," he replied.

Peter and Kate watched Gideon as he headed for the far side of the great oak. Their argument was not forgotten, but this was not the time to pursue it. Gideon appeared to glide over the moonlit meadow. He did not make a sound. The children crawled nearer to the carriage on their hands and knees so they could follow his progress. A smell of fresh damp grass rose up from the cold earth.

Peter rubbed dirt onto his face. "Camouflage!" he whispered.

"You've been watching too many films."

"I'll be lucky if I see another one ever again."

"Keep your voice down!" whispered Kate. "Anyway, there's not much point me blacking my face when I'm wearing a great big flouncy dress like this."

Peter and Kate crept forward a little farther. Parson Ledbury was telling the footpads about the prodigal son, and snatches of his story floated toward them. Will and Stammering John hung on his every word, reprimanding the son and sympathizing with the father.

"Ay, 'tis a child's fate to stray and a father's to forgive," said Will.

"I n-n-never had a f-f-father," said Stammering John.

"Even the lowest, the most wretched, the most undeserving . . . the foulest smelling fellow," commented the parson, pointing up to the stars, "need never feel he is without a Father up in heaven."

Joe Carrick sucked on a rabbit bone, feigning indifference, but listened nonetheless. By now Will was slumped on the ground, insensible to everything. Opposite them Ned and Stinking John looked on. Neither had drunk any brandy. Ned's gaze rarely left Joe, and his hand rested on his pistol.

Will Carrick groaned and appeared to roll over into the dark shadows. None of the footpads noticed, but Peter did. He nudged Kate and pointed.

"What's Gideon up to?" he hissed.

Kate shrugged her shoulders. After a few seconds Will, his face scarcely visible under his hat, reappeared and stood up. Peter held his breath. An owl hooted.

"Brrrrr," Will said, and shivered. He turned up the collar of his jacket. "The ground is damp," Will continued, mumbling. He limped in front of the parson, so drunk he could scarcely keep upright.

"Pardon me, Parson!" he said, slurring his words. "Call of nature."

Will then proceeded to trip up, landing on the ground in front of Ned. He leaned heavily against him as he tried to pick himself up. The bonfire illuminated the handsome face of the highwayman. Ned heaved him off bad-temperedly, and Will grunted as he vanished into the darkness to do his business.

Moments later Gideon reappeared out of the night as if by magic. He sat down next to Kate and shrugged off Will's jacket and hat.

"It wasn't Will! It was you!" exclaimed Peter.

Then Gideon held up Mrs. Byng's necklace and released it, letting the rope of diamonds trickle onto Kate's lap. Kate picked it up and dangled it from her fingers. It was heavy and still warm from being in Ned's pocket. The diamonds sparkled blue and white in the light of the moon.

"For safekeeping," he said to her.

"Wow!" she replied.

"'Tis a pity I could not have taken his pistol, too, but he held it in his hand."

Peter could just make out Gideon's expression as he stood with his back to the moon, and he could see that his friend was allowing himself a broad grin of satisfaction.

Gideon did not need to tell Kate the story of his namesake, as she already knew it. If it were possible, he explained, to convince Ned and the footpads that they were surrounded and outnumbered, then they stood at least a chance of frightening them off without too much of a fight. Gideon would ride in circles around the encampment, galloping first this way and then that, blowing his horn, while the children would shout and make as much noise to startle them with whatever they found to hand.

Gideon gave Kate his knife.

"Crawl under the carriage, Master Peter, and stay there until the signal. Mistress Kate, you must cut through Master Sidney's bonds and tell him that help is at hand."

The children nodded and Gideon disappeared once more. Kate's dress made crawling impossible.

"Grrr! I am so *sick* of being a girl in the eighteenth century!"

Peter frowned at her and put a finger to his lips. Frustrated, Kate scowled back at him. Then she tried to gather up the full folds of her skirt and lift them above ground level, but when she did that she couldn't see in front of her and she put her knee on a dry branch, which broke with a loud crack. Both children froze and peered through the spokes of one of the carriage wheels at Ned and the footpads lounging around the fire. The parson had stopped speaking and seemed to be gathering his thoughts. Joe Carrick turned his head around lazily, half-conscious of a noise he could not explain, but then a gust of wind buffeted the oak tree and the fire crackled and spit and he turned back unconcerned. However, things did not remain calm for long.

"Where is it?" shouted Ned so that every face turned to look at him.

"What are you yelling about now?" growled Joe.

"Who has it? It is you, Will Carrick, is it not? You filched it not a moment past!"

"Quick! Cut Sidney loose!" whispered Kate urgently to Peter. She thrust the knife at him. "I can't move in this stupid dress. Something's going to happen. I know it is. We'd better be ready."

Peter gave Kate the thumbs-up and scampered to the far side of the cart. "Don't move!" he breathed into Sidney's ear. "Gideon's on his way."

Sidney nodded his head a fraction to show he had understood and braced his arms so that they did not spring apart when Peter had finished cutting the rope.

Ned leaped over the fire to where Will was snoring gently and kicked him in the ribs. Will cried out with the pain and shock of it and sat up with a start. He had pulled his knife out and brandished it in Ned's face even before he had come to his senses.

"Get away from me, you puffed-up peacock, or as God is my witness I'll take your eye out," he said.

Ned did not flinch. "Hand it over!"

"Hand what over?" asked Will, eyeing Ned's pistol.

"This is the last time I do a job with the Carrick gang. I'd sooner throw in my lot with a herd of pigs."

A shot rang out and there were gasps and stifled screams all around. Ned clutched his chest and swayed back and forth for a long moment. Joe's pistol smoked. Stammering John stepped forward, uncurled Ned's fingers from his pistol, and gave him the gentlest of pushes with the tips of his fingers. The highwayman crashed backward into the grass. A large dark stain covered half of Ned's sky blue jacket. No one spoke. The only sound, apart from the crackling of the fire, was the slow rhythmic snore of little Jack's miraculously untroubled sleep.

Parson Ledbury knelt down to see to Ned, who was barely conscious.

"You are determined to enter the gates of hell, I see," he said to Joe.

Stammering John crossed himself. Joe gave the parson a murderous look. *Oh, please don't provoke him!* said Kate to herself, willing him to keep quiet. Luckily for the parson, something distracted him. Fearing he was to be next on Joe's list, Stinking John shot up and made a dash for the horses.

"I'm not a squeaker!" he shouted as he mounted one of the horses. "You're welcome to my share of the rhino. Don't shoot me, that's all. . . ."

Stammering John took aim with Ned's pistol and looked up at Joe for a decision.

"Save your powder," said Joe. "He won't cause us no trouble. He wouldn't dare. Stinking John always was lily-livered."

"Have you g-g-got the necklace, Will?" asked Stammering John.

"I don't know what you're talking about," he replied.

"I knew you had," laughed Joe. "There's no point denying it. You never could bear for anything to be taken off you. The way you forked him as if you was as drunk as a lord! Handsome!"

"Eh?"

Will was interrupted by Stammering John. "W-what was that?"

They all listened. Gideon's horn sounded in the distance— and then they could hear galloping that stopped abruptly only to start again a moment later. Then the horn sounded again, but this time it was nearer. Peter came to his senses, remembering what he was supposed to be doing, and sprinted out from under the carriage into the darkness. He kept on running, knowing he had to shout something, but couldn't think at first what it was Gideon had told him to say. Then it came to him. "Ahoy there!" he shouted. The phrase sounded a little on the nautical side, but that is what Gideon had said.

"Heave to, you slackers! My grandmother, God bless her soul, could walk faster than you landlubbers!" bellowed Gideon, sounding for all the world like a ship's bosun. "It's a fair old march to Lichfield and we have a dozen more shipmates to find before you can peel your boots off!"

Gideon's words rang out in the dark.

"By heaven, it's a press gang!" exclaimed Will under his breath. "There's a stroke of bad luck and no mistake."

"I d-d-don't want to serve in no navy," said Stammering John. "King George can keep his precious America—I don't want to d-d-die in some godforsaken land full of c-c-convicts and savages."

"No more do I," said Joe. "Sounds like there's a fair few of them. Fetch the prancers and be smart about it."

"Left, right, left, right, left, right . . ."

"Quickly, lads, they are almost upon us!"

Drunk and unsteady on their feet though they were, fear pushed the Carrick gang to career around the camp grabbing hold of their scattered possessions and the goods plundered from the carriage. Scarcely pausing to draw breath they shoved every-thing into saddle bags and threw them over the horses' backs.

Will could find neither his jacket nor his hat and took out his bad temper on Tom, whom he cursed roundly. In the confusion Will and Stammering John bumped heads so hard they both fell over backward, howling in pain.

"Shut your faces, you numbskulls," growled Joe, "if you don't want to blow the widd."

Peter joined in with Gideon, making his voice as deep and rumbling as he could: "Left, right, left, right, left, right, me hearties!"

Peter's efforts brought a smile to Kate's face underneath the carriage. She was attempting to restrain Sidney, who was struggling to get up to show he was not afraid. She clung on to his hands.

"It's not worth it, Sidney," she said. "They'll be away in a minute. They've already knocked your teeth out. I don't want to see you hurt any more!"

At her words Sidney stopped struggling, and Kate felt his fingers squeeze hers. She gently but firmly pulled her hands away.

Parson Ledbury was straining to catch what Ned was saying to him and so did not even look up as the Carrick gang made off with his precious horses, nor did he notice Joe Carrick kicking Tom away as he attempted to clamber up beside him.

"I've had a belly full of your scrawny features," Joe shouted at Tom. "We've had nothing but bad luck since you arrived. Go on! Crawl back to the stinking 'ole you came from!"

When Tom hesitated, Joe slapped the side of his head so hard that he fell to the ground, rolling over and over in the dry leaves.

When he came to a halt, he covered his head with his hands and didn't move. Then Kate watched, fascinated, as she glimpsed a small white mouse appear from under Tom's collar. He stroked it with one finger, then gently took hold of it and slipped it into his pocket.

"Parson," shouted Stammering John over his shoulder, "I can't see you t-t-taking to splicing the m-m-mainbrace. If I were you I'd m-m-make yourself scarce and be quick about it!"

Stammering John hesitated a moment before mounting one of the parson's chestnut mares. "Will you p-p-pray for us, Parson?"

"I shall not, you murderous coves!"

"N-n-no more than we deserve . . . Thank you, Parson . . ."

Joe grabbed hold of Stammering John's sleeve and slapped the flank of his horse.

"Move, you ninny, they are upon us!"

Joe cast a last look at the broken highwayman and spat at the ground. And with that the footpads rode off and vanished into the night.

After a moment Kate called out to everyone, "It's not a press gang! It's Gideon and Peter!"

"Thank the Lord!" exclaimed Hannah. "My nerves won't stand any more."

Sidney and Kate untied the driver, and Hannah ran over to help the parson with Ned. The parson knelt at Ned's side, puffing slightly with the effort of bending double.

"I did not imagine my life would be as it has been," Ned murmured. "Am I to die, Parson?"

"I am no doctor, Ned. But I think that you should make your peace with God."

Ned looked up at the stars twinkling through the leaves of the oak tree and let out a deep sigh.

"Are you in great pain?" asked Hannah.

"I feel nothing," he replied.

Hannah folded a handkerchief and placed it on the wound beneath his jacket. She bit her lip at the sight of the injury and pressed gently to try to stop the flow of blood.

Midnight's hooves announced Gideon and Peter's arrival. Parson Ledbury stood up and smiled broadly. He stepped forward and offered Gideon his hand, which he shook willingly.

"A press gang! An inspired notion, Mr. Seymour. Even footpads will go out of their way to avoid a press gang! I thank you, sir. I shall not forget this. You shall not go unrewarded."

Gideon inclined his head, suddenly unsure how to react to the parson. His gaze fell on Ned.

"To find everyone safe is reward enough, Parson. I heard the shot. I feared it was one of the party."

The parson turned to Peter and crushed his hand in his.

"Well done, my lad! I knew you would find out the meaning of bottom!"

"Parson Ledbury," said Kate, "Gideon stole back the necklace from Ned Porter."

She walked toward him, holding up the diamonds, which swayed and sparkled in the light of the fire. The parson gasped and then, grabbing hold of Kate's two hands, swung her round and round and did a little jig.

"Perhaps you would care to put on your jacket and trousers, Parson," suggested Hannah.

Kate laughed out loud.

"I feared it was lost forever!" cried Parson Ledbury. "I have been imagining the accusing expression on my dear cousin's face. . . . The necklace is quite irreplaceable, a family heirloom. Oh, happy day!"

With what strength he had left, Ned laughed, a little bitterly. He beckoned weakly to Gideon with one finger. Gideon knelt down next to Ned and took his hat off.

"So Will did not have the necklace. It was you, Mr. Seymour. I have taken this shot for nothing. You are a skillful cutpurse. It is no wonder that the Thief-taker does not wish to lose you."

"I have sworn an oath," Gideon replied. "I will neither betray Lord Luxon nor ever work for him again. He knows this."

An ironic smile passed over Ned's contorted features.

"I don't think he believes you, Mr. Seymour."

"Lord Luxon, a thief-taker!" exclaimed the parson.

Gideon stood up and walked away. He appeared angry with himself. Now Peter crouched down next to the highwayman.

"Why won't Lord Luxon let Gideon go if he's sworn not to betray him?"

Ned turned to look at Peter.

"Have you not heard tell of Mr. Seymour's skill? There is no one like him. He is Lord Luxon's favorite. He is more than his cutpurse—he is his conscience. The rest of the world might see Lord Luxon as the devil by any other name, but your Mr. Seymour is determined to see some good in him. Besides, a thief-taker can't let people walk away whenever they please—he is forced to make an example of him."

"I don't understand," said Peter. "What does Gideon know that makes Lord Luxon frightened to lose him?"

Ned laughed and then started to cough. A trickle of blood appeared at the side of his mouth.

"Master Schock, you must let him rest," said Hannah. "He has a grievous wound."

Ned, however, continued. "Your Mr. Seymour knows what every rogue in London knows—that nothing is stolen nor fenced, that no one is robbed nor killed, that no one squeaks on another nor pays the straw men to get 'em off, without the Thief-taker and his henchman getting to hear about it. Only for the rest of us, the Thief-taker is naught but a distant figure, an elegant gentleman in his fine coach. If you put us at the same table he wouldn't know us and we wouldn't know him. And as for the fops and lords and ladies that pay court to him—they don't know or even suspect the half of it. But Gideon—he's seen enough to have his master hanged at Tyburn ten times over. If I'd have been in Lord Luxon's shoes, your Mr. Seymour would have had his throat cut long ago."

Ned slumped back, exhausted, and Hannah motioned to Peter to leave before Ned was tempted to talk any more. She poured a little water into the highwayman's mouth. Ned's words horrified Peter. He glanced over at his friend, who was busy repacking the trunks whose contents were scattered all over the camp. Gideon was in even more danger than Peter had thought. It was easy to see why the Tar Man was so very determined to take him back to his master.

Peter walked over to join Kate, who was trying to persuade Tom to get up off the ground.

"We're not going to hurt you. We're not like the Carrick gang. We'll help you get home."

Sidney stood behind her. "Help this vermin!" he exclaimed. "Never!"

Kate lost her temper.

"Stop being such a pompous, stuck-up idiot!" she shouted. "Do you think you'd be any better than him in his shoes?"

Tom looked at Kate in wonderment through a crack in his fingers. Sidney seemed crestfallen. Peter could not help smirking, and Gideon, too, looked away for fear she would see his smile.

"Well," she continued hastily, giving Peter a cursory glance, "at least Sidney is brave—unlike some people who don't mind leaving their friends in the lurch—"

Kate stopped in full flow when she heard Hannah's gasp. They all looked over toward her, crouched down at Ned's side.

"The highwayman is dead," said the parson. He passed his hand over Ned's forehead and closed his eyelids.

It was at that moment that little Jack chose to wake up. He tottered sleepily over to Hannah. "I'm thirsty," he said.

"Oh, Master Jack," said Hannah. "Lord bless you!"

And she hugged him.

A Pact Made in Blood

*In which Inspector Wheeler goes on the warpath,
Peter and Kate make a solemn promise, and London
exposes some of its attractions and its dangers*

They had no choice but to spend the night under the oak tree. They made themselves as comfortable as they could, and although they were all hungry, at least the fire kept them warm. The knowledge that Ned's body lay stretched out on the other side of the carriage haunted their dreams. When Hannah had sung Jack a lullaby to get him back to sleep, he wasn't the only one who allowed himself to be comforted.

Nobody slept well. Peter least of all. It bothered him that Kate clearly thought so badly of him. *She must know how unfair she's being,* he thought, but still it bothered him. She'd said that Sidney was braver than he was! What had he done that was so great? Allowed Stinking John to knock his teeth out? And surely Kate must see that if Peter hadn't gone off with Gideon, things might have turned out a lot worse. And maybe it was mean of him to go off with Gideon without trying to include her—but it was meaner of her to imply he was acting like his dad, who always left him behind while he went off and did something important. Nor was it his fault that girls had to wear stupid big skirts in the eighteenth century and weren't allowed to do anything interesting.

He tried to stop thinking about it and instead forced himself to work out how many days they had been in the eighteenth century. Tomorrow, he decided, must be their sixth day. Which meant that at home, in four days' time, it would be Christmas. Not that his mother had yet decided whether she could spare the time to fly home to celebrate it with them. . . . She'd been so far away for so long. Strangely, it felt pretty much the same whether they were separated by eight thousand miles or two and a half centuries. Something tugged at him—was it anger? Or guilt at feeling angry? Or was it just that he missed her? Or perhaps he was frightened that he didn't miss her enough?

"Aren't you proud of her?" his dad had said. "Doing without her for a few months is hard but not too much to ask. This film is so important to her."

Except it wasn't a few months, it was more like a year and a half. And, yes, it was nice to be able to say to his friends that his mum was working on a film in Hollywood, and, yes, he'd been promised a couple of weeks' holiday in LA before too long, but all he really wanted was for her to come back home and for things to go back to normal. His dad was so bad-tempered when she wasn't around. Always on a short fuse, always too busy, always so critical. And when she did come home for a holiday, it was awkward at first—like having to get to know each other all over again—and just as everyone was beginning to feel comfortable, she would fly back to California.

Images of his mother came to him unbidden. Precious memories, silly things, momentous things: standing in a thunderstorm together, heads back, mouths wide open; her throwing a tub of chocolate mousse at him after he'd lied about taking some loose change, and then, as she scraped it off his clothes, her happy, infectious laughter; her waving good-bye to him at Heathrow, trying very hard not to cry the first time she left for Los Angeles.

Fluorescent spirals started to form in his mind. Peter opened his eyes. He lay on bare, ploughed earth, hard and white with frost, and directly above, a watery sun was trying to break through rippled white clouds. There was no sign of the giant oak tree, and in the distance he could hear the constant hum of traffic as if there were a motorway over the horizon. I'm back! he cried. I'm back! He stood up and tried to ignore the flickering dark borders that were trying to creep into the center of his vision. *If I concentrate,* he thought, *I can stay. I refuse to go back! I won't go back! I'll walk to the motorway and hitchhike back to Richmond.* He was conscious of a force being exerted on him with increasing pressure. He felt he was strong enough to resist it, but it was building up every second. For a moment—and he wasn't quite sure how he was doing it—he felt he was making headway. And then Kate's words pushed their way into his thoughts, just as a gust of wind suddenly flings open a window: "And you went off without giving me a second thought. . . ."

His concentration snapped, and a pool of darkness flowed over the pale wintry scene. After all his efforts he collapsed to the ground. He was back on the damp earth under the oak tree and no matter how hard he tried he could not manage to blur a second time. Peter felt cold and empty and alone. He had nearly managed to return home by what felt like sheer force of will. If only he hadn't thought of Kate . . . And now he was stuck in 1763 with a girl who thought he was a coward. For all he knew he might never be able to blur again. Might never see his parents ever again. He realized he was crying: He never cried, he had trained himself not to. His back heaved as he gulped silently for air. Suddenly he became aware of a hand resting lightly on his shoulder. Peter felt too ashamed to look up and kept his head buried in the crook of his arm. He tried not to sniff. Then he sensed someone lay a jacket over him, spread it out, and tuck it around his sides. The warmth soothed him, and soon he fell into a dreamless sleep.

To Gideon's and Peter's surprise, the cherry-picking boy kept his word and arrived shortly after daybreak with his father, a farmer with a good-natured nut brown face and hair streaked yellow by the sun and scraped back from his face in a neat ponytail. They brought two large wooden wagons with them. The boy was keen to get his second sixpence, which Gideon willingly gave to him. The farmer helped the party into one wagon and was beginning to load their luggage into another when he spotted Ned's corpse. He shrank back and put his rough, square hand to his mouth and took another, fearful look at the folk he had come to help.

"Do not be alarmed, my good fellow," said the parson. "We are no murderers. This is none other than the notorious highwayman, Ned Porter. We have had a narrow escape."

The farmer's curiosity was such that he took a surreptitious peep at Ned's face when he thought no one was looking, though he slapped the back of his son's head when he tried to do the same.

Tom was allowed to travel with them too, mainly thanks to Kate, but he had to suffer a stern warning from Parson Ledbury.

"I have my eye on you, lad. You have Mistress Kate to thank for your safe passage. If her faith in you proves to be mistaken, you can be assured that Newgate Gaol will be your next destination!"

The wretched boy cowered even more than usual and put his hand deep into his pocket, where, Kate guessed, he was gaining some small comfort by stroking his one friend in the world.

The farmer refused to have anything to do with moving Ned's body but agreed to get a message to the magistrate at Lichfield that afternoon. Parson Ledbury undertook to write a full account of the night's events and send it to him but said he was not prepared to delay their journey to London any longer, for they had an appointment to keep with no less a person than His Majesty King George III.

"I have the King's evil," announced Jack proudly to the farmer and his son, who looked suitably impressed.

Gideon and the parson covered Ned's face with his jacket and placed some leafy branches over him to protect him, at least for some little time, against the rooks and the foxes. The parson stood over him and said a few words. Already flies were beginning to buzz around him. How happy the travelers were to see the giant oak tree and the scene of the attack recede into the distance.

Gideon reluctantly put Midnight into the hands of Martin, the driver, who was no longer needed now that the party was to catch a stagecoach. After two knocks to the head in as many days, Martin was, in any case, happy to be returning home on a fast horse.

"Though I hope I might be spared any further encounters with any gentlemen of the road," he said.

The parson did his best to reassure him.

"I doubt, Martin, that the sight of you drooping over your horse would excite the interest of the least daring highwayman. He would have expectation of very slim pickings indeed to spare a poor wretch like you a second glance. Why, he is more likely to offer you a sixpence."

Gideon stroked Midnight's nose and wished horse and rider Godspeed. When the driver dug his heels in, Midnight responded a little too eagerly—they all watched poor Martin disappear out of sight clinging to the reins for all he was worth.

While the farmer's massive shire horses heaved against the weight of the wagons on the road to Birmingham, the party took it in turns to recount what had happened the previous night. Somehow it helped everyone get over the shock of the attack and the horror of Ned's murder. The farmer listened in rapt attention and then, when Hannah told him about the parson having to preach to the drunken footpads in a state of undress, he slapped his thigh and laughed out loud, begging the parson's pardon, at the thought of it. He could not stop repeating, "As I live, Ned Porter . . . As I live . . ." and was quite beside himself when the parson allowed him to hold Mrs. Byng's diamond necklace in his own hands. Gideon, who was driving the second wagon, piled high with luggage, happened to look back as the farmer dangled the jewels from his fingers, his eyes wide with awe. Gideon glared at the parson and raised his eyebrows. The parson met his gaze and hastily snatched back the diamonds, secreting them in his jacket.

"Faith, you've spent a more thrilling night in Shenstone than ever I have, and I was born and bred there!" the farmer said. "I shan't want for an audience at the Fox and Hounds tonight."

Thrilling, thought Kate, isn't what it had felt like at the time.

They stopped briefly at Aldridge for breakfast before making haste to Birmingham, where they hoped to catch the morning stagecoach to London. The farmer and his boy deposited them outside the King's Head, and having been thanked very kindly and paid two shillings for their trouble, they set off back toward Shenstone, their heads buzzing with tales of footpads and highwaymen.

As the party was so large, an extra coach was laid on for their party to travel in. Parson Ledbury handed over the princely sum of twenty shillings (which he was obliged to borrow from Gideon), and the party clambered in. A printed notice announced that

"God permitting" the London coach would depart at nine a.m. and would reach the Blue Boar Inn in Holborn at ten a.m. the following day, stopping only at four staging posts along the way to change the horses.

Gideon and Tom sat up on top with the driver and his guard, who carried a blunderbuss and a fearsome-looking cutlass in case of attack. The rest of the party were crammed into the carriage: It smelled of horse and stale sweat, but its steel springs made for a more comfortable journey than anyone had been expecting. The guard said that Dr. Samuel Johnson often took the stagecoach from Lichfield and swore that he had a better night's sleep than in any bed at a wayside inn. Nevertheless, the carriage bumped over interminable potholes and made frequent enforced stops while they waited for flocks of sheep and herds of cows to let them through. Often the roads were so bad the driver would take detours over farmers' fields to avoid getting stuck in the mud. Just after Oxford the driver stopped at a turnpike and paid to use a private road, which was much smoother in comparison and allowed them to make fast progress for a good while.

Whenever they passed another coach, the drivers and passengers would exchange greetings and pleasantries and wave their handkerchiefs out of the windows.

"This is a bit different from being stuck in lines of traffic on the M1," whispered Kate to Peter.

"Yeah," he whispered back. "But I wish we could stop at a service station for a Coke and a burger and chips."

The golden landscape swept slowly by. Day turned into night and night into day. Once they passed a village green where they saw, suspended from a gibbet, the body of a half-decomposed man swaying in the summer breeze. He still wore his three-cornered hat. Hannah would not let Jack look. Otherwise the journey was uneventful. The most exciting thing that happened was in Highgate the following morning when the driver lost his temper with a foppish young gentleman in a yellow jacket who refused to give way to him, nearly causing the carriage to run over a woman carrying a baby. He was driving a pretty, if slightly ridiculous-looking, one-seater chaise—a carriage built for one passenger—and was hurtling through the crowded streets paying no heed to the other road users.

The stagecoach driver cracked his whip over the horses' heads and skillfully drove off in hot pursuit of the one-seater, weaving between wagons and horse riders. He drew up next to him and started to force him, inch by inch, onto the side of the road, brushing the flimsy, ornate wheels of the chaise with the solid metal-rimmed ones of the coach. The gentleman, red-faced with fury, called out, "What the devil are you about, you impudent hound?"

The driver took pleasure in howling at him like a lovesick dog and then replied, "Have you not heard of hunting the squirrel? 'Tis a fine game—so long as both players can hold their nerve. . . ."

And with that, he urged the horses forward and compelled the one-seater to dive into the gutter, where one of its wheels collided with some debris. The chaise tipped sideways and the young dandy was deposited into the gutter. If his dignity was not already damaged enough, a gang of small boys then decided to pelt him with mud. Everyone laughed, even Tom, who had remained silent the whole trip.

The roads had become busier and busier, and Peter and Kate hung their heads out of the window, eager for their first glimpse of the London of 1763. And then they saw it, the greatest city in Europe, stretched out below them, set against a blue horizon made hazy by the wood smoke of tens of thousands of fires. A host of church spires rose up from a maze of streets that described the curving contours of the Thames. Soaring up majestically in the east, the tallest building in the city, was the great dome of St. Paul's Cathedral, and farther east still, the Tower of London. To the west, Westminster Abbey and St. James's Park. It was not the gigantic, sprawling city of the twenty-first century that Peter and Kate knew. You could walk from one end to the other in the space of an afternoon, and yet they recognized it straightaway like an old friend.

"It's so beautiful!" Kate gasped.

"It's so small!" said Peter who had seen London from high up on Hampstead Heath many times. "You can see the edges! It's surrounded by green. . . . And no Post Office Tower! No Big Ben! No Canary Wharf! No Centre Point! Not a single skyscraper! I wonder if there are this many churches in our century—because if there are, you can't see most of them behind everything else."

They stared, mesmerized, longing to get out of the coach and experience the city firsthand, all feelings of fatigue gone. At a quarter to ten the stagecoach came to a halt in the yard of the Blue Boar Inn at Holborn. The driver leaped down and opened the door. His passengers clambered out onto the granite sets of the street. Although they now stood on firm ground, after over a day of being constantly jolted over holes in muddy roads, they had the impression that they were still in motion.

Peter and Kate looked about them. The noise of the street reached them from the other side of the inn. Here in the yard it was scarcely calmer. The Blue Boar Inn, one of the largest coaching inns in London, was a hive of activity—they saw porters carrying trunks, bakers delivering bread, a butcher stooped nearly double with the weight of a whole side of beef on his back. And there was a smell. Peter sniffed the air, and a grin appeared on his face that no one could have understood. Eighteenth-century London in the summer had its own distinctive mix of odors: wood smoke and horseflesh, rotting vegetables and sewers, and fresh horse manure. But over and above that pungent mix there was a trace of a smell, something subtle and impossible to define but which Peter recognized. London still *smelled* like London. In a curious sort of way Peter felt he had arrived home.

The parson yawned extravagantly. "Upon my word, a more vexatious journey from Baslow Hall I cannot imagine! The stagecoach is a marvel of the modern age but does little for my aching back. Thank heaven we have arrived in civilization. It is wearisome indeed to go abroad fearing that every other fellow has his eye on your purse."

The parson stretched up his arms to relieve his aching back, and then reached down to touch his toes, which he would have managed were it not for the obstacle of his large belly. When he stood up again he found that a woman had planted herself in front of him.

"Won't you spare a farthin' for a poor widow wiv ten children to feed?" she asked.

She was so thin her bones jutted out from beneath her skin like furniture under dust sheets. She appeared to have no teeth, and she was swaying ever so slightly. Just visible underneath a frayed shawl, a baby was clamped to her bosom. The stench emanating from her was such that Kate, who stood right next to her, could not help retching. The parson reached into his pocket in search of a coin.

"And this must be the welcoming committee," commented the driver sarcastically. "Keep your money, Parson. I know her sort. She won't spend it on her poor starved children. It's gin she's after."

"So you'd begrudge me a drop of kill-grief, would you?" she hissed. "You in your fancy livery and a face like a pig's backside. What's it to you if the gentleman has a kind heart?"

The woman spat at the driver, and a large glob of spittle ran down his cheek. The driver wiped his face with his sleeve and pushed her roughly out of the way, and she and the baby fell in the mud.

Kate was mesmerized by the hate in her eyes. Hannah came forward and held out a penny, which the woman grabbed instinctively in a movement that reminded Kate of the way a chameleon shoots out its sticky tongue to catch a fly.

As the woman disappeared into the heaving crowd, Kate noticed the bruises on her arms and her bare, black feet. She turned to look at Peter, who was clearly thinking the same thing.

"So this is eighteenth-century London," he said.

Detective Inspector Wheeler crouched down and drew a line with his finger in the red dust gathered in a pile at the foot of the brick wall. He shone a torch at the wall where Dr. Pirretti's knife had effaced Kate's message. When he got up, his face was like thunder.

"Where are they now?" he asked Sergeant Chadwick.

"They arrived at the NCRDM lab half an hour ago."

"Then what are you waiting for?" barked the inspector. "Get me a car!"

The inspector stared around Dr. Dyer's office, his eyes resting on the piles of computer printouts covering the floor and the wall-to-wall photographs of deep space. Dr. Pirretti poured him a cup of strong black coffee.

"Sugar?" she asked.

"Two. Please."

A vein throbbed in his temple. His studied silence prompted the scientists to exchange anxious glances. Suddenly the inspector grabbed hold of the sides of Dr. Dyer's desk and leaned over it, glowering at the row of apprehensive faces.

"Don't insult my intelligence by trying to deny that you are all concealing something. If you know anything that could be helpful to us in our inquiries, I should like you to tell me. Now."

No one spoke. Inspector Wheeler turned to face Dr. Dyer.

"What in God's name is going on?" he exploded. "There are two hundred police officers involved in this case. It has national press coverage. Pleas for information are still going out on local news stations four times a day. The Police Commissioner is breathing down my neck, insisting on an early resolution to our investigations. And, meanwhile, the one man who seems to know something, the father of the missing girl, no less, sees fit to keep this information to himself!"

"I . . ." Dr. Dyer faltered. He was at a loss to know what to say. He passed a hand over his forehead.

"Dr. Dyer," growled the inspector, "if you don't want me to charge you with obstructing the police in their inquiries, I strongly suggest that you start talking."

Dr. Dyer looked around wildly at his colleagues.

The inspector walked right up to Kate's father and leaned in so close that Dr. Dyer could smell his breath. Dr. Dyer tried his best not to flinch.

"Have the children been launched into outer space?" asked the inspector sarcastically. "Has NASA invented an invisibility machine? Have they been abducted by aliens? Tell me!"

"I . . . can't," said Dr. Dyer.

"What do you mean, you can't?" shouted the inspector.

"He means," interrupted Dr. Pirretti, "that the information is classified. You will have to go through the official channels at NASA if you wish to have access to this information, and I doubt whether they will agree to it. However, I should like to assure you that we do not mean to obstruct your inquiries in any way."

"Nor help them either," retorted the inspector.

"I can give you the director of research's number at Houston, if you like."

"Please do."

Half an hour later Inspector Wheeler returned briefly to Dr. Dyer's office to inform them that NASA had been singularly unhelpful and that he would be contacting the Foreign Office to ask them to pursue the matter vigorously. No sooner had he swept out the door than the telephone rang. Dr. Jacob answered the call and put his hand over the receiver.

"It's Houston," he said. "They want to speak to you at once, Anita."

Dr. Pirretti took a deep breath, reached out her hand to take the phone, and then changed her mind.

"Tell them I'll ring them back later."

She ran her fingers through her wavy dark hair. "Now what?" she breathed.

The Honorable Mrs. Byng's brother, Sir Richard Picard, owned a grand five-story house in Lincoln's Inn Fields, five minutes' walk from the Blue Boar Inn. Gideon hired a hackney coach for a shilling and went on ahead to the house with the luggage. He asked Tom to help him before he took his leave of them. The rest of the party were glad to stretch their legs and go on foot.

"Richard is an accommodating fellow," commented the parson to Peter and Kate. "I have no doubt that he would be happy to have you in his house until you can find your uncle. Indeed, Richard will doubtless assist you in your search."

Kate and Peter smiled and nodded in thanks.

"This is going to be tricky," said Peter to Kate when the parson had turned his back.

"Don't worry," replied Kate. "It's just going to take a very long time to find this particular uncle. Anyway, we might have the antigravity machine soon, if we can find the Black Lion Tavern, that is."

Peter frowned. "That's not going to be the problem. It's whether we can persuade the Tar Man to hand it over."

"I know," Kate replied. "I've been thinking the same thing. But at least he told you where to find him."

"Yeah, but what does he want in return? He's not going to say, 'Of course you can have your machine back—no problem at all!' What have we got that he wants? We don't have any money, that's for sure."

Kate suddenly clapped her hand to her mouth. "Oh, no!" she said. "We *have* got something that he wants. Or rather, some-one."

Peter looked at her, puzzled, and then understood what she meant. Peter clenched his fists tight.

"Well, we're not going to give Gideon up to him no matter what he does to us!"

That first walk along eighteenth-century Holborn made such an intense impression on Peter and Kate that they could scarcely take it all in. They stepped into the street and joined the great crowd that streamed eastward and westward along High Holborn. All around them was the din of a thousand conversations, of hawkers selling their wares, of infants crying, of a gypsy playing his fiddle, of church bells, of horses snorting, and of wooden axles creaking. They walked along, craning their heads first upward, gawping at the fine high stone buildings and the huge colorful shop signs hanging from iron brackets, and then downward at the cobbled street as they tripped over a loose stone or sank ankle-deep into a muddy hole, spattering their clothes with stinking filth. Several times they became separated from their companions, and it was only the beacon of Jack's blond hair, shining in the sunlight as he rode astride the parson's shoulders, that saved them from becoming utterly lost in the heaving mass of people.

They rubbed shoulders with beggars and merchants, servants and laborers, street urchins and courtiers. Soon they began to pick out details in the ever-changing scene: black beauty spots on powdered white faces, greasy ponytails and three-cornered hats, wigs and turbans, cascades of lace flowing from wide sleeves, white stockings and polished black boots, exquisite embroidered court shoes with pointed toes and satin heels that had no business treading in the dirt of the street.

Every few yards a stallholder would accost them.

"Who will buy my lovely roses? Two a penny, four a penny!" cried a flower girl.

"Hot pudding and gray peas!" called out a plump woman stirring a pan of unidentifiable green mush.

They all soon learned to step aside when they heard the shout: "Chair!" or "By your leave, sir!" Saved by a quick shove from

Parson Ledbury, Sidney was nearly trampled underfoot by two bearers carrying a sedan chair. This one must have belonged to a great family, for it was upholstered in brocade and a coat of arms was embroidered in gold thread on the door. The two chair-men, who wore liveried uniforms, ran at breakneck speed through the street with their heavy burden—far too fast to be able to stop if anyone got in their way. As it raced by, Kate caught through the window a glimpse of turquoise taffeta, a painted fan, and ropes of pearls draped over creamy skin.

Peter felt Kate grab hold of his hand.

"This is something else, isn't it?"

"You're not kidding," Peter replied, and he thought, although he could not bring himself to say it, how much he would have loved his mother to be here. Once when she had been working on an historical film, she had shown him around the set. His mother had been so proud of all the authentic details that they had used. He could imagine the exact expression, the wide eyes and half-open mouth, that would have come to her face if she had been here with him and could have experienced all of this. A pang of sadness entered his heart, and for a moment he trudged along and desperately did not want to be in Holborn in 1763 with Kate and the Byng family. He wanted to be with his family, not a stranger in a time that was not his own.

When they had to cross the road, treading over the foul-smelling central gutter, they took their lives in their hands, darting among lumbering wagons, elegant chaises, carriages and four, and hackney coaches. Halfway across they saw a magpie pecking at a dead cat, his meal forever interrupted by the constant procession of vehicles.

At last the parson took them up a narrow street past a noisy tavern, where a woman in a revealing red dress sidled up to Sidney, took him by the arm, and said, "Come, my young sir, let us drink a glass together."

Sidney's jaw dropped and he stared at her, speechless. The parson grabbed him by the other arm and pulled him forward. The woman loosened her grip and laughed.

"Another day perhaps, my lord," she called out after him.

Suddenly they stepped out into the sunlight and saw the great expanse of calm green that was Lincoln's Inn Fields. Children were playing, a cow was grazing, and some ladies holding lapdogs were sitting on a bench. Around the edges of this tranquil square stood tall, elegant terraces. It was to one of the grandest houses, on the west side, that the parson led them. They walked through an ornate iron gate, flanked by two giant urns. The parson rapped on the door with a brass knocker in the shape of a dolphin, and a footman in full livery pulled open the heavy door. Finally they had arrived at their destination.

By late afternoon everyone had washed, put on a change of clothing, and eaten a late lunch. Sir Richard Picard was busy at the Treasury Offices in Downing Street but sent word that he would be back by eight to join them for a celebratory supper. Gideon asked the cook to give Tom something to eat before he left, and the kindhearted woman prepared him a feast of bread and chicken and ham washed down with a glass of cider. Peter and Kate sat with him in the dark basement kitchen. He ate greedily but could not bear to look anyone in the eye, although when Kate asked if she could hold his pet mouse, he took it out and let it scamper on his head and shoulders and run up his sleeves.

"She won't go to no one else," Tom explained. His voice was breaking, and he hit squeaky high notes and rumbling low ones in the space of a few words.

Gideon asked him if he had somewhere to go.

"Yes, yes, sir. I . . ." His voice trailed off.

"Where?" inquired Gideon. "To your parents' house?"

"I have no parents. Lodgings . . . I have lodgings," he muttered.

Peter and Kate said good-bye to the boy, and when Kate held out her hand he was too shy to take it and took a step backward. Peter was pretty sure he was close to tears. *Tom can't want to go home,* he thought. *It can't, in any case, be much of a home if he left it to hang around with the Carrick gang.*

Gideon gave Tom a sixpence and they watched him slip out the back door into the alley behind the terrace of houses.

"Poor wretch," commented Gideon. "God in his wisdom gives some of his children a heavy burden to bear."

Hannah insisted that Peter and Kate rest awhile after their long journey, but neither of them were tired and Kate soon joined Peter in his tiny attic room. They needed to decide how and when to approach the Tar Man without putting Gideon at risk. They couldn't agree, and after a while they stopped talking. Peter broke the silence.

"Kate," said Peter. "I'm sorry I went off with Gideon without you, but I wouldn't have gone back without you. Not deliberately, I mean. Don't you believe me?"

"I'd like to believe you, but . . . I don't *know*. I can't imagine anything worse than being cut off, all alone in 1763 with no hope of getting back."

"All right, then," said Peter, "I swear. I'll swear on anything you like, I'll not go back without you."

"You'll swear on anything?"

"Yes."

"Then let's make a blood pact. Give me your knife."

Kate took Peter's knife and, without flinching, pricked the tip of her finger with the point of the blade and squeezed until a bulging drop of blood appeared. She smeared it onto the palm of her hand. Then she wiped the blade carefully on her handkerchief and handed it back to Peter, indicating that he should do the same. When he had finished, she grasped his hand and held it tightly in hers.

"Say after me," she said. "I swear on my life."

"I swear on my life."

"That I shall never return to the twenty-first century without you."

"That I shall never return to the twenty-first century without you."

"There's no getting out of that promise," she said.

"I don't want to," he replied.

Their mood lightened and as they talked, they leaned out of the two small windows that looked out over Lincoln's Inn Fields.

They could see Gideon, sitting on a bench in the sunshine, reading a letter, a troubled expression on his face.

"Look," Peter said abruptly. "Isn't that Tom?"

"Yes, it is. What's he doing lurking behind the tree? I thought he was going home."

There was alarm in Kate's voice. They watched Tom look behind him toward someone they could not see and then point toward Gideon with his forefinger. Will and Joe Carrick darted toward their friend.

"Gideon!" they both screamed at the top of their voices.

As Gideon looked up, a sack was thrust over his head, his hands forced behind his back and tied with rope. The Carrick brothers pulled him toward a waiting carriage and threw him in. Peter and Kate ran out of the room and down the four flights of stairs three steps at a time and burst through the front door. The carriage had already disappeared. They ran down the narrow alley that led to High Holborn and stood looking at the sea of coaches, carriages, and wagons moving through the broad thoroughfare. If the carriage was there, they could not pick it out in this lot. And even if they could, what could they do? They trudged slowly back, defeated and disconsolate, to the bench where Gideon had been sitting. Peter picked up the letter that Gideon had dropped during the struggle, and folded and unfolded it mechanically. Set in the indecipherable copperplate writing was a thumbnail sketch of Gideon. It was a good likeness. *This must be from Joshua,* he thought. What would happen to Gideon's young half brother now? Peter passed the letter to Kate for her to look at the sketch. She said it was good and then they both slumped on the bench in horrified silence, heads bowed, looking at the ground.

The crunch of gravel caused them to look up. Standing before them, quivering in fear, was Tom. Peter flew at him and, before he knew what he was doing, grabbed hold of his neck in both hands.

"You betrayed us! You were a plant! You'd planned to do this all along! You're still part of the Carrick gang!"

Tom grabbed Peter's elbows, dislodged his grip with one easy movement, and shoved him backward so that he landed on his back, arms splayed, in the clover.

"They would have killed me else! I didn't choose to do it! If only you hadn't showed me such . . . consideration. Joe ain't got a kind bone in his body. You let me be. Please, Mistress Kate, take back the sixpence Mr. Seymour gave me!"

"I don't want your stupid sixpence!" she shouted. "I wouldn't take anything from a Judas! You deliberately led them to him!"

Tom sank to his knees and started to shake his head from side to side in distress as he talked.

"You don't know what Joe's like. And the Tar Man. They do . . . terrible things. I had to do it. Can't you understand?"

"So why are you still here?" burst out Peter. "Do you want us to forgive you or something? Because I won't. Not now and not ever. Get lost! Go away before you're taken away!"

Tom did not move. There was a pause while Peter and Kate stared at him, eyes burning with righteous fury.

"I've come to take you to where they're holding him. The Tar Man's got a secret holding place at the back of the Black Lion."

A look of terror suddenly passed over Tom's features, and he automatically reached into his pocket to stroke his mouse for comfort.

"I'll show you so long as you don't tell 'em as it was me what told you," he said. "You got to swear!"

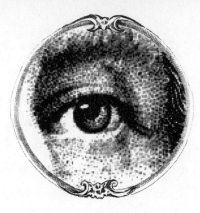

SIXTEEN

Two Covent Gardens

*In which the children finally make the acquaintance
of the Tar Man at the Black Lion Tavern
and then disrupt a juggler's street show*

Tom refused to help them if they told the parson, for he feared
that he would call a magistrate and have him instantly clapped
in Newgate Gaol. Nevertheless, Kate ran back to the house and
asked the aloof footman to tell the parson, when he awoke from
his nap, that Mr. Seymour had need of them and that they had
gone to the Black Lion Tavern in Covent Garden.

As they headed down Drury Lane, the air was heavy and
humid and the gutters stank in the early evening heat. A

storm was brewing and the rumble of thunder in the distance announced that it would not be long in arriving. If the crowds in High Holborn indicated the rich variety of life to be found in the capital and if Lincoln's Inn Fields was an oasis of calm for those who could afford it, then Covent Garden was a magnet for the low life of London. A feeling of creeping dread came over the children as they walked deeper and deeper into the Tar Man's haunt. Tom made them walk in the shadows against the walls, but their fine clothes made them stand out and drew malicious glances from doorways and from drunken groups spilling out of the boisterous taverns into the street. Tom kept his hand on his knife and stared out anyone taking an interest in his companions. He might have been timid with Kate and Peter, but this was his territory and he had learned to hold his own here. There was a fierce, shrewd, cunning side to him that they had not seen before.

"They know I'm protected by the Carrick gang," he told them. "Keep close to me and you'll come to no harm."

As they walked past the Rose Tavern, on the corner of Drury Lane and Russell Street, they saw a giant of a man lying in the mud of the street urging the driver of a wagon to ride over him. He called out to Tom, "Oi! Tom, lad. Where the devil have Joe and Will got to? I haven't seen hide nor hair of them these three weeks past!"

"You'll see them before the night is out, I don't doubt. They have a job to finish for Blueskin," shouted Tom.

As the wagon drew closer to the huge man, the crowd started to thump their fists and bang their glasses on the wooden tables.

"Feather-stone! Feather-stone! Feather-stone!" they chanted.

"He'll be crushed!" exclaimed Kate.

"Don't be anxious on his account, Mistress Kate. That's Featherstone, the porter at the Rose. He's got a ribcage like iron. He's forever doing it. It's how he's got so rich."

The broad wagon wheels sliced over him and the crowd went silent. Featherstone's body lay immobile in the road. After a dramatic pause Featherstone leaped to his feet and roared with laughter. A man in the crowd swore an oath and dropped a golden guinea into his hands. The rest of the crowd shouted and cheered.

In a side road off Drury Lane a great painted sign announced the Black Lion Tavern. Peter's heart sank. It seemed half a lifetime ago since he'd watched the Tar Man disappearing over the hill in Derbyshire, telling him to find him at the Black Lion if he wanted his machine back. He remembered the quivering horror he felt as he pretended to be unconscious. Don't hoodwink a hoodwinker, the Tar Man had told him. And what was it that Gideon had said? That above all they must never try to double-cross him . . . that they had little to fear from him as long as they gave him what he wanted? But what could they give him? He had the antigravity machine *and* Gideon. And now they would have to confront him, face-to-face.

"Wait here," said Tom as he edged down the side of the Black Lion.

He was only gone for two minutes at the most, but Peter and Kate were so scared by now it seemed an age. When he returned, they knew something was wrong.

"It's empty," he said in a flat voice. "They've already moved him. . . . I must make inquiries—someone will know. Nothing's a secret for long at the Black Lion. Follow me. Keep yourselves to yourselves and best not to talk to anyone as, pardon me for saying so, you do have a queer manner of speech."

Tom disappeared into the Black Lion. Peter and Kate followed and sat in a dark corner, trying not to return the curious looks of the unsavory clientele across the clouds of tobacco smoke. Kate wanted to cough but stifled the impulse for fear of drawing attention to herself. Peter felt his heart thumping wildly in his chest—all he really wanted to do was slip back out and run. He felt that every eye was on them, and Tom or no Tom, he was beginning to doubt whether they would get out of there in one piece.

Tom was talking quietly with the landlord when the door to a back room squealed open on its rusting hinges. The three Carrick brothers emerged from the shadows.

"No! No! No! That's all we need!" whispered Kate frantically, trying to hide her face behind her hands. "We've got to get out of here—if they see us, they'll kill Tom."

"And us, too!"

They stood up, trying not to scrape their chairs on the flagged stone floor.

"Why, if it's not y-y-young Tom," they heard Stammering John say. "I was a-wondering where you'd g-g-got to."

Peter and Kate sidled toward the door keeping their heads down, and once into the narrow alley they made a dash for it. After a few yards they found that their path was blocked by a man coming toward them. If Peter had not gasped in recognition as he came to a sudden stop, the man might not have given him a second look.

"Come on!" urged Kate, tugging at Peter's sleeve. She wondered why he was suddenly rooted to the spot, until she focused on the man, on the horrifying scar on his face, and on the way he was looking at her bright red hair.

She could not stop herself giving a small yelp of fear. "The Tar Man!" she breathed.

He gave a long slow smile of satisfaction. "Upon my word! So you found old Blueskin's haunt. Now there is a happy coincidence— the very children whose remarkable arrival I had the good fortune to witness and whose company I was resolved to seek out this very day. Why, I scarcely recognized you in your finery! But you don't want to be walking alone in these streets—it is not safe for gentlefolk such as yourselves."

The Tar Man paused, waiting for any kind of response. Peter and Kate could do nothing more than gawp up at him. Peter felt Kate reach out for his hand. There was something in the tone of the Tar Man's voice, something honeyed and treacherous, that made the hairs on the back of Peter's neck stand on end. He was gripping Kate's hand harder than he realized.

"I am told you go by the names of Miss Dyer and Master Schock."

Kate gave a slight nod of her head despite herself.

"Come, will you not drink a glass with me? For it is me you have come to see, is it not? Have you come alone? Yes? No? I see you have no great taste for conversation. Well, no matter, I shall soon find out how the land lies."

Peter's terror did not prevent him from absorbing every detail about this man whose mere existence weighed so heavily on him. When Peter had first seen him, in Kate's valley in Derbyshire, the Tar Man had been on the road for many days. Now he seemed neither as grotesque nor as unkempt as Peter remembered. Peter took in his intense, dark eyes; his Roman nose, large but not out of proportion; and his surprisingly good clothes: a jacket and breeches in pigeon gray, and fine buckled shoes worn with clean white stockings. There was something feline about him—his movements were rapid, yet confident and unhurried, and he seemed permanently on the alert. His hair was black and his skin weather-beaten and although he had shaved, the stubble was already showing through, giving a dark cast to his face. But the scar was as terrible as Peter remembered—a livid white arc between brow and jaw. Peter shuddered; the flesh must have been cut to the bone.

Peter and Kate followed the Tar Man into the Black Lion. He did not need to threaten them. His authority was such that somehow the possibility of making a quick getaway down the alley did not occur to either of them. As the Tar Man strode through the door of the Black Lion, Kate detected a slight swagger in his step. He struck a pose for a moment on the threshold, to survey the room and to make sure everyone was aware of his arrival. He enjoyed an audience. He turned slightly toward Peter and Kate and patted the back of his thigh, signaling to them that they should enter—which they did, feeling, thought Kate uncomfortably, like two dogs following at their master's heels. Almost at once half the tavern were on their feet, raising their glasses, lifting their hats, calling out greetings to Blueskin, as they called him, no doubt on account of his stubble.

The Tar Man waited pointedly by what was evidently his favorite table, and after a short but anxious pause its occupants got up apologetically and sloped off to sit somewhere else. The Tar Man indicated to Peter and Kate that they should sit down. They were soon joined by Joe Carrick.

"What the devil are this pair doing here, Blueskin?" demanded Joe Carrick, glaring at the children.

There was a part of Kate that wanted to rise to her feet and shout "Murderer!" at Joe, but here in the Black Lion Tavern, surrounded by his cronies and sitting next to Lord Luxon's henchman, she bit her lip.

"You took the words out of my mouth," said the Tar Man to Joe. "What, you are asking yourself, are Blueskin's intentions with regard to young Master Schock and Miss Dyer, who may not wish to keep their account of recent events to themselves."

Joe nodded.

"Well, I say to you, Joe Carrick, that, first, I should be obliged if you would be civil enough to wish me good day before you badger me with your questions and, second, that as I have private business with my distinguished guests, I'll thank you to wait for me at the Rose, where we have the matter of some gold and a dead highwayman to discuss."

Joe looked disgruntled and did not move.

"You were happy enough to take delivery of Mr. Seymour," he whined. "If they squeak—"

Before Joe could continue, the Tar Man was on his feet and

had barked at him so that the whole tavern could hear: "Meet me at the Rose as I asked. You and the numbskulls that ride with you! Don't overreach yourself, Joe, for my master's net reaches farther than you could ever run."

The Carrick gang headed toward the door.

"C-c-come on, Tom," said Stammering John over his shoulder.

"No, not him," said the Tar Man. "I've got business with young Tom."

Joe glared at him but said nothing and disappeared into the alley. At the Tar Man's invitation, Tom, white-faced and trembling, joined Peter and Kate at their table.

"So, young Tom, how rich were the pickings? How much of the parson's gold did they take?"

The Tar Man took hold of Tom's ear and twisted it—not, Peter noticed, with any particular relish for the pain he was inflicting. He did it because he needed the information and this was how to get it.

"Fifty-seven guineas, sir," Tom replied, grimacing.

"Is that right?" asked the Tar Man, looking at Peter.

"Yes," Peter replied hastily before the Tar Man used the technique on him.

The Tar Man let go of Tom's ear.

"Who does he take me for, the conceited blockhead? He told me twenty-five. Young Tom here has got more brains than all the Carrick gang put together, if only they would realize. Eh, Tom?"

Tom was too terrified to speak and looked in anguished despair at Peter and Kate.

Before she could stop herself, Kate exclaimed, "Don't worry, Tom—we'll protect you."

The Tar Man laughed out loud.

"Ah, I understand you now, Tom. They have *befriended* you! You feel gratitude. You want to help them."

Suddenly the Tar Man's expression changed and he spoke fiercely.

"Don't be a fool, boy! You are alone, as I was at your age. You cannot rely on such people in this world. They might throw you a few crumbs if it suits them, but you are not of their kind. They would be off at the first sign of trouble and you know it in your heart."

His tone softened, and he continued, "I give you fair warning, Tom. The Carrick gang is finished. But I've had my eye on you, and unlike Joe, I can see your worth. I could use a lad like you. There, young Tom, that is an offer you weren't expecting this day, I'll warrant! How would the role of Blueskin's apprentice suit you?"

Tom looked horrified, flattered, and incredulous all at once.

"Don't do it, Tom!" cried Kate.

Peter put his hand on her arm. This was perhaps not the greatest approach to take with the Tar Man, he thought, even though her comment only caused a wry smile to appear on his face.

Tom's pet mouse chose that moment to emerge from its master's collar. With lightning reflexes the Tar Man reached over to Tom's neck and grabbed hold of it. He held the white mouse by its tail and it swung like a miniature pendulum above the oak table. Tom stood up, petrified.

"Don't hurt it!"

The Tar Man scrutinized Tom's face and said, "And here is your first lesson: Love anything or anyone and it becomes your Achilles' heel."

He moved his arm slowly toward the candle burning in the middle of the table. The poor creature wriggled and squeaked.

"No!" cried Kate.

He dangled the struggling mouse high above the flame and gradually lowered it. Suddenly there was a whiff of singeing hair as the mouse's whiskers briefly passed through the flame. It squeaked uncontrollably. In a turmoil of pain and distress for his pet, Tom launched himself at the Tar Man, who coolly threw the animal high into the air toward the other side of the table, so that Tom was forced to interrupt his attack in order to leap after the mouse. He reappeared clutching the tiny animal and gently put her into his pocket.

"You would have done anything to stop me, would you not?" asked the Tar Man calmly. "Affection is a fatal weakness. Resist it."

Tom sat down, breathing hard, a terrible rage in his eyes.

"And the second lesson," said the Tar Man to Tom, "as you have this very moment shown us, is that anger is stronger than fear. Make anger your weapon, not your downfall, unlike most men."

"You beast!" shouted Kate. "No wonder someone gave you that scar. I dread to think what you must have done to them!"

"Such emotion, Miss Dyer! You would be surprised to learn how I got that scar. But I'll tell you how I got my scar if you tell me how to master that contraption of yours."

"I don't know anything—"

Peter interrupted her. "*I* know how to make the antigravity machine transport us anywhere we like," he said.

The Tar Man swung round to look at Peter. He had his full attention; his eyes burned with intense interest. Peter suddenly realized that it was not only Lord Luxon who desired the machine; it was also his henchman. Even though the Tar Man could not know what the antigravity machine could do, it was clear to Peter that the henchman wanted it badly. Kate looked at Peter, aghast.

"But," he continued, "in return I want you to release Gideon Seymour."

The Tar Man had recovered himself and was feigning little interest in Peter's bargain. "Now, that is a powerful high price, Master Schock. We have spent nigh on three weeks trying to persuade Gideon to return home. Gideon has scruples that sometimes blind him to the greater truth. Besides, Lord Luxon would be ill pleased, indeed, if I were to release Mr. Seymour before he has remembered why he should remain with those who appreciate his talents the most."

"You're not saying that Gideon won't want to come with us?"

"Gideon is as a brother to me and is fortunate enough to be the favorite of Lord Luxon. And surely you are old enough to know that it is those closest to us who cause us most grief? I can assure you that once he has been reunited with Lord Luxon, he will not want to return with you."

Peter and Kate looked at each other, unsure of how to react to what the Tar Man was telling them. He was very convincing even though they knew he must be lying. Kate turned to Tom.

"Gideon would never go back to work for Lord Luxon, would he?"

An unfathomable look passed between the Tar Man and Tom. Tom shrugged his shoulders nervously.

"It's not for me to say. Lord Luxon saved his life. It is common knowledge."

"But he made him *steal* for him!" cried Peter.

"Only from those who stole from his master," said the Tar Man.

"That's not the point! He's a good man! He didn't *want* to steal!"

"You have a lot to learn about the way of the world, Master Schock. But this I will promise you: Your mechanism intrigues Lord Luxon and he has taken a fancy to it. If you will open up its secrets to us, I will take you to Gideon and you can advise him in person to turn his back on those who have his best interests at heart."

Peter looked from the Tar Man to Kate and back again. He suddenly felt out of his depth. What should they do? If they refused to go with the Tar Man, what would he do to Gideon— and to them, for that matter? But if they went with the Tar Man and pretended to know about the antigravity machine, could he be trusted to take them to Gideon?

"What do you think, Kate?" he asked.

"I . . . *think* we should go," she said doubtfully. "But you've got to take us to Gideon first."

"Agreed, Miss Dyer! Come, I shall take you to him directly."

The four of them walked up Drury Lane, the Tar Man striding

ahead with Tom at his side, his hand resting lightly on the boy's shoulder. Peter and Kate followed, Kate struggling to keep up in her cumbersome skirt. *We're caught in his web,* thought Peter, *but what choice do we have if we want to get Gideon back—or the machine for that matter?* His hands were clammy with fear. Tom had told them that in this part of London you would be lucky to walk fifty yards without having your life threatened at least once. And it was true, nearly everyone they passed looked as if they would knife you for a sixpence, but what set the Tar Man apart, Peter decided, was that he was clever. Too clever. When he looked at you, you had the feeling that he saw more than you wanted him to see.

Thick purple clouds now covered the city, and when forked lightning illuminated the sky overhead, the crack of thunder followed almost instantly. A warm breeze started to gust fiercely, heralding the imminent cloudburst. At the corner of Russell Street they heard the sound of hooves galloping toward them.

"Master Blueskin!"

They all looked up and saw a large man with a lantern jaw astride a black horse. He wore a snowy white wig and what the children now recognized as a footman's uniform.

"Lord Luxon requests that you return with all haste—Mr. Seymour has escaped."

"Escaped! How in damnation did he escape?"

"I do not know, sir. All the doors were locked and bolted when we entered the room."

The Tar Man gave a snort of exasperation.

"Must I oversee everything myself? Tell Lord Luxon that I will be with him within the half hour."

He turned to the children. Peter and Kate exchanged triumphant glances.

"We must make our way to St. James with all speed. Follow me."

"Actually," said Peter, "there's not much point now, if you don't mind . . ."

"I said follow me," repeated the Tar Man coolly. "Lord Luxon anticipates meeting you with pleasure."

"Another time, perhaps," said Kate, looking around to see who would be likely to help them if she screamed. "Tom?" She looked pleadingly at him.

Tom could not meet her gaze and looked at the ground. The Tar Man took first Peter's and then Kate's elbow in a viselike grip and dragged them up Drury Lane. Tom trailed after them, an expression of anguish and helplessness on his face. A few drops of rain started to splatter on their hot faces, and soon they were walking through a torrential downpour.

The Tar Man continued at such an energetic pace that Peter and Kate quickly became out of breath. Suddenly, as a wagon weighed down with barrels of ale rolled past, spraying them with mud to shoulder height, Kate cried out in pain and fell against the window of a milliners' shop. Peter felt the Tar Man's grip loosen as he was forced to stop. Kate was now slumped at the bottom of the wall, and tears were running down her cheeks.

"What's wrong?" Peter exclaimed, kneeling down next to her.

"It's my ankle." She winced. "I can't walk."

To his surprise, she put her arms around his neck and put her head on his shoulder farthest from the Tar Man. She whispered furiously in his ear, "There's nothing wrong with me. There's only one way out of this—we've got to blur."

Peter wanted to say that there was a fat chance of that happening and ask if she'd always been able to cry at will, but instead he turned to the Tar Man and said, "Could we stop for a moment? She must have twisted her ankle. I'm sure she'll be all right in a minute or two."

Water dripped from the corners of the Tar Man's hat onto his already damp shoulders. He scrutinized Kate's face, evidently concluding that her tears and pain were genuine. *Well done, Kate!* thought Peter. *Oscar!*

"Tie this round your ankle, Miss Dyer," said the Tar Man, offering her his cotton handkerchief. "But kindly do not take too long to recover yourself, else we shall all drown."

He stood between the children and the street, legs apart and with his back to them, and turned up the collar of his jacket. Tom stood, looking vacantly at the window full of gorgeous hats decorated with ribbons and flowers and fruit, his eyebrows knitted together as if debating some weighty problem.

Kate had closed her eyes. Crouching down next to her, Peter did the same, trying unsuccessfully to ignore the voice in his head that was telling him that this was not going to work and that he would never be able to blur at will under these circumstances— if he ever could again, for that matter. Nothing happened, of course, but when he opened his eyes only a few seconds later, he realized that Kate was indeed beginning to blur—he had the vivid impression that she was dissolving in the rain.

"Blueskin!" he heard Tom cry in alarm.

Peter gulped, rigid with fright at the thought of what the Tar Man would do to him if Kate vanished and he did not. Out of the corner of his eye he was aware of the Tar Man turning his head to look at them. Careful not to touch her, Peter held out his hands toward Kate as if warming them in front of a fire. Was it wishful thinking that he started to feel himself sucked in? Now the Tar Man was kneeling down in the dirt next to them, staring at Kate with an expression of awe and fascination and terror. Now he was reaching out a trembling hand toward Kate. Peter took a giant leap of faith and somehow caught hold of this ineffable force, as if diving toward it, jumping without a parachute. The rain was thundering on the pavement like a drumbeat and seemed to synchronize with the fluorescent spirals that passed in front of him and through him. . . . The Tar Man's anguished cries reached him as though from a great distance.

"How is it done, confound them? As heaven is my witness, I will learn the secret if I hang for it!"

When Peter finally opened his eyes, feeling a little sick and dizzy and still crouched down on the ground, he saw black cabs and neon signs and crowds of theatergoers spilling out of Drury Lane Theatre onto the pavements. He laughed out loud in triumph.

"I did it!" he cried. "I can do it!"

Kate had stood up and was looking down at him, a broad grin on her face.

"You see! I *told* you that you could do it if you tried!"

"It's not a question of trying," Peter replied. "You just have to let go."

"Whatever," said Kate, and she pulled him up from the pavement. Her touch was peculiar—not quite right somehow—but there was no time to dwell on it.

"Let's get away from here before we snap back again," he said.

They started to jog through the crowded streets. No one seemed to notice them, or if they did they must have thought the children had come from a fancy-dress party or that their slightly watery appearance was due to the orange streetlights or one gin and tonic too many.

"It's getting harder to stay," said Peter, clutching at his side. It felt a little like getting a stitch, except there was a draining feeling too, as if somebody had pulled the plug out. "Do you feel the same, Kate?"

There were real tears in her eyes this time.

"Resist it as long as you can," she said. "We've got to work out how to beat it."

We can't just leave Gideon in the lurch, Peter thought, but did not say as much to Kate.

Soon they arrived at Covent Garden Piazza and, another century tugging at them unbearably, they stopped, exhausted, to concentrate their energies on straining against the mysterious force. They stood on the edge of a large circle of people cheering and clapping in time as a man in black leather underpants juggled with three live electric chainsaws.

"He's certainly got bottom," panted Peter.

"Hasn't he just?" replied a Japanese girl who was standing next to them. She had long bright green hair that shone like silk. She glanced over at them and said in an American accent, "Why are you so wet? I don't recall it raining." She looked back at the juggler and then, in a double take, immediately back at the children. "And how come I can see through you—are you part of the act? . . . Oh my God!"

The green-haired girl began to scream hysterically, pointing her finger accusingly at the children. The juggler lost his concentration and dropped one of his electric saws. More and more people spotted the children and, like a wave at a football match, started to scream and point in horror at Peter and Kate. The juggler's other two chainsaws crashed to the ground, and all three of them jiggered around and around as if possessed by an evil spirit. Several tourists trained their video recorders on the bizarre apparition.

Peter spoke into Kate's ear. "I'm slipping. I can't hold on much longer."

Kate looked at him and sighed resignedly.

"Okay," she panted.

By the look on her face Peter guessed she was in as much pain as he was. In an instant they were back in the rain, and forked lightning streaked across the sky illuminating a Covent Garden that was at once newer and older than the one they had left. Before they had time to recover themselves, a fine carriage pulled by a pair of chestnut mares drew up next to them, the door flew open, and Parson Ledbury got out, followed by a tall man whose coloring and features declared him to be without doubt the brother of the Honorable Mrs. Byng.

"Upon my word, where did you spring from?" asked the parson. "The piazza was empty one minute past. But it is good to see you! We have been tearing around the city like a band of demented monkeys trying to find you."

"Gideon!" exclaimed Peter as he saw his friend emerge from the carriage behind Sir Richard Picard. He was covered from head to foot in soot except where he had rubbed his eyes, so that he looked like an underfed panda.

"Lord Luxon's study has a broad chimney," he said by way of explanation. "When I heard where you had gone, I feared the worst. Thank God that you are safe."

"Miss Dyer, Master Schock," said Sir Richard. "I am delighted to make your acquaintance. But you are soaked to the skin! Come, let us return to Lincoln's Inn Fields, where we can get you warm and dry. Then tomorrow morning—when you have recovered from your adventure—perhaps you could tell me how it is that I saw you appear out of thin air in the blink of an eye?"

SEVENTEEN

Queen Charlotte's Promise

*In which Inspector Wheeler's exchange with Dr. Pirretti
takes an unexpected turn, George III lays his hands on
Jack, and Kate resorts to desperate measures*

Standing by the kitchen window, Mrs. Dyer pushed back a stray
lock of hair with a trembling hand. She watched her husband run
to the Land Rover and heard the screech of brakes as he swerved
to avoid the press pack who had been gathering in a ragged line
since early morning on the other side of the stream.

Detective Inspector Wheeler had sent over a constable to stand
at the gate. The journalists had been trying to get round him with
doughnuts and mugs of steaming coffee from their vacuum flasks,

but, so far at least, the cheerful policeman had succeeded in keeping them out of the farm.

Mrs. Dyer looked across the room at the Christmas tree decorated by Kate's own hand the morning that Peter Schock had come into all their lives, and then she glanced down again at the headline that covered half the front page of the newspaper.

GHOSTS IN COVENT GARDEN

Underneath the headline there were five color photographs that depicted Peter and Kate, hazy but perfectly recognizable, standing in the crowds in Covent Garden Piazza. They were wearing mud-spattered eighteenth-century costume, and with each successive picture they were gradually fading from view. In the final image a Japanese girl with bright green hair was screaming in horror, her eyes fixed on the empty space where Peter and Kate had been a second before. The caption underneath read: "Going, Going, Gone . . ."

How pale and tired she looks, thought Mrs. Dyer. *Almost as if she's in pain.* Then Kate's mother reread the newspaper article for the tenth time that morning:

Who are they? What are they? Are we looking at a hoax? Or could these images be the most convincing evidence to date of the existence of ghosts?

Hundreds of tourists in Covent Garden Piazza witnessed the astounding disappearance, apparently into thin air, of a girl and a boy dressed in outlandish historical costume.

Caught by a tourist's video camera, could these baffling images be portraits of Peter Schock and Kate Dyer, who disappeared from a NASA-funded laboratory in Derbyshire seven days ago? Recent photographs of the children, below, reveal a striking resemblance to these disturbing apparitions. Detective Inspector Wheeler, who is in charge of the case that has seen over two hundred police officers combing the Derbyshire countryside in search of the children, was unavailable for comment last night.

Mrs. Dyer stroked the photograph of Kate in her Year 7 photograph. Kate looked younger than her age in the picture. Her hair was tied back in two neat plaits and her school tie all crooked.

"Oh, Katie," she said. "I don't know how we'll do it, but we'll get you home somehow, my darling. I promise. I promise."

One of the security guards at the NCRDM laboratory, whose own children had often played with Kate and Sam at the farm, smuggled Dr. Dyer into the building without the press or the police being aware of his arrival.

"How are you doing? And the family?" he asked kindly. He had a lot of respect for Dr. Dyer, and it didn't seem right that such a man and his family should have to go through such suffering.

"We're all coping—in our own fashion. Sam's probably taking it hardest, even though he and Kate get on each other's nerves half the time. Kate's always been the sensible one. We all think that if anyone is going to come through this she will. Anyway, we haven't cancelled Christmas . . . not yet at least."

The security guard escorted Dr. Dyer to his office, where he was surprised to find Detective Inspector Wheeler in full flow. He had expected him to be in London, interviewing witnesses in Covent Garden. Presumably the inspector felt that he would get more answers here. And perhaps he was right, thought Dr. Dyer. He stood for a moment, silent and unnoticed in the doorway, listening to the policeman.

". . . and by lunchtime you can be sure that some bright young journalist will have managed to get hold of the pictures of the children floating above the supermarket car park. The editors of every newspaper in the land will be rubbing their hands together with glee! At last—proof that ghosts exist! But, you see, I don't think you believe in ghosts any more than I do. You know something. I am sure of it. And, with respect, Dr. Pirretti, American citizen or not, senior NASA official or not, if you don't change your attitude—and fast—I have a mind to charge you with police obstruction."

Anita Pirretti sat opposite the policeman, gripping a china teacup so hard that she was in danger of snapping off its handle. She had been through enough stressful moments in her life, however, to know how to appear relaxed and in control even when, on the inside, she felt about to crumble into a thousand pieces. She also wondered if she was coming down with something—these headaches and the peculiar ringing in her ears had been getting worse and worse ever since her arrival in Derbyshire.

"Please believe me," she said, taking a deep, calming breath, "when I tell you that I am sorry—truly sorry—that I am not in a position to give you the answers that you seek. It's true that some of the work undertaken in this laboratory is of a . . . sensitive nature—but I can assure you that even if I were to give you a detailed explanation of the purpose of our research here, it would not help you to solve your case."

Dr. Pirretti saw Dr. Dyer in the doorway and flashed him a brief smile.

"Ah, your partner in crime," exclaimed Detective Inspector Wheeler, standing up and pulling up a chair for Dr. Dyer. "Now I ask you, Dr. Pirretti, is this flushed and excited expression one that you might expect to find on the face of a father who has just seen a photograph, allegedly of the ghost of his child?"

"You go too far!" protested Dr. Pirretti.

"It's all right, Anita," said Dr. Dyer. "Inspector Wheeler, I've already told you that I don't believe in ghosts."

"Well, I am afraid that the parents of Peter Schock are not so sure what they believe after seeing this morning's newspapers. Perhaps you might have some explanation that might ease their anguish? I talked to them this morning, and to say that they are in deep distress is an understatement. Have you no grain of comfort which you would be prepared to toss their way?"

Kate's father could not look the inspector in the eye. Guilt and sorrow etched themselves across his face like cracks through ice.

Dr. Pirretti watched, in alarm, as Dr. Dyer responded to the policeman.

"I'd like you to tell Peter's parents that . . . that . . . they must not give up hope. All is not lost."

"What on earth is going on here?" shouted the inspector, banging his fist on the table. "Tell me what you know, damn it!"

An uneasy silence fell upon the room. Sergeant Chadwick cleared his throat nervously. His boss did not have what you might call an easygoing temperament, and by the look on the inspector's face, a storm, if not a hurricane, was brewing up behind those bushy eyebrows.

All of a sudden Dr. Pirretti let out a low moan and clapped her hands to both sides of her head as though she were trying to protect herself from a loud noise. She had turned very pale. Staggering forward a few steps, she swayed from side to side in the middle of the room. Inspector Wheeler caught her before she crashed to the ground, unconscious.

"Sergeant Chadwick," he shouted. "Call for an ambulance!"

The King's messenger arrived at Lincoln's Inn Fields shortly before seven o'clock in the morning. By the time Peter and Kate emerged for breakfast, vainly trying to work out how they were going to explain the blurring episode to Sir Richard, the whole household was already in a flurry of activity. Parson Ledbury, who was eating a second plate of scrambled eggs and deviled kidneys in the sunny, flower-filled dining room, explained the cause of all the excitement. It appeared that Queen Charlotte, who was due to give birth to her second child in barely a month's time, had, owing to the hot weather, decided to quit the city for the country. The royal couple would leave London the following day, and so the King would be unable to receive the party at the Court of St. James on the date that had previously been agreed to. However, since Sir Richard was a dear friend of the King's favorite, Lord Bute, and since the King and Queen were fond of children, Their Majesties would be pleased to receive Sir Richard informally that very afternoon at Buckingham House—along with his nephews and his guests from Derbyshire. Besides, the King let it be known that as he did not wish to reinstate the public ceremony of the laying on of hands to cure the King's evil, he would prefer to receive the Byng family in a private setting.

Gideon, due to his inferior social position, was not, of course, invited, and in any case, the parson told the children, he had left early that morning on an urgent errand. On the other hand, much to Peter's dismay and Kate's amusement, Sir Richard insisted that they come to Buckingham House to meet the King and Queen. They could thank the Honorable Mrs. Byng for their invitation. In a letter to Sir Richard his sister had explained how the children were of a good family—branches of which, Master Schock had told her, were to be found both in Germany and Scotland. It would be a comfort for the Queen if Master Schock could converse with her in her native German.

"How much German *can* you speak?" asked Kate once the parson had cleared his plate and gone upstairs to have his new wig fitted.

"I can only say one thing: *Sprechen Sie Englisch?*"

"What does that mean, then?"

"'Do you speak English?'"

Kate snorted with laughter. "That'll teach you to make stuff up! You're going to be in big trouble."

"Thanks, Kate. That's just what I need."

"Don't look so worried! I mean, they're hardly going to throw you into the deepest, darkest dungeon for not being able to speak German!"

"Oh, yeah? How do you know?"

Hired by Sir Richard at the last minute and at great expense, a small army of hairdressers, seamstresses, shoemakers, and wig-makers were let loose on the household to ensure that everyone, from the eldest to the youngest, looked the part on this most important occasion. On the advice of the tailor, Parson Ledbury's ample stomach was squeezed into a gentleman's corset to show off his new waistcoat to the best advantage. It was double-breasted and made from cherry red silk generously trimmed, with gold lace and two rows of gold buttons. The waistcoat was a triumph, but the parson hated fuss of any kind and was soon in a terrible temper. He could be heard roaring at the wretched servants through the closed door of his dressing room.

"Damn your eyes, sir, not so tight! Where is the point in cutting a fine figure for the King if one has not breath enough to speak?"

Finally, when all the preening and polishing and primping had finally stopped, they set off for Buckingham House in two carriages. The width of Kate's court dress meant that she had to have one side of the carriage all to herself. Like the parson's, her stays had been pulled so tight it was impossible for her to take a deep breath or to slouch. Peter, Sidney, and Jack sat opposite her. No one spoke—everyone was too excited at the prospect of being presented to the King and Queen. Peter had no idea what to expect, but the image of the Red Queen in *Alice in Wonderland* saying "Off with his head!" kept coming to mind whenever he thought what he should do if Queen Charlotte decided to speak German to him. He caught Kate smirking at his legs, which, in truth, looked very shapely in spotless white tights and high-heeled buckled shoes. Sir Richard's manservant had declared that Peter's evil-smelling sneakers were unacceptable attire for a young gentleman and had carried them at arm's length out of the room.

Sidney was sporting a new set of wooden false teeth, hastily fitted that morning by a so-called operator dentist in Mayfair. His tongue constantly explored the contours of this foreign object. It was taking all of Sidney's willpower not to pluck them out and throw them through the carriage window. However, the sight of Kate took Sidney's mind off his discomfort. His eyes were forever sliding over to her, taking in the ringlets that framed her heart-shaped face, the large gray eyes, the white skin lightly speckled with freckles, the silk gown in pale forget-me-not blue that set off Kate's red hair to perfection. Kate pretended not to notice, but Peter did notice, and he found Sidney's attention intensely irritating. He kept shoving him hard with his elbow but it had no effect at all. Sidney did not even try to shove him back.

Young Jack was more interested in what was going on outside. Every so often Sidney had to haul him back into the carriage by his breeches, for he was leaning dangerously far out of the window. It was worth it, though, for Jack was the only one to catch sight of the Venetian ambassador's enormously long, gilded coach, which disappeared into Whitehall like some glorious golden stretch limo. Sidney had heard tell of this marvel, but by the time he looked, it was too late.

The party was shown into a high-ceilinged drawing room that overlooked the gardens of the recently acquired Buckingham House. The room was sparsely furnished and there was a smell of beeswax and sun-heated carpet. Several gilt armchairs upholstered in maroon velvet were carefully placed around the room—although nobody showed any inclination to sit down—and there were fine rosewood commodes, mirrors with ornate golden frames, and two landscape paintings that depicted St. Paul's Cathedral and the Thames. Kate felt sure she recognized one of these paintings from a school trip to an art gallery in London. In pride of place stood a French longcase clock, at least seven feet high and fashioned from precious wood and intricately worked gold that gleamed richly in the soft light. King George III was fond of timepieces. When, on the stroke of three, George and Charlotte entered the room, Buckingham House echoed to the sound of a dozen clocks chiming the hour. The party had already been waiting expectantly for ten minutes. During this time Peter's stomach had started to rumble and Jack had got an attack of the hiccups. Jack's hiccups, which were unaffected by a strong thump between the shoulders from his elder brother, were miraculously cured by the shock of seeing the King of England walking toward him.

Sir Richard introduced the party to Their Majesties one by one, and the children bowed, or in Kate's case, curtsied, as they had been taught. Prince George, only a year old, was carried into the room by Elizabeth, Countess of Pembroke, one of the Queen's ladies-in-waiting. The King, in a scarlet jacket trimmed with gold, worn over a snowy white shirt and breeches, was not a handsome man, but he had a kindly, fleshy face with prominent pale eyes, thick blond eyebrows, and apple-red cheeks. He spoke in a clipped, abrupt fashion. Queen Charlotte was eight months pregnant but still wore court dress. She was a quietly pretty woman and was flushed with the heat. Her elaborate hairstyle was excessively high, and her ivory satin skirts were excessively wide. With all her younger brothers and sisters, Kate knew how tired and uncomfortable and hot a mother becomes in the last few weeks before she gives birth. It was no wonder, then, that in an outfit like that, Queen Charlotte sounded out of breath and was forever fanning herself with her beautiful painted fan.

Peter, who had presumed that King George and Queen Charlotte would be at least as old as his parents, was astonished when he saw the royal couple. Despite their regal bearing, their grand clothes, and the number of pearls and diamonds and gold buttons that adorned the royal couple, George and Charlotte seemed far too young to be the rulers of a great country and its colonies. They could be college students! Even Gideon and Hannah looked older! Peter took an instant liking to the King, whose manner was easy and natural. Queen Charlotte was a little more reserved, but her lady-in-waiting bent down to talk with Jack to put him at his ease. Soon the grown-ups were talking comfortably about this and that while Sidney, Peter, and Kate stood and listened politely or watched the baby prince totter from one pair of legs to another. Kate held out a finger for the toddler to hold. He grasped it with a hot, sticky hand and Kate pulled a silly face at him. He stared back with wide blue eyes and for a moment Kate thought he was going to cry, but he laughed instead, and for a moment the King and Queen looked pleased and proud. Suddenly Kate felt a pang of sadness, for she remembered learning that George III grew to heartily dislike his eldest son and that although he lived to a great age, the King died mad and alone. Tears sprang to her eyes and she thought what a terrible thing it was to know what was going to happen. She wondered, if she were to tell the King what the future could hold, whether he might somehow be able to alter the course of his life. But she decided it was not her place to say anything, and blinked away her tears.

Sir Richard shared George III's enthusiasm for clocks, and the King promised to show him a new acquisition sent to him by an horologist in Effingham, in Surrey. It was, he said, a quite remarkable piece—he had never seen anything like it. The clock was set in a gold bracelet, to be worn, if Sir Richard could imagine such a thing, on the wrist! The clock face was scarcely larger than a gold sovereign, and the inner workings were nothing short of miraculous! The King was anxious to know who had the skill to make such an impressive timepiece and had sent word to the horologist to track down its maker with all speed.

Meanwhile, every time Queen Charlotte opened her mouth

to speak, Peter looked fixedly at the floor, terrified that she would start speaking in German. Happily, she did not appear to be taking any notice of him whatsoever, and Peter began to breathe a little easier. In fact, he was beginning to feel a little bored, not to mention hungry, as they had not eaten lunch for fear of dirtying their finery, and he was becoming more aware how exceedingly hot and stuffy it was. He could feel the sweat trickling down his back. *Stupid tights and breeches and jackets! If this is a summer costume,* he thought, *what do they wear when it's cold?* He tugged at his collar, and when he looked up he found that Queen Charlotte had caught his eye and was smiling at him.

"It is very warm this afternoon, is it not, Master Schock? Shall we take a turn around the garden? There may be a little breeze, and we shall perhaps feel cooler under the shade of the trees."

Tongue-tied, Peter nodded violently.

"A capital idea," said King George. "Let us move out into the garden."

They walked together around and around in a huddled group under the spreading branches of some large trees. A small troop of dignified footmen in curled and powdered wigs followed at their heels. Kate thought that from the house they must have looked liked a small flock of sheep whom the footmen were failing to guide into an invisible enclosure.

Parson Ledbury told the King about their meeting with Erasmus Darwin in Lichfield and how Dr. Samuel Johnson's mother had been one of his patients.

"The young Dr. Johnson suffered from the King's evil just as my poor nephew, here. His mother sent him to London to be touched by Her Majesty, Queen Anne in the hope that his condition might be improved. And who knows if Dr. Johnson would have become the illustrious man of letters he is today had she not done so? Master Jack's mother, the Honorable Mrs. Byng, who is my cousin, would be eternally grateful to Your Majesty if you would consent to touch her own son."

King George listened and nodded and then bent over and lifted young Jack high into the air.

"Dr. Johnson," the King commented to Jack, "is a devilishly clever fellow. I have a copy of his *Dictionary* in my library. Though I admit I have never read it. Have you?"

The King supported the little boy in the crook of his arm. Jack shook his head slowly.

"Neither my grandfather, nor my great-grandfather," King George continued, addressing himself to the parson, "favored this kind of ceremony, although I know that Queen Anne and King Charles II touched many thousands who suffered from scrofula. I am not in the habit of laying on hands to cure the sick, but on this occasion I should be happy to oblige you if it would console his mother. Perhaps you, Parson Ledbury, would say a prayer."

The King put the boy down and there, on the grass beneath the trees, he placed his square pink hands onto Jack's blond head. Everyone followed the Queen's lead and lowered their heads while the parson prayed that if it be the Lord's will Jack's affliction might be cured.

When the impromptu ceremony was over, Jack, who had been

looking very solemn, turned to the King and Queen and on a signal from the parson bowed low and said, "I am much obliged to Your Majesties. . . . Pray accept a small gift which I have brought to ex—ex—"

"Express my gratitude," prompted Sir Richard.

". . . express my gratitude."

Then, reaching into his pocket, Jack drew out a small muslin bag tied with ribbon. The King took the bag and looked inside.

"Upon my word—seeds! Are you a gardener, my little fellow?"

"I am, Your Highness. They are seeds from my biggest cabbage. Mama says I grow the best cabbages in Derbyshire. The rabbits are fond of them too, and are grown very fat and greedy. It is most vexing!"

"If I were not King, Master Jack, there is nothing in the world I should rather do than grow cabbages. I am certain that the rabbits are vexatious, but at least they will teach you how to defend what you hold dear—which is a valuable lesson. However, if the problem becomes insurmountable, you must send word to me and I shall send a company of guards to Derbyshire to help you beat them down."

Jack beamed a huge smile of pleasure.

As the afternoon wore on, everyone sensed that the meeting was coming to an end. The parson had entertained everyone with a description of their encounters with Ned Porter and the footpads, and everyone had added details. But now the King and Sir Richard had started to talk about the growing crime rate in

London and the conversation had taken a serious turn. Peter was standing to one side of the group and overheard something about Lord Luxon. He was about to ask Kate what had been said when, to his horror, he saw Queen Charlotte advancing toward him.

"I understand that you have family in Germany, Master Schock," she said. "*Wie ich mich danach sehne, nach Preussen zurückzukehren. Wo lebt denn Ihre Familie nun, Meister Schock? Wann kamen Sie erstmals nach England?*"

Peter froze. He opened his mouth and closed it again. Queen Charlotte continued to look at him expectantly, a kindly smile on her face. There was only one thing for it. He was going to have to tell the truth.

"I was lying when I said I had family in Germany, Your Highness."

The Queen was taken aback. "But why would you lie about such a thing?"

The Queen pronounced her *W*s like *V*s in just the same way as Margrit, and suddenly Peter remembered eating meatballs with Margrit and his father on his last evening at home. He pushed the thought away.

"Because I didn't think Mrs. Byng would believe me if I told the truth."

"And what is the truth, Master Schock?"

"We were chasing a dog when somehow we collided with an antigravity machine—please don't ask what one of those is because I don't know. Anyway, somehow it carried Kate and me back two and a half centuries to 1763. Then someone stole it. . . . We belong in the twenty-first century and we can't get back—although I should be grateful if you wouldn't tell anybody."

The Queen looked at him without replying and then started to laugh. She moved away, still laughing, and Peter heard her comment to her lady-in-waiting, "What an amusing child, Elizabeth. How I envy him the freedom to imagine his world."

Everyone had started moving back to the house, and Sir Richard and the parson thanked Their Majesties for their generosity. Peter noticed the Queen studying him closely. The party walked back through the drawing room, where they took their leave of the King and Queen. At the last minute Queen Charlotte called Peter back and spoke to him quietly at the door.

"I believe you were serious, were you not?"

"I was, Your Highness," Peter replied.

"In which case, Master Schock, you must call on me if there is anything I can do to aid you in your difficult situation. You may be assured of my discretion."

"*You* would help *me*?" asked Peter.

"With all my heart," replied Queen Charlotte. "I know what it is to be far from home and unable to return."

Sir Richard ordered the coachmen to pick them up in Pall Mall so that he could take his visitors on a tour of St. James's Park. Peter wanted to catch a moment alone with Kate so that he could tell her what Queen Charlotte had said, but as Sidney was sticking to her like glue, he walked on ahead with Jack. They walked across the sun-bleached long grass past deer and chestnut-colored cows, along the canal where, according to Sir Richard, James I used to keep crocodiles, and then they continued on to Rosamund's Pond. It was here that Jack saw his first pelican. He was spellbound by the bird and refused to be dragged away. Peter sat down in the grass and absentmindedly watched the reflections on the water. Suddenly, out of the corner of his eye, he saw Sidney bearing down on him, a thunderous look on his face. Peter quickly stood up, convinced that Sidney was going to hit him—which he did, or at any rate he shoved Peter backward so hard that he staggered half into the pond. The pelican took off in fright.

"I am mortified beyond belief by what I have just learned! That a person of such beauty and quality is to be condemned to a union with a poor fish like you! It is nothing less than a tragedy."

Sidney looked down his nose at Peter, who stood half in and half out of Rosamund's Pond.

"What?" exclaimed Peter, too bemused to be angry.

"You frightened it away!" shouted Jack.

"Kate is a lady. You, sir, are an ass," continued Sidney, ignoring his little brother. "I will do everything in my power to persuade her to turn her back on this ludicrous arrangement."

With nostrils flaring and a final toss of his head, Sidney flounced off to walk alone. Peter decided he had better remove his foot from the water. Green weed clung to his white stocking, and his beautiful buckled shoe was stuck in mud at the bottom of the pond. He bent over and pulled it out of the water with a squelch. When he stood up, he saw Kate looking rather sheepish.

"What was that all about?" he demanded.

"I couldn't think what else to do! Sidney's been pestering me for days. . . . I told him we're engaged—that it was all arranged by our parents when we were babies."

Peter looked up to heaven. "Great," he said. "I've just dug my way out of one hole with Queen Charlotte, and now I've got some more playacting to do." He suddenly looked a little more cheerful. "Mind you, I don't mind being one up on Sidney. He really does have it coming to him. Come on, the future Mrs. Schock, you had better take my arm."

"Steady on," said Kate, stepping to one side. "There's no need to go that far."

Parson Ledbury and Sir Richard were a long way ahead by this time. The parson stopped to bellow at them all to hurry up if they wanted to see the Court of St. James's most recent resident, a diplomatic gift to the Queen, being taken for its afternoon walk. A baby elephant, perhaps eight feet high, presently came into view carrying its Indian keeper. It was escorted by two soldiers. Everyone save Sidney, who wished to know what the elephant ate before he went any nearer, walked up to the animal and soon found themselves the object of its soft and probing trunk. Not to be outdone by Peter, who was feeding it grass, Sidney planted himself stiffly in front of the elephant and braced himself as the animal gently explored the brass buttons on his jacket and his tightly curled hair. The barber's generous use of powder irritated the delicate lining of the elephant's trunk, causing it to have a sudden and violent sneezing attack. Sidney leaped behind a tree in fright and had to suffer the indignity of having the whole party, but especially Peter, laughing at him. Sir Richard tactfully suggested that they should bid farewell to the elephant and return home. However, as it was a hot day, he should be pleased to buy everyone a drink first.

"A can of milk, ladies! A can of red cow's milk, sir!"

At the Whitehall end of the park, close to the ranks of sedan chair-men waiting for customers, a pretty girl stood selling fresh milk. Sir Richard bought them all a china mug of frothy milk, still warm from the cow. Peter had one sip and spat it out in disgust. Sir Richard noticed and seemed mildly offended.

"I'm sorry, sir," explained Peter. "I normally only drink chilled milk."

"Chilled milk, Master Schock? I cannot understand you."

Sir Richard motioned to Peter and Kate to approach him. He spoke quietly to them.

"My sister's good opinion of you both has led me to welcome you into my house and to present you to the King and Queen of England. I hope that you will feel able to honor my trust in you by explaining to me your disturbing appearance in Covent Garden. I should also be curious to learn the reason for the concern on the Queen's face after she spoke to you, Master Schock. Pray meet me in my study at six o' clock. I shall also ask Mr. Seymour, if he is returned, and the good parson to be present at our interview."

Both children gulped and looked at each other.

"Of course, Sir Richard," said Peter. "We will be there at six."

"Yes," said Kate. "Me too. Six o'clock."

"What did you tell Queen Charlotte?" whispered Kate furiously in Peter's ear as Sir Richard walked away.

When Dr. Dyer came to visit Dr. Pirretti in the hospital that afternoon, he was surprised to find Sergeant Chadwick sitting outside her room.

"Surely a police guard is not necessary?" he exclaimed. "Dr. Pirretti is hardly a criminal!"

"Detective Inspector Wheeler's orders, sir," Sergeant Chadwick replied.

"How is she?"

"She seems as right as rain if you ask me. But they're going to keep her in for observation overnight."

Dr. Dyer tapped softly on the door and walked in. Dr. Pirretti lay flat on the bed, her head turned toward the window.

"Andrew?" she called out.

"Yes," replied Dr. Dyer, wondering how she knew it was him. *She must have seen my reflection in the window,* he thought.

"Andrew. Tim's machine . . . the time differential. It's directly proportional to the quantity of antigravity generated."

"I beg your pardon?"

"The time differential produced is directly proportional to the quantity of antigravity generated."

"You mean you think we could control how far backward in time the antigravity machine could travel? Well, it's a nice idea . . . But I thought you were supposed to be resting. How are you feeling now?"

He walked around to the other side of the bed and looked at her. She seemed to be fast asleep and breathing deeply.

"Anita?" he said softly. "Anita?"

She did not reply, and after looking at her peaceful face for a couple of minutes Dr. Dyer tiptoed out.

"She's asleep," he said to Sergeant Chadwick as he made his way to the lift.

LORD LUXON BADE ME ENTER WITH ALL THE WARMTH AND SOLICITUDE OF A LONG-LOST FRIEND. WE SAT IN HIS LIBRARY, AMIDST HIS BELOVED BOOKS, WHOSE COMPANY I KNEW HE WOULD RATHER SEEK THAN THAT OF MOST OF HIS ACQUAINTANCES, DID THEY BUT KNOW IT. A SHAFT OF SUNLIGHT PENETRATED THE DARKENED ROOM SO THAT HE SAT IN A GOLDEN CIRCLE, RESPLENDENT IN BLUE SILK, HIS STANCE AND EXPRESSION BELYING EVERYTHING I KNEW HIM, IN MY HEART OF HEARTS, NOW TO BE. YET FACE-TO-FACE WITH HIM WHO HAD SAVED MY LIFE AND GIVEN ME FOOD, SHELTER, A POSITION IN SOCIETY, AND MORE— HIS TRUST—I FELT MY RESOLVE TO BE SHAKEN. WHO WAS I TO STAND IN JUDGEMENT ON HIM? I FELT TONGUE-TIED AND LONGED TO ESCAPE MY SEAT AND STRIDE ABOUT THE ROOM TO EASE MY AGITATION.

"HOW I HAVE MISSED YOUR PRUDISH, DISAPPROVING STARE," HE SAID TO ME AT LAST, SMILING INDULGENTLY AT MY AWKWARDNESS.

"I CAN SEE THAT YOU ARE ANGRY, GIDEON," HE CONTINUED, "AND I DO NOT BLAME YOU, GIVEN THE MANNER OF YOUR ARRIVAL YESTERDAY. I AM HAPPY INDEED THAT YOU ARE RETURNED TODAY OF YOUR OWN FREE WILL—ALTHOUGH I CANNOT DENY THAT I AM PUZZLED AS TO YOUR MOTIVES."

HIS EASY CHARM DISARMED ME—AS IT OFTEN DID—AND I

DROVE MY NAILS INTO THE PALM OF MY HAND AS I SCREWED UP MY COURAGE TO TELL HIM THAT I HAD TURNED MY BACK ON MY OLD LIFE FOREVER AND WOULD NOT FOR THE WORLD BE SUCKED BACK INTO IT.

"MY LORD, I HAVE COME HERE TO BEG YOU TO BE MERCIFUL AS I KNOW YOU CAN BE—NOT TOWARD MYSELF BUT TO MY HALF BROTHER, JOSHUA, AND TO TWO YOUNG FRIENDS WHO ARE A LONG WAY FROM HOME."

"MERCIFUL? AM I THEN SOME BLACK-HEARTED TYRANT BENT ON CRUELTY? WHAT HAVE I DONE TO YOU THAT YOU SPEAK OF ME IN THIS WAY? WHERE IS THE EVIL IN OFFERING YOUR HALF BROTHER A POSITION IN THIS HOUSE? AND WAS IT I WHO TOOK THE MAGIC BOX FROM THE CHILDREN? SURELY I AM NOT SO WICKED AS YOU WOULD PORTRAY ME, MY FRIEND."

WHETHER THE PAIN ON HIS FACE WAS REAL OR CONTRIVED, I FELT MYSELF AT THAT MOMENT TO BE THE MOST UNGRATEFUL WRETCH THAT EVER BREATHED.

—*THE LIFE AND TIMES OF GIDEON SEYMOUR, CUTPURSE AND GENTLEMAN, 1792*

EIGHTEEN

Into the Net

*In which the children answer some difficult questions
and Gideon walks into Lord Luxon's net*

When Peter and Kate had finished speaking, there was an awful silence. Sir Richard's study was small and stuffy, and the resounding *tick-tock* of his brass carriage clock seemed to reverberate around the room until it pulsed like a heartbeat.

Suddenly Sir Richard leaned forward, his fine-featured face strained and concerned. He exclaimed gravely, "Can you swear that what the children have told us is true, Mr. Seymour?"

Peter and Kate stared at the carpet, subdued and ashamed that they had concealed the truth from those who had shown them such kindness.

"I can swear to it," said Gideon. "I witnessed their arrival. I saw the machine appear out of thin air on the slopes of a valley not five leagues from Baslow Hall. The children were attached to the device by I know not what force. After some little time had elapsed, the nature of this force was suddenly altered. Attraction was replaced by repulsion and the machine appeared to hurl Master Peter and Mistress Kate high into the air and onto the hard ground. At first I feared that they were dead. I can also swear that they do not understand how this astonishing journey has come to pass. All they ask is that they may return home to their waiting families."

"So you have *no* recollection of your passage through time?" asked Sir Richard.

Peter and Kate shook their heads.

"And this capacity you have discovered for . . . *blurring*, as you call it—does it happen spontaneously, of its own accord, or can you control it?"

"Both," replied Kate.

"Although it's been a few days since either of us blurred without intending to," said Peter, "as if we're . . . I don't know what the word is . . . stabilizing, settling into 1763. But we've been finding it easier to blur when we want to—Kate especially—"

"The only trouble," Kate said, interrupting, "is that once we've blurred back to our time, we can only stay a few minutes. We get pulled back to your time. It actually hurts to resist."

"Would you say that it is the machine that is pulling you back?" asked Sir Richard.

"Ooh. I'd not thought of that," replied Kate. "I wish my dad were here to ask. I don't know. Maybe."

"Do you consider that you have need of the machine in order to return to the twenty-first century permanently?"

"We don't know that either—but I think it's our best bet if we can't blur home."

Sir Richard leaned back in his chair and smoothed the hair back from his temples.

"Astonishing," he said. "Quite astonishing. How infinitely mysterious life is. Well, my dear Parson, what do *you* make of all this?"

"Sir, my mind struggles to make any sense whatsoever of all that I have heard. On first meeting Master Schock and Mistress Kate I fancied I detected a certain . . . foreignness . . . about their attire and manner of speech, but upon my word, I have never heard a more astounding thing in my life! However, I pride myself on being a good judge of character, and I am of the opinion that these children do not intend to mislead us. Else we are all demented and are merely deluding ourselves that we are in good Sir Richard's study talking about journeys through time."

"If you like," offered Kate, "we—or I—could try to blur now."

She looked at Peter, who shook his head. "I'm not sure that I could right now."

Kate stood up with a swish of her blue silk dress. She closed her eyes and held herself very still. Peter was suddenly aware how used he already was to the idea of blurring. Seeing the look on his host's face, he was reminded just how weird it must seem. He shuffled uncomfortably in his seat and observed the reactions of Sir Richard and the parson. Peter knew without even needing to look at Kate that she was beginning to blur. He was becoming attuned enough to the process to sense the ripples in time caused by Kate's passage from one century to another. He reached out his hand toward her, and instinctively he knew that, just like in Covent Garden, Kate could have pulled him back with her. It would almost have been like hitching a lift. He drew back his hand. Now when he looked across at her, she was already becoming fuzzy around the edges. Soon she was transparent, like an image printed on gauze, and soon after that she was gone. The parson crossed himself while beads of sweat stood out on Sir Richard's forehead—he looked truly terrified.

"What devilry is this?" breathed Sir Richard.

"It is not devilry!" burst out Peter. "It's not some kind of black magic, if that's what you're thinking. Kate is not a witch! It's science! It's physics! It's something to do with gravity or dark matter, or both. Just because you don't understand something doesn't make it evil. Does it?"

Gideon put his hand on Peter's shoulder.

"Calm yourself, Master Peter. It would be surprising, indeed, if the sight of Mistress Kate blurring did not strike terror into a man's soul when he saw it for the first time. Why, even you—"

"I'm sorry, Sir Richard," said Peter. "I didn't mean to be rude. But now that we've told you the truth, we don't want to be burnt as witches or be forced to answer lots of questions about the future.

After all, we could tell you about inventions that will change everything, how wars are going to be fought, which country will become the most powerful on earth. . . . I don't know how time works, but I'm pretty sure that we oughtn't to talk about what will happen in the future. Well, as little as possible, anyway."

Sir Richard was, in fact, too shaken to take in the enormity of what Peter was saying to him. He just stared blankly at the space where Kate had been a moment ago. The parson, however, was paying more attention.

"Which country will become the most powerful on earth?" he asked.

"You wouldn't believe me, Parson Ledbury. Anyway, I don't think I should tell you in case it makes you do something that changes the future."

"I undertake, on my honor," replied the parson, "not to believe a word of what you tell me. I shall tell no one, nor shall I act on anything I hear within these four walls. Will that do, Master Schock? Please, I should like to know before I wake from this dream."

"Oh, all right, then," said Peter, who could not resist seeing the look on the parson's face. "England will soon lose control of America and it will become the richest and most powerful country on earth. By our time, America is the world's only super-power."

"America? Nonsense! No, I cannot believe it!" exclaimed the parson, becoming very red in the face. "More powerful than England?"

"Much."

"More powerful than France?"

"Oh, yes. Much more."

"Ah, well. That is some small comfort. . . . Upon my word . . . America! . . . I should not dare tell anyone, in any case, for fear of being lynched."

"And America builds a spaceship that carries men to the moon."

"Now I know I am but dreaming," said the parson.

"And in the future," interjected Gideon, "they do not condemn the weak and the poor to a life of misery or a life of crime. They don't hang men for stealing food to prevent their children from starving."

"Look!" cried Sir Richard suddenly. "Mistress Kate!"

Like a photograph forming in developing fluid, Kate started to materialize. It was mesmerizing and rather beautiful. Peter alone sensed an infinitesimally small jolt as her form fixed itself in 1763 once more.

"Peter!" she immediately exclaimed, beaming with happiness. "They know about us blurring! Our parents must know that we're not dead! They won't have given up."

"How do you know?"

"In our time this is an office. There's a photocopier in the corner and there was a girl reading a newspaper and having a crafty cigarette and blowing the smoke through the window. Anyway, she didn't notice me at first and I just stood there looking at her. Something made her look up and she noticed me. She was so shocked she forgot to breathe out the smoke and she started to choke. She was coughing and the tears were running down her face, but she managed to refold her newspaper back to the front page, and she tapped it with her finger and held it up for me to see. "Is this you?" she spluttered. When I looked, I saw that there was a picture of us in Covent Garden—someone had caught us on film blurring. The headline said 'Going, going, gone!'"

"Wow!" said Peter. "That's fantastic! What did you say to her?"

"I only just managed to say anything. It was really hurting by that time, but I managed to say 'I'm in 1763' and give her the thumbs-up sign. The last thing I saw was her picking up the telephone."

"I do not pretend to grasp the half of what you say, Mistress Kate, but are we to understand that your parents know that you are lost in a different century?" asked Sir Richard.

"Well, they will now!" replied Kate triumphantly.

"And so will they be able to travel here to get you? Do they have a machine like the one you seek?"

Peter looked at Kate, but he already knew how she was going to react. He watched as her face crumpled and she sat down heavily in the chair and the tears started to roll down her cheeks. *For someone who is so clever and brave,* he thought, *Kate can be seriously embarrassing.*

"I don't think that there is another machine," said Peter, as Kate was incapable of replying. "It was part of a scientific experiment. It was an accident that brought us here, and I don't see how they could come and get us."

Gideon stood up and walked over to Kate, where he knelt next to her and put his hand on hers.

"Do not let despair darken your heart, Mistress Kate," he said. "There is always hope and you are not alone. You shall have the antigravity machine, I swear it. And sooner than you think."

"How so, Gideon?" asked Sir Richard.

"I visited Lord Luxon this very morning."

"You did what?" exclaimed Peter. "But he kidnapped you only yesterday!"

"I am certain stealing the machine was the Tar Man's doing. It is not in Lord Luxon's nature to order such a thing."

"I bet he didn't offer to give it back, though!"

"I truly believe he would have returned the machine—even though it is a treasure which Blueskin craves—had I not angered him by begging him not to employ Joshua, my half brother."

"Joshua is apprenticed to Mr. Hogarth in Covent Garden, is he not?" asked Sir Richard. "He is a fine engraver, I hear."

"Mr. Hogarth is old and in ill health. Lord Luxon offered to employ Joshua and in so doing hoped to persuade me back into his household."

"My dear Gideon," said Sir Richard. "You should have mentioned Joshua's difficulty to me before. I should be happy to help him find a position."

"Thank you, Sir Richard! Thank you!"

"So how can we get the antigravity machine back, then?" asked Kate.

"Lord Luxon said . . . that as the Tar Man and I both desire it, we must ride for it."

"What the devil does he mean by that?" asked the parson.

"The machine is hidden in the family crypt at Tempest House

in Surrey. Blueskin and I are to ride from Lord Luxon's London residence in St. James to Tempest House. The first of us to reach the crypt wins the prize."

"Ride against the Tar Man!" declared the parson. "You must not agree to his terms! Against such an adversary you would risk more than the loss of the machine, of that I have no doubt."

"No, Gideon," said Sir Richard. "You would do better to denounce Lord Luxon. I know that he wields great influence and he may think that his position in society is impregnable, but—if you could conquer your tender scruples—your testimony against him would bring him down."

"I owe Lord Luxon my life. I have sworn an oath. You know that I shall not betray him."

Sir Richard sighed and shook his head. "Your sense of honor does you justice, Gideon, but I consider that you are wrong in this. However, you know my views on the matter and I shall not lecture you any further. So, you appear to have only one choice, Gideon. You must ride."

"I am prepared to do so."

"When is the race to take place?"

"Dawn tomorrow."

"Then I shall attend you," said Sir Richard.

"And I," said the parson.

Gideon smiled his thanks and said, "If modesty permits me to say so, good sirs, I ride well. I can easily outrun Blueskin—and he knows it."

"All the more reason," said Sir Richard, "for you to be on your guard and for your friends to ensure fair play."

•   •   •

Sergeant Chadwick showed Kate's parents into a gloomy and windowless interview room in Bakewell police station. A sickly yellow light shone onto a long table, around which Peter's mother and father, a girl of about seventeen wearing pink lipgloss, and Detective Inspector Wheeler sat awaiting their arrival. Mr. and Mrs. Schock immediately got up and greeted Dr. and Mrs. Dyer. For a moment the two mothers clung to each other. Mrs. Dyer wanted so much to be able to tell Mrs. Schock about Kate's message, etched into the wall of her school, but knew that she must not. As she moved away, Mrs. Dyer wished it could have been Peter instead of she who had detected the citrus tang of his mother's perfume, felt the softness of her woollen coat, and sensed the tremulous emotion in her voice. It struck her that after all of this she would never again take for granted all those little details that add up to our own impression—never complete—of those we love. Mrs. Dyer looked down at her own old tweed coat that always picked up Molly's dog hairs and wondered if this formed part of Kate's idea of her. . . . She tried to create a picture of her daughter in her mind's eye, as clear a picture as she could. It was surprisingly difficult. The image kept shifting. No one memory was good enough. No one memory was precise enough. And then she thought that all she really longed for was her daughter's warmth and weight and the smell of her hair and the sound of her laughter—evidence of her physical presence. When would this waiting stop? Would it ever stop?

Meanwhile the inspector was asking her husband how Dr. Pirretti was bearing up. Dr. Dyer told him that she had left hospital and was feeling back to normal. The hospital doctor had told her that the most likely cause of her collapse was stress, so he had advised her not to overdo things.

"Is she going to return to America?" asked Inspector Wheeler.

"No . . . not yet," replied Dr. Dyer.

The policeman observed Dr. Dyer coldly and blew his nose before proceeding to start the meeting.

"Good morning, ladies and gentlemen. I am sure you are all wondering why I asked you here this morning on such short notice. So let me introduce you to Sarah, Sarah Kain, who is on work experience at a legal firm based in Lincoln's Inn Fields. Sarah has kindly agreed to come up from London in order to give you her remarkable testimony in person."

The inspector looked expectantly at Sarah, who was a sweet-faced girl with dark bobbed hair. Sarah smiled self-consciously but said nothing.

"So, Sarah . . . In your own time . . . ," prompted the inspector.

"Hi," she said nervously. "I'm ever so sorry about your kids. . . . It must be awful for you. . . . The inspector asked me here to tell you about something strange I saw yesterday. You see, I think I saw Kate. Well, part of her at any rate—"

"What do you mean?" asked Mrs. Dyer in alarm.

"Well . . . she didn't look very solid, more like you'd expect a ghost to look if you know what I mean. . . . I was doing some photocopying. It was a big print run—hundreds of copies—so I sat down and read the paper for something to do. I don't know what made me look up, but when I did, there she was, standing in the middle of the room. She was wearing a gorgeous dress—just like out of a costume drama. Her hair was in ringlets and everything."

"What color was the dress?" asked Inspector Wheeler.

"Er . . . blue . . . yes, pale blue."

"Go on," said the inspector.

"I knew who it was straight off. I'd just been looking at the headlines and those photographs taken in Covent Garden. Anyway, I started to cough for some reason—probably the shock of seeing her—and I couldn't get any words out, so I held up the newspaper. I pointed to the photograph of the girl and boy disappearing. 'Is that you?' I managed to say. Well, she had a good look, and then stared right at me and said, 'I'm in 1763. Tell them I'm in 1763.' And then she disappeared—not instantly, like turning off the telly or something, more a sort of gradual fade-out, if you know what I mean."

"Could you repeat what she said?" asked Dr. Dyer.

"'I'm in 1763. Tell them I'm in 1763.' Oh, and I forgot to say that she did a thumbs-up sign as well."

The inspector saw Dr. Dyer looking at his wife and mouthing "1763" to her.

"Didn't she say anything about Peter?" cried Mrs. Schock. "What does it mean? Is this some elaborate hoax? You're not expecting us to believe that our children have gone back in time, are you, Inspector? Or are we supposed to believe that our children have died and these are their ghosts?"

"Forgive me, Mrs. Schock," said the inspector. "I thought you would rather hear this from Sarah herself than from the newspapers. The press agreed to hold the story until you had been informed of the development."

Poor Mrs. Schock burst into tears, and her husband sat stiffly next to her, his arm around her shoulders, but he was clearly as distressed as she was. Dr. and Mrs. Dyer, the inspector noted, were emotional but in a quite different way. Dr. Pirretti was not going to cave in to his questioning, he could tell that already, but he wondered just how much pressure Dr. Dyer could take before blurting out what he knew.

"Why did you have to subject my wife . . . all of us . . . to this?" asked Mr. Schock. "It seems to me that the press are going into a hysterical frenzy and for all we know this is just another crazy story made up in the hope of getting into the headlines. . . . Why did you ask us here?"

Sarah gasped. "I've come all this way to tell you in person . . . and you accuse me of lying!"

"The children's parents are under a lot of stress, Sarah," explained the inspector calmly. "Please don't take it personally— we're all very grateful to you."

"Yes, thank you," said Mrs. Dyer.

"Yes, very grateful indeed," said Kate's father.

"But in answer to your question, Mr. Schock," the inspector continued, pushing back his chair and starting to pace around the room, "I asked you all here not to give you answers but to admit to you our failure, despite many hundreds of man-hours, to come up with any concrete leads. None. As I have said many times before about this case, it truly is as if the children vanished into thin air. All we have to go on are these baffling sightings, of what? Ghosts? Supernatural beings? At any rate they do, at first sight, appear to look like Kate and Peter. Kate was seen on the school playing fields—which I myself witnessed from a distance—then she was seen in a school common room. Both of them were spotted in a supermarket car park and then in Covent Garden, and now, Kate in Lincoln's Inn Fields. So they are on the move. And, as they have been wearing different clothes in each new sighting, they appear to have access to a well-stocked wardrobe. Not something normally associated with ghosts."

The inspector stopped pacing and sat down again and looked directly in everyone's face in turn.

"I don't believe in ghosts, ladies and gentlemen. I don't believe in the supernatural. But I *do* believe that there is a logical explanation for what has happened to Peter and Kate. My hunch is that it has something to do with the research going on at the laboratory where they disappeared. Someone must know something. Someone *always* knows something. And I am waiting for that someone to tell us what he or she knows."

The policeman stopped talking and waited. The silence made everyone profoundly uncomfortable. Dr. Dyer cleared his throat and the inspector looked directly at him. Mr. and Mrs. Shock, bemused, watched Inspector Wheeler staring at Kate's father, and their expressions changed. Surely Dr. Dyer of all people couldn't be concealing something?

"Very well," said the inspector. "It looks as though the mystery is not going to be cleared up today. Thank you all for coming. I shall, of course, keep you informed of any new developments. Sarah, Sergeant Chadwick will give you a lift to the station."

Five minutes later Inspector Wheeler peered through the venetian blinds of a window overlooking the car park. It was with great satisfaction that he watched Mr. Schock punching Dr. Dyer so hard he fell backward over the bonnet of his Land Rover.

NINETEEN

A Race Against Time

*In which the parson insults some macaronies
and displays his knowledge of horseflesh,
and Gideon rides against the Tar Man*

The day of the race dawned. The July sun shone down on St. James's Park and the quack-quacking of ducks and mooing of cows drifted over toward Lord Luxon's five-story house, which overlooked Bird Cage Walk. Quite a crowd had already gathered in front of the house.

Grooms were attending to a pair of powerful stallions, full of energy and raring to go. They whinnied and snorted and had to be restrained from galloping off into the park. One was white and the other black. There were two carriages waiting outside the house: a coach and six in black and gold, bearing the crest of Lord Luxon, and a small but well-sprung two-seater carriage with high wheels, belonging to Sir Richard. Several footmen, carrying refreshments on large silver trays, were moving between two distinct groups of people. The first comprised Sir Richard, Sidney, Parson Ledbury, Peter, Kate, Hannah, and Jack. The second, at some yards distant, was made up of a dozen or so wealthy young men, still dressed in showy if somewhat disheveled costumes from the night before. They were all talking and laughing very loudly, and many of them seemed unsteady on their feet. They made frequent requests for more wine. Some of them wore extremely high wigs with tiny hats perched on top of them, whose sheer silliness made Peter want to laugh out loud.

"Look at these *fops* and *macaronies*, Sidney," commented the parson under his breath, making what he said perfectly audible to everyone. "If this is what travel to France and Italy does to one's sense of fashion, I should strongly advise you to stay at home."

One of the young men, who, Peter noticed, was not only wearing white powder but also lipstick and a black beauty spot, turned toward the parson and hissed like a snake.

Sir Richard tactfully encouraged his party to move away from the pretty young men in order to take a look at the horses.

"Fine-looking beasts, the pair of them," pronounced the parson, who was of the opinion that anything he did not know about horses was not worth bothering about.

"Yes," agreed Sir Richard. "There is not much to choose between them. This race will be won by the rider."

"Just think," said Kate to Peter, "we might have the antigravity machine back by evening! This could be our last day in 1763!"

Peter did not know how to reply. He knew how good a horseman Gideon was, but given that his opponent was the Tar Man, Peter found it difficult to feel confident.

Suddenly the front door of the house opened and out into the hazy sunshine stepped Lord Luxon. He stood on the stone stairs dressed entirely in pale cream silk. Hannah, who was lifting up Jack so that he could pat the white horse, let out a little gasp. "Upon my word, is he not the handsomest man you ever saw? I have heard tell of his elegance and good looks, but the reality surpasses all expectation."

"Oh, Hannah!" exclaimed Kate, exasperated. "Lord Luxon kidnapped Gideon only the day before yesterday! What does it matter what he looks like?"

"I beg your pardon, Mistress Kate," said Hannah. "Of course, Gideon is very handsome too."

Lord Luxon waited for his boisterous friends to settle down and spoke in a strong, clear voice that carried across the park.

"Good day to you all, ladies and gentlemen! I am happy indeed that our two contestants can count on such a distinguished audience to send them off on this fine morning. They are asked to ride, without stopping, from this place to my family's crypt in the churchyard adjacent to Tempest House in Surrey. The first to reach the crypt shall win fifteen guineas, as well as some small trinket both gentlemen have taken a fancy to, which will be found therein."

There were cheers all round. Lord Luxon smiled broadly. Shutters started to open in neighboring houses, and people dressed in nightgowns and turbans hung out of windows to watch the spectacle.

"I have already wagered that one of our brave contestants will be the first to finish, but I shall not admit which one I favor! I have had brought up from my stables in Surrey these two racing horses, which I see you have all had the chance to admire. Magnificent creatures, the pair of them, as I am sure you will agree, both sired by a champion of Arab blood. And so, without more ado, ladies and gentlemen, it remains for me to introduce the contestants and for each to choose his horse! Please raise your glasses to Mr. Seymour and Master Blueskin!"

On cue Gideon and the Tar Man emerged from the hall and stood on the step next to Lord Luxon, who put an arm around each shoulder. The small crowd cheered and clapped.

"What a monster!" Peter heard Sir Richard say under his breath.

Peter wondered if he referred to Lord Luxon or the Tar Man. Then Lord Luxon took a golden guinea from the pocket of his waistcoat.

"Heads or tails, gentlemen?"

"Heads," said the Tar Man.

"Very well, tails," replied Gideon.

Lord Luxon tossed the coin high into the air. It spun several times, catching the sun's rays as it did so. It fell into Lord Luxon's outstretched palm, and he slapped it onto his wrist and lifted up his hand to reveal the golden guinea.

"Heads," he declared. "Which horse do you choose, Master Blueskin? Black or white?"

"Black, my Lord," replied the Tar Man, and then, putting his face right up to his adversary's, continued, "Black, eh, Gideon, like my heart!"

There was general laughter, but those of Lord Luxon's friends who had placed bets on Gideon booed good-humoredly.

"You have made a poor choice of animal, Master Blueskin," responded Gideon, "for the white is the stronger horse, although in the circumstances I should be the last to complain."

Peter and Kate whooped, which provoked a raised eyebrow from Sir Richard, while the rest of the party, along with several of the fops, cheered heartily. "Huzzah!" they cried. "Huzzah!" The Tar Man's supporters booed. Jack thought all this was great fun.

Two footmen now appeared in the doorway carrying a long-case clock, which they placed with the utmost care on the top step.

"It is now five and half past," declared Lord Luxon. "The inimitable Mr. De Courcy here has agreed to officiate and will start the race on the stroke of six o'clock."

The macaroni who had hissed at the parson stepped forward and bowed low to the crowd with a flourish of his handkerchief.

"Gentlemen, may the best man win!"

Then Lord Luxon climbed into the coach and six, and with the crack of a whip the carriage thundered away toward the Thames and, twenty-five miles to the southwest, Tempest House. Lord Luxon's lace handkerchief fluttered from the window as his carriage disappeared out of sight. A boy, dressed in the same ornate livery as the driver, stood at the rear of the carriage, one hand in his pocket. He looked over at Peter and Kate but quickly turned away when his gaze was returned, as if he were ashamed to be seen. Suddenly Kate realized who it was.

"Tom! It's Tom!" she said to Peter. "I can't believe it! He must have taken the Tar Man up on his offer!"

"I guess it's difficult saying no to the Tar Man. I wonder which is worse, being a member of the Carrick gang or becoming the Tar Man's apprentice?"

"Poor Tom. Maybe he'll escape one day," said Kate. "I hope so. I liked him."

"Even after what he did?"

"Well, he didn't have a lot of choice, did he? And he did try to help us."

While they waited for the race to begin, Sir Richard, always the diplomat, had gone over to talk with Lord Luxon's friends. He was having an animated conversation with De Courcy, who made dramatic gestures with his hands to emphasize every point that he made. Peter and Kate moved toward the rest of their party, who were now clustered around the proud white horse, patting its neck and feeding it blades of fresh green grass. As they drew closer, the parson asked Kate to stand next to Hannah in front of the animal so that he could discreetly examine its hooves. Being able to function as a moveable screen was, thought Kate, perhaps one of the very few advantages of wearing a skirt the width of a sofa. She stood with her back to the horse, pretending to take an interest in the macaronies' antics and listening to the grunts and groans of the parson. "Damn his eyes!" she heard him say. Finally he stood up and Kate turned around. He was angry and red in the face.

"I knew it! Some villainous fellow—and I can guess who—has put a nail in the hoof. Skillfully done, too. All but invisible—had I not pulled it out, the beast would have been lame after ten miles."

Kate had never seen Gideon look so furious, and she watched him as his eyes searched the crowd for the Tar Man. He spotted him and sprang up with the intention, Kate was sure, of challenging him. The parson stopped him.

"Trust me, Mr. Seymour, say nothing for the time being. Let him think that you are unlikely to get beyond Richmond. I have a happy idea. Sidney, why do you not regale our friends with an amusing story while I attend to a small matter."

The parson then laughed affectedly and said loud enough for everyone to hear, "Very droll, Sidney, very droll. Come, Jack, you wanted to see the ducks."

Then he caught hold of Jack's hand and walked into the park. Hannah hurried after them. Peter and Kate exchanged looks. *What on earth,* thought Peter, *is the parson up to?* Sidney did as he was asked and told them his best stories about Parson Ledbury. Even Gideon, who was preoccupied with the race, burst out laughing when he heard how the parson had attempted to set light to damp firewood in the drawing room at Baslow Hall by using gunpowder, and had ended up destroying the chimney.

Soon they saw the parson returning with Hannah and Jack. He walked straight up to the Tar Man and offered him his hand. The Tar Man eyed him suspiciously.

"To the victor the spoils!" Parson Ledbury said. "May the best man win!"

The Tar Man slowly took his hand and shook it.

"Thank you, Parson. I have no doubt that the best man will win."

Parson Ledbury stroked the stallion's black neck and stood back for a moment to admire its physique.

"Dashed fine horse, sir, dashed fine. I do not mind admitting that I have never seen a prettier piece of horseflesh in my life. Were it not for the fact that you are riding it, Master Blueskin, I might be tempted to put ten guineas on him."

The Tar Man threw back his head and laughed, and the parson's attention was taken by his scar.

"You would offend good Mr. Seymour if you did, Parson, for you must know that he does not approve of gambling."

"Pish pash! Life is too short to deprive oneself of such small pleasures," he replied. "But, tell me, for I am curious. That handsome scar of yours, Master Blueskin, it bears all the marks of an encounter with a sabre. Did you perchance earn it in His Majesty's service?"

"Most of my acquaintances know better than to make personal comments of that nature," the Tar Man replied, allowing a menacing smile to linger awhile on his lips. "But I have taken a fancy to you, Parson Ledbury, so I shall tell you the truth about my scar, as you might appreciate the irony of it. This is how I got my war wound. I was sent to fetch my brother in from the barn where he was playing. I was nearly grown by then but he was still very young, scarcely able to talk. I found him perched on top of a cart, whirling around and around with a scythe my father used for cutting hay. It was too heavy for him and he lost his grip. I watched it flying through the air toward me. I dived to one side, which no doubt saved my life, but it still cut me deep, as the scar bears witness. My brother ran back to his mother without knowing what he had done. They did not find me until the next morning and, when they did, would not believe my story, so convinced were they that it was my appetite for fighting that was responsible for my injuries."

"Did you find it in your heart to forgive your brother?" asked the parson.

"Forgive him? I should rather thank him. This scar is eloquent. It promises much, does it not? It strikes terror into the souls of those who would cross me—little do they know that it is the work of one who had not seen his third birthday. . . . However, he is dead, as are the rest of my brothers and sisters. The fever took them all, or so I am told."

"I am sorry for it," said the parson. "That must have been a grievous blow, indeed."

"No. My family felt no great tenderness toward me, and I returned their feelings."

The parson did not know what to reply so said nothing.

Jack was feeding the black stallion with the last of a large bunch of grass they had brought back from the park. He looked up at the Tar Man and asked, "Is it on account of your brother that you cannot hold your neck straight?"

The question caused all of the Tar Man's good humor to drop from his face, and the parson realized the child had overstepped the mark. He hastily lifted Jack onto his shoulders.

"Well," he said, "I shall take my leave of you, Master Blueskin, and shall await news of the race with bated breath."

The parson strode away with a huge grin on his face. Hannah and Jack, too, looked very pleased with themselves as they rejoined the party, trying to look as casual as they could.

Sir Richard, who had managed to extricate himself from the excitable Mr. De Courcy, said, "Something's afoot. What is the cause of such merriment?"

The parson was chuckling too much to speak and covered his face with a handkerchief. Hannah spoke for him.

"Someone had put a nail in the hoof of Gideon's horse. If the parson had not found it, the poor animal would have been lame within a matter of miles."

"But we must inform De Courcy!" exclaimed Sir Richard. "This is shocking!"

The parson stopped laughing and shook his head violently.

"We must do no such thing! Let them think the horse will go lame—it will give Gideon the advantage."

"The parson is a good horse doctor," continued Hannah. "He always treats our horses when they get sick at Baslow Hall. He has found an herb in the park that will cure all manner of minor ailments when taken in very small quantities. Taken in larger quantities it is liable to make a horse's bowels a little irritable for some hours afterward."

"You mean . . . ," said Kate.

Hannah nodded. Kate tried hard to keep her face straight. Neither Sir Richard nor Gideon looked at all pleased.

"Well," said Sir Richard. "It's too late to do anything now. I am going to ride to Tempest House myself in the interests of fair play—although it seems that we are not playing by the rules ourselves."

Sir Richard climbed into his two-seater carriage and took hold of the reins.

"Until tonight!" he cried to the party, and then, to Gideon, "May God be with you, my friend!"

The carriage moved off. Suddenly Kate caught hold of Peter's arm.

"One of us should be there too," she exclaimed. "How will Sir Richard know if it's the antigravity machine? Quick, Peter, run after him—I'll never catch him in this stupid dress."

Without even bothering to reply, Peter raced after Sir Richard in his carriage.

"Sir Richard! Sir Richard!" he cried.

"Whoa!" called Sir Richard to the two chestnut mares.

The horses slowed down just long enough for Peter to leap up. He turned around in his seat and waved back at Kate.

"Good luck!" she shouted.

Kate sighed. She would have liked to have gone too. *Clothes in this century,* she thought, *have a lot to answer for.*

•   •   •

As the clock struck six, Gideon and the Tar Man mounted their steeds, and the flamboyant Mr. De Courcy pointed his pistol to the sky.

"On your marks, gentlemen," he cried, striking a pose. "On the count of three! One! Two! Three!"

With a whiff of gunpowder and an earsplitting blast that echoed around St. James's Park, De Courcy discharged his pistol, sending both the riders and a small flock of starlings on their way. The black-and-white stallions plunged into a headlong gallop. Kate watched Gideon's white shirt billowing in the breeze and saw the Tar Man crack his whip once and then crack it again—only this time Gideon nearly lost his seat and clutched at his shoulder.

"He struck Gideon!" she cried.

There were boos but also some cheers. Kate's spirits sank. Was Gideon a match for the Tar Man? It suddenly struck her that if Gideon did not win back the antigravity machine, she might never see her family again. The two riders disappeared into the distance and the crowd went eerily silent. The race had begun and there was nothing she could do now but wait.

Sir Richard had hoped that his carriage would catch and out-run Lord Luxon's heavy coach and six, but he had not counted on Lord Luxon's procuring fresh horses on Richmond Hill. As Sir Richard's horses tired, the gap between them grew gradually wider again, and soon Peter lost sight of the shiny black carriage with Tom perched on top, barely recognizable in his smart new uniform. Sir Richard took the main Portsmouth Road through Esher and on to Cobham, a route that he knew because of his frequent visits to Mr. Hamilton's pleasure gardens at Painshill Park. By midday they had reached Effingham, where they asked for directions to Tempest House. They spoke little, as Sir Richard needed to concentrate to avoid hitting any stone or pothole, which could, at this rattling speed, tip over the lightweight two-seater. Yet the silence between them was an easy one, and Peter enjoyed seeing the countryside flying past them as they hurtled over the rough roads.

Half an hour's ride beyond Effingham, amidst rolling hills and lightly wooded valleys, they caught their first glimpse of Tempest House. It was set in landscaped grounds that afforded views of a large lake, and lush fields dotted with sheep as far as the eye could see. It was, as Gideon had described it, a great estate, and the house itself was perhaps five times the size of Baslow Hall.

In the circumstances, Sir Richard was reluctant to impose on Lord Luxon's hospitality and decided to wait for the two contenders outside the tall iron gates at the head of the tree-lined drive to Tempest House. Sir Richard predicted that the wait would not be a long one, but he was wrong. An hour went by, then two, and they started to become concerned. They saw, from a distance, tiny figures emerge on a balcony at the top of Tempest House, and they guessed that Lord Luxon was scanning the landscape with his spyglass.

It was hot and flies buzzed around the horses. Sir Richard and Peter had drunk all the water and had nothing to do but pace up and down the country lane leading to the house. Peter's eyes ached from focusing on the horizon for so long. At half past three they heard the sound of horses galloping up the drive. There were three riders, one of whom they recognized as Lord Luxon.

"I'll warrant they've spotted something," said Sir Richard.

They climbed back into the carriage and drove a little way down the lane. Peter screwed up his eyes against the sun, and then he saw it—a tiny white speck in the far distance.

"It's Gideon!" shouted Peter. "Gideon's won!"

"The Lord be praised!" said Sir Richard, letting out a huge sigh of relief. "I was beginning to fear the worst."

The tiny white speck approached at a snail's pace.

"Why is it taking him so long?" asked Peter.

Sir Richard did not answer, but the look of relief was turning into an expression of concern. Peter wanted to ride to meet him, but Sir Richard was anxious that they could be accused of helping Gideon. He did not want to give Lord Luxon any excuse to disqualify him. They looked behind them and saw that Lord Luxon and his attendants had stopped at the iron gates—he raised his hand in greeting but did not approach them.

Finally the white horse came close enough for them to see. At first they feared that the horse was riderless. Then they saw that Gideon was slumped over his horse's neck.

As he passed in front of them, Peter shouted, "Gideon! You're here! You've made it to Tempest House!"

"What ails you, Gideon?" called out Sir Richard.

Gideon lifted his head a couple of inches and shook it from side to side. He started to come to his senses. He glanced over at

Peter and tried to smile—but he had a badly cut lip and a black eye, and when he pushed himself up, he winced and clutched his side.

"Oh, no!" exclaimed Peter. "What happened?"

"Forgive me, Master Peter, I did what I could. I was winning for much of the race, but Blueskin knew a shortcut in Abinger Forest and decided to even the odds."

"What did he do?"

"He pulled me off my horse and left me in the woods. I am not badly hurt—mainly my pride. I should have been on my guard against such a thing. I was lucky—Blueskin drove off my horse but he is a faithful animal and he came back for me. How long ago did he arrive?"

"The Tar Man, you mean?"

"Yes."

"He hasn't!"

"Blueskin has not arrived?"

"No."

"Then I have won?"

"Yes, Gideon," shouted Sir Richard. "You have won!"

Suddenly Gideon found the strength he thought had failed him, and he dug in his heels and urged the white horse forward.

"It looks like the parson's horse medicine worked!" said Peter, keeping his voice low.

"And it seems that you are to have your antigravity machine after all!" said Sir Richard. "I wish Mistress Kate were here to witness Gideon's triumph!"

They all followed Gideon as he rode past the iron gates and acknowledged Lord Luxon.

"Well done, indeed, Gideon!" they heard him shout. "I have won my wager. To the crypt!"

They continued some little way up the country lane, and soon they reached a small stone church. Everyone dismounted and walked through the churchyard toward an imposing crypt bearing the Luxon's family crest. Holding himself very stiffly on account of his bruised ribs, Gideon walked to the door and placed his hand on it. There was a smattering of applause.

"What kept you so long, Gideon?" asked Lord Luxon. "I have been waiting these three hours past to claim my winnings! I see that you have defended yourself against Master Blueskin. He lives, I take it?"

"He lives, my Lord, and was in better health than I the last time I saw him."

Peter and Sir Richard could contain themselves no longer and rushed up to congratulate him.

"Well done, indeed!" exclaimed Sir Richard.

Peter patted him on the back, which made Gideon wince.

"Whoops! Sorry!" he said, and then whispered, "We stand a chance of returning home now, thanks to you."

"So, Mr. Seymour," said Lord Luxon, "it is time for you to claim your prize. Master Blueskin will be ill-pleased. He has set his heart on this curious device. But it is not the first time that you two have not seen eye to eye. There has always been bad blood between you, eh, Gideon?"

Lord Luxon took out an ornate brass key from his pocket and

unlocked the door of the crypt. The hinges groaned as he pushed open the double doors. He gestured for everyone to enter. They stepped from the bright sunshine into the dark and musty crypt, and blinked. Peter's eyes slowly adjusted to the dim light, and he looked around him for his first sight of the antigravity machine since that first day in the valley in Derbyshire. Peter swung around. He could see no sign of it. The crypt was empty.

"What is the meaning of this?" Lord Luxon cried.

Everyone looked at one another, confused and angry and suspicious.

"Where is the machine?" demanded Lord Luxon.

No one spoke. The only sound was the gentle roaring of the wind through the great copper beeches in the churchyard. What small amount of light there was in the crypt suddenly diminished as the unmistakable silhouette of the Tar Man appeared in the doorway.

"Blueskin!" exclaimed Lord Luxon.

The Tar Man scarcely had the breath to speak and did not waste time with pleasantries.

"He has not won! He is disqualified!" he shouted. "My horse, who was the picture of health this morning, became suddenly sick. I should have known that little wretch was not feeding him grass! They have fed him some evil herb and he is too weak to race. I have run the last five miles."

Lord Luxon turned to Gideon.

"I can scarce believe this! Mr. Seymour, whose conscience is without smear or stain, has *cheated*? What do you have to say for yourself?"

Sir Richard intervened.

"As we are on the subject of cheating, apart from the small matter of Master Blueskin attacking Gideon during the race, I must tell you, Lord Luxon, that we found a nail driven into the hoof of the white stallion with the clear intention of laming the beast. An upset stomach is hardly comparable! Besides, it was neither Gideon's idea to feed herbs to the horse nor did he execute or approve of the plan."

"Master Blueskin," said Lord Luxon. "Do you know anything about a nail?"

"I do not, my lord. Although I have a suspicion that some of your lordship's friends—who have wagered princely sums on my winning the race—may well know more than I."

"I admit it is not an implausible explanation," commented Lord Luxon. "And do you deny attacking Mr. Seymour?"

"I do not! But surely there are no rules against one rider challenging another? I used no weapon. We are evenly matched, would you not say, my lord?"

"That is true enough. In fact, I should say that you are as evenly matched as your horses."

"Except that Mr. Seymour has ensured that his horse had the advantage!"

Sir Richard exploded: "Do you expect us to accept the word of your henchman without question?"

The remark appeared to anger Lord Luxon.

"Henchman? What kind of term is that to describe Master Blueskin? What need have I for a *henchman*? He manages my estate. I suggest you choose your words more carefully, Sir

Richard, given that you and your party are charged with a most dishonorable act."

Lord Luxon turned to Gideon.

"Mr. Seymour, did you embark on the race knowing of this vile plot against your opponent?"

"I cannot deny that I did."

Peter was expecting an outburst of anger. Instead he detected in Lord Luxon's expression the traces of a profound disappointment.

"Then I must disqualify you, Gideon," Lord Luxon said flatly. "I declare Master Blueskin to be the winner by default."

"I must protest!" exclaimed Sir Richard. "The race has not been won fairly, I accept that—but why impose a forfeit on one side and not the other? What of the attempt to lame Gideon's horse? What of Master Blueskin's attack on Gideon? And as for Gideon, it was not he who fed bitter herbs to the horse!"

"You protest too much!" shouted Lord Luxon. "You are a cheat, sir, or you aid and abet cheats."

It was at that moment that the Tar Man realized that the antigravity machine was nowhere to be seen. He interrupted his master, crying out in panic, "But where is the prize, my lord?"

"It is gone, as you can see! It is a mystery!"

"Gone!" exploded the Tar Man. "Then they have taken it! They did not trust us to hand it over—they have stolen our machine!"

"The device was never yours!" cried Gideon. "This is naught but a trick! If truth were known, Master Schock's machine was never here in the first place!"

"You go too far, Gideon!" Lord Luxon was incandescent with fury. "Your arrogance is extraordinary! I have been your protector long enough. You leave my service against my will and to the detriment of the estate, and you take it upon yourself to disapprove of my affairs at every turn. Enough is enough, Gideon. I shall court your good opinion no more. You are a liar and a cheat and—what is more—a *thief.* I will thank you to accompany me back to London. I shall deliver you into the hands of the magistrate and I will bring a charge against you of fraud and theft!"

Although it was past one o'clock in the morning, Kate was still awake when she heard voices in the hall. She ran downstairs in her white nightgown. Peter and Sir Richard stood on the black-and-white marble floor and shrugged off their jackets. One look at Peter's pale face and his bowed shoulders and she knew the result of the race without having to ask.

"He lost, then. Where is he?"

"He didn't lose," said Peter. "But the machine was missing from the crypt and Lord Luxon accused us of stealing it. And because the parson fed that stuff to the Tar Man's horse to make him sick, Gideon was disqualified."

"Oh, no!" exclaimed Kate.

"And there's worse. Much worse."

"Tell me!"

Sir Richard answered. "Lord Luxon has taken Gideon to the magistrate and has charged him with stealing his property. Gideon has been imprisoned."

"Gideon gave me these for safekeeping," said Peter.

He could hardly get the words out. He held up the horn that Gideon's father had given him, and his small spyglass. Peter slumped onto the bottom step of the curved staircase, sank his head against the wrought-iron banisters, and finally gave in to the tears that he had been struggling to hold back since seeing Gideon, his hands tied behind his back, being pushed into an open cart bound for Newgate Gaol.

TWENTY

Newgate

In which Gideon languishes in Newgate prison,
the children meet a famous author,
and a chance meeting leaves Kate overjoyed

The coach driver stopped outside St. Sepulchre's Church. It was
the bells of this church that tolled for the condemned on hanging
days, when a procession of carts took them on their final journey
to Tyburn. Opposite St. Sepulchre's, on the other side of Newgate
Street, the group saw the high stone walls of the infamous prison
rising up before them. They walked through massive iron gates
and stopped underneath the motto *Venio sicut fur,* which Parson
Ledbury translated for them as "I come as a thief."

Sir Richard turned to Kate and Peter. "It is not too late to change your minds. I understand that Gideon is your friend, but there is no shame in turning away from such a place."

"No, no, I'm fine," lied Kate.

"Yeah, me too," said Peter.

Damp and despair seemed to leach out of the stones of the oppressive building. The walls of the entrance were decorated with the shackles and chains and iron fetters used to restrain the prisoners. Peter had expected Newgate prison to be closely guarded and for there to be strict routines and procedures. Yet the opposite seemed to be the case. There were no guards in sight, but a crowd of wretched folk was swarming in and out of the grimy forecourt. The visitors saw mothers followed by ragged hollow-eyed children, and they saw men and women of all ages, most of them in rags, and many of whom seemed to be crippled or lame, or raving or dead drunk. No one appeared to be in charge. Instead there was an atmosphere of barely contained chaos.

"We've got to get him out of here!" whispered Peter to Kate.

With sinking hearts Peter and Kate followed Sir Richard to the keeper's lodge, where he found a prison guard who was willing to take them to see Gideon. The guard was drinking beer with some other turnkeys, as they were called, and Sir Richard had to buy him another beer and pay him five shillings for the privilege. The turnkey took them to the master's side of the prison and into an inner courtyard, where the holding cells were to be found.

Parson Ledbury had warned Peter and Kate what to expect. He told them about the terrible stench, the roaring and howling of the prisoners packed in rooms far too small to contain them, the "hellcat women," who screeched abuse at passersby, and the multitude of hands that reached out through the windows in the hope that someone would drop money into their palms so that they could buy bread from the jailers. Peter and Kate knew Newgate prison was going to be hard to stomach, yet that knowledge did not prepare them for the gut-twisting reality. Oh, the nauseating, putrid, poisonous stink of it! The parson handed out the vinegar-soaked handkerchiefs that Hannah had supplied to put over their mouths and noses. The turnkey pulled the parson out of the way just in time as the contents of a chamber pot splattered in front of them. He bawled at the wild-eyed prisoner up above, who responded in kind with a stream of oaths. And the noise! Sir Richard had described it as the Newgate roar—a maddening cacophony of sounds: voices bellowing, shouting, howling, swearing, singing, calling from one cell to another . . . and then the clanking of chains, tankards being banged against metal bars, heavy doors clanging shut. It made Kate's ears ring and her nerves jangle. A hand suddenly shot out from a grated window and grabbed hold of her dress. She screamed with the shock of it, wanted to cover her ears and eyes, wanted above all to get out of there. She started to tremble uncontrollably. She did not want to go any nearer, did not want to see Gideon in this hellhole and be powerless to do anything to help.

"Please take me out of here," she said simply to Sir Richard.

Sir Richard nodded. "Tell Gideon I'll come and see him tomorrow," he said, and escorted Kate back to the carriage.

The parson and Peter continued to follow the turnkey down a series of corridors.

"This is the cell you require, gentlemen," said the turnkey.

He unlocked a door, and they walked into a room smaller than an average classroom. As Peter stepped inside, the stench, the noise, and the heat struck him like a blow to the head. The guard, the parson, and Peter stood in a narrow gangway, metal bars between them and the thirty or forty prisoners, young and old, men and women, who remained here twenty-four hours a day. Some of them were shackled to the wall or the floor, some of them sat or lay on the bare wooden shelves that served as beds, but most of them were on the move. A woman was slumped against the bars in a drunken stupor, her jaw hanging open and a bottle of kill-grief clutched loosely in her hand. Peter saw a squat man with bulging eyes creep up behind her and deftly remove the bottle of gin from her grasp.

Peter could not see Gideon at first. The cell was a snake pit, bodies writhing and weaving between each other. Peter was aware of a curious noise that was noticeable over and above the general din. He couldn't pinpoint it until he looked down, and then he saw what it was. The floor was covered with a thick carpet of lice, and whenever anyone moved their feet, there was a crunching sound as a few more were crushed into the ground. Peter shuddered.

Parson Ledbury and Peter breathed through their handkerchiefs, their eyes darting everywhere for a glimpse of Gideon.

"These conditions are intolerable!" said the parson to the turnkey.

"They get used to it—if they don't die first," the turnkey replied.

Suddenly Peter spotted him. Gideon seemed to be the only prisoner who was completely still. He stood leaning against the far wall. His eyes were closed and, miraculously, Peter saw the faintest trace of a smile pass over his features. Someone must have stolen his shirt and his boots, for he was dressed only in a pair of breeches. His encounter with the Tar Man had left its mark: One eye was still badly swollen, and large purple and yellow bruises were clearly visible on his chest. Peter cringed as he saw that Gideon was having to stand in all these lice in bare feet.

"Gideon!" he shouted.

Gideon's eyes shot open and looked in Peter's direction. His face lit up but instantly turned serious. He pushed his way toward the metal bars.

"You should not have come," he said. "I would have wished to spare you this. I am ashamed to be seen in this place."

Parson Ledbury had already taken off his jacket and was now pulling off his shirt, which he pushed through the bars to Gideon.

"Here, Mr. Seymour; it is too big, but you are very welcome to it," said the parson.

Gideon took it gratefully and immediately put it on.

"You are very good, Parson. Thank you."

"I am not very good, Mr. Seymour, and I have come to ask your forgiveness for what I did yesterday. I fear that my interference is responsible in part for your sorry plight."

"Do not blame yourself, Parson," replied Gideon. "I have been a thorn in Lord Luxon's side for too long. I have been expecting something of the sort—it was only a matter of time. However, I do regret, most sincerely, our failure to win back the machine for Peter and Mistress Kate."

"We brought you some food," said Peter.

He then thrust the bundle of bread, cheese, and roast chicken and the flagon of wine they had brought through the bars. This was a mistake because invisible hands immediately snatched it, and Gideon's dinner was dispersed throughout the cell with lightning speed, causing unseen scuffles within the mass of bodies.

"No!" cried Peter uselessly. "Give it back!"

The turnkey laughed. "You cannot expect good table manners from wild dogs."

The parson glared at him.

Gideon said resignedly, "You cannot blame them. They have been here longer than I, and if they have no money they cannot buy food. Half of them are starving."

Parson Ledbury looked sadly at all the faces crowded behind the iron bars—anger and hatred, misery and utter hopelessness stared back at him.

"Mr. Seymour," said the parson, "we have come to tell you that you are not abandoned. We shall do everything in our power to secure your release. Do not lose hope."

"I shall not lose hope. I am innocent of the crime of which I have been accused. I put my faith in God and in my friends. And I thank you for coming with all my heart, Parson Ledbury, but please, I would ask you to leave now. I do not wish Master Peter to linger here—Newgate has a habit of persisting in men's dreams."

"As you wish," replied the parson, "but I shall return with Sir Richard on the morrow."

"Good-bye, Peter," said Gideon. "Tell Mistress Kate that she must not lose hope."

"But I wanted to stay. I wanted to keep you company for a while," Peter started to protest.

"Mr. Seymour is right," said the parson. "We will be better employed hiring the finest lawyer in London to represent him at his trial."

They caught the attention of the turnkey and asked him to let them out. At the last minute Peter turned around and said to Gideon, "What were you smiling at when we arrived?"

Gideon managed another smile. "They have locked up my body, but they can imprison neither my mind nor my soul. I was taking a stroll by the stream in the valley where you caught the trout, feeling the sun on my head and breathing in the good air."

On their way out Parson Ledbury asked the turnkey how much he would charge to put Gideon into a less crowded cell and to get him some decent food to eat.

"Twenty guineas for a room with five prisoners, or five hundred pounds will buy you the best lodgings in Newgate."

"Twenty guineas! Five hundred pounds!" exclaimed Parson Ledbury. "Why, that is a king's ransom! Here, have five guineas on account. I will return tomorrow, when I shall give you the rest. I shall expect to see Mr. Seymour in more salubrious surroundings and with a good dinner inside him."

"But what about the people who cannot afford to pay you?" asked Peter. "What happens to them?"

"Why, they should have thought of that before they took it into their heads to break the law."

"But it's not fair!" shouted Peter, burning with righteous rage and tears welling in his eyes. "It's wicked to treat human beings like that! You are an evil man! You should be in that cell, not Gideon!"

The parson interrupted Peter and pulled him firmly away.

"Thank you, Master Turnkey. Until tomorrow."

When they were out of earshot of the turnkey, he continued, "It would be wise to resist provoking the man on whom your friend is dependent for his every need."

Peter and the parson joined Kate and Sir Richard in the carriage.

"How was he?" Kate asked.

"How do you think?" Peter replied bitterly. "It is the most disgusting, horrible place I've ever seen. They'd stolen his shirt and his boots. It stank worse than the elephant house at the zoo. The floor was crawling with lice. I don't think he wanted me to see him like that."

Sir Richard opened the door and called up to the driver, "Take us to John Leche's chambers, Middle Temple!"

Sir Richard took note of Peter's pale tear-stained face and the way Kate sat, hunched up and a frown etched onto her forehead, her hands pulling distractedly at her handkerchief.

"To be separated from your families and everyone you know," he said softly, "is hard enough, but to have to witness the cruel incarceration of your friend as well must seem more than you can bear. Yet I tell you that you are not alone and that this will pass. All this will pass and you *will* know happier times again. In the meantime I promise you that Gideon's stay in Newgate prison will be short. John Leche is an excellent man and a fine lawyer. I am certain that he will prove Mr. Seymour's innocence to the world."

While Sir Richard tried to comfort Peter and Kate, a clerk of the court, wearing a dusty black robe, was hurrying out of the Old Bailey. The great law court was conveniently placed next door to the prison, and the two buildings were linked by an underground tunnel. The clerk hurried across the street and into Newgate prison, where he approached the turnkey who had shown the way to Gideon's cell.

"Good day, Samuel," said the clerk. "You look displeased with the world this morning!"

"Good day to you, Ethan. Nay, "tis nothing. After nigh on ten years of protecting society from this den of thieves and felons, I am accustomed to the ingratitude of the public."

"Ay, Samuel, ingratitude is our lot in life. However, I have urgent business to attend to and must ask you to fetch a certain Gideon Seymour, who is required to appear in court at two o' clock."

"I have just come from him! He was brought here but last night! I happen to know that his friends have not yet had the occasion to hire a lawyer, let alone one who can appear at such short notice."

"That is as may be," replied the clerk, tapping the side of his nose, "but there are people interested in this case who have great influence. I should get him into court without delay, if you know what's good for you. I hear that the straw men have done good business this day, and rumor has it that there's a thief-taker involved whom you would be foolish to cross. I also happen to know that the King is leaving the city tonight and the Recorder of London must send him reports of all forthcoming executions before sunset."

"Executions! What crime has Mr. Seymour committed? He seems a gentle sort of fellow."

The clerk shrugged his shoulders. "What crime indeed."

For a moment the turnkey was tempted to run over to the carriage that was just moving away, to tell the parson about Gideon's imminent trial. Then he remembered how Peter had called him an evil man, and he decided instead to return for a while to the keeper's lodge. After another beer or two he would get around to escorting his prisoner through the dank tunnel that linked Newgate prison to the Old Bailey.

They had lain awake for hours. Sleep had finally released his wife from her torment, but Peter's father was still struggling to make sense of what the office girl had told them. How could this be true? How could his son be lost in a different century? And what, if anything, did Dr. Dyer know? The last time he had punched someone, he had been at school—and it had not got him anywhere then, either. Dr. Dyer had told him nothing. Yet he found himself agreeing with Inspector Wheeler—Kate's father definitely had something he wanted to conceal.

Slowly, so as not to disturb his wife, Mr. Schock crept out

of bed, got dressed, and went downstairs. The brightly lit hotel lobby was deserted. He walked past the giant Christmas tree and through the automatic glass doors. Tomorrow would be Christmas Eve. It was a freezing cloudless night and the stars shone down on rows of expensive cars in the hotel car park. His breath came out in great clouds of steam. Were these same stars shining down on Peter? *In the great scheme of things,* he thought, *our lives are over in the blink of an eye, and yet there are times when each moment seems to last an eternity.* He tried to remember what it felt like to be happy and free from worry, but found that he could not.

Mr. Schock walked slowly up the steep road, his feet crunching on the icy tarmac. At the brow of the hill he stopped and looked across the valley, almost blue in the moonlight.

"I hate you!" Unless or until Peter was found, those would remain his son's last words to him. His course of action suddenly became very clear. If the police could not find his son, then he would. He would go to the NCRDM laboratory. He would track down this NASA scientist and would make her tell him what she knew. He would do whatever it took to get Peter back. He would not stop until, one way or another, he had found his son and could tell him to his face that he was sorry and that he loved him.

While Sir Richard was briefing the lawyer in his chambers in Middle Temple, Parson Ledbury took Peter and Kate for lunch to a "chop house" at the corner of Fleet Street and Hanging Sword Alley. Having given Gideon his shirt, the parson's outfit provoked a few curious looks, but he did not let this bother him. He did his best to cheer up the children and convinced them that Mr. Leche would have Gideon out of Newgate prison in no time. He ordered beef and oyster pie for everyone, which even Peter, who was not overly keen on eighteenth-century fare, admitted was delicious. This was followed by a lemon syllabub that Kate quite liked and Peter could have done without. As Peter did not appear to care for the dessert, Parson Ledbury asked the serving wench to bring some cheese for him. She brought him a fat slice of Stilton, which Peter would have eaten had he not noticed the half a dozen weevils that shared the plate.

"Starving ourselves will not help Mr. Seymour suffer the pangs of hunger," commented the parson, which instantly made Peter and Kate regret having let a morsel of food pass their lips.

While Parson Ledbury attacked a second helping of syllabub, Peter looked through the diamond-paned window at the street outside. A golden-haired dog trotted past, and suddenly the incident with Molly and the Van de Graaff generator came back to him. It seemed so long ago. How, if they couldn't get hold of the antigravity machine, were they ever going to get home? The year 1763 was rapidly losing any charm it might once have held for him.

Meanwhile Kate could not resist eavesdropping. Two gentlemen at an adjacent table were having an animated conversation. A large bulky fellow who had spilled gravy down his shirt and who spoke in a booming voice even louder than Parson Ledbury's, was being questioned on all manner of subjects by his young companion. His neck and face were badly scarred and he was blind in one eye. His companion had untidy dark hair and a pronounced

Scottish accent. The large man seemed to hold strong opinions about everything under the sun.

Every so often, when the older man said something particularly witty, the young one would hastily scribble down his words in a small blue notebook.

"Parson Ledbury," Kate whispered, "I think we're sitting next to Dr. Samuel Johnson!"

"Upon my word, you don't say! We must introduce ourselves at once!"

He twisted around in his seat and called out, "Pardon me for interrupting you, gentlemen, but do I have the honor of addressing Dr. Johnson, creator of the first dictionary of the English language?"

The large man confirmed that he was indeed Dr. Johnson and that he was the author of such a book. The parson told him that he had recently had the pleasure of talking with Erasmus Darwin in Lichfield. Dr. Johnson nodded politely and commented that he was a fine doctor who deserved his reputation, and while he could not say that he found his company altogether agreeable, there were doubtless many who did. . . . The parson went on to describe their meeting with King George and told Dr. Johnson that a copy of the *Dictionary* could be found in the King's own library. Dr. Johnson seemed most flattered and invited the parson and his companions to join them at their table. He introduced the young Scotsman as Mr. James Boswell and invited the parson to present himself and his young friends.

On hearing that Peter and Kate were recently arrived in London, he asked Kate how she found the city.

Kate giggled a little and grew pink and then pulled herself together and said solemnly, "Well, Dr. Johnson, I say that when a man is tired of London, he is tired of life."

"Prettily put, Miss Dyer, most prettily put. Mr. Boswell, I think you would do well to write that down."

Mr. Boswell obediently copied down the sentence while Kate grinned from ear to ear. *What is she up to?* wondered Peter. When Mr. Boswell had finished writing, he told them that he was about to depart on a long trip to the continent but that he would miss London exceedingly. The parson agreed that travel was an excellent way of broadening one's mind but advised him to avoid the temptation of copying foreign fashions. It was not, he said, admiration that he felt on seeing someone dressed in the continental manner but the strong desire to push its wearer into the mud of the street.

Dr. Johnson laughed appreciatively and said, "I have recently returned from France and must confess that I find the French a gross, ill-bred, untaught people. . . . What I gained by being in France was learning to be better satisfied with my own country. And you, Master Schock, how do you find London? Do you not think it earns its reputation as being the greatest and most civilized city in the world?"

"I like the French!" exclaimed Peter. "We go there for holidays and I've got a French penfriend! And their food is brilliant, and they're good at soccer. . . . And as for London being civilized . . ."

Peter was momentarily lost for words as all the things he missed about his own time and all the things he hated about 1763 flooded into his head. The anguish that he had felt since his arrival seemed to boil up inside him like lava pushing against the cracking membrane of a volcano. He could contain his anger no longer. *Oh, no,* said Kate to herself under her breath. She sensed what was coming. Dr. Johnson, Mr. Boswell, and the parson waited expectantly for Peter to continue.

"Civilized! . . . I don't even know where to start. Where I come from we don't have open sewers running down the street and serve cheese with animals living in it. There are toilets that flush and supermarkets where you can get good, clean food, and what wouldn't I give for a bottle of Coke and some ice cream . . . or a Chinese takeaway and a good film. . . . Oh, you wouldn't understand. But you can go for a ride in the countryside without getting attacked by highwaymen or footpads, and if someone does try to rob you, you can telephone 999 and a police car will come and arrest them. And you can walk down the street without seeing hundreds of starving people and cripples. There are doctors and hospitals if you get sick, and people aren't so poor that they're forced to steal and get put into prison where they're treated worse than any animal."

"Peter," said Kate softly, "it's not their fault. They don't know."

The parson was lost for words. Dr. Johnson exchanged amused glances with his young companion.

"Decent provision for the poor is a true test of civilization, and your concern does you credit," he said. "But tell me, *999, police cars?* Here are some terms that do not appear in my dictionary. Perhaps you would be good enough to elucidate, Master Schock?"

"The police stop people breaking the law. Police cars are how they get about. And a car is like a carriage only without horses and much, much faster. When they are after someone, they have flashing lights on top of their cars and their sirens wail."

"Their sirens wail?"

"Yes, they go *nee-noo, nee-noo, nee-noo* . . ."

Mr. Boswell and Dr. Johnson burst out laughing.

"Nee-noo, nee-noo, nee-noo!" they cried gleefully until tears ran down their faces.

"Master Schock is feverish and I fear his imagination has become overheated," said Parson Ledbury swiftly. "However, you must excuse us, gentlemen, pressing business awaits us."

The parson stood up and practically lifted Peter out of his seat, but he would not be silenced and continued angrily, "And your dictionary, Dr. Johnson, has meant that millions of schoolchildren have to waste hours and hours learning stupid spellings when they could be playing football—"

The parson pulled him away and Kate followed behind, giving a nervous little wave to Dr. Johnson as she closed the door behind them.

"Extraordinary!" said Mr. Boswell.

"A hot-headed young fellow," commented Dr. Johnson. "Fancy liking the French . . . but he had bottom."

The three of them slipped out into Fleet Street. It was hot and steamy and the streets were busy. Parson Ledbury plucked off his wig to mop his bristly head with a handkerchief.

"By your leave!" shouted a chair-man, and they all knew by now to get out of the way quickly. They squeezed against a wall while the sedan chair thundered past.

"Well, Master Schock," said the parson sadly, "you have given the good doctor something to think about, at least. I grasped but half of what you said, but I understood that you disapprove of your forebears. . . . Are we so uncivilized?"

"No! . . . Well, yes, some things *are* better in our time. But a lot of things are much worse. We can fly to the moon but we're destroying our own planet. To be honest, until I saw Gideon in Newgate, I was beginning to prefer the eighteenth century. I am sorry, I didn't mean to be rude."

"You spoke from the heart, Master Schock. There is no cause to be sorry."

They made their way back toward Middle Temple to rejoin Sir Richard. The parson walked ahead, forging a path through the bustling crowds. The air was thick with the cries of street hawkers, the rumble of heavy wagons, and the barking of dogs. On the opposite side of Fleet Street a girl stood on a box singing a ballad. Her voice was so clear and so sweet, quite a crowd had gathered around her. To their amusement a dog was howling, trying to sing along with the girl.

Kate laughed. "Can you hear that dog?"

Peter asked Kate what had amused her so much when she answered Dr. Johnson's question.

Kate grimaced. "I probably shouldn't have said that."

"Why not?"

"It's one of Dr. Johnson's famous sayings—you must have heard it: 'When a man is tired of London, he is tired of life.' I couldn't resist it."

Peter screwed up his forehead while he thought about the

consequences of Kate repeating Dr. Johnson's own saying to him before he had, in fact, said it. Except that Kate had already heard it in order to repeat it. So who said it first—Kate or Dr. Johnson? And would the answer to this question be different if they returned to their own time?

"Don't!" Kate laughed. "You look like your brain is going to pop."

Caught in the throng behind them a dog was barking incessantly. Kate stopped and put her head on one side.

"What is it?" asked Peter.

"Oh, nothing," said Kate. "For a minute, I thought . . . No, it's nothing."

The parson's attention was taken by a stall selling spinning tops and painted wooden figures—soldiers and gentlemen and farmers, and even Jack Ketch, the hangman at Tyburn.

"Mistress Kate," he asked, "which shall I choose for young Jack? A farmer, would you say? Or a soldier like his father?"

Kate picked up a rosy-cheeked farmer. "This one—so he can remember his visit to King—"

She never finished the sentence. A lightning streak of honey-colored fur passed in front of Peter's eyes as a golden Labrador launched itself at Kate's chest. She was instantly knocked backward onto the flimsy toy stall, which tipped over, sending all the wooden figures clattering onto the granite cobblestones. The dog barked ecstatically and its long pink tongue licked every inch of Kate's face.

The street hawker struggled to put his stall upright at the same time as he fended off two small boys who were attempting to make off with his goods. The parson had grabbed hold of the dog's solid middle and was heaving it off Kate. Peter's attention, however, was elsewhere. . . . He was staring at the red-haired man with a freckled face who had come to a sudden halt in front of them. A name—could it have been "Molly"?—was fading from the man's lips.

Kate tried to recover herself and stood up, panting heavily. She wiped her face with the back of her hand.

"It can't be," she said, looking at the yellow Labrador that was struggling to escape from the parson's grasp. Bewildered, she glanced over at Peter, and as she did so her eyes met those of the man with the red hair. They gazed numbly at each other, and the rest of the world seemed to fade silently away. Father and daughter each stared out at this familiar stranger as if from a great distance. For a long moment no one else existed and the only sound Kate heard was the beating of her own heart. Suddenly Kate let out a deep, shuddering gasp from the very core of her being and the world came flooding back. She became aware of Molly's frantic barking.

"Dad!" she screamed and flung her arms around him.

"The Lord be praised!" exclaimed Parson Ledbury, letting go of Molly so that she could leap around Kate and her father like a young puppy.

Peter watched the scene, a huge grin on his face, not quite knowing what to do with himself. How had Dr. Dyer got here? It was nothing less than a miracle! And then a feeling pushed its way into his mind and took form without Peter wishing it to—but it came anyway. *Why hasn't my father come?* he thought. *If Kate's father can find his way back, why can't mine?*

TWENTY-ONE

The Straw Men

*In which Dr. Dyer explains the
disappearance of the antigravity machine,
and Gideon's situation goes from bad to worse*

They wanted to be able to speak freely and could not do so with Sidney present. Sir Richard had the idea to ask his neighbor to take Sidney with him to the cockpit in Bird Cage Walk, where he often spent the evening. He gave his nephew three guineas to bet on the cockerels and made him promise faithfully not to tell his mother. Sidney, whose parents had always forbidden him to frequent such places and had never allowed him to gamble, was even happier when his uncle explained to him that Master

Schock had wanted to go but Sir Richard had felt that he was too young for such a venue.

So it was that the rest of the party gathered around a candlelit table in Lincoln's Inn Fields to celebrate the arrival of a man not due to be born for another two hundred years. Dr. Dyer was clearly overjoyed that, against all the odds, here he was sitting at the same table as his daughter. As they ate, he continually put down his fork to hold Kate's hand in order to convince himself that he was not dreaming. Molly lay on Kate's feet gnawing at a knuckle of veal and refused to be moved from her beloved Kate even when Kate got pins and needles.

"If only I could phone your mum to tell her that I've found you," said her father.

Peter and Kate all took it in turns to tell Dr. Dyer what had happened to them since their arrival, everyone interrupting and commenting and adding another detail. Dr. Dyer was stunned by how much they had lived through in such a short space of time. They had encountered footpads and highwaymen, the King and Queen of England, Erasmus Darwin, not to mention Dr. Johnson. They had seen the inside of Buckingham House as well as Newgate prison. When Kate told her father about Ned Porter's murder and how they had been kidnapped by footpads, he went very quiet and stroked her cheek.

"I cannot thank you enough for the kindness you have shown to Kate and Peter," he said to Sir Richard and the parson when he realized just how much he owed to the Byng family. "And Gideon Seymour, too—if Gideon had not stumbled across the children in Derbyshire, I do not like to think what could have happened to them. It is tempting to think that fate had a hand in all this. I look forward to thanking Gideon in person. I agree with Kate that we cannot think of trying to return home until he is freed from Newgate prison."

"Do you have the *means* of returning home, Dr. Dyer?" asked Sir Richard.

"Andrew, please call me Andrew. Yes, I believe I do—at least I hope I do—but more of that in a moment. First there is something I must know. There is a massive police hunt underway in the twenty-first century, as I am sure you can imagine."

"Ah," said Parson Ledbury, "999. Police cars."

"Mmm," continued Dr. Dyer. "Well, given how Peter and Kate disappeared, it's not surprising that the police have not come up with anything. There was your message, of course, Kate, etched into the wall at your school—very clever idea, by the way, well done. Naturally we erased it before the police saw it."

"Erased it? Why?"

"Because we, I mean the NASA scientists who came over to help and I—"

"NASA?" asked the parson and Sir Richard.

"They build space rockets," explained Peter quickly.

"The future sounds damned tricky, does it not, Sir Richard?" said the parson. "I think we are better off where we are, what?"

Sir Richard laughed. "I am sure you are right and yet there is a part of me that longs to see what we will achieve, the progress we shall have made."

"I should be satisfied with your own time," said Dr. Dyer. "From what I have seen, we have lost much that should not have been lost, and although great scientific discoveries will be made, I am sorry to say that mankind does terrible, terrible things to itself over the next centuries." He sighed. "Where was I?"

"NASA scientists," said Kate. "Why you erased my message."

"Ah yes. We decided that if, as we were beginning to suspect, you had gone back in time, we did not want the public to get to know about it. You don't have to think very hard to come up with some of the potential dangers. For instance, my history is not very good but England has just won the Seven Years War, yes?"

Sir Richard nodded. "Yes, the Treaty of Paris was signed in February."

"Well, what is to stop some fanatical Frenchman traveling back in time with a large bomb and blowing up the English fleet at a crucial moment? France wins, and bang goes the Treaty of Paris."

The parson looked horrified. "It cannot be! You cannot come back and take away our past! We have earned our history—it is ours!"

"But we already have," said Dr. Dyer. "We've just got to try and minimize the damage, leave, and never come back."

The parson looked shaken.

"I promise you that, as soon as we return, the antigravity machine and all its documentation will be destroyed."

"Is everyone concerned with this antigravity machine of the same opinion, Andrew?" asked Sir Richard.

"I believe so."

"Then have a care, for whoever holds this knowledge has a power greater than any army."

There was a long and profound silence. Dr. Dyer squeezed Kate's hand. It was Kate who spoke first.

"Well, don't keep us in suspense, Dad! How *did* you get here?"

"I will tell you, I will, once you've told me how you two managed to appear like ghosts in the twenty-first century, leaving a trail for me to follow from Bakewell to Lincoln's Inn Fields."

"Oh yes! We haven't told you about blurring! But surely you must have blurred—how long have you been here?"

"About a week."

"But that's as long as us!"

"I know. Carry on. And no, I haven't 'blurred' as you call it. Not once. Tell me what happens when you do."

Kate and Peter struggled to explain to Dr. Dyer what blurring felt like, how at first they blurred without realizing what was happening, and how subsequently they had learned to blur at will.

"So it doesn't happen to you of its own accord anymore?"

"Doesn't seem to. The last time we both blurred together without meaning to was days and days ago. We popped up in a supermarket car park! We got some very funny looks, I can tell you!" said Kate.

"I know you did. I've seen the photograph!"

"No! Someone took a picture of that, too?"

"Yes, you two are celebrities, for what it's worth. But tell me, you say that when you blur, you soon get pulled back?"

Peter and Kate nodded. "It hurts," said Peter.

"You get sucked back and you can't resist it for very long," said Kate. "It's a horrible feeling."

"Fascinating. I wonder why it hasn't happened to me—or Molly for that matter."

"Kate finds it easier to blur than me," Peter said.

"Well, girls are best!" said Kate.

"Could you blur now, so I could see?" asked Dr. Dyer.

"For pity's sake!" exclaimed Parson Ledbury. "Not during supper! I can assure you that it is a perfectly bloodcurdling sight and will give us all indigestion."

Dr. Dyer laughed. "Tomorrow, perhaps. When our stomachs are empty. Why don't I tell you my story, then . . ."

The telephone call came, he told them, on the morning of Christmas Eve. Sam was still refusing to come out of his room, but the rest of the family was sitting around the Christmas tree. It was pointless trying to pretend that this was a normal Christmas, but for the little ones' sake they were playing Snap! and charades. Ever since Kate had vanished, the sound of a telephone always made the grown-ups apprehensive. A desperate wish for good news was always accompanied by the fear that this call could bring the bad news they had been dreading. Dr. Dyer picked up the receiver. It was one of the security guards at the NCRDM laboratory. He had been making a routine check on the office that Dr. Dyer shared with Tim Williamson when he heard a message being recorded on their answering machine. It was an unusual message, and he made a note of the number in case it was important.

Kate's father decided to make the call immediately. He got through to the estate manager of a property owned by the National Trust in Surrey. It was called Tempest House.

"Tempest House!" cried everyone at once. "But that's—"

"Lord Luxon's country estate. I know—I found that out for myself."

The estate manager told him that a piece of equipment with a NCRDM security label on it had turned up inexplicably inside the Luxon family crypt. It was a total mystery how the object had got in there, as the crypt was securely locked. Not only that, there was also a crazed tramp in the crypt who fled like a trapped bird as soon as the doors were opened. The estate manager presumed that it was a student prank.

"It was your mum who suggested taking Molly," said Dr. Dyer, "and thank goodness she did. I got straight into the Land Rover, and three hours later I was standing in the crypt. It was Tim's antigravity machine all right, and it seemed undamaged. I watched Molly sniffing about and hoped she might pick up your scent. She didn't, but funnily enough there was a strong smell of fish. . . . I think I'd convinced myself that you were going to come back for Christmas—the one present your mum and I had prayed for. As I stood there, trying to calm down, the tramp crept back into the crypt. One look at him and I knew he wasn't mad—he was from the eighteenth century. I asked him what the date was."

"What did he say?" asked Kate.

"Twenty-sixth July 1763."

"Yesterday!" exclaimed Sir Richard.

"Yes. Anyway, it was after talking to him that I realized what I must do."

"Who was he, Dad?"

"A poacher. He had been fishing for carp in Lord Luxon's lake. He used the crypt as a hiding place when he thought he had been spotted. There were a couple of loose tiles in the roof and he would squeeze through and drop down into the crypt. He thought Lord Luxon was up in town, but the lord had appeared unexpectedly that morning, and the poacher had thought it best to make himself scarce until it was safe to leave the estate. Only when the poacher landed on the floor of the crypt and lit a candle as he usually did, did he discover that he wasn't in fact alone. There was one of Lord Luxon's liveried footmen in there with him. The poacher was so startled he took a step backward and fell over something. That was the last thing he could remember.

"Of course, it was the morning of the race!" exclaimed Peter. "So they *had* put the machine in the crypt. . . . It wasn't a trick."

"Go on," said Sir Richard. "I am beginning to understand."

"And so," continued Dr. Dyer, "I had the proof I needed that the antigravity machine was indeed responsible for Kate and Peter's disappearance and that it had gone both backward *and* forward in time. If the children were still in 1763 and their only hope of returning was this machine, I had no choice. I had to get it back to you. I telephoned your mother, Kate. And do you know, she did not hesitate for a second. "Go," she said. "Bring my Katie back.""

Kate burst into tears.

"Don't cry, love. I have hidden the machine on Hampstead Heath. I *shall* get you back to your mum—and Peter to his—I promise. And you know that I don't break my promises."

Peter looked down at the table.

"How did you know that the machine would return you to 1763?" asked Sir Richard.

"I didn't, but what else could I do? I had to try."

Kate grabbed hold of her father's hand and squeezed it.

"There are various settings on Tim's antigravity machine, and a dial. I reasoned that if the machine had gone forward and backward over an identical time span, so long as none of the settings had been interfered with, the machine stood at least a decent chance of being able to replicate that journey. And it did, give or take a few days. Bizarrely, two days before it happened I had visited one of my NASA colleagues in the hospital. She said something to me whilst she was apparently asleep. She told me that the time differential is directly proportional to the quantity of antigravity generated. She couldn't remember saying it afterward.

"Ooh, that's spooky!" said Kate.

"I know. And it's not something I would want to write up in a scientific journal, either, but it did give me the courage to switch on the generator. But she could be right—perhaps there is a direct relationship between energy output and the lapse in time."

He then described how the poacher had helped him move the machine out of the crypt and into the Land Rover, for Kate's father did not want to risk getting to 1763 and then being locked in the crypt! Dr. Dyer drove to Abinger Forest—a truly terrifying journey for the poacher, but he gamely helped unload the antigravity machine once they had arrived. Dr. Dyer said that he had no recollection whatsoever of switching the machine on but remembered waking up in the woods in the middle of the night, owls hooting overhead, and the poacher long gone. Molly was fast asleep beside him and appeared none the worse for her experience.

"We couldn't remember anything about our journey either, could we?" said Kate to Peter.

"No. I couldn't even remember who you were at first."

"But we are talking about short-term memory loss, here, aren't we?" asked Dr. Dyer anxiously. "I mean, you don't have any difficulty recalling the names of your friends at school or the name of the prime minister, do you?"

"Now you come to mention it . . . ," said Kate.

"What?" said Dr. Dyer.

"What were you saying? I can't remember."

"Very funny, Kate. As I was saying, Molly and I woke up in the middle of Abinger Forest. The next day I sold my gold watch to a master clockmaker in Effingham for twenty guineas, hired a horse and cart, and made for London, where I hid the machine on Hampstead Heath and rented some rooms in Highgate. I knew that at some point you were going to turn up in Covent Garden or Lincoln's Inn Fields, so Molly and I have been searching for you ever since."

"When you say 'watch,' Andrew, do you mean a pocket watch small enough to be worn around the wrist, by any chance?" asked Sir Richard.

"Yes, I do."

"In which case I can tell you that King George himself is in

possession of your timepiece! No wonder there was such amazement at the delicacy of its mechanism!"

There was so much more to say and so much more to ask, but
after all the excitement everyone was beginning to grow tired.
Molly was snoring gently at Kate's feet. The candles were low and
Parson Ledbury kept dropping off to sleep and waking up with a
start. At half past eleven Sir Richard suggested that they resume
the conversation the next day. He had an appointment to keep
at Newgate with Gideon and Mr. Leche at nine o'clock, and he
wondered if Kate's father would be prepared to join them.

"I should be honored," said Dr. Dyer. "I should like to be able
to shake his hand. I can, in any case, swear on oath that Gideon
did *not* take the antigravity machine. Although I am not sure that
it would be a very good idea for *me* to explain the circumstances
of its disappearance."

Kate and Peter waited in Sir Richard's carriage outside St.
Sepulchre's Church while Dr. Dyer, Sir Richard, Parson Ledbury,
and the lawyer, Mr. Leche, went to visit Gideon. A quarter of an
hour later the four men appeared at the iron gates. Mr. Leche, a
sallow-faced man in a tightly curled wig, shook hands with Sir
Richard and, with a slight bow to the others, strode away at a
furious pace in the direction of the Old Bailey. He did not look
pleased. Neither did the others. They stood at the gate talking to
each other urgently with angry expressions on their faces.

"Something's wrong," said Peter. "What's Sir Richard doing?"

Sir Richard was waving down a hackney coach. He climbed in

and was followed by the parson. Dr. Dyer watched as the driver turned the carriage through a hundred and eighty degrees and set off at a great speed toward Holborn and the west.

"What's happening?" cried Kate as her father climbed in next to them. He called up to the driver to take them back to Lincoln's Inn Fields.

"I've got bad news to give you, I'm afraid. Gideon's case was heard at the Old Bailey yesterday afternoon."

"But he was only arrested the day before yesterday!"

"I know. Lord Luxon clearly knows whose strings he can pull. . . . Gideon was convicted of seven instances of theft—all valuable items and all the property of Lord Luxon."

"But he's innocent! How could they find him guilty with no proof?"

Dr. Dyer called up to the driver to stop for a moment. They had just passed in front of the Old Bailey. Dr. Dyer peered through the window.

"What is it?" asked Kate.

"Look," he said. "Sir Richard was telling me about them. Can you see that group of men standing in front of the law courts? Look at their shoes."

"They've got something sticking out of them," said Peter.

"It's straw. They call them the straw men. They'll go into court and swear anything you like under oath—for the right price. That's how they got Gideon."

"We've got to do something!" cried Peter. "Pay some other straw men to say something different. Ask for a retrial! There must be something we can do!"

"Mr. Leche says it's too late."

"But why? How long must Gideon stay in that awful place?"

"Gideon wasn't sentenced to imprisonment. He is to be hanged at Tyburn on the next hanging day—which is on the first of August, in five days' time. The Recorder of London has already delivered the names of the condemned to the King."

Kate cried out in horror. "No!" she exclaimed "No, it can't be!"

Peter was so shocked that he could not say a word. He had been so sure that Gideon would have been out of Newgate today, or tomorrow at the worst. Now he felt weak with the shock of it, winded as if someone had punched him in the stomach.

"It can't be true!" he murmured.

"I'm afraid that it is true. Gideon had already been moved to the condemned hold, so we could not even speak to him. Although the turnkey told us that he was not in despair."

"Then we must go to Buckingham House and explain what has happened!" said Peter. "Queen Charlotte will help us—she said she would."

Peter was shaking with emotion. Dr. Dyer assured him that Sir Richard and Parson Ledbury were doing all they could. They were going at this very minute to the Court of St. James to prepare a petition to send to King George. Hopefully, as long as he got it in time, the King would pardon Gideon if Sir Richard could present a convincing enough case.

"What do you mean, as long as he gets it in time?" asked Peter.

"Unfortunately," said Kate's father, "the King and Queen have already left London for the country. To make matters worse,

Sir Richard heard that King George has plans to visit the Earl of Northumberland at Alnwick Castle on the Northumberland coast."

"Oh, no!" said Kate. "That's hundreds of miles away!"

"Yes, Parson Ledbury said that it would take between two to three days to reach Northumberland, even if you changed horses frequently."

This last news was too much for Peter. "He's going to die!" he wept. "Gideon is going to die because of us. And there's nothing we can do about it! We shouldn't have let him ride in that race!"

Kate put her arms around Peter and held him tight. She did not contradict him. After all, she thought sadly, if it weren't for Gideon helping them, he would probably be back in Derbyshire by now, settled in Hawthorn Cottage and about to start a new life as the Honorable Mrs. Byng's new estate manager.

"You found a true friend in Gideon, didn't you?" asked Dr. Dyer.

Peter could only nod his head.

Sir Richard and Parson Ledbury worked tirelessly on Gideon's behalf. They tried to see Lord Luxon at his London residence in Bird Cage Walk and were told that he had returned to Tempest House. So they rode on horseback to Surrey and presented their cards at the door. Lord Luxon refused to see them, and when they tried to force their way in he had them thrown out. As they galloped away from Tempest House, Sir Richard turned around and saw Lord Luxon observing their departure from the topmost balcony.

"Murderer!" Sir Richard roared at him. "I knew your father—

he would be ashamed! You condemn Gideon for being a better man than you!"

Lord Luxon turned his back on them and retreated into his mansion.

By nightfall Sir Richard and Mr. Leche had put together a document that they hoped would prove Gideon's innocence or at least put into doubt the court's verdict. A messenger was sent with all speed after the King and Queen, with the instruction to go on to Alnwick Castle if King George had already left for Northumberland.

Now all they could do was wait. The following day was a Sunday, and they heard that Gideon had attended a special service for the condemned in Newgate Chapel. The Ordinary, as the Newgate clergyman was called, preached a sermon while those who were shortly to die sat around a black coffin placed in the center of the chapel. Gideon was not allowed visitors but Sir Richard sent food and wine to the prison twice a day and paid a turnkey handsomely to ensure that it was Gideon who got it.

When Dr. Dyer saw how hard the children had taken the news about Gideon, particularly Peter, he was keen to distract them. The three of them went on long walks to explore the city. He bought a small leather-bound book in Fleet Street in which he made copious notes, and bemoaned his lack of a digital camera several times a day. He took enormous delight in the language and the food and the customs of the age. He liked to imitate the parson: "Gadzooks, sir!" he would say at every opportunity and, "Upon my word!" and, to a waitress in a chop house recommended by Sir Richard,

"Confound your Beef Tremblante, madam. I'm for plain eating. Bring me a pork pie and a tiff-taffety cream!" which made even Peter laugh out loud. They sat in coffeehouses and listened to wags and dandies exchanging witticisms, and men of letters engaging in serious debate; they watched gentlemen take snuff and gesticulate with foamy, lace handkerchiefs, and saw ladies throwing seductive glances to their beaux over fluttering painted fans. They admired the extravagant costumes of the day and noted the stink of the people wearing them. . . . They witnessed the life of the street from hackney coaches and once, thrillingly, from sedan chairs.

One evening, walking through the maze of narrow streets beyond St. Paul's Cathedral, they looked up, trying to get their bearings. Dr. Dyer remarked on how many churches they could see.

"All these spires rising toward the heavens. It's all banks and insurance companies in our time. Thank goodness St. Paul's survived the Second World War."

"I'm beginning to hate knowing what is going to happen," said Peter. "We did tell Parson Ledbury that America is going to be a superpower—it was worth it just to see his face!—and Kate let on to Erasmus Darwin that his grandson was going to go down in history. . . . But thinking about the First World War and the Second and the Holocaust and Hiroshima . . . I really wish I didn't know. And it makes you wonder if there's any way you could stop it."

"Dad," said Kate, "do you think our time will be affected because we have come here?"

"I don't know. I guess we'll find out when we get back. And there's something that's been really bothering me. You know how the poacher got transported to the twenty-first century on the day of the race, on July twenty-sixth?"

"Yes. And . . . ?"

"Well, I arrived with the poacher on the twenty-first, and what's bugging me is this: How many poachers and antigravity machines were there between the twenty-first and the twenty-sixth? Think about it."

Kate and Peter stopped walking and looked at each other, frowning.

"But that's not possible. I mean, how could that be?" asked Peter.

"It makes my head hurt," said Kate. "Surely it must be against the laws of nature or physics or something."

"Well, I can only think of two explanations, neither of which makes me feel any better. The first possibility is that for five days there were duplicate poachers and antigravity machines. The second possibility relies on the parallel worlds hypothesis. Put simply, to avoid a time anomaly like this one, the universe splits at the point of conflict. In other words, by coming back in time with the poacher, I am responsible for the creation of a duplicate universe."

"You mean there's one universe where Peter and I are still alone in 1763 without any hope of getting back and there's this one where you're here with the antigravity machine?"

"Exactly."

"Then the same would be true of when we arrived!" exclaimed Peter. "There'd be one universe where Kate and I left your laboratory and went back for lunch and another one when we were sent back in time."

"I know," said Dr. Dyer. "But take your pick—duplicate poachers or duplicate universes. Although no doubt there's an entirely different explanation we haven't thought of."

". . . and I woke up and it was all a dream," said Kate.

"I wish!" said Dr. Dyer.

Peter liked Dr. Dyer very much but he did not feel as easy being in this threesome as he did when it was just him and Kate. And, of course, the presence of Kate's father highlighted for him the absence of his own. Although they kept busy, for Peter the hours passed slowly, as if in a dream. There was always a part of him that was thinking of Gideon and hoping for the arrival of a messenger from the King, always a lingering feeling of guilt that somehow this was all his fault. Meanwhile Molly stuck to Kate like a limpet, never letting her mistress out of her sight, just in case she disappeared again.

It was during these long days of waiting that they decided to tell Sidney and Hannah the truth about who they were. They also told Jack, but he did not really understand and soon went back to playing with the skittles his uncle had bought him. At first Hannah seemed to take the news in her stride; then, after half an hour, she became hysterical. However, a glass of Sir Richard's best Madeira wine calmed her down, and she admitted that she always found Peter's and Kate's manners a little peculiar and, having seen both children's sneakers, said that she was disappointed that shoes in the future were quite so unsightly.

It took a long time to convince Sidney that they were telling the truth, for he suspected that Peter was trying to make a fool out of him. Kate had to ask Sir Richard to confirm their story, and when he did, Sidney threw himself into a rage because he had not been told earlier.

"Could I not have been entrusted with this secret? You have been toying with me, Mistress Kate! It cannot have escaped your attention that my affection for your person has been growing with every day. Why could you not have found it in your heart to tell me that I was scattering my hopes on barren ground!"

"But I didn't . . . ," protested Kate, taken aback by Sidney's outburst. She watched him traipse tearfully off to Lincoln's Inn Fields, where he sat alone on a bench.

"Oh dear, poor, poor Sidney," said Kate, looking at him from the drawing room window. "I didn't realize . . ."

Peter stood at her shoulder. "He'll get over it," he said, a tad unsympathetically.

Dr. Dyer looked over at Kate and Peter and smiled to himself.

When, eventually, Sidney returned to the house, Sir Richard had a quiet word with him in his study. When Sidney came out, he found Kate and apologized to her for his hasty words. He offered to do anything he could to ensure her safe return home.

"Sidney's not bad once you get to know him, is he?" commented Kate to Peter once Sidney was out of earshot.

"I suppose not," he replied.

On the evening of July thirty-first everyone gathered in the drawing room of Sir Richard's house in Lincoln's Inn Fields. They had to make a decision. Would they go to Tyburn to witness the hanging of Mr. Gideon Seymour the following day?

They talked late into the night. If the King had decided to pardon Gideon, the messenger might well arrive too late. Everyone was of the same mind: They could not, they agreed, permit Gideon to die alone. They would not abandon him. They would all go to Tyburn, from the eldest to the youngest.

TWENTY-TWO

Tyburn

*In which the party gathers at Tyburn,
the Tar Man makes an unexpected appearance,
and this story comes to an end*

The day was too sunny for a hanging day, thought Kate as they set out for Tyburn in two carriages. Sir Richard rode on horseback behind them. In the distance the bells of St. Sepulchre tolled for the condemned. The streets were thronged with people going to see the executions. It was a public holiday and the crowds were relaxed and loud and cheerful. There was much laughter and singing, and street hawkers sold their oysters and puddings and gray peas while people with tankards of ale gathered outside the numerous taverns that lined the route between Newgate and Tyburn. Suddenly, as the party was approaching the Oxford Road, the crowd started to roar behind them, and the shouts reached their carriage like a tidal wave. The procession of carts that carried the condemned from Newgate to their place of execution—the day's entertainment—was on its way. Sir Richard rode up to the carriage window that Peter, Kate, and her father shared with Parson Ledbury and told them that he was going to ride back up High Holborn to meet the carts. He wanted to know if Peter would like to come with him. Peter did not need to be asked twice. He opened the door and clambered onto Sir Richard's horse.

Before departing, Sir Richard rode alongside the carriage for a moment and addressed its occupants: "This will be an ordeal for us all. Hope for the best outcome but prepare yourselves for the worst."

Sir Richard then rode on to speak to Sidney, Hannah, and Jack.

"We will meet again at Tyburn!" he shouted. "May God be with us all this day!"

Then he turned his horse around, and he and Peter set off in pursuit of Gideon, cutting a passage through the heaving mass of Londoners.

Peter could not distinguish Gideon at first. There were three carts, each one surrounded by half a dozen uniformed guards on horseback carrying pikes. The four highwaymen who were to be hanged alongside Gideon were tied up in pairs. Gideon had a cart to himself and, like the other prisoners, he shared it with his own coffin. His arms were tied with the rope he would be hanged with, and he was facing backward. The condemned men had all been given a loose linen shirt to wear over their clothes and a kind of soft cap. It was impossible for Sir Richard to get close to Gideon because of the guards and all the people pushing up against the cart. The leader of the gang of highwaymen was notorious but popular with the crowd, and as the carts rolled slowly through the Oxford Road the condemned were cheered, and weeping girls threw flowers at the gang's leader.

"Gideon!" Peter shouted until he was hoarse. Eventually Gideon responded and scanned the crowd for a familiar face. When he spotted Peter, his face lit up and he smiled and nodded, for he was unable to wave. Sir Richard forced his way closer to the cart.

"Do not lose hope!" shouted Sir Richard. "There is time for the King's pardon to arrive yet! Do not lose hope—there is still time!"

Peter waved and waved and gave Gideon the thumbs-up sign and smiled as hard as he could, even though he felt that his heart was breaking. Then Sir Richard was forced to fall back, and they followed Gideon's cart, always keeping him in sight so that he knew he was not alone. After an hour the procession stopped at a tavern so that the prisoners could have a last drink, and, as Sir Richard commented, any delay that would allow the King's messenger to arrive in time was very welcome.

Then the carts set off on the last stage of their journey. Progress was slow through the packed streets. However, by half past ten they left London behind, and the rolling hills of Middlesex came into view. By a quarter to eleven they caught their first glimpse of the place of execution: Tyburn.

Thirty thousand people were crammed around a simple wooden scaffold against a setting of green fields. The sun was now high in the sky and it was becoming uncomfortably hot. A single oak tree rose up against the horizon, offering some shade for those lucky enough to be able to sit beneath its branches. The crowd was chaotic. Soldiers and children jostled with beggars and gentlemen for a good spot. Some were on horseback and some were standing, packed like sardines, on carts and wagons. Children sat perched on their parents' shoulders. Many carriages, including the two owned by Sir Richard, were scattered around the perimeter of the crowd. Those with money sat on specially constructed wooden stands called Mother Proctor's Pews. Sir Richard rode to the back of the stands and pushed his way along the edge of them until he and Peter had a clear view of the scaffold.

When the carts arrived, the crowd went quiet. Peter looked frantically around for any sign of the King's messenger. How could he spot him? It was hopeless. They needed more time! Please let them have more time! He hoped the highwaymen would be hanged first to give the messenger a few more precious minutes to arrive. And then Peter realized what a terrible thing he had wished for and felt ashamed. He looked around him at the grotesque spectacle. It was shameful. Why were all these tens of thousands of people drawn here? Why were they compelled to look at another's death? What did they get from it?

Peter looked over toward Mother Proctor's Pews, where Lord Luxon sat. He had hired, as was his custom, two full rows of seats, at enormous expense. He was surrounded by pretty women dressed in white with flowers in their hair, and by fops and maca-ronies, all of whom were in high spirits and eating chicken legs and gulping down wine from the bottle. Lord Luxon, too, was all in white. But he was not eating. Behind the forced smile of a gracious host at a social gathering, his fragile mask was beginning to crack. It seemed to Peter that his wild eyes revealed some of the guilt and horror he must now surely feel.

Sir Richard, too, was observing Lord Luxon. "That man," he said coldly, "will reap what he has sown in this world, or in the next."

But it was not the highwaymen who were to be hanged first. Peter's heart sank as he watched Gideon's cart being guided underneath the gallows. The guards helped him to his feet, untied the rope that bound his arms, formed it into a noose, and put it around Gideon's neck. There was a murmur of excited anticipation from the crowd.

"No!" screamed Peter uselessly. "He's innocent! You can't do this!"

Sir Richard turned to Peter. "We must now despair of the King's pardon arriving in time. Are you ready to play your part?"

"I am."

The Newgate Ordinary climbed up beside Gideon and read from a small black Bible. Peter saw his friend's lips move in prayer.

Suddenly a slight young man with brown hair similar to his own pushed forward toward the cart. Peter saw Gideon start at first in surprise, and then put his arms around the weeping figure.

"It's Joshua, Gideon's half brother," exclaimed Sir Richard, tears welling in his eyes. "I must go to him. I visited Joshua two days ago on Gideon's request to tell him that he must on no account come to Tyburn and that he could rely on me to find him another position. I pity him for he has no one else in the world. Wait here while I fetch him—Joshua should not be alone and perhaps he can help us."

Sir Richard dismounted and then seemed to change his mind.

"Peter, I fear there may not be enough time. You must get to the carriage by yourself as quickly as you can. Are you able to ride my horse through this crowd?"

"I'll do my best, sir."

"Good."

Sir Richard set off toward the scaffold, shoving people roughly out of his way in his haste. Peter watched Joshua clinging to his half brother. Peter felt he should be up there with him too. He wanted so much to say sorry for all of this—if it weren't for him and Kate and the stupid antigravity machine, Gideon would be safe and sound in Derbyshire. . . . He remembered Gideon telling the Honorable Mrs. Byng at Baslow Hall that he should be happy if he did not see Tyburn again in his entire life. And here he was, scarcely two weeks later, with a noose around his neck. Gideon must not die! He must not die! Peter did not even notice that his own face was wet with tears. He looked over at Lord

Luxon in Mother Proctor's stands, and a rush of hatred surged through him. He wanted to drag him off the wooden stands and place *him* under the gallows instead. He wanted to—

"Peter! Peter!" It was Kate's high voice that reached him across the crowds. "Move! Get here *now*!"

Peter did not need to be told twice—he urged Sir Richard's horse forward, screaming at people all the while to get out of his way. It became easier as he approached the perimeter and the crowd grew less dense. Soon he managed to rejoin Kate and the parson at the carriage, and he clambered in. Kate took hold of Peter's hand and together they watched through the window and waited.

Sir Richard, meanwhile, had managed to reach Gideon's cart and had peeled the wretched Joshua from his half brother. Sir Richard then plunged back into the crowd, dragging Joshua behind him, but not before he had embraced Gideon and whispered "Courage!" into his friend's ear. Parson Ledbury motioned furiously to them from the carriage window to hurry up, until his attention was suddenly taken by a commotion on the scaffold.

Just as the Newgate Ordinary was climbing out of the cart, a man in a three-cornered hat leaped onto the scaffold, scattering a group of confused soldiers as he did so. He raised his hands high above his head for silence. A single soldier jumped onto the scaffold next to him, but the man with the hat possessed such authority that when he gestured to the soldier to wait until he had finished speaking, the soldier merely stood there meekly and obeyed. Gideon, the noose around his neck, looked on, amazed.

Kate gasped.

"It's the Tar Man!" Peter exclaimed.

The Tar Man waited until he had got the crowd's attention before speaking. He pointed an accusing finger directly at Lord Luxon in the front row of the stands.

"It is not too late, my lord, to stop this execution!" the Tar Man cried. "He is innocent of the crime, as well you know! I ask you to admit that you have been mistaken about Mr. Seymour!"

Lord Luxon stood up, and although clearly shocked to see his henchman, he remained an elegant and dignified figure and only the tendons in his neck belied his cool exterior. He clutched a lace handkerchief.

"I am surprised to see you at Tyburn, Master Blueskin. I thought it was your custom to avoid all places of execution. But you are impertinent, sir. Mr. Seymour has been found guilty of his crimes and must pay the penalty this day. I pray you withdraw from this place, as you do not appear to have the stomach for justice."

The Tar Man's scar glowed white in the strong sunshine as he returned his employer's haughty stare. "I believe it was on account of my strong stomach that you hired me. Come, my lord, it is easy to draw hasty conclusions from scant evidence, and I have received information about Mr. Seymour that, shall we say, makes me urge you—*strongly*—to withdraw your allegation. For is there anything more odious than to permit a man to hang for a crime he did not commit?"

"You speak out of turn, Blueskin. I shall expect an explanation of your intolerable outburst later."

"Then as God is my witness I denounce you as a liar!"

The crowd gasped. The Tar Man was well known and his name spread like a brush fire from one side of the crowd to another—"Blueskin!" was on everyone's lips. "Blueskin! Blueskin!"

"Guards, remove this man at once!" barked Lord Luxon to the soldiers standing to attention around the scaffold. "This man is surely in league with the condemned felon!"

Peter could scarcely believe this turn of events. Since when did the Tar Man care about Gideon?

"What's he up to?" he said to Kate. "The Tar Man is Gideon's worst enemy!"

"I don't know, but it sure looks like Lord Luxon's got on the wrong side of him."

The Tar Man, a dark, feline figure, jumped down in one bound from the scaffold and started to push his way toward Lord Luxon, who feigned indifference. Sensing trouble, the sergeant sent half a dozen soldiers after the Tar Man, and, with difficulty, they overpowered him. The Tar Man was not cowed but stood within spitting distance of his employer, straining against his captors, his arms forced behind his back.

"The new gamekeeper arrived from Abinger this morning and let slip something he shouldn't have," he hissed into Lord Luxon's face. "After a little persuasion he admitted that you had spoken of the matter with him. Can it be true what he told me about Mr. Seymour?"

What color there was in Lord Luxon's cheeks faded away. He remained silent.

"Damn your eyes, Luxon. Admit it or deny it, but don't play with me!"

The soldiers dragged the Tar Man away. "Is it true!"

At first the crowd did not know how to react, but then, when they saw Lord Luxon standing up and trying to slip away, a great booing and hissing began, and people started to throw anything they could lay their hands on at the retreating figure, who lacked the courage to witness the consequences of his actions. Fruit, oyster shells, and bread were catapulted into the air. Lord Luxon lifted up his arms to protect himself. Several of the fops and macaronies were hit by the projectiles that failed to reach their target. Not one of them came to Lord Luxon's aid. The holiday atmosphere had vanished, and the crowd was transformed into a mob. The sergeant knew that if he was to prevent a riot he was going to have to escort Lord Luxon away as quickly as possible. Within moments a circle of soldiers had surrounded the lord and were maneuvering themselves, turtle-like, away from the scaffold and the chanting mob.

"Excellent!" exclaimed Parson Ledbury. "You'd have thought the Tar Man was in league with us! Why, we are already rid of half the guards, and the crowd is whipped into a frenzy without us lifting a finger!"

Sir Richard and Joshua reached the carriage. This was no time for introductions. Peter and Kate were pushed into the larger carriage and the blinds firmly shut. Sir Richard, the parson, Dr. Dyer, Joshua, and even Jack, who held Hannah's hand tightly, were given large metal dishes and hammers and rods. Sidney was given a snare drum.

"Go now! Go to your places and follow Sidney's lead. As soon as Gideon has spoken his last word, make enough noise to bring down the angels from heaven!"

With the Tar Man under armed guard behind the scaffold and Lord Luxon escorted from Tyburn, the crowd had grown calmer. The officer decided that it would be best to get the hanging of the wretched Mr. Seymour over and done with before his audience got bored and fractious. Jack Ketch, as all hangmen were called, appeared on the scaffold, and an expectant hush descended on the crowd. They had come to see a man die, and they hoped he would die well, and so grew quiet in order to be able to hear his last words.

Gideon Seymour was unknown to the vast majority of the crowd, but the Tar Man's support of him predisposed them in his favor. Thirty thousand pairs of eyes focused on the small figure with a rope around his neck. Gideon stepped forward and spoke. His voice rang across the fields of Tyburn, and the crowds shuffled forward in order to hear him the better.

"I do not deny that I have done wrong," he said in a loud, strong voice that trembled only slightly. "And before God and the people I say that I truly repent of my sins. But I am not guilty of those crimes of which I am accused. Nor have I led a more wicked life than that of my betters who have seen fit to bring me here to this accursed place. I stole food when I was starving, and I know that I am not alone here in having to choose between life and breaking God's law."

There were murmurs of approval.

"Yet I tell you that I have seen the future and in that distant land there will be justice! No one shall be driven by poverty to a life of crime and deceit! Live in the hope that better things are yet to come and that if individual men are wicked, the heart of our nation is sound, and we shall create our own paradise on earth."

The crowd now broke into cheers. Flowers were thrown onto the scaffold.

"Life is sweet, my friends! Do not waste a moment of it! Fare thee well!"

Gideon took out a coin from his pocket and presented it to Jack Ketch. The hangman took a step closer to Gideon and adjusted the rope around his neck. Girls in white dresses took out their handkerchiefs. The crowd drew its breath, but then, abruptly, the staccato beat of a drum sounded from the back of the scaffold. And all around them there was the clanging of metal on metal, and shouts, and the sound of pistols being discharged. No one knew where to look. The soldiers were in disarray, wondering where to go to put a stop to the uproar. After a few moments a single note of a horn silenced the disturbers of the peace. The horn sounded again, rich and clear. Everyone was searching for the horn player. Jack Ketch stepped away from Gideon, unwilling to proceed during this commotion. Then gasps could be heard, and people started to point at two figures hovering on the top of a black and gold carriage.

"Look!" went up the cry. "Angels are come among us!"

Peter and Kate, dressed in white and gold, with wreaths of golden leaves upon their heads, stood like statues, balanced on small metal stands that from a distance were invisible. They appeared to be floating.

Then Peter pressed Gideon's horn to his lips. He blew again, three long notes as if to gain the crowd's attention. And then Kate began to sing: at first just notes and trills, all very high and melodious, and then, when she had everyone's rapt attention, she sang words, too.

"Help him, oh my people!" she sang. "For he is without sin. Do not let the blood of an innocent man stain this soil! Help him, oh my people! Let him be lifted on your shoulders and delivered into the arms of those who love him. Help him, oh my people! Help him!"

Kate then gestured for Joshua, Dr. Dyer, and Sir Richard to join her. They had just arrived, panting, from their positions along the circumference of the crowd. They climbed up onto the roof of the carriage and stood on either side of Kate and Peter with arms open as if in supplication. At this point, and to the astonishment of the crowd, the two angels gradually started to fade and in another moment they had disappeared into thin air. For a second there was total silence. No one spoke and no one moved. And then pandemonium broke out: People screamed and clung to each other.

Sir Richard looked anxiously over at the scaffold. What was the crowd going to do? Inside the carriage Peter and Kate struggled to pull off their costumes and peeped out through a crack in the blinds. They waited an agonizing minute, scarcely daring to breathe. . . . Then they made out a group of men clambering onto the scaffold.

"Come on, lads!" a gruff voice shouted. "You heard 'em!"

On the cart Gideon felt the rope being removed from his neck and found himself being carried down into the crowd. He was passed over people's heads like a raft, hundreds of hands helping him on his way over this sea of well-wishers. It was not only Gideon who was saved; the crowd also cut the bonds of the highwaymen, who made their escape without the soldiers being able to lift a finger to prevent them. The officer bawled frantic orders at his men but to no avail. The Tar Man, too, slipped away, unnoticed in all the confusion.

Peter opened the carriage door, and Gideon was deposited at his feet. Sir Richard and the parson piled in after him.

"I am saved!" cried Gideon. "God has granted me a second chance! Thank you! Oh, thank you!"

Everyone had tears in their eyes.

"No problem," said Peter. "Any time."

Kate burst out laughing and Peter had to agree that nothing he could think of saying could quite match up to the occasion. Gideon pushed himself up and sat down heavily on the leather seat of the carriage, letting out an enormous sigh of relief. He looked at Peter, who was still crouching on the floor of the carriage, and grinned at him and pushed him over with the sole of his foot.

"Did you have to wait until the noose was around my neck? Could you not have rescued me before I thought I was about to depart this earth?"

"Well, we didn't want to disappoint the crowd. . . . They were looking forward to it," replied Peter, handing Gideon's horn back to him.

Gideon laughed and took back his horn. "It would have glad-dened my father's heart to see how his horn helped to save his son."

"And we had welcome if somewhat puzzling assistance from your adversary!" said Sir Richard. "I cannot say I understand it, but I am glad the Tar Man chose so opportune a moment to discover his fondness for you! He will soon be seeking a new employer—for after today's outburst I doubt Lord Luxon will tolerate him under his roof!"

"I fancy the Tar Man has had enough of employers," replied Gideon. "I know it is his ambition to be master of his own des-tiny. Besides, you misread his motives, for I can scarce believe that it was my plight alone that provoked his compassion. I am certain that it was his own young self that he saw on the scaffold today, falsely accused and hanged, not me. When first he came to Tempest House, Lord Luxon was rash enough to promise to help him clear his name."

"I see," said Sir Richard. "A foolish thing to break one's prom-ise to the likes of the Tar Man! Although I wonder if there is more to the Tar Man's actions than you suspect. But come, my friends, we have no time to lose. This is not the fastest of carriages, and we must not squander whatever advantage we have."

Sidney, Hannah, Jack, and the parson climbed up into the second carriage, then Sir Richard rapped on the carriage roof as a signal to the driver that they were ready. The carriages set off at a gallop for Hampstead Heath, and there was nothing the soldiers could do to stop them. The crowd watched clouds of dust rise into the air as Sir Richard's carriages receded into the distance, and, unlike Mr. Seymour and his rescuers, the crowd had a good view of the Tar Man clinging on for dear life to the back of the second carriage. The day's entertainment was over, but as hanging days went, this had been a good one.

The afternoon sun filtered through the leaves of a densely wooded part of Hampstead Heath. They had concealed the carriages as best as they could and had come on foot to the place where Dr. Dyer had hidden the antigravity machine. One of Sir Richard's grooms had stood guard over it since morning and had waited here with Molly and a fast horse provided for Gideon's escape. It had been a difficult day for Molly, and her relief was plain when she was reunited with Kate. After all the jubilation and congratulations, the tears and the laughter in the two carriages, a somber mood had descended on the company. This was to be good-bye. Gideon must go into hiding, and Peter, Kate, and her father were to return to their own time if they could. Nor could they spend any time on long good-byes, for the soldiers would be fast on their heels. Dr. Dyer removed the bracken he had used to conceal the antigravity machine and positioned Kate, Peter, and Molly around it.

Kate broke away and hugged little Jack and Hannah.

"I hope King George has cured you of the scrofula, Jack. Make sure to grow lots more cabbages—if the rabbits eat them, you know what you can threaten them with!"

"Were I to live to be a hundred, I should never meet a finer person than you, Mistress Kate," said Sidney. "God bless you and Godspeed!"

Kate kissed his cheek, and Sidney put his hand to the spot where she had kissed him and kept it there. "Have a happy life," she said. "I hope all of you have happy lives!"

The parson kissed Kate's hand. "I shall forget all about America, but I shall not forget you," he said.

Kate was beginning to become tearful again, and for once Peter did not blame her. He followed Kate's example and shook everyone's hand warmly, even Sidney's.

"Good-bye," said Dr. Dyer. "I cannot thank you enough. And I know that Kate's mother and Peter's parents, too, would join me in my heartfelt thanks."

"You have been so good to us, Sir Richard," said Peter. "Thank you for everything you have done."

"I count it a privilege to have known you," replied Sir Richard. "I shall often think about the time you spent with us, and I shall dream of a future with you all in it."

Everyone suddenly became aware of horses' hooves.

"Quick!" said Sir Richard. "There is no time to lose."

Peter, who had so much to say to Gideon, was not going to get the opportunity to say anything at all. He glanced over at his friend, who stood side by side with Joshua, whom Peter so resembled.

"Peter," said Dr. Dyer. "We must go."

The three of them and Molly clustered around the antigravity machine. Peter looked up at Gideon and tried to smile. He had not even been able to say good-bye. He saw Kate holding her father's hand, and then he looked back at Gideon. The thought came into his head that in the short space of time he had known him, Gideon had done things for him that his own father never had. He had rescued him, probably saved his life; not only that, he had put his own life in danger. He had been a true friend. He had been there when he needed him. Gideon had *trusted* him. And now, because Gideon had come to his and Kate's aid, he was going to be alone and on the run. An impulse came over Peter that was too strong to resist. He *couldn't* go without saying good-bye, without saying thank you.

"Ready?" asked Dr. Dyer.

Kate nodded her head and tightened her grip around Molly's collar, but Peter suddenly darted toward Gideon, arms out-stretched. Kate saw Dr. Dyer move his hand toward the starter switch and she screamed at Peter.

"Peter! No!"

Peter swung around just in time to see the Tar Man spring, seemingly from nowhere, into the position Peter had just vacated. Molly's snarl alerted the rest of the party to the intruder. Gideon's warm smile vanished and he instinctively threw Peter back toward Dr. Dyer and Kate. The Tar Man glanced over at Gideon, and for a brief moment there was an unfathomable look in his eyes. The tips of Peter's fingers sank into the liquefying edges of the antigravity machine. It was too late. A wave of nausea swept over Peter before he was flung backward, every atom repelled by the arcane function-ing of the device. He looked up, and in that split second before all was lost, he saw the Tar Man, dark eyes burning, triumph and terror etched in equal measure on that hateful face; he saw Dr. Dyer, eyes wide with horror; and then he glimpsed Kate, his Kate, who had sworn never to leave without him. Her hand reached out toward him and her mouth was open in a scream that rang in Peter's ears long after it had stopped. And above them all, emanating from the reflective dome at the top of the machine, he saw—or did he imagine that he saw?—a pulsating wave of fluorescent spirals that shot into infinity and vanished.

Hannah and Jack screamed. Gideon and Joshua stepped forward to lift Peter from the ground. He stood, unsteady on his feet, his eyes fixed to the spot where the antigravity machine had been. The Tar Man traveled to the twenty-first century, and Peter was stranded in 1763. No one spoke. The only sound was that of horses' hooves drawing nearer and nearer every second.

"Go! Go now! Go with Gideon!" Sir Richard managed to say. "Take this gold and send word when you can."

He put a bag of coin into Gideon's hand. Gideon mounted the horse, and the parson pushed Peter up behind him.

"Take this," said the parson, thrusting Mrs. Byng's diamond necklace into Gideon's hands. "Deliver it to my cousin and tell her that I have offered you the use of Hawthorn Cottage for as long as you need it."

"You would trust me with Mrs. Byng's necklace?"

"I misjudged you, Mr. Seymour," said the parson. "I would trust you above all men."

Gideon met the good parson's gaze and bowed his head in thanks.

Joshua reached up to grasp Gideon's hand.

"I'll send word when I can," Gideon said. "Sir Richard has promised to find a position for you."

"You can count on me, Gideon, be assured of that, but if you do not leave on the instant, I shall be visiting you once more in Newgate Gaol! Go now and Godspeed to you both!"

Gideon dug his heels in, and the horse galloped into the cover of the wood. Peter held on to Gideon and looked over his shoulder, his mind blunt with shock. He had a last impression of a forlorn group, still as statues, too stunned to do more than watch them disappear into the trees.

Sir Richard and the parson thought it best that they all walk out to meet the soldiers who had come to arrest them. No doubt they had discovered the carriages, which had been hastily and not very well hidden. Sidney, Joshua, Hannah, and little Jack followed behind, all of them shaken by what they had just witnessed. There was, as the parson said, no point skulking in the undergrowth when half of London could testify to what they had done. However, they were surprised to find not soldiers but the King's messenger with an escort of men.

The messenger recognized Sir Richard at once and dropped down off his horse. With a low bow he put a rolled parchment that carried the King's seal into Sir Richard's hands. The parson stood side by side with him.

"His Majesty King George III is pleased to grant Mr. Gideon Seymour a pardon and bids you instruct him that he is a free man."

The parson and Sir Richard exchanged glances. The messenger was exhausted and out of breath. He had ridden for three days and two nights to deliver the King's pardon, only to see it greeted with crestfallen expressions. He had hoped for something better.

• • •

Gideon urged Sir Richard's bay mare through Hampstead Heath under cover of the trees, and then, by the quietest routes he could find, they made for Highgate Hill. He turned around frequently to check on Peter, who would not respond to anything he said. Peter's forehead bounced against Gideon's back; he was awake, but his eyes were firmly closed, and he was conscious only of fluorescent spirals rolling sickeningly and without end across the landscape of his mind. Kate's scream still resonated in his ears.

"Do not lose heart, my young friend," said Gideon. "We might be on the run, but you must not doubt that we *will* find a way to get you home."

Halfway up Highgate Hill, Gideon stopped and turned the horse around so that they could both see London spread out before them.

"Look," he said.

Peter looked. He took in the great dome of St. Paul's and the Monument, a tall white column surrounded by a cluster of city churches. His eyes traveled over all those parts of the city that now held such vivid memories for him: Holborn, Covent Garden, Lincoln's Inn Fields, and, toward the west, St. James's Park and Buckingham House. How different it was from the London of his time. Would he ever see his London again? Would he forget what it looked like? Would he forget what his mum and dad looked like? He swept the thoughts away. He could not think about all that now. Instead he inserted, in his mind's eye, the Post Office Tower, Canary Wharf, the Houses of Parliament. He made himself conjure up the sounds of his century: the incessant roar of the traffic, the background grumble of overhead planes, sirens, car radios, the ringtones of mobile phones. . . . Suddenly, despite himself, a broad grin appeared on Peter's face.

"The Tar Man will be terrified of the twenty-first century!"

Gideon's blue eyes focused on the city stretched out beneath them. A cool wind blew strands of blond hair from his face.

"Do not underestimate him; he is more resourceful than you know. I fear it may be the twenty-first century that will be terrified of the Tar Man."

Author's Note

When writing about the eighteenth century in *Gideon the Cutpurse*, I have tried, wherever possible, to be historically accurate and to offer a glimpse of what it might have been like to live in 1763. However, this is above all an adventure written to entertain, and not a history textbook, and I hope readers will enjoy distinguishing between historical fact and historical fiction.

Acknowledgments

I began writing *Gideon the Cutpurse* for the best of reasons: because I wanted to. It is very easy to start a novel, less so to finish it. And if, over the course of five years, the germ of an idea grew into a series of novels, it is in large part thanks to those who enthused me in the first place, those who encouraged me to keep at it, and those who lent me their literary talents to help me get it ready to go out into the world. Looking now at the list of people I have had the pleasure of meeting, it strikes me that although writing is necessarily a solitary occupation, it certainly has its compensations!

I feel that I should first acknowledge my debt to the historian Lucy Moore, whose works on eighteenth-century criminal London caught my imagination in the first place. I heard her speaking on the radio one morning in June 2000, and by the end of the afternoon, I had already planned out the story of *Gideon the Cutpurse* in broad brushstrokes. I consulted many works on the period, but books that rarely left my desk are Liza Picard's *Dr. Johnson's London* and Michael Brander's *Georgian Gentleman.* I should also like to thank David Lewis for lending me his copy

Acknowledgments

of *The Newgate Calendar*—without this often gruesome book I should never have created one of my favorite characters, the Tar Man.

For their constant encouragement and literary expertise my thanks are due to my novelist friends: Stephanie Chilman, Kate Harrison, Jacqui Hazell, Jacqui Lofthouse, and Louise Voss. I should also like to thank my first adult readers, Heather Swain, Liz Facer, Anne-Marie Nation-Telleray, and Catherine Pappo, and my first young reader, Rachel Walsh. I am extremely grateful for all their comments. Thanks, also, to all in the Department of English and Comparative Literature at Goldsmiths College for their support and, in particular, to Blake Morrison, and to Maura Dooley for all her insight and encouragement. I should also like to thank Maura's daughter, Imelda, for her reaction to the book. I am grateful to Brigitte Resl for translating Queen Charlotte's dialogue into German.

I am indebted to the Arts and Humanities Research Council for supporting my continuing research into story development at Goldsmiths College. My grateful thanks.

Without my involvement with and help from PAWS (Public Awareness of Science), an organization that promotes the depiction of science in the arts, I doubt whether I should have dared to write about time travel—albeit fictional! My thanks to Barrie Whatley and Andrew Millington at PAWS.

I feel especially fortunate to be represented and published by a literary agency and a publisher who have shown such belief in *Gideon the Cutpurse* and its sequels. My grateful thanks to: Caradoc King, Judith Evans, Christine Glover, and Linda Shaughnessy at

ACKNOWLEDGMENTS

A P Watt, and to Ingrid Selberg, Venetia Gosling, Joanna Moult (London), and Elizabeth Law (New York) at Simon & Schuster.

Finally, I should like to thank my husband, for his endless encouragement and curiosity about the universe, and also my children, Louis and Issy, who have at various times been my guinea pigs, critics, and editors. *Gideon* was written for them, and it was through reading the novel to them in installments that the plot was refined and developed. There is a large part of all of them in this story.

L. B.-A.

COMING IN
SUMMER 2007

The Tar Man

BEING THE SECOND PART OF
THE GIDEON TRILOGY